COBRA
GUARDIAN

COBRA WAR, BOOK TWO

BAEN BOOKS by TIMOTHY ZAHN

Blackcollar: The Judas Solution

Blackcollar
(contains *The Blackcollar* and
Blackcollar: The Backlash Mission)

The Cobra Trilogy
(contains *Cobra, Cobra Strike,* and *Cobra Bargain*)

COBRA WAR
Cobra Alliance
Cobra Guardian
Cobra Gamble

COBRA
GUARDIAN

COBRA WAR, BOOK TWO

TIMOTHY ZAHN

COBRA GUARDIAN

Copyright © 2011 by Timothy Zahn

A Baen Books Original

Baen Publishing Enterprises
P.O. Box 1403
Riverdale, NY 10471
www.baen.com

ISBN: 978-1-4391-3406-1

Cover art by David Mattingly

First printing, January 2011

Distributed by Simon & Schuster
1230 Avenue of the Americas
New York, NY 10020

Library of Congress Cataloging-in-Publication Data

Zahn, Timothy.
  Cobra guardian / Timothy Zahn.
      p. cm. — (Cobra war ; bk. 2)
  ISBN 978-1-4391-3406-1 (hc)
  1. Space warfare—Fiction. I. Title.
  PS3576.A33C568 2011
  813'.54—dc22

                                                                    2010042440

10 9 8 7 6 5 4 3 2 1

Pages by Joy Freeman (www.pagesbyjoy.com)
Printed in the United States of America

Dedication

To the men and women of the
United States Armed Forces.
Thank you for your service.

CHAPTER ONE

The first indication that it was going to be one of those days was when the cooker burned the leftover pizza Lorne Broom had planned to have for breakfast.

"Oh, for—" he choked off the curse before it could get out past his throat, old habits of propriety kicking in as he glared at the cooker. This was the third time this month the stupid thing had gone gunnybags on him, and with everything else weighing on his shoulders he had precious little patience left for balky appliances.

Or, better even than a curse, he could deal with the balky cooker once and for all. A single, full-power fingertip laser blast into the cooker's core would turn the thing into a conversation-piece paperweight. A shot with his arcthrower would send the cooker beyond paperweight status into a slagged heap that even the revivalist Earth artist Salvador Dali would have been proud of. Even better, a blast from his antiarmor laser—

Lorne took a deep breath, forcing down the surge of frustration. A blast from his antiarmor laser would not only blow a hole through the cooker, but also through the kitchen wall, the wall behind that, and possibly the wall beyond that into the building corridor. At that point, he could say good-bye not only to the cooker, but to his damage deposit as well.

With a sigh, he unloaded the burned pizza and pushed the cooker back into its niche at the back of the counter. The depressing fact was that Cobra salaries had been on a steady downward slide for the past two years, and even with the extra hazard pay he got out here at the edge of Aventine's expansion area, he simply couldn't afford to dump uncooperative appliances. Not when there was still a chance they could be repaired.

Unfortunately, he couldn't afford to dump a ruined meal, either.

He picked away as much of the blackened cheese as he could without giving up on the meal entirely. Then, taking the plate over to the breakfast nook, he keyed his computer for the news feed and sat down to eat.

The news, as usual, was right up there with the quality of his meal. The late-year election season was heating up, and puff ads by incumbents and hopefuls were starting to crowd out the usual selection of business and service commercials. Viminal, the latest addition to the Cobra Worlds, announced that its population had just passed the twenty-two thousand mark, and Governor Conzjuaraz was taking the opportunity to remind Aventinians that there was a world's worth of good land out there going cheap.

And right at the end, almost as an afterthought, came a report that there'd been another spine leopard attack at the edge of a settlement out past Mayring in Willaway Province. Five of the big predators had been involved, killing three settlers and injuring eight others. The local Cobras were already on the hunt in hopes of catching and killing the family-pack before it struck again.

The report was only an hour old, but already two of Aventine's most outspoken politicians had jumped on it with their usual and predictable stances as the news switched over into commentary. Governor Ellen Hoffman had gotten on record first, pointing to the incident as proof that the government needed to budget more money for Cobra recruitment and training. Senior Governor Tomo Treakness was right behind her, sympathizing with the victims while at the same time managing to imply it was partially their fault for moving out into the planet's wilderness areas in the first place instead of filling up the cities and farms the way good sociable people were apparently supposed to. He also made it clear that he would vigorously oppose pouring more money into the MacDonald and Sun Centers, declaring that the incident proved that an expansion of the Cobra program wasn't the solution.

By the time Lorne finally turned off the feed in disgust, the worst taste in his mouth was no longer that of burned pizza.

He loaded the dishes in the washer for later, giving the cooker a baleful look as he did so and wondering once again how long he could keep his shaky finances a secret from the rest of his family. His brother Merrick, who had been assigned to the small Cobra contingent in Capitalia, was paid even less than Lorne was, but the Cobra barracks attached to the MacDonald Center had rooms that went for a quarter of the price of even Lorne's miniscule apartment. Besides that, Merrick had parents and grandparents right there in the city with him, whose houses he could go to for meals on a regular basis. Especially since with his gourmet skills he could bargain for those meals with the offer to cook them.

Someday, Lorne vowed to himself, he really should learn how to cook something.

He was fastening his tunic and heading for the door when his comm buzzed. He pulled it out, frowning at the ID as he keyed it on. What in the Worlds was Commandant Yoshio Ishikuma calling for when Lorne would be there in another fifteen minutes? Keying it on, he held it to his ear. "Broom."

"You left your apartment yet?" Ishikuma asked.

"Just heading out now," Lorne assured him.

"Well, when you hit the door, break left instead of right," Ishikuma said. "There's an aircar coming in from the Dome to get you."

Lorne felt his stomach close into a hard knot around his breakfast. "What's happened?"

"No idea," Ishikuma said. "But they're not coming with an armed guard, so whatever you've been doing in your off-hours you can relax about."

"Like we actually have any off-hours," Lorne said, trying to sound his usual flippant self even as his stomach tightened another couple of turns. Had something happened to his father or sister on Caelian? On that hell-world, death could come in a splintered heartbeat, and from any of a hundred different directions.

Or could someone have found out where Lorne's mother and Merrick had disappeared to?

"Just remember that it could always be worse," Ishikuma said. "You could be on burial duty in Hunter's Crossing."

"Yes, I heard about that," Lorne said grimly. "We sending anyone to help in the hunt?"

"So far, they haven't asked," Ishikuma said. "But it might not matter. If Willaway is getting an uptick in spiny activity, we could see the same thing here by the end of next week. So whatever the fancy desks in Capitalia want with you, close it down fast and get your tail back out here."

"Don't worry," Lorne promised. He pulled open the building's front door and turned left toward the airfield eight blocks away. "By the way, if they're calling me in to tell me they want to shower us with new funding, how much do we want?"

"Chin-deep ought to do it," Ishikuma said. "No need to be greedy."

"Chin-deep it is," Lorne agreed. "See you soon."

"Just watch your back," Ishikuma warned. "These days, every Cobra in the Worlds has a bull's-eye tattooed there."

"Understood," Lorne said. "I'll be back as soon as I can." He keyed off the comm and picked up his pace.

It was definitely going to be one of those days.

The aircar waiting on the field had Directorate markings on it, which meant the vehicle and its driver were attached to the fifteen most powerful people in the Cobra Worlds. Given the violent political polarizations currently swirling around those fifteen people, Lorne expected the driver to present as neutral and nonaligned an attitude as it was possible for a human being to achieve.

Sure enough, the other greeted Lorne with exactly the correct degree of cool courtesy as he ushered him into the passenger section. He quickly and efficiently got the vehicle into the air, and then spent the next two and a half hours saying absolutely nothing.

They put down in the private landing terrace behind the Dome, the two-decades-old governmental building that had been named after the much larger and more dramatic structure in the main governmental center of the distant Dominion of Man. Lorne had always thought the name here to be more than a little pretentious, given that the Dominion held sway over seventy worlds—possibly more than that now—while the Cobra Worlds numbered a paltry and underdeveloped five.

Still, it could have been worse. They could have named the center after one of the previous governor-generals, very few of whom had been worth naming anything significant after. At least, not as Lorne read his family's history.

The driver had called ahead, and there was a young woman with a red-and-white shoulder band waiting when Lorne emerged from the aircar. "Cobra Lorne Broom?" she asked briskly.

"Yes," Lorne confirmed, slightly taken aback by her open face and genuinely pleasant smile. Either her job was secure enough that she didn't have to worry about keeping her head below the political firestorms, or else she hadn't been at the Dome long enough to have learned the driver's studied caution and neutrality.

"Welcome to the Dome," she said, holding out her hand. "I'm Nissa Gendreves, secondary assistant to Governor-General Chintawa."

"Nice to meet you," Lorne said, taking her hand in a brief handshake. The woman had a good, firm grip. "What exactly does a secondary assistant do?"

"All the unpaid, unglamorous, and dirty jobs no one else wants," she said straightforwardly and unapologetically, her friendly smile going a little dry. "Though I think that in this particular case someone must have slipped up." She gestured to a door behind her, flanked by two Cobras in semidress uniforms. "If you'll follow me, the governor-general is waiting."

She led the way through the door into a nicely appointed hallway filled with other governmental types. The older ones—the governors, syndics, and top bureaucrats—mostly moved at sedate walks, as befit their noble status and venerable ages. Those of Nissa's age or slightly older moved much faster on apparently less dignified errands. Most of the latter group, Lorne noted, had assistant or aide shoulder bands of various colors. "What did you mean that someone must have slipped up?" he asked as they headed toward the center of the building.

"I meant that acting as your escort is hardly one of the dirty jobs," Nissa said. "You're something of a celebrity, you know. Or at least your family is."

"Was," Lorne corrected. "Not so much anymore."

"Perhaps, but they certainly were once," Nissa conceded. "I read about your mother when I was a little girl, the first female Cobra and all. Even if the Qasaman mission didn't come out the way everyone hoped, she was still the first woman to step up and take the challenge. That makes her someone special."

"I've always thought so," Lorne murmured, wondering what Nissa would say if he told her that the official history of the Qasaman mission was pretty much a complete and bald-faced fabrication. Wondered what her response would be if he told her that his mother had actually succeeded in every damn thing they'd sent her to Qasama to accomplish, and a whole lot more.

But it wasn't worth the effort. Nissa was young and idealistic, and that sort of revelation would either upset her or simply convince her that Lorne was a biased and untrustworthy observer. Nissa had passed through the Worlds' school system, and as he himself had learned, that system never let truth get in the way of the official line. "So what am I doing here?" he asked instead.

"I really don't know," she said. "But Governor-General Chintawa seemed very anxious to see you."

"So it's just the governor-general who's waiting for me?" Lorne probed gently.

"I don't know—he didn't have me on conference call," Nissa said dryly. "Come on, Cobra Broom. I know your family was well-known for its political machinations, but pumping me for information isn't going to get you anywhere."

"Yes, I can see that," Lorne said, pushing back a fresh flicker of annoyance.

Still, that one, at least, *did* have a certain ring of truth to it.

There was a secretary and another pair of Cobra guards stationed outside Chintawa's private office. The former looked up and silently nodded Nissa toward the door, while the latter moved a step farther apart to indicate their own acceptance of the visitors' right to pass unchallenged. One of the Cobras caught Lorne's eye and gave him a microscopic nod of acknowledgment as Nissa led the way between them and pushed open the door.

Lorne had visited the governor-general's official office once or twice, that large and photogenic chamber where public business, meetings, and interviews took place. He'd never before seen Chintawa's private office, though, and his first impression as he followed Nissa in was that a Willaway windstorm must have swept through overnight. The oversized desk was almost literally covered with scattered stacks of papers, though none of the stacks seemed to be more than a few pages deep. The floor-to-ceiling shelves were crammed with books, awards, and dozens of small mementos Chintawa had collected during his years on the political scene, all arranged haphazardly without any of the calculated symmetry or eye appeal of the similar shelves in the official office. There were no windows, but across from the shelves was a group of nine displays, all of them set to different news channels with the volume down and simul transcriptions crawling across the pictures. Directly across from the desk, where it was the first thing Chintawa would see when he lifted his head from his papers or his computer, was a full-wall montage of scenes from different parts of the five Cobra Worlds.

"Cobra Broom," Chintawa said, smiling as he looked up. "Good of you to come. Please, sit down." He gestured to a chair at the corner of his desk. "Can Nissa get you some refreshment?"

"No, thank you," Lorne said as he crossed to the indicated chair and sat down.

Chintawa nodded to Nissa. "Dismissed."

"Yes, sir." Nissa's eyes flicked once to Lorne, and then she was gone.

"Impressive young lady," Chintawa commented as the door closed behind her with a solid-sounding thunk. "I'm sure you didn't get much of a feel for her on the short walk from the landing terrace, but she really is quite bright."

"Well read, too," Lorne murmured. "She was telling me all about my family history."

"Now, now—you're way too young to go all cynical on me," Chintawa chided mildly. "Anyway, she's young yet. Idealistic. Believes what she reads in school. She'll learn." He leaned back in his chair. "But I didn't ask you here to talk about your family's past. I brought you here to talk about your family's present."

Lorne frowned. "Excuse me?"

"Specifically," Chintawa continued, "I want to know where your mother is."

Lorne felt his heart seize up inside his ceramic-laminated rib cage. Had Chintawa somehow found out about his mother and brother's quiet and incredibly illegal trip to Qasama? "She's somewhere in the wilderness out past Pindar," he said, managing with a supreme effort to keep his voice steady. "Didn't Merrick tell Commandant Dreysler that when he requested temporary leave?"

"Yes, he did," Chintawa said, eyeing Lorne closely. "And at the time I was willing to let it slide."

"What do you mean?" Lorne asked, and immediately cursed himself for doing so. Now he was going to have to hear Chintawa's answer, and he was pretty sure he wasn't going to like it.

He was right. "Please, Broom," Chintawa scoffed. "Jin Moreau Broom, the first woman Cobra, who single-handedly took down a traitorous Qasaman and his Troft allies, suddenly going all to pieces in the Esserling scrubland just because her husband and daughter have gone off on a visit to Caelian?" He snorted. "You forget that as governor-general I have access to *genuine* Cobra Worlds' history."

"We really should see about getting that published someday," Lorne said stiffly. "As to Mom being upset about Dad and Jody going to Caelian, I didn't realize Cobras weren't allowed to be concerned about their loved ones."

"Of course she's allowed to be concerned," Chintawa said. "But going off to commune with nature simply isn't her style."

"People's styles change."

"Not that much they don't," Chintawa said flatly. "More significantly, people worried about their loved ones don't deliberately go incommunicado for days at a time. We've tried both their comms—repeatedly—and get nothing but their voice stacks."

"Maybe they just don't feel like talking to anyone in the Dome."

"Or maybe they aren't out crying in the wilderness at all," Chintawa countered brusquely. "They're with your great-uncle Corwin, aren't they?"

Lorne blinked, the sheer unexpectedness of the question bringing his mad scramble for a good defensible position to a skidding halt. "*What*?" he asked.

"No games," Chintawa said sternly. "I've been keeping track of Corwin Moreau's work over the years. I know that right now he's trying to develop a type of bone laminate that might ease some of the long-term anemia and arthritis problems. The fact that your mother and brother have suddenly disappeared tells me he's reached the point where he's ready to do some field tests with actual Cobras."

"That's ridiculous," Lorne said with as much dignity as he could drum up on the spur of the moment. It *was* ridiculous, actually—Uncle Corwin had been working on and off on the Cobra medical problems for most of Lorne's lifetime, and as far as Lorne knew he'd never gotten any traction with any of them.

But Chintawa obviously didn't know that. And in fact, the more Lorne thought about it, the more he realized the governor-general's suspicions made for a much better cover story than even the one he, Merrick, Jody, and their dad had come up with.

"It's not ridiculous, and I frankly don't care what any of them is doing," Chintawa said. "The point is that I need your mother here, and I need her here now."

"What for?"

"Something important and confidential," Chintawa said. "Also something I think will help put your family in a better light than it's been in for the past several years." He smiled faintly. "She's not in trouble, if that's what you're wondering."

If you only knew, Lorne thought grimly. "It would certainly be nice to have the record set at least a little straighter," he said, "though it would probably be terribly confusing to people like Nissa. You say you need her right now?"

"By noon tomorrow, actually," Chintawa said. "If absolutely necessary I could probably postpone the ceremony a couple of days."

Lorne frowned. "Ceremony?"

Chintawa smiled faintly. "You'll know when your mother knows," he said. "Until then, it's my prerogative to be mysterious."

"In that case, it's my prerogative to take my leave," Lorne said, standing up. "If I hear from her, I'll be sure and let her know you're looking for her."

"Just a minute," Chintawa said, his voice darkening as he also stood up. "That's it?"

"What do you want me to say?" Lorne countered. "That I'll bring my mother in whether she wants to be here or not? I can't promise that. If you want to tell me something that'll sweeten the pot, I'll be happy to hear it."

"You want the pot sweetened?" Chintawa rumbled. "Fine. Tell her that if she isn't here, other people will get all the credit and she'll get nothing. *And* they'll get to put their own spin on it, which will leave the Moreau name right where it is. In the historical gutter."

Lorne snorted. "With all due respect, sir, my family stopped caring about who got credit for what a long time ago. And unless you're planning to nominate my mother for sainthood, it's going to take more than anything you can do to put our family name back where it deserves."

"Certainly not if you aren't willing to make some effort of your own," Chintawa ground out. "If you can't see that, why should I waste my time trying to help?"

"I don't know," Lorne said sarcastically. This was probably not the direction his mother or father would take the conversation, and certainly not where Uncle Corwin would go. But he didn't have their verbal finesse, and he simply couldn't think of anything else to try. "Maybe because you see some political gain in it for yourself?"

Chintawa's face darkened like an approaching thunderstorm. "How in the Worlds did you grow up in the Moreau family without learning anything about politics?" he demanded. "It's not a zero-sum game, you know. What's gain for me can also be gain for you."

"And all you need for that gain is to put my mother up on a stage like your private sock puppet?" Lorne suggested.

Chintawa muttered something under his breath. "Get out of here," he ordered. "Just get out."

"As you wish, Governor-General Chintawa," Lorne said formally, starting to breathe again as he stood up. It had actually worked. He'd made Chintawa so mad at him that he didn't even want to see Lorne's mother anymore.

Now if Chintawa would just stay this mad long enough for Lorne to get out of Capitalia and back to DeVegas Province, this whole thing might blow over. Or at least quiet down long enough for his mother and brother to finish up their mysterious errand on Qasama and get back home.

He'd made it halfway to the office door when Chintawa cleared his throat. "And where exactly do you think you're going?"

Lorne stopped but didn't turn around. "I'm going back to my duty station," he said over his shoulder. "As per your orders."

"I've given you no such orders," Chintawa said. "But since you bring it up, let's do that, shall we? You're hereby relieved of all other duties and tasked with the job of finding Cobra Jasmine Moreau Broom and bringing her to the Dome."

Lorne turned around, feeling his mouth drop open. "*What?*"

"You heard me," Chintawa said. The thunderstorm of anger had passed, leaving frozen ground behind it. "Until your mother is standing in front of me, you're not going back to Archway or anywhere else."

"This is ridiculous," Lorne protested. "I have work to do."

"Then you'd better persuade your mother to come in, hadn't you?" Chintawa said. "Otherwise, you'd better get used to living in your parents' house again."

"This is illegal and out of channels. Sir," Lorne bit out. "Barring a declared state of emergency, you can't counteract standing orders and assignments."

"You're welcome to appeal to Commandant Dreysler," Chintawa said. "But I can tell you right now that the orders will be cut before you even reach his office."

For a long moment the two men locked eyes. "Fine," Lorne said stiffly. It was clear that Chintawa had his mind made up. It was also clear that Lorne himself didn't have the faintest idea of what to do now.

But he knew who might. "I'll need a way to get to Uncle Corwin's house," he continued. "Cobra pay doesn't stretch far enough to cover car rentals."

Chintawa reached over and touched a switch on his intercom. "Nissa, come in here, please."

He straightened up again, and the staring contest resumed. Thirty-two seconds later by Lorne's nanocomputer clock, the door opened and Nissa stepped inside. "Yes, sir?" she asked, a slight frown creasing her forehead as her eyes flicked back and forth between the two men.

"Until further notice, you're assigned to Cobra Broom," Chintawa told her. "Check out a car and take him anywhere in or around Capitalia he wants to go. If he wants to leave the city, call Ms. Oomara first and have her clear it with me."

"Yes, sir," Nissa said, her forehead clearing as she apparently decided whatever was happening was none of her business. "Cobra Broom?"

Lorne held his glare another second and a half. Then, turning away from Chintawa, he stalked across the room, past the girl, and out the door.

It was going to be one of those days, all right. And then some.

Corwin Moreau listened silently as Lorne described the morning's events, occasionally nodding in reaction to something his great-nephew said, his fingertips occasionally rubbing gently at the arm of his chair in response to some inner thoughts or musings of his own.

"And so I came here," Lorne finished, looking briefly over at Aunt Thena, who had listened to the tale in the same silence as her husband. "It might not have been very smart, but I couldn't think of anything else to do."

"No, you did fine," Corwin assured him, looking questioningly at Thena. She gave a slight shrug in return. "Is the young lady still waiting out there? We should at least invite her in for lunch."

"I don't know if she's there or not," Lorne said. "Probably not—I told her I'd be here for a while, and she told me she has family a couple of blocks away. Maybe that's why Chintawa gave her the job of carting me around in the first place. He probably figured I'd go to ground here, and she might as well have someplace of her own to wait for me."

"Or else she got the job because he thought you might open up to someone who wasn't a hardened politician," Thena offered. "It's an old trick, and not beneath Chintawa's dignity."

"Certainly not if lying isn't," Lorne growled.

Corwin cocked an eyebrow at him. "What did he lie about?"

"Oh, come on," Lorne scoffed. "This whole secret ceremony thing? How obvious can a lie get?"

"Well, that's the point, isn't it?" Corwin said thoughtfully. "It's such an obviously ridiculous cover story that one has to wonder whether it might actually be true."

Lorne frowned. "Have you heard something?"

"No, not a whisper," Corwin said. "But I'm hardly in the official gossip ring these days."

"Besides being obvious, the story's also pointless," Thena added. "As a Cobra, your mother is still a reservist, and hence subject to immediate call-up by the governor-general for any reason. He can order her to appear at the Dome, or order you to go get her, with no explanation needed."

"Maybe," Lorne said. "But right now it doesn't really matter why he wants her. What we need is a way to stall him off. And I can tell you right now, he didn't look to be in a stalling mood."

"Not if he's willing to pull a Cobra in from frontier duty," Corwin agreed heavily. "Especially right after a major spine leopard attack in the same general region. Any chance he could be persuaded to accept the story that she and Merrick are off on a retreat somewhere?"

"No," Lorne said. "And in fact, he pointed out the logical flaw in it: that they wouldn't go off without leaving some way of contacting them."

"Yes, that was always the weak spot," Corwin said heavily. "I should have come up with something better."

"You didn't have much time," Thena pointed out. "Besides, there was no way to guess that anyone would take more than a passing interest in their absence."

"I suppose," Corwin conceded. "So now what?"

"Well, we can't pretend they're hiding here," Thena said slowly. "If Chintawa is determined enough to get a search warrant, a few patrollers could pop that balloon within half an hour."

"So again, they're somewhere else," Corwin said. "Someplace where Lorne presumably can try to call them."

"Right now?" Lorne asked, pulling out his comm.

"Yes, this would be good," Corwin confirmed, looking at his watch. "You've been here just long enough to have consulted with us, and for us to have decided together that this is worth breaking into her solitude. Go ahead—your mother first."

Lorne nodded and punched in his mother's number. "I presume this is purely for the benefit of anyone who might decide to pull my comm records later?"

"Correct." Corwin hesitated. "It'll also put all the rest of us in a slightly better legal position should the worst-case scenario happen."

Lorne felt his throat tighten. That scenario being if his mother and brother got caught sneaking back onto Aventine from Qasama and were brought up on charges of treason.

At which point, of course, all of Uncle Corwin's caution would go scattering to the four winds, because Lorne was absolutely not going to hunker down behind legal excuses while two of his family stood in the dock. He would be right up there with them, as would his father and sister. And probably Uncle Corwin and Aunt Thena, too.

At which point Chintawa and the Directorate would have to decide whether they really wanted to risk the kind of political fallout that could come of prosecuting the whole family.

Lorne almost hoped they did. He would use the occasion to make sure the true story of his mother's original mission to Qasama got brought up into the open from the shallow grave where Uncle Corwin's political enemies had buried it.

"Hello, this is Jasmine," his mother's voice came in his ear. "I'm not available right now, but if you'd care to leave a message..."

Lorne waited for the greeting to run its course, recorded a short message telling her to call as soon as it was convenient, and keyed off. "Now Merrick?" he asked.

Corwin nodded, and Lorne went through the same charade with his brother's voice stack. "That sound okay?" he asked when he was finished.

"Perfect," Corwin said. "Another half hour, I think, and it'll be time to try again." He squinted toward one of the windows that looked out onto the walkway leading between the front door and the gate at the edge of the grounds. "Meanwhile, let's put our heads together and see if we can come up with a plan."

"We can do that while we eat," Thena said firmly. "If we're all going to end up in jail tonight, we might as well have a good meal first."

Lunch was, Lorne assumed, up to Thena's usual culinary standards. He didn't know for sure because he didn't really taste any of it. His full attention then, and for the rest of the afternoon, was on their conversation and brainstorming.

He continued to call his mother and brother at half-hour intervals, leaving messages that under Uncle Corwin's coaching gradually increased in anxiety and frustration. It would take a preliminary indictment and court order to tap into those messages, he knew, but at this point he wouldn't put anything past Chintawa.

Late in the afternoon the governor-general himself called, looking for a progress report. In complete honesty, Lorne told him that, no, the missing family members weren't at Uncle Corwin's, and that he hadn't been able to get hold of either of them by comm. Chintawa ordered him to keep trying, and hung up.

The three of them were sitting down to dinner when Nissa called to ask Lorne if he would be needing her to drive him anywhere else. Lorne assured her that he would be staying the night, and that he'd be sure to call her if and when he needed to go somewhere. She reminded him that she was always available, should he change his mind, slipped in a subtle reminder that wandering off without her would get both of them in trouble with Chintawa, and wished him a pleasant good evening.

"You'd better watch that girl," Corwin warned after Lorne relayed the conversation. "She may come across as a wide-eyed ingenue standing high above the political mud, but she clearly knows how to find and push a person's buttons."

"What, because she told me she'd get in trouble if I ditched her?" Lorne scoffed.

"Exactly," Corwin said. "Take it from someone who once played on that same field. She's got your profile down cold, and I don't think she'd hesitate to bring the lasers to bear if she was ordered to do so."

They finished dinner, which Lorne again assumed was excellent, and continued talking well past sundown and into the night. A hundred plans were brought up, discussed, and ultimately discarded, and by the time Lorne said his good-nights and headed to the guest room they were no further toward a solution than they were when they'd started.

He slept fitfully, waking up for long stretches at a time. Probably the city noises, he told himself, which he was no longer accustomed to after all the time he'd spent fighting spine leopards at the edges of civilization.

It was still dark, and he'd finally fallen into a deep sleep, when he was jolted awake by the trilling of his comm.

He grabbed the device and keyed it on, his first half-fogged thought that Merrick and his mother were back on Aventine and were returning his calls. "Hello?" he croaked.

"It's Nissa," Nissa's voice came, quivering with tension. "Get dressed—I need to get you back to the Dome right away. I'll be there in five minutes—"

"Wait a second, hold on," Lorne interrupted, his brain snapping fully awake at the simmering panic in her voice. "What's going on?"

"There's no time," she said. "An astronomer at North Bank picked up a fleet of ships—Troft ships, they think—heading eastward towards Capitalia from orbit. And none of the ships register on radar."

Lorne felt his muscles tense as the full implications of that fact blew away the last wisps of sleepiness. "I'll meet you at the gate," he said, and keyed off. Dropping the comm on the bed, he grabbed for his clothes.

He'd been afraid the call was bad news about his mother and brother. It was far worse...because there was just one type of ship designed not to show up on traffic control's radar.

Warships.

A century ago, the Dominion of Man had set up the Aventine colony, ostensibly as a way to get rid of the Cobra war veterans, but also as a deterrent to the Trofts against launching future attacks on Dominion worlds. Barely twenty-five years later, the colonists' connection to the rest of humanity had been closed, but the deterrent effect of the Cobras' presence had remained.

Until now. It was unbelievable. It was insane. But apparently, it was also true. The Cobras' century-old bluff had been called.

Aventine was under attack.

CHAPTER TWO

"The secret to a contented life," Paul Broom commented sagely as he scraped bits of green spore off his silliweave tunic, "is to find a comfortable morning routine and stick with it."

Jody Broom paused in the process of scraping her own tunic and gave her father one of the disbelieving stares she'd worked so hard to master during her teenage years. "You really want to be saying things like that when I have a razor in my hand?" she asked.

"But I thought this was the life you'd always dreamed about," he said, turning innocent eyes on her. "Out here in the wilds of humanity's frontier, degrees in animal physiology and management firmly in hand, cutting an impressive swath through—" He indicated the tunic in his hand. "Well, through tiny little creatures growing on silicon clothing."

"Oh, this is the life, all right," Jody said sourly, turning back to her work. "It's also been occurring to me more and more lately that I could just as easily have turned my impressive animal management degree into the field of hamster breeding."

"Hamsters? Pheh," her father scoffed. "Where's the fame and glory in that?"

"You ever see a hamster go rogue?" Jody countered. "Or worse, a whole herd of them?"

Paul gave a low whistle. "I had no idea how dangerous—" He

broke off, shifting his scraper to his other hand and flashing a fingertip laser blast across the room. Jody turned in time to see a coin-sized buzzic drop to the floor. "How dangerous livestock that size could be," he continued, his eyes carefully sweeping the room. "I'm grateful now that you didn't choose to go into that line of work. Get down a bit, would you?"

Jody dropped into a low crouch, wincing as her father fired four more laser shots over her head into the wall and ceiling. There were four more thunks, louder ones this time, and she turned to see four freshly killed thumb-sized flycrawlers smoldering on the floor behind her. "I think they're getting bigger," Paul commented.

"Almost big enough to take on my hamster farm," Jody agreed, her throat tightening. "How in the Worlds are bugs that size getting in?"

"The boys must have missed a spot," Paul said, crossing the room and peering down at the insects. "Maybe in one of the upper corners or alongside a window where a vine's taken root and started pulling the plaster apart. You let them get a foothold and start a crack, and that's all they need."

Jody went to her father's side. Already tiny spots of green were starting to appear on the burned insect carcasses as microscopic airborne spores found something to eat and set to work with a vengeance. And once the flycrawlers settled in, she knew, the micewhiskers would be right behind them, and before long it would take a Cobra to clear them all out.

Luckily for Jody and her two teammates, they had one. "Have I mentioned lately how grateful I am you came along on this trip?" she asked her father.

"Once or twice," he assured her. "I was just trying to think of that poem. 'Big fleas have little fleas upon their backs to bite 'em. And little fleas something something.'"

"'And little fleas have lesser fleas, and so *ad infinitum*,'" Jody quoted. "Except that on Caelian, the whole process seems to work backwards."

There was a double thunk as the airlock door one room over opened and closed, and Jody turned to see Geoff Boulton and Freylan Sonderby walk into the room. "Okay, the house is all scraped," Geoff announced briskly as he brushed at some dust on his tunic sleeve. "Ready to head out as soon as—" He stopped as he suddenly seemed to notice the odd way Jody and her father were standing. "What is it?" he asked.

Paul gestured silently to the floor. Geoff threw a look at Freylan, and the two young men crossed to Jody's side.

For a moment no one said anything, but simply stood in their semicircle staring at the dead insects as if it was some sort of funereal viewing ritual. Then, Freylan stirred. "It's the southeast corner," he said. "There's a flange up there that I've never thought looked quite right."

"And you didn't do anything about it?" Geoff asked, a dark edge to his voice.

"I thought it was all right," Freylan said with a sigh. "It looked solid enough, just a little oddly shaped."

"What did Governor Uy tell us when we first got here?" Geoff demanded. "Odd shapes, odd fittings, and odd colorations are the first signs of trouble. Blast it all, Freylan." He waved a hand in disgust. "Come on—show me where it is."

"You won't be able to reach it," Freylan said, a sort of kicked-dog look in his eyes as he headed back toward the door. "The step stool isn't tall enough. We'll have to find a ladder we can borrow."

"I can get up there," Paul volunteered. "Let me finish with my tunic and I'll go with you."

"Go ahead," Jody said. "I'll finish your tunic."

"What, go out in my underwear?" Paul asked, sounding vaguely scandalized as he gestured to his silliweave singlet.

"People in Stronghold go outside in their underwear all the time," Jody growled, warning him with her eyes. This wasn't the time for jokes.

Fortunately, he got the message. "We'll be back in a minute," he said. He gestured Freylan ahead of him, and the two men left the room.

"I'll do that," Geoff growled, holding out his hand as Jody picked up her father's tunic. "You've got your own to do."

"I've got it," Jody said firmly, half turning and bumping his arm aside with her shoulder as he tried to take the tunic from her. "You go make sure the packs are ready."

"Are you mad at me for telling Freylan he screwed up?" Geoff demanded. "Damn it all, Jody, this is *Caelian*. You screw up here and you get eaten alive."

"Yes, I remember the lecture," Jody said as she started scraping the bits of green off the tunic. "I also remember that none of us has exactly been the pride of the litter as far as screw-ups are concerned."

"We've been here eleven days," Geoff growled. "Screw-up incidence is supposed to be on a downward curve by now."

"It is," Jody said flatly. "And jumping down Freylan's throat isn't going to flatten the curve any faster."

Geoff hissed between his teeth. "You're sorry you came along on this fiasco, aren't you?"

"I didn't say that."

"But you're *thinking* it."

Jody didn't answer, but kept working at the tunic. There wasn't supposed to be anything organic in the material for the little green spores to eat, but as the wind blew the spores themselves through the Caelian air, it also blew along microscopic bits of their food.

And as her father had pointed out, letting even harmless spores get ahead of them was the first step on the road to disaster.

"I said you were thinking it," Geoff repeated into the silence, a fresh edge of challenge in his voice.

Jody took a deep breath. So he was in the mood for a fight, was he? Fine. She was willing to oblige. "I came along because I thought my training might help in figuring out a solution to this place," she said stiffly. "But that wasn't the reason I was invited, was it?"

A sudden shadow flicked across the anger and frustration in Geoff's face. "What are you talking about?" he asked carefully.

"I'm talking about the *real* reason you asked me to join you and Freylan out here," Jody said. "It wasn't my animal training you wanted at all. It was—"

She broke off at the sound of the double doors opening again, and turned her attention back to the tunic she was supposed to be scraping.

But before she did, she had the slightly guilty pleasure of seeing a look of shame briefly cross Geoff's face.

"That was the spot, all right," Paul announced as he and Freylan came into the room. "It should be all right now."

"At least until the next vine gets a grip," Freylan muttered, still brooding over his failure to catch the chink earlier.

"When it does, we'll deal with it," Paul said calmly. "How are we doing in here?"

"Almost ready," Jody said, giving her father's tunic a final inspection. Geoff, she noted, had quietly slipped into the other room where the packs were stacked. "Yes, it's done," she confirmed, handing it over. "I wonder what you do if you're allergic to this stuff."

"You probably itch a lot," Paul said, giving the tunic a quick once-over of his own and then slipping it on. "Either that, or you get used to walking around naked."

"Not you personally," Freylan added hastily, his cheeks reddening.

Jody turned back to her own unfinished tunic, a smile sneaking onto her face despite her grouchy mood. Freylan could be so adorably awkward sometimes. "I know," she said over her shoulder to him. "But at least you'd still have your skin."

"Speaking of skin," Paul said, stepping smoothly in on top of Freylan's embarrassment, "did you get anything more from that red-tail?"

"Not really," Freylan said, and Jody could hear the relief in his voice at the return to safer scientific ground. "I'm still ninety percent convinced that odor has something to do with it. But there's too much overlap between the red-tail and the groundsniffer for me to figure out what the key might be."

"If it's there at all," Paul warned.

"It's there," Freylan said firmly. "*Something*'s there. Otherwise, the spores and other vegetation would attack *all* hair and fur, instead of just everything from five or six millimeters out."

Jody grimaced, running her fingers over the stubble that had once been a lovingly-cared-for head of hair. The very first thing they'd been ordered to do when the *Freedom's Fire* lifted off Aventine en route for Caelian was to shave their heads and body hair. Of all the unpleasant aspects of their brief time here, that was the one she still couldn't get used to.

But it wasn't like there was any choice in the matter. Caelian's rich and aggressive plant life attacked anything with even a trace of organic, carbon-bearing material in it, the skin of living beings the only exception to that rule. And much as she missed her hair Jody had no wish to wake up every morning with her body covered by little green spores.

In and of themselves, the spores wouldn't have been so bad. They loved to settle on and eat the natural fibers and synthetics that made up most clothing, but that was a slow process and would hardly leave a person running home from the shops clutching rags to her chest, despite the way her father had made it sound.

The problem was that vigorous Caelian plants attracted voracious Caelian animals. The first to come were always the insects, from buzzics to flycrawlers all the way up to some that Jody hadn't seen yet but was told could be mistaken for small birds. The insects would start eating the plants, inevitably moth-chewing some of the clothing material in the process, and eventually a person *would* be running home covered in nothing but rags and insects.

But it got worse. Brushed-off insects attracted carrion eaters, plants and animals both, which attracted larger animals, which attracted still larger animals, which finally attracted the massive, tiger-sized predators who could take on human-sized prey without even blinking.

It was how all planetary ecologies worked, of course. The problem was that on Caelian it worked faster and more violently than on Aventine or any other world humanity had run into over the centuries.

Worse yet, even by Caelian's own harsh standards, the ecology seemed to work harder and faster against humans than against its own members. It was as if the planet itself resented the newcomers who had pushed their way into its private biological war and had mustered all its combined forces in an effort to force them off.

"But at the same time odor can't be the whole story," Freylan went on into Jody's musings, "because artificial odor applications don't do any good, or at least nothing has that's been tried. It has to be some combination of things no one's figured out yet."

"Well, I hope someone does so soon," Paul said, making a face as he worked his shoulders against his tunic. "I don't mind mineral-based houses and furniture, but this clothing is about as uncomfortable as anything I've ever worn in my life."

"I've heard there are supposed to be a couple of companies on Aventine that are working on alternatives," Freylan said. "But with a potential customer base of less than five thousand, I doubt they're working very hard."

Geoff poked his head around the doorway. "We going to talk all morning, or are we going to check on the trap?" he asked crossly. "Come on, come on."

"We're ready," Paul said, meeting the younger man's irritation with the steadfast calm Jody had found annoying when she was growing up and had only gradually learned to admire.

"Ready," Jody confirmed, giving her tunic one last sweep of the razor and slipping it on.

"I'll grab my pack and go get the aircar started," Freylan volunteered, slipping a bit gingerly past Geoff and heading for the door.

"I'll go with you," Paul said, and followed him out.

Geoff looked at Jody, and she could see him wondering if she was going to drag them back to the conversation the others' arrival had interrupted. But Jody's anger had cooled to mere annoyance. She simply returned his gaze in silence, and after a moment he nodded. "Okay, then," he said with forced briskness. "Let's go see if we've finally got ourselves a gigger."

"Yes, let's." Jody gestured toward the door. "After you."

The first colonists on Caelian, knowing from the assessment teams the kind of aggressive ecology they were up against, had envisioned a series of small towns encircled by high walls to protect against the larger predators, with the settlements connected by a network of roads made by clearing, sterilizing, and melt-paving wide pathways through the forest.

It hadn't worked out that way. The ceramic walls had worked for a few months, but eventually the stubborn airborne spores had managed to get a foothold, and once that happened the rest inevitably followed. Stronghold's replacement wall, this one not of ceramic but stainless steel, worked better, but even with periodic scraping its surface had become badly pitted.

The roads hadn't worked at all. The effects of standard burning lasted a few days at the most, and even sterilizing burns were only good for a few weeks at a time. The fifty-meter-wide clear zone outside Stronghold's wall, plus the larger rectangle adjoining it to the south that acted as the planet's spaceport landing area, were cleared every two weeks. Ground vehicles were still of some use inside Caelian's six remaining towns, but outside those walls aircars were the only practical means of transportation.

The forest beyond Stronghold's clear zone was as teeming with life as anywhere else on the planet, and in theory the team could have worked their traps right there. But Geoff and Freylan had wanted to get a little farther from any effects of human civilization, miniscule though those effects might be, and had opted instead for a hillside about five kilometers northwest of the main gate.

The four of them had spent their first day on Caelian burning off a small section of ground to serve as a landing pad for their rented aircar. Six days later they'd repeated the process. Now, only four days after that, not only had most of the grasses come back, but several small bushes had taken root as well. Jody winced at the teeth-tingling screech of thorns against metal as Geoff set them down on the pad, wondering how much of a bite the fresh scratches were going to take out of the rental's damage deposit.

But at least they'd finally nailed a gigger. As Geoff shut down the aircar's engine, she could hear the small predator's outraged snarling a dozen meters away.

"Sounds like we've got one," Freylan said with a mixture of relief and excitement as he started to open his door.

And stopped as Paul touched his shoulder. "My turn to go out first," the older man said mildly.

"Right," Freylan said, his voice muffled with embarrassment.

Mentally, Jody shook her head. Back on Aventine, when she'd first been brought aboard the project, she'd noticed Freylan's tendency to get so focused on some part of his work that he totally forgot where he was.

In Capitalia, that could be an embarrassment. On Caelian, it could get you killed.

Paul climbed out of his side of the aircar, closing the door behind him, and for a minute he stood with his back to the vehicle, his head moving slowly back and forth as his enhanced vision and hearing scoped out the section of forest closest to them. Jody held her breath, wondering which variety of Caelian's fauna would decide to check out the intruders this time. The forest had gone quiet, almost as if in anticipation of the drama about to take place...

Abruptly, Paul leaned over, brought his left leg up, and fired a burst from his antiarmor laser into a stand of bushes behind the aircar. There was a piercing scream, and with a crackle of broken branches a screech tiger half leaped, half fell into view between two of the bushes. Paul gave the area another slow sweep, then gestured the all clear.

"Man, those things are big," Geoff muttered, his eyes on the dead screech tiger as he climbed gingerly out of the car.

"Amazingly quiet, too," Paul agreed. "Especially considering their size. I didn't even know it was coming toward us until I picked up its infrared signature."

"I sure hope we find some kind of breakthrough before we have to go that far up the food chain," Freylan said feelingly as he looked at the screech tiger. "I *really* don't want to have to take blood and tissue samples from a live one of those."

"A hearty amen to that," Jody agreed, tearing her eyes away from the dead predator and looking around. The usual midmorning lull in the wind was right on schedule, and the still air around her seemed to press in with a sense of watchful foreboding. "Let's grab the gigger and get out of here before the scavengers pick up the scent."

Their animal trap was simplicity itself, consisting of a rectangular mesh box set up with its floor and sides bunched together and held loosely at ground level beneath a layer of leaves and over a deep hole dug in the ground. The minute an animal put its weight on the mesh, the floor was designed to collapse, dropping the animal into the newly formed box while a spring-loaded lid swung over from concealment to seal off the top. Jody's contribution to the contraption had been the set of cylindrical free-spinning tubes around each of the mesh's main wires, which were designed to send the captured animal's legs straight through to hang uselessly in midair in the hole instead of leaving them inside the box proper where the animal could make full use of its claws to try to escape.

The trap had worked perfectly on the team's first two captures, and as Jody reached the hole and peered down through the mesh top she saw that they were now three for three. The gigger was lying on its belly inside the box, rocking back and forth as it tried to get some kind of purchase with its feet, jabbing uselessly at the sides with the pair of hollow mouth tusks it used to impale and then suck the blood from its victims.

"Ugly little beasts, aren't they?" Geoff commented as he squatted down and started brushing the leaves from the two carrying bars that ran through the top of the cage. "Freylan, you want to get the other end?"

"Hold it," Paul said sharply. "Everyone be quiet."

Jody froze, the other two following suit. In the unmoving air the forest around her was alive with quiet sounds, muted chirps and soft buzzings. She strained her ears, wondering anxiously just how big the predator was that her father had heard sneaking up on them.

And then, somewhere in the distance, she heard a rumbling roar. Not the roar of any of Caelian's predators, but the roar of approaching aircraft. *Big* aircraft. She turned toward her father, frowning, as the sound rapidly intensified.

And suddenly, a pair of large ships shot past to the south, their upper sides visible for just an instant above the trees. The roar cut off suddenly—

"Alert!" Governor Uy's voice crackled abruptly from their aircar's comm. "All Caelians! Troft gunships have landed at Stronghold. We are under—"

The voice cut off. "Dad—?" Jody began.

"Shh," Paul said, a darkness in his voice that Jody had never heard there before. She listened to the sounds of the forest and the sudden thundering of her own pulse.

And then, drifting through the still air, she heard the distant, muffled crack of an explosion. Followed by another, and another, and another.

She looked at Geoff's taut face, and at Freylan's pale one, and at her father's grim one . . . and slowly, it dawned on her that the unthinkable had happened. The Trofts had invaded Caelian.

The Cobra Worlds were at war.

CHAPTER THREE

Nissa was waiting when Lorne reached the gate at the end of the walkway. "Any ID on the ships yet?" he asked as he dropped into the seat beside her.

"They're Trofts," she said tautly as she pulled back onto the deserted street and shoved her foot against the accelerator, sending the car leaping forward like a scalded leatherwing. "What else do we need to know?"

"Whose demesne they're from, for starters," Lorne said, grabbing at the armrest for support and fastening the restraints across his chest and hips. "It might also be nice to know if anyone's been threatening us or is an unhappy customer or something."

"I don't know anything about that," Nissa said, taking a corner dangerously fast. "Governor-General Chintawa said not to use the comm any more than I had to—he wanted to keep the system open for emergency use."

She had pulled onto Cavendish Boulevard, the main thoroughfare leading into the central part of the city, when the western sky abruptly lit up with the red firefly glows of a hundred distant grav lifts. "Here they come," Lorne said, pointing.

"Oh, God," Nissa breathed, her voice sounding half strangled. "What do we *do*?"

"We keep going," he told her, peering past the girl's head and trying to gauge the ships' speed. Two minutes, he estimated,

27

maybe three, and the armada would be right on top of them. He and Nissa should make it to the government section of the city by then, but probably not to the Dome itself. "Can you get any more speed out of this thing?" he asked.

"I don't think so," Nissa said, leaning forward a little as she presumably pressed harder on the accelerator. There was no change in the car's speed that Lorne could detect. "Where are we going?" she asked.

"The Dome, right?" Lorne countered. "That's where Chintawa told you to bring me."

"Yes, but—" She flashed a look at him. "Aren't *they* going to the Dome, too?"

"They're probably going everywhere in Capitalia," Lorne said grimly, ducking his head a little lower to try to get the best view out her window that he could from his angle. The ships were still coming in, but they were also spreading out, and he saw several of the ones in back drop precipitously out of sight below the skyline as they headed for landing points in the western parts of the city. "Where does this car live?"

"What?" Nissa asked, sounding confused.

"Is it usually parked in the main car park?" Lorne clarified. "Because there's a private tunnel connecting that to the Dome itself. Right?"

"Yes, but I'm only a second assistant," she said. "I can't use it."

"I don't think this is going to be a morning for arguing regulations," Lorne said. "If we can make it to the car park—"

And with a sudden thundering roar, the leading edge of the Troft armada shot past above them.

"Pull over!" Lorne snapped as the car bucked violently in the crosswind of the spacecrafts' slipstreams. An instant later he was thrown against the restraints as Nissa slammed on the brakes, fighting the car to a skidding halt beside the curb.

Just as a tall, shadowy ship settled on its grav lifts into the center of the intersection two blocks directly ahead.

"Out!" Lorne ordered, popping his restraints.

"But—" Nissa protested, pointing at the Troft ship, towering over the shorter buildings around them.

"I said *out!*" Lorne said, reaching over and releasing her restraints himself. Out the windshield he could see another, more compact set of grav lifts glowing their way out of the sky toward them, apparently aiming for a spot directly in front of the big warship. Pushing open his door, he got a grip on Nissa's arm and hauled her out of the car.

"What are you doing?" she gasped, struggling in his grip. "Let me go—"

Ignoring her protests, Lorne pushed her down into a crouched position against the side of the car. "Quiet," he muttered, looking cautiously over the hood. Ahead, the incoming grav lifts he'd seen resolved themselves into a small transport that was settling to the pavement about fifty meters in front of the looming Troft warship.

"Great," he muttered under his breath. A troop carrier, undoubtedly. Another minute, and they would be up to their eyebrows in Troft soldiers. "We have to get to cover," he murmured to Nissa. "Any ideas?"

"The car park's over there," she said. "Up there on the left."

Lorne grimaced. Unfortunately, the structure she was pointing to was right beside the Troft warship, directly beneath one of the stubby wings sticking out from the ship's flank up near the crest.

Wings that seemed curiously lumpy and decidedly non-aerodynamic, now that he focused on them. Frowning, he keyed in his vision enhancers' telescopic setting.

And hissed between his teeth. The wings didn't look aero-dynamic because they had absolutely nothing to do with the ship's flight characteristics. They were nothing more or less than the supports for a set of incredibly nasty-looking weapons clusters: pylon-mounted lasers and missile tubes both. "Forget the car park," he told Nissa, looking around them. Most of the nearby buildings were either retail businesses or office space for the myriad of support groups and hangers-on that always collected around governmental seats of power. At this hour, with dawn only now starting to break in the east, all those buildings would be unoccupied and locked down tight.

But the four-story structure directly ahead of them on their right had the look of an apartment building. An upper-class one, too, if the stone facing and fancy balconies were anything to go by. If they could get in there before the soldiers appeared...

Too late. Even as he looked back at the transport he saw the side loading hatches swing ponderously down.

Only it wasn't a squad of Troft soldiers who swarmed out onto the deserted street.

It was a pack of spine leopards.

Beside him, Nissa gave a muffled gasp. "Are those—?"

"They sure are," Lorne said grimly.

And suddenly it was more urgent than ever that he and Nissa get off the streets. The spinies looked a little wobbly as they walked around, as if the trip in the transport had left them groggy or disoriented. But that wouldn't last long. The minute they caught human scent out here, they would be on the hunt.

Nissa knew it, too. "You have to kill them," she said urgently, her voice trembling. "Before they get to us."

Lorne gazed at the animals, his heart sinking. There were at least fifteen of the beasts out there, plus however many more might still be out of sight in the transport's hold. Did Nissa really think a single Cobra could take on that many all by himself?

And then his stomach tightened as he finally got it. Of course no single Cobra was up to this kind of challenge. It would take a group of them, working together, to take down that many predators.

Right in the shadow of the Trofts' heavy lasers and missiles.

"You have to kill them," Nissa pleaded again.

"Maybe later," Lorne said, shifting his eyes back to the apartment building. Earlier, before the transport had unloaded its cargo, the distance to the front door had looked reasonable. Now, with spinies roaming the streets, the trip was a lot more problematic.

"What do you mean?" Nissa demanded, her voice starting to shake again. "You can't let them stay out here on the streets. You have to get rid of them."

"Quiet," Lorne bit out, looking around. With the whole area deserted, any sudden movement on his and Nissa's part would instantly draw the attention of both the Trofts and the spinies. Movement was always noticeable, and in this case movement would probably be fatal.

Unless something else started moving first.

"Are the keys still in the car?" he asked, peering in through the window.

"No, I've got them," Nissa said, holding up a closed fist as she started to move toward the car door. "Can they get through the doors or windows?"

"Probably," Lorne said. "Give me the keys, then find a place to duck down and don't move until I tell you."

She turned bewildered eyes on him. "What? You want me to stay out *here*?"

"Until I tell you," Lorne repeated, pushing her gently but firmly a meter back from the car. Prying the keys from her frozen fist, he climbed back into the car, stretching out on his stomach across the front seats. He fitted the keys into the starter and turned it on.

"What are you *doing*?" Nissa called from behind him.

"Hopefully, creating a diversion," Lorne told her, easing his head up to windshield height and turning the steering wheel toward the transport and the milling spinies. "You have anything I can use to hold down the accelerator?"

"Like what?"

"Never mind," Lorne said, prying up the floor mat and rolling it up as tightly as he could. He folded the slightly floppy cylinder over once and wedged it between the lower dashboard and the accelerator. It wouldn't stay in place very long, but with luck it would stay there long enough. Pressing his left hand down on the brake, he shifted the car into gear with his right. Then, setting his right hand against the inner edge of the driver's seat, he shoved hard on the seat, launching himself backward through the open door and simultaneously pulling his left hand off the brake.

He'd hoped to move backward fast enough to make it out of the car before the vehicle picked up too much momentum. But he wasn't quite fast enough. The edge of the doorframe clipped him across his shoulder as the car leaped forward, sending a quick jolt of pain through the shoulder and upper arm and spinning him partway around. An instant later he was clear, the doorframe narrowly missing the side of his head as the car curved away from the curb, and he got his hands under him just in time as he slammed full length onto the hard pavement. The car straightened out of its sharp turn as the steering system's self-alignment kicked in, leaving it rushing more or less in the direction of the Troft transport.

And for the next few seconds, the spinies grouped around the ship would have something more urgent to look at than a couple of distant humans. "Come on," Lorne muttered, pushing himself up and grabbing Nissa's arm. "That building right there," he added, nodding toward the apartment as he pulled her to her feet. "Keep low, and *go*."

She was on the move before he'd even finished the sentence, with no need for the shove he'd planned to give her if she'd needed added encouragement. Lorne gave the car and the spinies one last look, then followed.

They were halfway to their target building when the street lit up with a brilliant flash of blue light. Lorne twisted his head around as the sizzling thunderclap of the high-power laser blast slapped across his ears.

Just in time to see the car he'd sent rolling down the street explode.

Nissa shrieked something unintelligible, her reflexive yelp nearly drowned out by the crackling of flame from the burning car and the creaking thud as it twisted violently around and flipped over onto its side. Putting on a burst of speed, Lorne caught up with the girl, grabbing her around the waist and pulling her along with him, trying to reach safety before the Troft gunners in the ship out there raised their aim.

They were five meters away when the door was abruptly flung open. "Come on!" someone shouted to them. Leaning into his stride, Lorne kicked full power to his leg servos, his skin tingling with heat from the blazing car and crawling with anticipation of the laser blast that would disintegrate him where he stood.

And then they were there, charging through the open door and into an ornately decorated lobby. Lorne caught a glimpse of dozens of people in night-robes and slippers standing tensely around the darkened room—

"Whoa!" a middle-aged man directly in front of them gasped, holding up his hands.

Lorne tried to stop, but he had too little time and too much momentum. With his arm still around Nissa's waist he crashed full tilt into the older man, sending all three of them sprawling onto the thick carpet.

"Sorry," Lorne said, scrambling to his feet and throwing a quick look over his shoulder. "Someone close that door. Lock it if you can."

"You think a *lock's* going to keep them out?" someone demanded in a sort of moaning snarl.

"Just do it," Lorne ordered. He watched long enough to make sure it was being done, then turned back and offered a hand each to Nissa and the man. "You okay?" he asked.

"I think so," Nissa said in a shaky voice as she took Lorne's hand and let him help her to her feet.

"I'm fine," the middle-aged man seconded, ignoring the prof-fered hand and getting up on his own. "Didn't expect you to be coming in so fast."

"Didn't expect to find someone in our way," Lorne said. "Sorry."

"It's okay," the man said, lowering his voice. "I'm just glad you got here at all."

Lorne frowned. "Oh?"

The other glanced around and lowered his voice still more. "My name's Poole," he said. "I'm an assistant to Senior Governor Tomo Treakness."

Lorne felt his stomach tighten. Treakness, the single loudest and most virulent anti-Cobra voice in the entire Cobra Worlds Directorate. "I guess I need to work on my aim," he said.

Poole frowned. "What?"

"Never mind," Lorne said, feeling a flicker of embarrassment. No matter how Treakness treated the Cobras, a comment like that was uncalled for. "Is the governor aware of what's happened?"

Poole frowned a little harder. "What do you mean?"

"I mean does he know about that," Lorne said patiently, waving a hand in the direction of the Troft warships and the spine leopards.

"Of course he knows," Poole said. "Why do you think you're here?"

It was Lorne's turn to frown. "What?"

"That's why Governor-General Chintawa called you," Poole said, as if it was obvious. "You've been assigned to escort Governor Treakness."

"Escort him where?"

"Where else?" Poole glanced at Nissa, then looked back at Lorne. "Out of the city."

Treakness's apartment, as befit the senior governor's exalted rank, was on the top floor, with a northern exposure that pre-sumably gave him a panoramic view of the city center, Dome, and the distant mountains.

At the moment, though, it was clear that his view was nowhere near the top of the governor's considerations. "About time," he snapped as he opened the door and stepped aside, gesturing the three of them inside with short, imperious movements. "What did you do, Poole, sit them down and discuss the weather?"

"No, sir, of course not," Poole said hastily as he ducked his head in deference. "I brought them up as soon as they arrived."

"So the delay is *your* fault?" Treakness demanded, shifting his eyes to Lorne. "Or hers?"

"We got here as fast as anyone could have," Lorne said, returning the governor's glare. "But of course, at the time we were under the impression that we were urgently needed for serious duty."

Treakness's eyes narrowed. "Meaning?"

"Meaning we've just been invaded, and this is hardly the time for anyone to run whimpering away with his tail between his legs," Lorne said. "Particularly senior governmental officials."

"I agree," Treakness said icily. "If you see anyone doing that, you're authorized to shoot him down."

"Really," Lorne said. "Do you want a running start? Or do you want it right here?"

Treakness threw a look at Poole. "I *did* tell them," the other said. "Just like you told me. I told them we were leaving the city."

Treakness hissed between his teeth. "You are useless, Poole. You know that?" He turned back to Lorne. "Yes, we're leaving the city. No, we aren't running."

"Well, that's clear," Lorne said sarcastically.

"You don't need an explanation, Cobra Broom," Treakness ground out. "All you need to do is follow orders."

"Great—except I don't really have any, do I?" Lorne countered. "I haven't heard word one about any of this from Chintawa."

"And you're not going to any time soon, either," Treakness said heavily. "The whole comm system's down, either destroyed or jammed."

"Cobra Broom!" Nissa snapped.

Lorne turned. She was standing by one of the windows, gazing down at the street below, a look of horror on her face. "The other Cobras. They're here."

Lorne felt his throat tighten. "Hell," he muttered, hurrying to her side.

There were Cobras down there, all right. Five of them, all wearing the semidress uniforms of the Dome security force, working together in deadly efficiency as they lasered, stunned, and otherwise methodically worked their way through the spine leopards the Trofts had turned loose on the streets. Already five of the spinies were down, and Lorne's memory flickered with the all-too-familiar acrid odor of burned flesh and muscle and bone.

"We have to warn them," Nissa breathed.

"About what?" Treakness asked as he and Poole took up positions at the other side of the window. "They seem to be doing all right."

"You don't get it," Lorne said darkly, his mind swirling with useless plans. The comms were being jammed, which probably meant the field radios were also useless, even if Lorne had had one with him. A warning flash through the window from his own laser? That would do nothing but distract and confuse them.

And going down there would only get him killed along with them.

"Don't get what?" Treakness demanded.

"There!" Poole said, jabbing a rigid finger. "Look!"

Lorne lifted his eyes from the carnage going on below them. All across the city, a dozen or more of the tall Troft warships could be seen across the skyline, the whole scene faintly lit by the reddish light from the east. Poole was pointing at one of the ships that had taken up position due west of the governmental center.

And as Lorne watched, the reddish sheen on its hull was suddenly joined by a flicker of sharper blue light from somewhere beneath it.

"They're using the spinies to draw out the Cobras," Lorne said, his voice distant in his ears. "And then they're killing them."

The words were barely out of his mouth when the ground below them and the buildings to either side lit up with another, eye-searing blue flash.

And when he looked down again, he saw the smoldering bodies of his fellow Cobras sprawled on the pavement.

For a long minute no one spoke. Then, Poole took a shuddering breath. "Oh, God," he said, very quietly.

With an effort, Lorne turned away from the grisly sight. Across the city to the northeast, another of the Troft ships was flickering with blue light. "Governor, how many Cobras are in the city?" he asked. "Any idea?"

"There are a little over three thousand on Aventine," Treakness said. For once, Lorne noted almost absently, there wasn't a single trace of arrogance or self-importance in the man's voice. "But of course most of them are in the outer provinces. There can't be more than—I don't know. Maybe two or three hundred in Capitalia proper." He hunched his shoulders.

"They didn't let them kill all the spine leopards first," Nissa said quietly, still gazing down through the window.

"What?" Poole asked.

"They didn't let the Cobras kill all of them," she told him, pointing. "There are still five of them alive out there."

"Of course not," Treakness said bitterly. "After all, once they've suckered the Cobras into the open there'll still be the patroller corps to deal with. Broom, we've got to get out of here."

Lorne felt a sudden flash of anger, as bitter and lethal-edged as the Troft lasers. How *dare* this stupid, pompous fool just casually brush aside the deaths of his comrades down there—men Treakness himself had probably passed at doorways in the Dome's halls a hundred times—as if nothing had happened? "Is that all you can say, Governor?" he snarled, curling his hands into fists and taking a step toward the other.

Treakness held his ground, meeting Lorne's eyes without flinching. "Yes, I know what just happened," he said quietly. "But we can't help them now. Under the circumstances, I don't think we ever could have. What we *can* do is try to make their sacrifice mean something."

"Like what?" Lorne demanded.

"We have a mission," Treakness said. "An urgent errand that Governor-General Chintawa has ordered us to do." He nodded microscopically toward the window. "There were fifteen spine leopards out there, ready to kill anyone who stepped outside. Now, there are only five. If we're going to go, this is the time to do it."

Lorne took a deep breath, forcing back the anger and the heartache. Treakness was still a fool. But he was also right. "You say we're leaving the city," he said. "Where are we going?"

"There's a Troft freighter waiting at Creeksedge Spaceport," he said. "A Tlossie freighter, to be exact."

"And?"

"And the Tlossies are on our side," Treakness said. "Or at least, they're not against us. The point is, the ship's master has agreed to take me to his demesne-lord to plead our case for assistance."

Lorne felt the first stirrings of hope. The Tlos'khin'fahi Demesne had been one of the Cobra Worlds' best trading partners over the past several decades. If they could be persuaded to come into this—whatever the hell *this* was—it could make all the difference between defeat and victory.

Unfortunately, the invading Trofts undoubtedly knew that, too. "What if the invaders don't let him leave with you aboard?"

"I think they will," Treakness said. "This particular shipmaster happens to be the demesne-lord's second heir. There's a fairly rigid protocol between demesnes on such matters." His lip twitched. "Especially since if we do it right they won't know we're aboard."

Lorne grimaced. "Which I presume means they don't want to fly over here and pick us up."

"Even if they were willing, we can't risk it," Treakness said. "We'll just have to go to him."

"What's our timing?"

Treakness seemed to brace himself. "Ingidi-inhiliziyo—that's the heir—has given us until tomorrow daybreak," he said. "Otherwise, he says he'll have to lift without us."

"Terrific," Lorne muttered under his breath. Creeksedge was only about twenty kilometers away as the leatherwing flew. Under normal conditions, a reasonably healthy person could probably walk it in four hours.

But conditions here were far from normal. And they weren't likely to get any better anytime soon, either.

He turned and looked out the window, his eyes drifting across the city skyline, his stomach tightening into a hard knot. Forest territory, plains, streams or small lakes—those he understood. He'd lived with that kind of terrain for the past three years, and he could travel those places with the confidence of knowing where the dangers lurked and the knowledge of how to evade or neutralize them.

But this was a city occupied by enemy soldiers and warships. He didn't have the faintest idea how to function here.

"Governor, we're wasting time," Poole murmured urgently.

Treakness ignored him. "Broom?" he asked.

Lorne looked at Nissa and Poole. Both of them were watching him, their faces rigid with fear and helplessness.

And slowly, it occurred to him that whatever uncertainties he was feeling, the other three people in the room had it far worse. They were political creatures, adept at conference room maneuvering and backstage deals, but at their core they were just civilians.

Lorne might not know the techniques of urban evasion and combat, but at least he knew how to fight.

"Like Mr. Poole said, we're wasting time," he said, putting as much confidence into his voice as he could.

"That we are," Treakness said, managing to sound relieved and annoyed at the same time. "Took you long enough. Poole, go get my bags from the bedroom."

"Whoa, whoa," Lorne said as Poole started to leave the room. "What kind of bags? What's in them?"

"The things I need for a trip to the Tlossie demesne world, of course," Treakness said. "Clothing, credentials, papers—"

"Forget 'em," Lorne interrupted. "Everything except the credentials—you can take those."

"What do you mean, forget them?" Treakness said, sounding annoyed again. "You want me to have to explain to a demesne-lord in his own audience hall that I've been wearing the same clothes for the past week?"

"I'd worry more about how you're going to explain to the Trofts right here in Capitalia why you're packed for a long trip," Lorne countered. "You can take your credentials and any food bars or bottled water you have. That's it."

"Fine," Treakness bit out. "Poole, go to the kitchen—there's an emergency bag in the cabinet above the cooker and some bottles of water in the cooler."

"Better split everything into four packs," Lorne added as Poole made for the kitchen. "Nissa, go help him."

"Yes, sir," Nissa said, and followed Poole out of the room.

Leaving Lorne and Treakness alone. "We're bringing her, too?" Treakness asked quietly.

"You were thinking of leaving her here alone?"

"Frankly, yes," Treakness said evenly. "Troft history indicates they don't mistreat their conquered peoples, at least as long as the conquered peoples behave themselves. She could stay here in my apartment—there's plenty of food—and try to ride it out. And you know as well as I do that a party of three will be easier to sneak past Troft sentries than a party of four."

"Why not just make it a party of two, then?" Lorne challenged. "Leave Nissa someone to talk to while she's hunkered down here."

"Poole comes with me," Treakness said firmly. "Bad enough that you won't let me take proper ceremonial clothing. I am *not* traveling without an assistant. Period."

"Fine," Lorne said with a shrug. "In that case, neither am I."

"Nissa Gendreves isn't your assistant."

"She is now," Lorne said. "If you don't like it, try to remember that this mess is at least partially your fault. If you'd headed directly to Creeksedge the minute North Bank picked up the incoming ships, you could have had your feet up in the Tlossie freighter before the first invaders even landed."

"Believe me, I'd rather have done it that way," Treakness said. "But there was a small fly in the batter." His glare sharpened a few degrees. "You."

Lorne frowned. "What's that supposed to mean?"

"You're the son of Jasmine Moreau," Treakness told him. "For whatever ridiculous reason, the Tlossies seem to have been impressed with the Moreau name over the years."

"Have they, now," Lorne said, permitting himself a small smile. "You'll have to send them a copy of the official report on my mother's mission. I'm sure that'll cool any ardor they feel for us."

"I'm not going to argue politics with you, Broom," Treakness growled. "This isn't the time for it. The bottom line is that, for whatever reason, you're high up in the Tlossies' estimation, and Chintawa insisted that you accompany me to their demesne-lord. So we waited for you." He jerked a hand toward the window. "You see the result."

Lorne grimaced. If Chintawa had just said something to Nissa when he'd called her . . . but that was water over the rim now. "Well, we'll just have to do the best we can," he said.

"I suppose we will," Treakness said with just a hint of sarcasm in his voice. "You have a plan?"

"I have the start of one," Lorne said. "This building have an east entrance?"

Treakness nodded. "It opens into the service street."

"That's where we go out, then," Lorne said. "It's out of sight of the warship, and with luck the spinies won't have gotten back there yet. We'll head south for a couple of blocks, by which time we should have some idea of how well they've got the city covered. Hopefully, at that point or shortly thereafter we'll be able to turn west and head toward Creeksedge."

"And the spine leopards?" Treakness asked. "I presume this ship isn't the only one that's released them out into the streets."

"We'll deal with them as necessary," Lorne said. "If the Trofts didn't grab family groups, they should split up as soon as they realize the city's open and start marking off individual territories for themselves. If there *are* any family groups, unfortunately, they'll probably stick together, at least for now." He gestured toward the east. "And of course, once we're at full daylight, I'll be able to use my lasers out in the open without it being as obvious as it would be right now. Something the Trofts might not have thought about when they planned their attack for dawn."

There was the sound of footsteps, and he turned as Nissa and Poole returned from the kitchen, four belt bags in hand. "We divided up the food and water," Poole said, offering one of his bags to Treakness. "Oh, and we also divided the medical kit from the emergency bag, too. I hope that's all right."

"Of course it's all right," Treakness growled, snatching the belt bag from the other's hand. "Just because Cobra Broom said to take just the food didn't mean you were supposed to turn off your brain."

Poole winced. "Sorry," he muttered.

Lorne suppressed the retort that wanted so badly to come out. If this wasn't the time to talk politics, it also wasn't the time to lecture Treakness about courtesy toward subordinates. "Here's the plan," he said, looking at each of them in turn. "Governor Treakness will take point when we hit the street—he lives here, so he presumably knows this neighborhood best. Nissa, you'll walk behind him to his left; Poole, you'll walk to her right; I'll bring up the rear a little to Poole's right where I can see what's coming from ahead but will also be able to take on anything that comes up from behind. Everyone is to walk as quietly as you can, and no talking unless it's absolutely necessary—I'll need to have my audio enhancers going in order to keep track of what's going on around us. We'll start by heading south, but our ultimate route will depend on the positioning of the Troft ships, the deployment of their troops, and what the spinies decide to do. Got it?"

"Got it," Treakness said for all of them.

"Good," Lorne said. "And from now on, everyone is to call me *Lorne*, not *Cobra Broom*." He took a deep breath. "Okay. Let's go."

CHAPTER FOUR

The explosions from the direction of Stronghold had faded away into the forest chatterings when Paul called them all back into the aircar for a council of war.

It was, Jody remembered distantly as she closed her door, her parents' favorite term over the years to describe formal family discussions. Never in her life had she imagined that she would ever take part in real council of actual war.

If the expressions on Geoff's and Freylan's faces were any indication, they were thinking the same thing.

"First things first," Paul said when the last door had been sealed. "What we've just heard is real. It wasn't a mistake, a joke, or a misinterpretation. Caelian has been invaded."

"But why?" Geoff asked, his voice barely above a moan. "It doesn't make sense."

"Well, it obviously makes sense to the Troft demesnes involved," Paul pointed out. "Otherwise, they wouldn't have done it. But that's not something we're going to figure out now. Nor should we waste a lot of time on it. Our first task is to consider what we're going to do with the situation we've been handed."

"We have to get out of here," Geoff said tightly. "We have to—well, we have to get *out*, that's all."

"And go where?" Paul asked. "Running away from something is useless in and of itself, Geoff. You have to run *to* something."

"There's Aerie," Freylan suggested hesitantly. "It's only fifty kilometers away. Or we could try Essbend. That's one-thirty."

Geoff snorted. "And what, you think the Trofts might have missed them?"

"It's possible," Freylan countered. "At less than five hundred people each, they're certainly small enough. Anyway, what would it hurt to try?"

"Well, for starters, it'll burn a bunch of fuel," Geoff growled. "Not to mention time."

"Actually, I think Freylan's right," Paul said. "Though it's probably more a matter of the Trofts not bothering with the other towns than it is of them having missed seeing them. Unfortunately, wherever we go, it can't be by aircar. As of right now, all travel is strictly on foot."

Geoff stared at him in disbelief. Freylan's face actually paled. "What are you talking about?" Geoff demanded. "I was kidding about the fuel—we've got practically a full tank."

"And any invasion force worth its pay will be watching closely for enemy aircraft," Paul told him. "*All* enemy aircraft, military or civilian. We get above treetop level, and chances are they'll be right on top of us."

"So we don't go that high," Freylan suggested. "There must be ways to maneuver through the forest instead of going over it."

Geoff hissed contemptuously. "Have you *looked* out there lately?"

"Unfortunately, Geoff's right," Paul said. "Unless we can fly this thing sideways, we're not getting through any of that."

"Well, we're sure not taking a fifty-kilometer walk," Jody said firmly. "Not through a Caelian forest."

"Agreed," Paul said. "And since those explosions were likely the comm towers being destroyed, we're not going to be calling anyone for help, either."

"Wait a second," Geoff said. "How do you know those were the comm towers?"

"I don't," Paul said. "But it's a fair enough assumption. Trofts don't go in for wholesale slaughter, and there was barely enough time for the town to even notice them, let alone launch some kind of attack that the Trofts might have been reacting to. Given the timing, the first explosion was almost certainly the primary tower, from which it follows that the others were probably the secondary ones."

"The timing?" Geoff asked, sounding bewildered.

"There was a fifteen-second gap between the cutoff of Uy's transmission and the sound of the first explosion," Freylan murmured. "Three seconds per kilometer for the sound to get here. Didn't you ever count seconds after a lightning flash?"

"Right," Paul said. "Which is also why I said earlier that you were probably right about Aerie and Essbend and the other towns not being attacked. The only reason I can think of to destroy the comm system instead of temporarily jamming it is to permanently keep Stronghold from talking to possible allies. No reason to waste perfectly good explosives on the towers if those allies are also pinned down."

"So our job is to hang tough and see if the other towns got Uy's message and are able to do something about it?" Jody asked.

"That's one option." Her father cocked an eyebrow. "The other would be to see whether we can do something about it ourselves."

Geoff's eyes widened. "You're joking. *Us*?"

"Why not?" Paul countered calmly. "Most of their attention's going to be focused on Stronghold, not out here."

Geoff shook his head disbelievingly. "You're not joking, you're insane. Look, I know you Cobras are supposed to be real hotshots at this sort of thing, but come *on*."

"It can't hurt to go back and poke around a little," Jody offered, trying hard to match her father's outward composure. Her skin was crawling at the thought of deliberately walking into enemy territory, but there was no way she was going to let Geoff and Freylan know that. "Anyway, if we get caught, as long as we don't make threatening moves the Trofts will probably just put us in the town with everyone else."

Freylan whistled softly. "Insanity must run in your family."

"Very possibly," Paul conceded. "I'm open to other suggestions."

"Well, *I'm* not going," Geoff said flatly. "You three want to play hero, go right ahead. But I didn't sign up for any suicide missions."

For a moment the aircar was silent. Then Freylan stirred. "That's fine," he said. "You can stay here. Just make sure you cook that gigger all the way through or you might end up with parasites."

Geoff frowned at him. "What are you talking about? There's a full survival kit back there with a couple dozen ration bars."

"Thirty, actually," Freylan said. "But we're going to be on the move, and won't have time for hunting or cooking. Certainly not that close to the Trofts." He waved a hand around them. "You, on the other hand, will have the time *and* the distance *and* the trap. Perfect conditions for living off the land."

"You can't be serious," Geoff protested. "You want me to *leave the aircar*? Alone?"

"Why not?" Freylan said coolly. "We're going to."

"But not alone," Geoff said, his voice taking on an edge of pleading. "You can't expect me to—" He shot a hooded look at Jody. "Jody, tell him."

"I'm sorry, but he's right," Jody said, working hard to keep a straight face. Despite the desperate danger they were in, watching Geoff the glib manipulator being verbally outmaneuvered by his quieter, more socially awkward friend and co-worker was just too funny. "Or you could come with us. That way you won't be alone."

"*And* you won't have to cook," Freylan added.

Geoff shot him a glare. "Yeah, I get it," he growled. "Cute. Both of you."

"So it's agreed," Paul said. "We stick together, and go see what's happening with Stronghold." He lifted a finger. "And in case you're working on your worst-case scenarios, let me set your minds at ease. No matter what the situation is back there, I'm not going to ask any of you to do any fighting."

"Yeah, thanks," Geoff muttered. "That makes it sound *so* much better."

"What do you want us to do?" Freylan asked.

"You three get the survival bag out and start sorting everything into smaller, carry-size packs," Paul instructed. "There may be some fold-up backpacks in there you can use. I'll go and see if I can scope out the best route."

"I'll come with you," Jody volunteered. "If we're not going to take samples from that gigger, we need to either release it or kill it. I'm not leaving it in the cage to starve to death."

"Better just kill it," Freylan suggested. "You don't want it turning on you when you open the lid."

"And it's not like the forest is likely to run out of the damn things," Geoff added sourly.

The wind was picking up again as Jody and her father left the aircar and made their way south up the hillside. "Clever of them to come during the midmorning lull," Paul commented as they walked. "The spores stop flying, ribbon vines stop flowing and twisting around where they might snag landing gear and get into opening hatches, and the major predators stop moving around until the wind starts covering their movements again. Perfect time to land—"

He spun around and Jody felt a sudden jolt of mild disorientation as she caught the edge of his sonic blast. A trio of striped saberclaws burst through the tall grass and bushes, staggering toward them, and there were three quick thunderclaps as Paul sent an arcthrower blast into each of them. "—and consolidate their position," he finished, turning his head back and forth in a quick sweep of the area. "Whoever this is, they've done their homework."

"But why?" Jody protested, blinking hard to shake away the last of the sonic's effects. "Why would anyone invade Caelian? What in the Worlds could they possibly want here?"

"I don't know," Paul said grimly. "But my guess is that if they're *here*, they're everywhere else, too."

Jody swallowed. "You mean Aventine."

"And Palatine and probably Esquiline and Viminal, too." He looked sideways at her. "I wouldn't worry about Lorne, though," he added. "The Trofts can't possibly have enough troops to occupy the entire planet. As long as he stays out in the expansion region, he should be okay."

"Unless Chintawa had time to call everyone back to the cities," Jody said.

"Not if the Trofts were as fast there as they were here," Paul pointed out. "But either way, Lorne's fate is out of our hands, and you need to set it aside. Our concern right now—our *only* concern—is our own survival."

They reached the top of the hill, which turned out to be already occupied by a stand of hookgrass. Paul used his fingertip lasers to burn a path through it, and a moment later they were standing at the crest gazing away to the south.

It was a stunning view, a panorama of multiple shades of green highlighted with swathes of light blue, red, and yellow. The original assessment teams had been astonished at its beauty during their first survey flights over the forests, and Jody herself had had her breath taken away as she watched on the *Freedom's Fire*'s viewscreens during their arrival.

Now, after less than two weeks on the ground, she couldn't even see the beauty anymore. All she could see was how the forest provided the perfect habitat for huge insects, painful or poisonous plants, and deadly predators.

"We'll start by following that ridge," her father said, pointing to a low, mostly treeless crest meandering its way through the greenery. "We'll be open to view from above, but we won't have as many trees for the arboreal predators to jump at us from."

"The Trofts ought to be too busy for a while to organize overflights, anyway," Jody said, trying to visualize the map of the region. "I think that'll take us most of the way to the river. I wonder if the survival kit includes an inflatable boat."

Paul grunted. "I wouldn't trust if even if it did," he said. "Way too many things with sharp teeth infesting the waterways here. Let's go deal with that gigger and get moving. We're going to be pushing our available daylight as it is."

They retraced their steps back to the aircar, where Geoff and Freylan were busily sorting out the survival pack's contents, and continued past to the gigger still rocking back and forth inside its prison. "I presume you'd like to keep the trap itself intact?" Paul asked as they gazed down at the growling predator.

"If possible," Jody said, frowning. The gigger was growling up a storm, complete with a set of subsonics she could feel right through the ground.

"Okay." Paul lifted his hands, aiming his fingertip lasers at the predator's head—

"Wait," Jody said suddenly.

Her father paused, his thumbs resting on his trigger fingers. "Trouble?"

"I'm not sure," Jody said, gazing down at the gigger. "You remember when we first got here, a screech tiger moved in and you had to shoot it? I'm not absolutely sure, but I don't think the gigger was growling during that time."

Slowly, Paul lowered his hands. "Interesting," he said. "Walk me through it."

Jody huffed. "I've hardly even got it myself."

"Then walk both of us through it."

Jody chewed her lip. "Okay. Assume I'm right about the gigger's moment of silence. It could just mean that he heard or smelled the screech tiger coming and wanted to keep a low profile. Except that from everything I've read on Caelian ecology the predators here don't usually eat other predators."

"Though it's a rare animal indeed that'll turn down a free lunch," Paul pointed out. "If the gigger realized he now fell into that category, it would be all the more reason to shut up when he knew something bigger was in the area."

"Maybe," Jody conceded. "In which case, this whole train of thought has already stopped in the station."

"Or?" Paul prompted.

"Or it could be something more complicated," Jody said slowly. "If the gigger is announcing his presence and claiming his territory... only then he stops when something bigger with a better claim to that territory comes along..." She shook her head. "I don't know, Dad. There's something going on here—I'm sure of it. But I don't have any kind of real grip on it yet."

For a moment they stood silently, gazing down at the rumbling gigger. "Well, when you run out of theory, it's time for an experiment. You feel up to carrying a double load of survival equipment?"

"Probably," Jody said, frowning at him. "Why?"

He gestured down at the cage. "If we each take a double load, it'll free up Geoff and Freylan to carry our new friend here. A little five-kilometer stroll through the forest would be the perfect way to observe his growling habits in the wild."

"Ooh, I don't think they'll go for that," Jody said doubtfully. "That trap is heavier than it looks. Especially with a full-grown gigger inside."

"Let's ask them," Paul suggested. "Maybe they'll surprise you."

To Jody's surprise, they did. "Interesting," Geoff said, frowning thoughtfully as he stuffed food bars and water purification tablets into one of the backpacks. "I don't think anyone's gone that direction before."

"And why would they?" Freylan agreed as he finished with one of his two backpacks and started on the second. "I don't think there's any known ecology where that kind of interspecies territorial hierarchy exists, at least not the kind you're suggesting. Land and mate wars usually only take place between members of the same species."

"It might explain why Caelian has so little predator-on-predator killing, too," Geoff said. "Damn. Wouldn't it be a real kick if the solution to this mess was nothing more complicated than everyone carrying around a recording of screech tiger screeches?"

" 'Course, your population will be totally deaf within three weeks," Freylan said dryly. "But there should be a way to engineer active-cancellation earplugs to filter out most of the sound."

"So you don't mind dragging him along?" Jody asked, still not quite believing they were going for this so enthusiastically.

"No problem," Geoff assured her. "Freylan, you think you can rig up something so that we can carry the bars on our shoulders instead of having to actually hold them the whole way?"

"No problem," Freylan assured him. "We can probably even use the spare straps from the survival kit to rig cross-shoulder harnesses so the guy in back can see over the cage." He gave Jody a tentative smile. "Great idea, Jody."

"Well, let's not award ourselves any prizes yet," Jody warned. "It could easily just be a gigger trying not to attract attention."

"Which is fine, too," Geoff said. "If and when he shuts up it'll mean we need to be extra careful to watch for something big to come at us. Okay, so Freylan and I will rig the cage and carry the gigger, while—"

"Snouts," Freylan said.

They all looked at him. "What?" Jody asked.

"That's his new name," Freylan said. "Snouts."

Jody looked questioningly at Geoff. The other just shrugged. "He used to name his lab equipment back at school, too," he said. "Don't worry, it's harmless. So like I was saying, Freylan and I will carry Snouts, and you, Jody will carry all the packs."

"She'll carry two of them," Paul corrected. "I'll carry the others."

"Sorry, but you're the sole defense of this little expedition," Geoff said, shaking his head. "That means you need to be free and unencumbered at all times."

"I think you're underestimating my abilities," Paul said mildly. "Besides, with a little luck, I'll be able to hear or see any trouble coming long before I need to use any of my combat reflexes."

Geoff snorted. "If we had any luck, we wouldn't be sitting in the middle of a Troft invasion."

"No, he's right, Dad," Jody said reluctantly, eyeing the four bulging backpacks. "I guess we shouldn't have wasted time dividing up the kit."

"Not at all," Geoff soothed. "It'll be easier to distribute the weight around your shoulders and hips this way."

Jody narrowed her eyes slightly at him. "You're enjoying this, aren't you?" she challenged.

"As much as I've enjoyed anything in the past ten minutes, pretty much," he agreed. He smiled, the old confident Geoff smile that had won the group so much of their corporate funding over the past few months. "If it helps any," he added, "and should the need arise, I'll also be available to do all the cooking."

"Oh, yeah," Jody said, nodding. "You're enjoying this."

"Probably not for long," Freylan said, reaching to the seat beside him and picking up a pair of stun sticks. "Here—you should probably carry one of these. Geoff, you want the other one?"

"Just a minute," Paul said as Jody gingerly took the two weapons and started to hand one to Geoff. "Do any of you know how to use one of those?"

"We all took the intro course aboard the *Freedom's Fire*," Jody reminded him.

"Yes, I sat in on that," Paul said. "Let me rephrase: has any of you ever actually *used* anything like those?"

"I had a fencing unit in high school," Jody offered.

"Did the foils generate current in the half-megavolt range?" Paul asked pointedly.

"Well, no," Jody conceded.

"Then your answer would be no," Paul told her. "Either of you?"

"No," Geoff said as Freylan shook his head.

"Then they stay in the bag," Paul said firmly. "Unless you've had actual training—and that shipboard lecture doesn't qualify—they'll be more of a danger to you than to anything you're likely to meet out there."

"Yes, but—" Geoff began.

"They stay in the packs," Paul said firmly. "Trust me. Some of the animals here are big enough to take a jolt that would kill you outright."

"Maybe we should just leave them here, then," Freylan suggested. "They're pretty heavy for something we can't use."

"No, let's take them," Paul said. "They may be useful in setting up a perimeter wherever we wind up spending the night. Just make sure they're locked in the off position before you put them back in the bags."

"They are," Jody confirmed as she handed the weapons back

to Freylan. "Anyway, don't worry about the weight," she added. "*I'll* be the one carrying them, remember?"

"So let's grab everything and get going," Paul said, opening his door. "Time to hit trail."

"Just no hiking songs," Jody warned. "I've heard you sing, and this planet hates us enough as it is."

CHAPTER FIVE

At Lorne's direction, Treakness led the group down a back stairway, out of sight of the Troft warship, which would hopefully
also allow them to bypass the nervous residents Lorne and Nissa
had left in the lobby.

They reached the back door to find that a smaller group was
likewise milling around the smaller area there. But everyone
seemed preoccupied with his or her own thoughts and concerns,
and none of them challenged the intentions of four people foolish
enough to venture out into the streets of a freshly occupied city.
Certainly none of them asked to come along. Lorne opened the
door a crack, confirmed that nothing was moving nearby, and
the group slipped out into the early morning gloom.

By this time, Lorne knew, Capitalia would normally be starting
to come to life. Traffic would be picking up as merchants arrived at
their stores for pre-opening checks, restaurateurs began preparing
the day's dishes, and early-rising office workers got a jump on the
traffic and headed in to tackle the work waiting on their desks.

But not today. Today, the rising sun might as well have been
looking down on a ghost town.

Or at least a ghost neighborhood. Over the thudding of the
group's footsteps in his enhanced hearing Lorne could pick out
the confused-sounding rumbles of multiple spine leopards as
they tried to figure out the unfamiliar surroundings they'd been

unceremoniously dumped into. Behind the sounds of the animals he could hear muffled metallic whirrings and clanks as the Trofts in their warships finished locking down their landing gear, tested the gimbals on their wing-mounted weapons, and probably prepared their troop deployment.

"Where is everyone?" Nissa shouted.

Lorne jumped, cursing, as he quickly dialed back his audios. "Sorry," Nissa said, her voice this time sounding more like the murmur the question had actually been.

"Where do you think they are?" Treakness growled before Lorne could answer. "You expect them to all rush outside to see the pretty fireworks?"

"I was asking about the Trofts, sir," Nissa countered stiffly. "Shouldn't they be moving troops into the Dome or the patroller stations or something?"

"Don't worry, that'll happen soon enough," Lorne said. "My guess is that they're waiting for the spinies to sort themselves out into territories, maybe draw a few more Cobras or patrollers into the open—"

And with his audios off, he was caught completely off guard by the spine leopard that appeared suddenly from behind an under-drop trash container across the street and charged.

Reflexively, Lorne took a long step to his right, perpendicular to the spiny's path, putting some distance between himself and the others. A flick of his eye set a target lock on the predator's head, and he shifted his weight onto his right foot. He would let it close about half the remaining distance, he decided, then swing his left leg up and nail it with an antiarmor laser shot. Maybe a quick burst with his sonic a step or two before that, just to slow it down—

"Lorne!" Nissa gasped.

—and in that frozen second he belatedly remembered where he was and who he was with. Not out in the Aventinian wilderness with his fellow Cobras, but in a city with a trio of helpless civilians. Civilians who couldn't fight, couldn't get out of the way, and probably didn't even have enough sense to duck.

And the spine leopard was charging directly toward them.

Lorne cursed under his breath, leaping back again to put himself between the civilians and the predator, realizing in that same instant that he couldn't use his planned response. An audible sonic, a visible flash, and he would have every Troft in range converging on this street.

Which left him only one option.

The spiny had made it two more steps, with maybe six more and a short leap to go, by the time Lorne had his original head shot cancelled and a new targeting lock on the front of the animal's neck where it met the lower jaw. Then, bracing himself, he squatted down and fell backwards, doing a controlled roll from hips to shoulder blades onto his back. He heard Nissa gasp something else as the spine leopard, sensing wounded prey, shifted direction slightly and bore straight down on him. As the predator shoved itself off the pavement into what it surely expected to be a killing leap, Lorne triggered his antiarmor laser. His leg servos, responding to the spiny's position and Lorne's own programmed target lock, swung his left leg up to meet the incoming threat.

And as Lorne's heel connected solidly with the attacker's throat, the laser finally fired, burning instantly through muscle and throat and brain.

The spine leopard's momentum kept it moving, caroming off Lorne's foot and flying over his body. But the creature was dead long before it thudded to the pavement.

"What the *hell* was that?" Treakness demanded as Lorne rolled back up onto his feet.

"It's called saving your lives," Lorne said stiffly. Going over to the dead spine leopard, he scooped it up in his arms, hearing the faint sound of his arm servos as they took the predator's weight. "You might say thank you."

"*Thank* you," Treakness growled. "What I *meant* was why didn't you just shoot the damn thing instead of playing patty-cake with it?"

Poole cleared his throat. "I think he was trying not to let the Trofts see the flash—"

"Shut up, Poole," Treakness cut him off. He was still glaring, but Lorne could see the anger starting to fade as he realized his aide was right. "Fine, so you're brave and strong *and* clever. Now what?"

"First, we find a place to stash the evidence," Lorne said, looking around. The closest stashing place was the trash container where the animal had been hiding. "Wait here," he said, and crossed the street to the bin.

He'd hoped he would be able to dump the carcass inside, but

the overhead conduit that carried the building's trash out to the bin fit too snugly for him to slip the animal through. He had to settle for shoving the animal behind the bin, pushing it as far out of sight as he could.

The others were looking nervously around when he rejoined them. "Come on, come on," Treakness muttered. "Another two blocks and we'll hit Palisade Park. Mostly low buildings around it, so we should be able to see all of the nearby Troft ships from there."

"Sounds good," Lorne said, glancing around at the five- and six-story structures rising up around them. "Again, no talking unless absolutely necessary, and keep those footsteps *quiet*."

They had made it halfway down the next block when Lorne began to pick up the distant hum of motors and the dull thuds of thick metal hitting pavement. They had covered another quarter block when the rumble of heavy-duty engines—a lot of them—began.

They had reached the next street, and Lorne was peering carefully around the corner building, when the rumble of engines became a line of boxy vehicles lumbering past along Cavendish Boulevard a block away, each heavily armored and sporting a swivel gun on its roof.

"What is it?" Treakness murmured.

Grimacing, Lorne stepped back and gestured for him to look. Treakness eased his head around the corner, watched for a few seconds, then drew back again. "So much for getting to the park," he said tightly.

"The Trofts?" Poole asked anxiously.

"No, the Ghirdel Pastry Express truck," Treakness snarled. "Use your *brain*, Poole."

"Enough of that," Lorne ordered. "Everyone be quiet a minute."

The others froze. Lorne keyed up his audios again, trying to hear beyond the roar of the traffic rolling past a block away. As far as he could tell, that particular convoy was the only one in the immediate area. "It just seems to be that one bunch," he said, lowering the audios. "Any idea where they might be going?"

"That seems like way too much firepower just to take down the Five Points patroller station," Treakness said thoughtfully. "I'm guessing they're sending those personnel carriers to some central place, probably Five Points, where they'll set up a command base and send the rest of the vehicles out in ones or twos to block and control the rest of the major intersections." He gave Lorne a look of strained patience. "Yes, I *have* studied a bit of military theory, thank you."

"But if they block all the intersections, how are we going to get past them?" Nissa asked nervously.

"That's the question, all right," Treakness agreed. "Hopefully, our brave and clever Cobra escort will come up with something brave and clever."

"Hold it," Lorne said, holding up a hand as he caught a flicker of grav-lift red reflecting from the side of one of the buildings to the east. Reflections were always tricky, but whatever it was definitely appeared to be moving in their direction. "Someone's coming," he said, looking around for the entrance to the building beside them. It was about twenty meters back along the street, beneath a small sign that read WEI KEI'S. "We need to get to cover."

The door was locked, but his fingertip lasers made quick work of the mechanism. The four of them slipped inside and Lorne pulled the door mostly closed again behind them.

As he did so, he saw one of the Trofts' transports settle into the intersection one block north. He stood motionless, the door still open a crack, and watched as the side hatches opened and another group of spine leopards strode out onto the street.

"What is it?" Treakness's voice came from behind him.

Lorne eased the door closed. "More spine leopards," he said.

"Terrific," Treakness growled. "Now what?"

Lorne looked around. They were standing in a narrow exit hallway stretching between the door and an unlit dining room, with a kitchen area visible through a wide doorway to their right. Obviously, Wei Kei's was a restaurant. "I need to find a way up to the top floor," he said. "See if I can spot a clear route west."

"Good idea," Treakness said, peering over at the kitchen. "We'll stay here. Poole, go check out that kitchen and see if you can find us something to eat."

Poole's eyes went a little wide. "Uh—sir, do you think we should do that?"

"This is a restaurant, Poole," Treakness said brusquely. "I'm a senior governor, this is an emergency situation, and I'm hungry. Go get me something to eat."

Poole swallowed visibly. "Yes, sir," he said, and hurried through the doorway into the kitchen.

Nissa touched Lorne's arm. "May I come with you?" she asked, her voice strained. "An extra pair of eyes might be useful."

"Yes, take her," Treakness seconded. "Don't be too long."

"It won't be safe for her," Lorne said between clenched teeth. Apparently, Treakness didn't want witnesses while he raided the restaurant's kitchen. "I'll have to go back outside to get to the main building entrance, and there's a new crop of spinies that's just arrived out there. I may have to do some quick dodging to get around them."

"We don't have to go outside," Nissa said. "There's an inside entrance, too, near the front of the restaurant. I've seen it the couple of times that I've eaten here."

"We'll check it out." Lorne eyed Treakness. "If anyone comes down from the apartments while we're gone, your job is to keep them calm."

"I know what my job is," Treakness said coolly. "You just remember what *yours* is."

The stairway Nissa had mentioned wasn't exactly a true inside stairway, but ran from the street parallel to the restaurant's southern edge. But there was another access door just inside the street entrance that opened up into that corner of the dining room. Again, it was locked, and again Lorne's lasers took care of that. Pulling open the door, they slipped into the stairway and headed up.

The stairway was fairly narrow, covered with sturdy but inexpensive carpeting, lined by undecorated walls. There were four apartments on each floor, each taking up one corner of the building, with a second stairway and a small elevator at the far end of each of the long landings. The landings themselves were deserted, but a quick tweaking of Lorne's audios at each stop picked up the sounds of people moving around inside the apartments.

"Which one do we want?" Nissa asked as they arrived at the top floor.

"This one," Lorne said, nodding toward the southwest apartment. Stepping to the door, he knocked.

For a moment there was no response. Lorne knocked again, then keyed in his audios. Someone was definitely in there, several someones, all of them trying very hard to be quiet. "Hey!" he called. "We need to look out your windows."

There was another short silence. Then, Lorne heard stealthy footsteps approaching. "Who is it?" a nervous voice called through the door.

"It's Nissa Gendreves from Governor-General Chintawa's office," Nissa called back before Lorne could answer. "It's urgent that we come in."

There was one final pause, and then Lorne heard the clicking as the longlock was disengaged. The door opened a crack and a tense, unshaven face peered out. "I'm Nissa Gendreves," Nissa repeated. "This is Lorne Broom."

"What do you want?" the man asked suspiciously, looking back and forth between them. "What the hell's going on out there?"

"That's what we're trying to find out," Lorne told him. "A quick look out your windows, and then we'll be gone."

"I don't think I've seen you before," the man said, his eyes narrowing as he studied Lorne's face. "Who do you work for?"

"He's with Senior Governor Treakness," Nissa said, stepping forward past Lorne and giving the door a gentle but firm push. The man grimaced, but backed out of the way, and Nissa walked past him into the apartment. Lorne followed, staying close behind her. "You're one of Syndic Priesly's aides, right?" Nissa added over her shoulder.

"Yes," the man said as he closed the door behind them. "Kovas Brander. Why didn't anyone tell us this was going to happen?"

"Because nobody knew," Nissa said as the three of them strode past a pair of bedroom doors and into the living room. A tense-looking woman was sitting on a narrow couch, clutching two silent, wide-eyed young children to her sides. "It's all right," Nissa added, nodding to them. "We're with Governor-General Chintawa's office."

"Yes, I heard," the woman said nervously. "Do you know what's going on?"

"So far, only that Capitalia's been invaded and is on its way to being fully occupied," Lorne told her as he and Nissa crossed to the windows and eased back the curtains.

Lorne had expected to see armed Troft soldiers spilling out of the armored vehicles they'd seen earlier, lasers held high as they roamed the streets of their newly conquered city. The aliens out there *were* definitely soldiers, garbed in visored helmets and heavily armored versions of the same leotards the species usually wore, with heavy laser rifles slung over their shoulders.

But they weren't exactly roaming, and the five-meter-long cylinders they were hauling out of the troop carriers didn't look like weapons. Frowning, Lorne focused on two of them as they lugged their burden over to the building on the southwest side of the intersection he and Nissa were looking down onto. The Trofts set the cylinder upright against the building's corner, and as Lorne keyed in his infrareds he spotted the subtle yellow flashes as the cylinder was molecularly welded to the building.

And then, to his astonishment, the Trofts began to unroll the cylinder into a fine mesh, working their way northward across the street.

"What in the *Worlds*?" Nissa breathed.

Lorne didn't answer, frowning in confusion as the Trofts reached the other side of the street, pulled the mesh as tight as they could, and again welded it to the corner of the building there. A quick slash from a plasma torch cut the rest of the roll free, and the two aliens picked it up and headed north toward the next open space.

"They're fencing off the street," Brander said disbelievingly from beside Lorne.

"He's right," Nissa confirmed. Pressing the side of her ear to the glass, she looked as straight down as she could. "They're putting one up on this side, too."

"But that's crazy," Brander protested, "I mean, hell, you can cut the stuff with a torch—I just saw them do it. How do they think it's going to keep us in?"

Lorne focused on the fence the Trofts had just created. Five meters tall, the same height as the fences around most of the major wilderness towns.

And then, he got it. "You're missing the point," he said, stepping around Nissa and moving to the far southwest corner of the room. From his new vantage point he could see a few blocks down the side street the Trofts had just blocked off, far enough to see a similar double barricade being erected around the major avenue three blocks away. "They're not trying to keep us *in*. They're trying to keep the spine leopards *out*."

"The *what*?" Brander asked.

"You're right," Nissa said, her voice suddenly taut. "Oh, God."

"What spine leopards?" Brander demanded.

"They're bringing in spine leopards," Nissa told him. "We've already seen two transports letting groups of them out onto the streets."

"And it looks like there are more on the way," Lorne said, nodding toward a pair of distant transports as they disappeared beneath the city's skyline.

Brander cursed under his breath. "Where are the damn Cobras?" he demanded. "Isn't that why we've got them, to handle things like this?"

Lorne turned toward him, a sudden surge of anger tightening his stomach— "They *are* handling it," Nissa said, throwing Lorne a quick warning look. "Or they were. We saw five of them out in the street, taking out that first group. They were doing fine until the Trofts killed them."

"And they didn't fight back?" Brander demanded. "Well, *hell*. What are we paying them for anyway?"

"Brander, go see to your family," Lorne ordered, jerking his head toward the woman and children. "Nissa, I need you over here, please."

Brander made as if to speak, took a second look at Lorne's expression, and seemed to think better of it. Turning, he walked back across the room.

"I'm sorry," Nissa said quietly as she stepped to Lorne's side.

"Yeah," Lorne growled back. Of course she was sorry now, now when it was too late to do anything. Where had her sorry been back when people like Treakness were demanding the Cobra program be gutted to save a few *klae* from the budget?

For that matter, where had the people of the Cobra Worlds been when Treakness had first won his seat by making loud promises to support those cutbacks? Were the people who'd voted for him and his allies even now staring out their windows at the Troft soldiers and vehicles, cursing the Cobras just like Brander had for not saving them?

He took a deep breath, striving for some of his father's and brother's inborn calm. The past was the past, and so were its mistakes and conceits. Holding onto it would just siphon off mental energy that he desperately needed elsewhere. "Stand here and look due west," he told Nissa, motioning her to the corner of the window. "You see how the street three blocks away is also being fenced in?"

"Yes," she said. "You think they're crosshatching the city?"

"I don't think so," Lorne said. "Why bother fencing both sides of the same street if they're just doing a crosshatch?"

"Corridors, then?" Nissa suggested. "Maybe they're setting up patrol routes that their soldiers can use without worrying about spine leopard attacks."

"If that's the plan, they're in for a rude awakening," Lorne said. "Like Brander said, that mesh may keep spinies out, but you can cut it with a torch. We do that, and they'll be in the same boat we are."

"Humans of Aventine," a computerized voice called faintly from somewhere below them. "Humans of Aventine, awake and listen."

"Do these open?" Lorne called to Brander, running his fingers along the window's edges as he searched in vain for a catch.

"Yeah, I'll get it," Brander said, bounding up from the couch and hurrying over. He did something, and the window swung open a few centimeters.

"Humans of Aventine," the Troft voice came again, much louder and clearer this time. Lorne nudged up his audios as the voice ended, and caught three distinct and distant echoes. Apparently, the Trofts were delivering the same message simultaneously across the whole city. "Humans of Aventine, awake and listen."

"We *are* awake, you son of a chicken," Brander muttered. "Get on with it."

"Humans of Aventine, in payment for the crimes of your government, you are now under the rule and authority of the Trof'te Assemblage. If you cooperate without resistance, you will not be harmed, and will be permitted to continue your daily lives.

"Your first orders are the following: For the next three hours you are to remain inside your residences or other interior locations; when the three hours have ended, you will have permission to emerge, but only into the fenced zones which we are currently building. All humans traveling outside those zones will be subject to immediate death.

"Also at the end of those three hours, your chief leaders will meet us in the assembly center known as the Dome, where detailed instructions will be delivered to them. Any of the chief leaders who fails to attend will also be subject to immediate death."

Lorne looked sideways at Nissa, and found her looking back at him. Would the invaders even know who all the governors and syndics were? Probably. Everything else that had happened, from the coordinated predawn invasion to the efficient fencing work, indicated that they knew what they were doing. They would spot Treakness's absence, all right, and they would certainly call Chintawa on it.

Hopefully, the governor-general could work up a plausible story for them. If not, their already tight timetable was likely to get a lot tighter.

"One final order," the loudspeaker below boomed. "Any human who hides or assists an armed patroller or a *koubrah*-soldier will be punished. Any human who exposes the existence and location of an armed patroller or *koubrah*-soldier will be rewarded."

The loudspeaker fell silent...and Lorne felt a shiver run up the back of his neck. A day ago, back in the expansion region, he would have dismissed any such carrot/stick ploy as a pathetic waste of time. He knew the people out there, and there was no way they would turn on him or the rest of the men who risked their lives on a daily basis to protect them.

But he was in the city now, surrounded by people with Brander's same attitude of contempt or indifference toward those guardians. What would *they* do with the handful of Cobras still among them? How big would the promised rewards and threatened punishments have to get before the betrayals started?

Or would the carrots and sticks not even be necessary? Would the people turn in the Cobras simply out of spite for their perceived failure in preventing the invasion in the first place?

He could feel Nissa's eyes on him. Deliberately, he didn't look back at her. "Sounds like that's it for now," he said, forcing his voice to remain calm. "Come on, we'd better get back downstairs."

"Wait a minute," Nissa said slowly.

Lorne turned, to find that he'd been wrong about her looking at him. In fact, she was frowning out at the cityscape below. "What is it?" he asked.

"This doesn't make any sense," she said, pointing down the side street. "That's Broadway over there, the one they're fencing off. It's mostly shopping, with the Gregorius Omni a block north and the Wickstra Performing Arts Center four blocks south."

"Okay," Lorne said, pulling up his own somewhat hazy memories of the central city's layout. "So?"

"So most of the residences in this area are *between* here and there," Nissa said. "In fact, almost all of them are, since there aren't even many of these store-and-apartment setups on Broadway. Nearly everything there above the shopping levels is office space."

"Again, so?" Lorne said, still not seeing where she was going with all this.

"So all those apartments and homes are outside the fences," Nissa said. "How are the people in there supposed to get to the fenced-in areas the Trofts are setting up?"

"Oh, hell," Lorne said as it finally clicked. "You're right, they *aren't* going to get there. Not without help." He hissed contemptuously. "Brilliant. Carrots, sticks, *and* bludgeons."

"What do you mean?" Brander asked, frowning.

"He means they're expecting the Cobras to go in and get the people out," Nissa murmured.

"Thereby giving the Trofts yet another free shot at them," Lorne said. "If the spinies don't get them first."

He took one final look at the fence construction going on along the street, then took Nissa's arm. "Come on," he said. "We need a consultation."

The restaurant had filled up in the time they'd been upstairs. There were upwards of twenty people in the dining room, a few still in nightdress and robes but the majority properly dressed. They were mostly clumped together in small groups, as had been the case back in the lobby of Treakness's apartment building, whispering nervously among themselves as they gazed out the windows at the construction going on outside.

All eyes turned to Lorne and Nissa as they came though the door, and for a moment the whispering went silent. But Lorne merely nodded a wordless acknowledgment to them and headed across the room toward the rear corner table where Treakness and Poole had taken up residence. A moment later, as it became clear that the newcomers had no fresh information to share, the whispering resumed.

"You enjoy your snack?" Lorne asked as he and Nissa sat down in the table's two empty seats.

"It was adequate," Treakness said coolly. "I presume you heard the announcement. How did things look from up there?"

"About like they do from down here," Lorne said. "The Trofts are busy fencing off this street and Broadway. Probably others, too, but Broadway was as far as we could see."

"Wait a minute," Poole said, frowning. "*Just* this one and Broadway?"

"*And* others they already said they couldn't see," Treakness growled. "Pay attention."

"No, no, that's not what I meant," Poole said, fumbling the words. "I meant what about the streets *between* here and Broadway?"

Treakness rolled his eyes. "They already said—"

"What Poole means," Lorne cut him off, "is whether the people living on those other streets are being thrown to the wolves. The answer is, yes, they are."

Treakness's lips compressed into a thin line. "I see," he said grimly. "So in other words, the Trofts are letting us choose between hundreds of civilian casualties and sending our remaining Cobras back out into the open."

"That about sums it up," Lorne agreed. "So what do we do?"

Treakness hissed thoughtfully. "Well, for the next three hours, at least, we do nothing," he said. "We're pretty well stuck here until the Trofts' quarantine period is up. After that…" He shrugged. "I suppose that particular decision will be landing in Chintawa's lap. Lucky him."

"Shouldn't we at least alert him as to what's going on out here?" Lorne asked. "And while we're at it, we should also find out what's happening back at the Dome. It might be nice to have some idea about the tactical landscape once we *are* able to move."

"My, aren't we enjoying our military jargon," Treakness said with an edge of sarcasm. "Unfortunately, the Trofts have jammed the comm system. Until they unjam it—if they ever do—the tactical landscape is going to be a discover-as-we-go proposition."

Poole stirred uneasily. "This isn't good," he murmured. "I don't think we can afford to just sit here for three hours."

"Good point," Treakness said. "Maybe we should try jogging in place."

"Please stop that," Nissa said suddenly.

"Stop what?" Treakness asked, frowning at her.

"Stop treating Poole that way," Nissa said. "I know you're frightened. We're all frightened. It doesn't help for you to keep picking on him."

"You think that my ignoring stupidity will be an asset in getting us through this?" Treakness countered.

"Your disagreeing with something doesn't make it stupid," Nissa said stubbornly. "And in fact, I agree with him. I don't think we can afford to just give up the next three hours."

Treakness looked at Lorne. "Well?" he challenged.

"If you're looking for support, look somewhere else," Lorne said. "I agree with them."

Treakness lifted his hands, palms upward. "Strength, resolve, and unanimity. How wonderful for us all. But unless you also have a cloak of invisibility, none of that will get us a single meter outside that door."

"There must be a way," Nissa insisted. "Maybe we can building-hop. You know: go in the front door, through the building, and out the back."

"And how exactly will that get us across Cavendish Boulevard?" Treakness asked, waving at the activity taking place outside the restaurant's windows. "You think that if we walk nonchalantly enough, the Trofts won't notice us?"

"What about the storm drain system?" Lorne asked. "That runs under the streets, right?"

"Yes, it does," Treakness said. "Do you have any idea how the system is laid out?"

Lorne grimaced. "No," he conceded.

"I do," a voice said from behind Lorne.

Lorne turned around, startled. While the four of them had been talking—reasonably quietly, or so he'd thought—all other conversation in the restaurant had once again ceased.

And to his uneasy surprise, he found that the whole crowd was silently watching them.

He focused on the man who'd just spoken. He was middle-aged and bulky, with a lined face and a rigid expression. "I beg your pardon?" Treakness asked.

"I said I know the drainage system," the man told him. "Been working down there for most of the past twenty years."

"You could show us how to get through it?" Treakness asked.

"I *could*, sure," the man said, eyeing Lorne. "The question is, *should* I?"

Lorne frowned. "Meaning . . . ?"

"Meaning he wants payment," Treakness said calmly. "A reasonable enough request. How much?"

"See, it's not so much quick cash as a long-term investment that I really need," the man said, still looking at Lorne. "Boils down to who pays better. You, or the Trofts."

"What, that thing about rewards and punishments?" Treakness scoffed. "You really think you can trust anything they say?"

"Yeah, actually, I can," the man said, finally turning his eyes away from Lorne and looking at Treakness. "See, I've read my history, Governor Treakness. I've read about the Troft occupation of Silvern and Adirondack during the Dominion-Troft war. Seems to me that when they promised something to the people there, they delivered on it."

"I wouldn't put a lot of weight on that if I were you," Lorne warned. "There are hundreds of Troft demesnes in the Assemblage, each with its own way of doing things. Just because the group that attacked the Dominion played by those rules doesn't mean this bunch will."

"I think it's worth the risk," he said. "Especially since they can get me something that maybe you can't."

"And what would that be?" Treakness asked.

The man looked behind him. "You folks mind?" he asked, raising his voice. "This here's a private conversation."

For a moment, no one moved. Then, a white-haired, leathery-skinned man in the middle of the group snorted and turned away, heading toward one of the tables by the windows. As if on signal, the others followed suit, moving back and re-forming themselves into their conversational clusters closer to the windows.

The man watched until they had all moved out of earshot. Then, grabbing a chair from one of the nearby tables, he pulled it over, nudging it in between Poole and Nissa. "Let's start with what exactly *you* want," he said as he sat down. "Then I'll tell you what *I* want."

"Actually, let's start with your name," Treakness said, pulling a small comboard from his jacket pocket. "No offense, but I want to make sure you can do what you claim you can."

The man gave him a twisted smile. "Aaron Koshevski," he said. "Address, apartment two-oh-one right above you. Occupation, mechanical and structural maintenance engineer."

Treakness nodded and started punching in the data. As he did so, Lorne looked back at the other people in the dining room, wondering what they were making of all this. But they seemed to have already lost interest, their attention back on the Troft soldiers working on their fencing project.

"All right, Mr. Koshevski," Treakness said, setting his comboard down on the table. "You do indeed appear to be who you say you are. What we want is to head west, obviously without interference from the Trofts. How can you help us do that?"

"How *far* west?" Koshevski countered. "Creeksedge Spaceport? Crystal Lake? The corner of Twenty-Eight and Panora? I need some idea of where exactly we're going."

"To the lake," Treakness said without hesitation. "Though I'm obviously not expecting the drainage system to get us that whole distance."

"You got that one right, anyway," Koshevski said with a grunt, his eyes narrowing with concentration.

Lorne looked at Nissa, noted her compete lack of expression, and adjusted his own face accordingly. Of course they weren't going to Crystal Lake—that area with its expensive houses and rolling parklands was a good thirty kilometers past the spaceport. But Treakness obviously had no intention of giving a total stranger their actual destination. Especially a total stranger who'd already hinted that he might prefer making a deal with the Trofts.

"Okay, here's what I can do," Koshevski said. "I can get you about nine kilometers west through the system, to somewhere around Ridgeline Street. Past that point, with the lower water table and better drainage, they put in smaller conduits that you won't be able to get through."

"Nine kilometers will be a good start," Treakness said, nodding. "What do you want in return?"

Koshevski pursed his lips. "My brother's family lives in an apartment building on West Twenty-Third, between Toyo and Mitterly," he said. "It's a residential area, not very fancy, about four kilometers southwest of here. From the way you were talking earlier, I'm guessing their block's going to end up in one of the unfenced zones."

He folded his arms across his chest. "Here's the deal. You get them to one of the safe areas, and I get you to Ridgeline Street."

"Can we get close to their building through the drainage system?" Treakness asked.

"I can get you practically to the front door," Koshevski said. "But Danny's wife has Jarvvi's Disease and won't be able to get through the conduits. You'll have to get them to the safe zones at street level."

"Fair enough," Treakness said. "Very well, you have a deal."

"Uh...sir?" Poole spoke up hesitantly. "Are you sure—?"

He broke off at an almost casual glare from his boss. "We'll want to leave as soon as possible," Treakness said. "How do we get in?"

"There's an access point right out there," Koshevski said, jabbing a thumb toward the rear of the restaurant. "Mid-block, about fifty meters north."

"Any special tools necessary for opening it?"

Koshevski shook his head. "All it takes is muscle." He looked Lorne up and down. "You got muscle?"

"We have muscle," Treakness confirmed, pushing back his chair and standing up. "Let's go."

The others followed suit, and as Lorne stood up he glanced one last time around the dining room.

And felt a shiver run up his spine. He'd been wrong earlier about everyone's attention being on the Trofts outside. One of them, the white-haired man who'd led the group retreat earlier at Koshevski's insistence, was sitting alone at one of the tables.

Watching them.

The man's gaze flicked to Lorne, and for a moment they locked eyes. Then, casually, the other turned away, as if there was nothing of interest there, that he'd just happened to be looking in that direction.

"Coming?" Treakness asked.

Lorne gazed at the white-haired man for another moment. Then, taking a deep breath, he turned away. "Yes," he told Treakness. Whether the other man had recognized Treakness, or whatever else his interest in the group might be, there was nothing Lorne could do about it now. At least the other had been too far away to eavesdrop on the critical parts of their conversation.

"Good," Koshevski said, taking Lorne's arm and pointing down the corridor toward the rear door. "After you."

There was a lone spine leopard wandering the street when Lorne eased the rear door open and stepped outside. The predator turned at the sound of the door, or possibly at the scent of fresh prey, and for a moment it eyed the rash human who had invaded its territory. But either it wasn't yet hungry, or else it hadn't finished staking out that part of the block as its territory. With a sniff and a brief flaring of its foreleg spines, it turned and walked away. "Clear," Lorne murmured over his shoulder, stepping aside and giving the rest of the street a quick look. No one was visible, human or Troft. "Where's this access point?"

"Right there," Koshevski said, pointing toward a round metal cover set flush into the street midway down the block, colored and textured to match the pavement around it. "Gripper holes in the edge—just grab them and pull straight up."

Lorne nodded and headed off down the walkway at a quick jog. He reached the cover, got his fingers into the gripper holes, and pulled. The cover was heavier than it looked, but his finger locks and arm servos were more than up to the task, and with a little effort he levered it up.

Treakness and the others were there by the time the way was

clear. "You first," Treakness murmured, gesturing Koshevski down into the dank-smelling hole.

Koshevski nodded. Sitting down on the edge of the hole, he found one of the two sets of embedded rungs with his feet and started down. Treakness was right behind him, followed by Poole, followed by Nissa. Balancing the cover on its edge, Lorne stepped into the opening and worked his way a couple of rungs downward. Then, spreading his legs and balancing himself, he picked up the cover and lowered it back into place, plunging them all into nearly total darkness. Keying in his opticals, he got his hands on the rungs and started down.

He'd gone only a few steps when, warned by the sound of footsteps and rustling cloth, he was able to key down the enhancers just as Treakness turned on the flashlight from his pack.

A minute later he arrived at the bottom, and found himself in a small chamber with meter-and-a-half-diameter cylindrical conduits leading off horizontally in four directions. "We go this way," Koshevski murmured, taking the flashlight from Treakness and shining it down the southward conduit.

"Why can't we just go west?" Treakness asked.

"Could, but won't," Koshevski said. "My brother is on West Twenty-Third, remember? Follow me. And be quiet—sound travels real good in here."

Bending over, he stepped into the conduit and headed off, the light bobbing drunkenly as he walked along the curved surface. Treakness followed, his hands splayed awkwardly to both sides for balance. Poole was again close behind him. Nissa paused long enough to give Lorne a strained smile, then followed.

Grimacing, Lorne watched them go, feeling a sudden twinge of claustrophobia as he eyed the narrow opening. But it was better than facing Troft lasers. Bending at the waist and the knees, he eased his way into the conduit. If this worked, he reminded himself firmly, they were going to gain almost half the distance to the spaceport and get a significant jump on the Trofts' efforts to lock down the city.

If it *didn't* work, this was going to be a very uncomfortable place to get caught in an ambush.

But there was nothing to do now but see it through. Keying up his audios as much as he dared, keeping a wary eye on their rear, he hurried to catch up.

CHAPTER SIX

It was five kilometers back to Stronghold as the aircar flew. By foot, Jody knew, it would be seven or eight. On Aventine, even the longer trip would be no more than a brisk two-hour walk. With a good nine hours remaining until sundown, she had wondered earlier what her father had meant with his comment about pushing their available daylight.

Within the first fifty meters of their journey, she'd figured it out.

The spores and other tiny plants that rode the Caelian wind were bad enough inside Stronghold. Here, away from the protection of the town's high wall, they were far worse. They whipped across her face and hands, tickling her ears and neck, and generally making a nuisance of themselves.

There were larger versions as well, versions that seldom made it into Stronghold. Some of those had tiny hooks designed to catch on something—anything—that would provide an opportunity for growth. They could actually sting if one of the hooks managed to snag a particularly sensitive section of skin, reminding Jody of her first experience on an Aventinian beach, when a rising wind had whipped sand across her face.

And of course, the eddy currents created by the trees and landscape meant that the whole spectrum of airborne plants could come from any direction, not just that of the prevailing wind.

The insects were out in force, too, following right behind the spores. In theory, since the spores didn't attach to living skin, the insects didn't have any reason to land on Jody's face or hands and try to take a bite. In actual practice, a lot of them did anyway. Others, the clumsier ones no doubt, simply lumbered into her, bouncing off and continuing on their way. The majority, content with merely swarming around the intruders, added their own layer of distraction and irritation.

Jody had known about all that from their previous times outside the town, and had mentally prepared herself for it. What she hadn't expected was the ferocity of Caelian's larger forms of plant life.

Stronghold was kept largely devoid of native plants, except for the handful that had been cultivated or were in the process of becoming so. She'd seen some of those, and of course she'd also seen the vegetation that had covered their testing area landing site before she and the others had burned it off.

It somehow had never occurred to her that perhaps Geoff and Freylan had chosen that spot precisely because of its lack of the nastier forms of Caelian plant life.

But all those forms were here now, splashed across the ridge that her father had chosen as their path. There were plants that tried to tangle her feet, and others that grabbed onto her trouser legs with tiny or not-so-tiny hooks, barbs, and thorns and tried to either trip her or shred the silliweave material. Other varieties exuded poisons or skin irritants or adhesives, the latter rather like Aventine's native gluevines, only worse. And even the innocuous plants did their bit to conceal tangled tree roots, ground insect mounds, or more dangerous plants.

In view of all that, it was probably remarkable that the group made it a full hundred meters before they had their first accident.

It happened to be Freylan, though in retrospect Jody realized it could have been any of them. Carrying the rear poles of the gigger's cage, he got his foot caught in a tangle of vines and sprawled facefirst on the ground. That by itself wouldn't have been so bad, but his left hand unfortunately hit the low hill of one of Caelian's antlike insect forms. This species was fortunately not poisonous or even biting, but enough of them got up his sleeve before he could disengage that he had to strip off his entire outfit in order to get clear of them.

Jody dutifully faced away from the situation, which was why she missed the additional drama of her father lasering a pair of orctangs that tried to take advantage of the party's preoccupation and creep up on them.

They got Freylan put back together and continued on, only to run into a patch of blue lettros fifty meters later lurking beneath a stand of solotropes. Paul was able to burn away just enough of the patch's end for them to get around it, but barely ten meters further on they hit a line of blue treacle that went all the way down the ridge on both sides. That meant there was no going around it, which meant Paul had to not only cut their way through the plants themselves but then use his arcthrower to systematically flash-burn a path through the adhesive that the lasered plants leaked all over the ground. That single patch took over half an hour to pass.

Midway through the operation they were attacked by two whisperlings that Paul had to kill. At the far edge of the patch, just as they were starting to pick up some speed again, he had to fend off two hooded clovens. Through all of it, Snouts never stopped growling once.

The next incident was Jody's, involving a nest of micewhiskers that she managed to kick as she was trying to avoid a patch of hookgrass, and left her with a bruise on her forehead and some madly itching scratches on her cheek. Her father and Geoff took the brunt of the next one, when a branch Paul was cutting fell the wrong way and sent some tendrils of poison shink whipping across both their faces. The resulting inflamed scratches not only itched, but hurt as well.

Still, the animal attacks were the most serious threat. Fortunately, Paul was mostly able to hear or see them coming in plenty of time to thwart them.

The sun was nearing the western horizon, and Jody estimated they'd covered about six of the seven or eight kilometers back to Stronghold, when one of the attacks finally got through.

With one final sizzle of charged vegetation, the last bit of poison shink blocking their path blackened and curled away. "Okay," Paul said, peering forward at the immediate terrain ahead, then lifting his head to survey the multiple arches of tree branches stretching out above them.

Jody looked up, too, eyeing the brilliant greenery distrustfully. Many of the trees they'd passed beneath during that long afternoon had featured lower branches that were dead and leafless and had thus provided little cover for anything larger than a nest of split-tails.

Not so this bunch. This bunch had apparently choked out all competing large vegetation, with the result that their branches had more or less free access to the region's daily quota of sunlight. That, along with the spiral arrangement of the branches, meant that it was worthwhile for nearly all of those branches to sprout leaves to catch that sunlight.

Which meant pretty much anything could be hiding up there.

Jody didn't like the look of the path. Not a bit. But they had little choice. A brief reconnoiter had showed a huge patch of green treacle to their left, and an equally large expanse of impassible marshland to their right. The only other option was to backtrack and find another route, and with the forest having grown steadily denser as they traveled there was a good chance they would find themselves in a similar situation somewhere else down the line anyway.

The others had clearly, and probably just as reluctantly, come to the same conclusion. "Are we going, or aren't we?" Geoff, at the cage's rear, growled as the seconds ticked past without anyone moving. "Come on, I don't want to be out in the open when the sun goes down and the predator night shift starts."

"Good point," Freylan agreed reluctantly. He took a deep breath. "Okay—"

"Hold it," Paul said suddenly. "Listen."

Jody frowned, straining her ears. What had he heard?

"Uh-oh," Freylan said quietly, twisting half around to look over his shoulder at the cage.

And Jody felt her breath catch in her throat as she suddenly got it.

For the first time in hours, Snouts had gone silent.

"You three wait here," Paul said, starting to ease forward past Freylan. "I'll check it out."

"Hold it," Geoff said. "All things being equal, if something decides to jump us I'd rather be up there with you than back here alone."

"I agree," Freylan seconded.

Paul's lip twitched, but he reluctantly nodded. "If it'll make you feel better," he said. "But stay a couple of paces back, and don't crowd me."

They set off, Paul in the lead, followed closely by Freylan, the swaying cage, and Geoff. Jody walked at Geoff's left, keeping her eyes moving and making especially sure to keep an eye behind them. During the past half hour an odd haze had begin to take over her mind, no doubt brought on by a day's worth of fear, fatigue, and adrenaline overload.

And they still had a good kilometer or two to go. At this point, she wasn't at all sure she was going to make it.

"Jody, you have those stun sticks handy?" Geoff murmured in her ear.

"Handy enough," Jody said, frowning at him. "Why?"

"Why do you think?" Geoff muttered. "Let me have one."

"Dad said you weren't supposed to," Jody reminded him.

"I don't care what he said," Geoff bit out. "Hand it over. Now."

Jody threw a quick glance forward. Her father, his attention on the area ahead and above them, didn't seem to have heard the exchange.

And suddenly she realized that she would rather like to have a weapon handy, too. Sliding open the fastener on one of the two packs hanging across her chest, she pulled out the two stun sticks and handed one to Geoff. "Be careful with it," she muttered.

"Don't worry," he said. Shifting it across to his right hand, he clicked off the safety catch and rested his thumb on the activation switch. Swallowing hard, wondering what her father would say if he caught them with the weapons, Jody did the same.

They'd gone ten more paces when the entire grove exploded in ululating howls and a dozen snarling, wolflike animals leaped from the branches above them.

Reflexively, Jody dropped into a crouch, turning half around as two of the animals hit the ground three meters away and charged toward her. Vaguely, she heard herself screaming at them in turn as she frantically tried to activate her stun stick.

But somehow, her madly searching thumb couldn't seem to find the switch. The nearest of the predators had opened its jaws wide, giving her a horrifying glimpse of sharp teeth and a bright red mouth.

Abruptly a brilliant flash of blue light slashed across the animal's flank. The creature twitched violently in midstride, then nose-dived onto the matted ribbon vines. Its partner dodged to the side, opened its own jaws, then also fell as a second antiarmor laser shot took it out.

And then, Jody's scrabbling thumb found the stun stick's activation button, and the sizzle of half a megavolt of electricity joined the cacophony of howling filling the grove. Something moved at the corner of her eye, and she swung around, trying to bring up the stun stick to intercept it.

She didn't make it. The creature slammed into her, its jaws stretching toward her throat, its body shoving her arm and the stun stick violently to the side. The impact turned her whole body into instant jelly, and her suddenly hazy brain realized she was being slammed to the ground. Her head hit the ground hard...

The darkness evaporated, and she found herself lying on her back in the grass. Freylan was kneeling over her, his arm stretched out rigidly, whipping the crackling stun stick in his hand back and forth in a hundred-eighty-degree arc, yelling defiantly at the pack of animals still filling the grove with their howls. Jody tried to roll away or get up and help, but her body inexplicably refused to move.

And then, someone shot past above Freylan's head, and Jody rolled her eyes to the side and saw that it was her father. He landed in front of the snarling animals, sending servo-powered kicks at the nearest ones while his fingertip lasers flashed death at those out of kicking range. Two of the animals leaped at him from behind, but before they could make contact he threw himself into a low leap over the ones in front of him. He hit the grass and rolled, and as the two animals leaped again, his antiarmor laser flashed twice, sending their charred bodies to thud against the ground. The rest of the pack turned to the attack, only to find themselves in the middle of a three-prong laser barrage.

A few seconds later, the last of them was dead.

The sizzling of Freylan's stun stick, audible now that the howling had stopped, also went silent, and she looked up to see Freylan lower the weapon to his side, his whole body shaking with reaction. He took a careful breath, gave one final look around the grove, then looked down at Jody. "You all right?" he asked.

"I do' know," Jody said. The words came out embarrassingly slurred, her mouth as numb as the rest of her. "Wha' ha'n'ed?"

"We were attacked by a pack of—I don't know what; call them tree wolves," Freylan said. "Your dad did a spinning sonic blast to try to slow them down, but I guess when one of them slammed into you, it bumped you and the stun stick over into Geoff."

Jody grimaced. Or tried to, anyway—she had no idea whether her facial muscles were even responding. "An' the curren' go' all th'ee o' us," she muttered.

"Yeah," Freylan said. He looked somewhere to his left, his face hardening. "With Geoff taking the brunt of it."

Jody felt a sudden flash of horror roll through her useless body as she remembered her father's warning that the stun sticks could deliver a lethal jolt. "Is he a' right?" she breathed.

"I don't know," Freylan said grimly. "He's still breathing, though."

"No thanks to you," Jody's father's voice came from the direction Freylan was looking, an uncharacteristic anger in his voice that made Jody wince. "*Or* to him. What in the *Worlds* did you two think you were doing?"

"I'm sorry," Jody said. Her mouth was starting to come back now, and with an effort she managed to turn her head.

Geoff was lying on his back on the ground, his eyes closed, his face pale. Paul was kneeling over him, busy pulling the cap off a hypo, the survival kit's medical pack laid open on the ground beside him. "Yeah," Paul rumbled. "Sorry."

"We were afraid," Jody said, knowing even as she said them how lame the words sounded. That was an excuse, not a reason, and her parents had never much liked excuses. "We thought that if...no. We weren't really thinking at all, were we?"

"No, you weren't," Paul ground out as he slipped the needle into Geoff's arm and pressed the plunger. "There's a reason why you need training to use a weapon. *Any* weapon." He held his fingers against Geoff's neck for a few seconds, then looked up at Jody. "But I think he'll be okay," he added, the anger starting to fade from his voice. His eyes flicked to Freylan. "How about you, Freylan?"

"I'm all right," Freylan said. He looked back down at Jody, as if suddenly realizing how close he was still kneeling to her, and got stiffly to his feet.

Only then did Jody see the blood-stained slashes in the side of his silliweave tunic.

"Freylan!" she gasped, struggling to get her body working again.

"Don't worry, it's okay," Freylan hastened to assure her. "They hurt, but they don't feel very deep."

"What happened?" Jody demanded, running her eyes over the rest of his outfit. There didn't seem to be any damage anywhere else.

"Nothing serious," Freylan said. "When the first tree wolves attacked, your father had to get out of their way so that he could set up his counterattack." He shrugged. "One of them got through before he could do that."

And then, suddenly, Jody understood.

She turned to her father again, her eyes tracing out the tension lines in his face and throat, the repressed anger still simmering there. Only it wasn't her and Geoff he was primarily angry at.

It was himself.

Jody closed her eyes, a wave of frustration and sympathy flowing through her. From the very beginning of the Dominion's Cobra project a hundred years ago, the men who volunteered to become their elite soldiers were carefully screened, not just for mental and emotional stability, but also for the kind of outward-centered personalities that would permit the downplaying of their personal desires and the elevation of the lives and safety of the civilians they would be fighting for. That screening had gotten tighter and more sophisticated over the years, but the goal was still the same: to create warriors who were able and willing to give their lives if necessary for their people and their worlds.

Only the military planners who'd created the Cobras' equipment hadn't seen it quite that way. The combat reflexes programmed into their nanocomputers weren't designed so that Cobras could throw themselves into self-sacrificing lunges into enemy fire in defense of the small and helpless. They were designed to get the Cobra himself out of harm's way, therefore permitting him to survive long enough to launch his own counterattacks against the enemy.

Even if it meant abandoning one of the small and helpless to take the brunt of the attack alone.

Freylan clearly understood that. But not everyone did. Jody had heard heartbreaking stories from her brothers and their friends about incidents in the Aventinian frontier, incidents where Cobras had lived and civilians had died. Every one of those stories had been told with a catch in the Cobra's voice, and usually a stiff drink in the Cobra's hand.

It wasn't a problem that was going to go away, either. The Dominion had given the Cobra Worlds the equipment necessary to reproduce the Cobra equipment, but not the ability to reprogram the nanocomputers.

There was a groan from Jody's side. "Geoff?" she called, trying again to get up. She halfway succeeded this time, rolling part of the way up onto her side. "You okay?"

"Thin' so," he said, his voice as slurred as Jody's had been a minute ago. "Kind o' nu'. Thin' it's gettin' better—startin' t' hurt now."

"Oh, good," Jody said.

"Just lie there for a few more minutes," Paul said, collecting the medical pack and standing up. "Your turn, Freylan. Let me help you with that tunic."

"It wa' 'y faul', Co'a Broo," Geoff called as Paul stepped over to Freylan and the two of them started easing off Freylan's bloodied tunic. "I m-mean m-my fault. Not Jody's."

"I appreciate knowing that," Paul said. "I hope *you* appreciate now that stun sticks aren't toys." He flashed a look at Jody. "Both of you."

"Trust me," Jody said fervently, trying to sit up. Once again, she was halfway successful. "What's the plan?"

"There's no point in trying to get any farther tonight," Paul told her, peering at Freylan's gashes and selecting an anti-infection salve from the kit. "After I get Freylan fixed up, I'll see what I can put together in the way of a shelter."

Jody looked around at all the predator corpses scattered around them, corpses the scavenger insects and carrion animals were already flocking to. "You think it'll be safe here?"

"As safe as anywhere else," Paul said. "If this pack of tree wolves permanently held this territory, we can hope it'll take any other predators at least until tomorrow to realize they're gone and move in."

"Unless they share the area with a nocturnal batch," Freylan warned, wincing as Paul applied the salve.

"In which case, again, we're in no more danger here than a hundred meters down the road," Paul said. "Let me get some sealant and bandages on this, and then the three of you can rest while I build us a shelter."

Jody expected the shelter to be something simple, perhaps a hedge of uprooted thorn bushes with a few well-placed treacles gluing it all together.

She was wrong.

By the time she was able to fully sit up, her father had burned off a three-by-four-meter area about ten meters upwind of the scattering of dead tree wolves. By the time she was able to stand up and hobble around, he'd begun lasering down some of the smaller trees, cutting them into sections, and lugging them to the cleared area. By the time her fine-muscle control had recovered to the point where she was able to start assembling the survival pack's silliweave tent, he'd put together a waist-high barrier enclosing the campsite on three sides.

And by the time Geoff had also recovered from his encounter with the stun stick, the sun was going down and the tent was nestled snugly inside a chest-high barrier that would give pause to even the most determined predator.

Clearly, her father had had a lot more frustration to work out than she'd realized.

"The last step will be to string the extra support wire across the entrance once you're settled down in there," Paul said as Jody and the others finished collecting the rest of the equipment and supplies. "I can tie in the stun sticks and rig a pressure switch so that anything that hits the wires hard enough will get a good jolt. That and the barricade should keep anything serious from getting through from the sides."

"And the top cover and support poles should be springy enough to bounce off anything that leaps in from the top," Freylan said. "At least, that's what the manual said is supposed to happen."

"We'll probably get a chance to see how that works," Paul said grimly. "Make sure you've done any business you need to do out here, then get inside."

"What about Snouts?" Freylan asked, nodding toward the gigger snarling quietly in its cage. "We just going to leave him out here?"

"You want him in there with us?" Geoff countered.

"He was a good early-warning system for the tree wolves," Freylan said doggedly. "He might do the same for the nighttime predators, too."

"Only if they run the same territorial game the daytime ones do," Geoff said.

"It's still worth a try," Paul decided. "You two put him next to the tent, and I'll string the wire so that he'll be inside the perimeter. Just make sure to position him where his tusks can't poke through the tent and hit something."

Jody watched as the two young men maneuvered the cage into

position, then stood aside and let them slip through the tent flap. "You want any help with that?" she asked as her father started unspooling the wire.

"No, I'm all right," Paul assured her. "Go on in and get settled. Make sure you leave me enough room just inside the flap where I can get out if there's trouble."

"I will." Jody took a step toward him and lowered her voice. "It wasn't your fault, you know, that the wolf got through to Freylan."

"Yes, I know," Paul said, a hint of his earlier frustration briefly touching his voice. "You know it, too. Does that knowledge make you feel any better?"

Jody grimaced. "Not really."

"It doesn't for us, either." He sighed. "I don't know, Jody. Maybe people like Treakness are right. Maybe it's time for the Cobras to fade gracefully into the sunset."

Jody peered at him in the gathering gloom, a knot forming in her stomach. This didn't sound like her calm, cool-headed father. "Not sure the middle of a Troft invasion is the right time to hand in your resignation," she warned.

"Fine, so we don't fade away, but instead go out in a blaze of glory," he said. "Same end result."

"That's nonsense," Jody insisted. "The Cobras are the best—"

"The Cobras are a hundred-year-old tactical concept, Jody," he interrupted quietly. "Surely there must be better and more practical weapons available by now. Combat suits, exoskeletons, remote drones—something."

"Okay, so you're old," Jody said. "Not all military doctrines go out of style, you know. There's this little something called *concentration of firepower* that I believe has been around since, oh, the invention of reliable firearms. It might go back to the longbow, too. Not sure about that."

Paul shook his head. "Hardly the same thing."

"There's also the old, time-tested doctrine of never trusting conclusions, strategic or otherwise, that you reach when you're tired," Jody continued. "So finish with your wire and stun sticks and get some sleep. If you really want to walk to the scrap center, tomorrow will be soon enough."

Paul snorted. "You sound like your mother," he said. "Except the scrap center part."

"Probably because if you head there she logically has to go

with you," Jody said, her mind flicking briefly to her mother and brother on Qasama, wondering what the problem was that her mother's old friend Daulo Sammon had called them there to solve. Something incredibly thorny, no doubt.

But at least they weren't in the middle of a Troft invasion. "But the principle still holds," she added. "Namely, listen to the women in your family."

"A principle that I believe predates even concentration of fire-power," Paul said, some of his usual dry humor finally peeking through.

"Absolutely," Jody said, starting to breathe a little easier. "And while you mull that over, toss me the end of that wire. The sooner we get this thing strung, the sooner we can both get some sleep."

CHAPTER SEVEN

Traveling through the drainage conduit wasn't nearly as bad as Lorne had expected it to be. Once he got past that first touch of claustrophobia in the narrow confines, he was able to configure his back and knee servos to take most of the strain off his muscles and joints as he walked.

Unfortunately, the trip wasn't nearly so easy for the others. The hunched-over, bent-knee postures they had to adopt quickly changed from awkward to uncomfortable to agonizing. By the time the group had covered their first half kilometer they were having to pause every few minutes to stretch aching backs and knees. The conduit's interior was also somewhat slimy, making footing treacherous, and as knees and backs began to give way, the number of slips and tumbles increased dramatically. Eventually, all of them except Koshevski and Lorne were forced to walk with their hands pressed against the ceramic at both sides, their palms walking across the repulsive surface in an effort to maintain their balance.

They had been underground for three hours, and had covered a little under three of the four kilometers to Koshevski's brother's apartment building, when they heard the faint sound of the Troft loudspeakers wafting down from overhead. Lorne keyed up his audios, and despite the confusing echoes in the conduits he was able to get most of the message.

"Well?" Treakness asked when the voice from above had faded away.

"They've finished the fencing and people are now being allowed outside," Lorne relayed. "And they again reminded everyone that there's a bounty on patrollers and Cobras."

"That it?" Koshevski asked, an odd expression on his face.

Lorne looked at him . . . and it occurred to him that, working in the conduits all these years, the bulky maintenance engineer had probably learned how to sift through the confusing echoes and decipher what was being said in the streets above. "They're also now specifying the bounty," he said evenly. "Anyone fingering a Cobra gets a transfer into one of the safe zones for themselves and their family, plus a week's worth of food. Anyone who assists a Cobra gets transferred the other direction, *out* of the safe zone."

"Yeah, that's what he said, all right," Koshevski said, a grim smile twitching briefly across his face. "Thought you might try to pull a fast one and skip that part."

"Why would he?" Treakness asked, eyeing Koshevski. "It's not like anyone here would ever think of betraying him. Right?"

"Of course not," Koshevski said. "We ready to get moving again?"

Treakness inclined his head. "After you."

Another hour had passed, and they were nearing Toyo Avenue, when the faint sound of another Troft announcement came distantly from above them. "What did they say?" Treakness asked when the loudspeakers fell silent.

"I couldn't tell," Lorne said, shaking his head. "It was too faint for me to get anything."

"We're between access points," Koshevski said, looking around. "I didn't get any of it, either."

"He sounded mad, though," Nissa murmured uneasily.

Lorne thought back. Now that she mentioned it, there *did* seem to have been a harder edge to that particular communiqué.

"You're imagining things," Treakness said brusquely. "We're almost there, right?"

"That's our exit, right there," Koshevski said, pointing to a faint sheen of diffuse light about fifty meters ahead. "We should probably let your Cobra go up first, of course."

"Of course," Treakness said.

Three minutes later, Lorne was climbing back up to street level, wincing a little as he was finally able to stretch his back and knees fully straight again. He reached the top of the shaft, pausing there for a moment with his audios at full power. But if there was anything moving up there, he couldn't hear it. "Seems clear," he whispered down to the others. "Stay there while I take a look." Bracing his feet on the rungs on the opposite sides of the shaft, he got his hands beneath one edge of the cover and eased it upward.

He found himself looking down a narrow street lined with medium-sized apartment buildings, a double row of neatly trimmed trees, and a handful of parked cars. He could hear the murmur of people in the distance, but they were too far away for him to pick anything out of the sound and from his vantage point he couldn't see them. Easing the cover back down, he turned himself around to the other side and again lifted the cover.

And nearly lost his balance as a spine leopard snout jabbed suddenly through the opening squarely in his face.

"Whoa!" Lorne jerked back from the snapping teeth, reflexively dropping the cover onto the predator's snout and pinning the creature in place.

The spine leopard was still struggling to free itself when Lorne's fingertip lasers, cutting zigzag paths through bone and flesh and brain, finally destroyed enough of the predator's decentralized nervous system to kill it.

"What the hell is going on up there?" Treakness called tautly.

Lorne took a deep breath and flicked a fingernail sharply against the spine leopard's nose, just to make sure. "I found the block patrol," he called back.

"Trofts?"

"Spine leopard." Setting his feet again, Lorne lifted the cover and peered out. "It's clear—come on up." Sliding the cover over onto the pavement beside him, he climbed the rest of the way out of the shaft.

Koshevski was the next one out. "It's that one over there," he said, pointing to the building to the left of the one directly across the street from them.

Lorne glanced both ways down the still-deserted street. Apparently, the spine leopard he'd killed had had this block to himself. "Go," he told Koshevski. "Get the door open, then stay there and keep it open for the others."

Koshevski nodded and took off, running as fast as his bulk would allow. By the time he reached the door and started pounding on it, Treakness was also out of the shaft and following after him. Poole had joined the group, and Nissa was nearly there, when the door was finally flung open and they all piled inside. Lorne slid the cover back into place over the shaft, then scooped up the dead spiny's carcass and sprinted to the apartment building.

Koshevski was still holding the door as ordered, his eyes wide as he watched Lorne approach with his burden. "What the hell are you doing?" he asked.

"Can't leave it out there for the Trofts to trip over," Lorne explained as he slipped past the other into the relative safety inside. "Is there a trash bin or shed or something where I can dump it?"

"Yeah, there's a bin out back," Koshevski said, pointing down the hallway.

"Thanks," Lorne said. "Go tell your brother to get his family ready to go. Which apartment is it?"

"Four-oh-two," Koshevski said, heading for the stairs. "The door'll be open for you."

"Right," Lorne said, turning around carefully in the cramped space. "I'll be up in a minute."

"I'll go with you," Poole volunteered, ducking gingerly past the spiny's snout and stepping out in front of Lorne. "I can get the doors and lids and stuff."

"Poole—" Treakness began threateningly.

"I'll be all right," Poole said quickly. "I mean, if it's all right with you."

Treakness grimaced, but then nodded. "Be quick about it," he growled. Turning, he headed up the stairs. Nissa gave Poole a quizzical look of her own and followed.

"Thank you, sir," Poole called after them. "I'll get the door," he added to Lorne, and hurried down the corridor.

Lorne caught up with him at the rear door. "Thanks," he said as Poole unfastened the lock. "Push it open, but stay inside, just in case. I'll go first."

"Yeah, just a second," Poole said, leaving the door closed and peering down at the dead spine leopard in Lorne's arms. "I'd like a quick look here, if you don't mind."

"Sure," Lorne said, frowning. "First one you've seen up close?"

"No, not really," Poole said absently as he began probing the fur between the animal's shoulders with his fingers. "I was just wondering…"

He trailed off, his face suddenly tightening. "What?" Lorne asked.

Poole took a deep breath. "Did it occur to you to wonder," he asked, "how the Trofts managed to sneak onto Aventine for the hours or days it would take to collect all the spine leopards they've been dumping in Capitalia this morning?"

"I—" Lorne paused. With all the more immediate problems to deal with, he suddenly realized he *hadn't* gotten around to wondering that. "So how did they?"

"They didn't." Poole touched the section of fur he'd been studying. "The skin under the fur here is heavily calloused, over a region fifteen or twenty centimeters square. I'm no expert, but it seems to me these are the kind of calluses an animal could only build up if something with sharp claws routinely hung onto the skin there."

Lorne stared at him. "Are you suggesting…?"

"I'm not *suggesting*, Cobra Broom," Poole said bitterly. "I'm *saying* it. This spine leopard came from Qasama.

"The Qasamans and Trofts have made an alliance."

Lorne looked down again at the carcass in his arms, his head spinning. No—that couldn't be right. Qasaman paranoia coupled with their awareness of how the Trofts had tried to manipulate their world thirty-two years ago would surely make such an alliance impossible.

Or would it? Even a culture as heavily steeped in its own past as the Qasamans' could change. Could a new generation of Shahni have decided to break with their traditions, to work with the distrusted Trofts in order to strike back at the hated Cobra Worlds? Was that the crisis situation the mysterious message from Daulo Sammon to their family had been referring to?

Was that alliance the crisis situation that his mother and brother had flown right into the middle of?

"Broom?"

Lorne started. "Sorry," he apologized. "I was just wondering if that's really possible."

"Looks pretty possible from where I'm standing," Poole said heavily. "And if it is, we're in worse trouble than we thought. As Koshevski said, Dominion history says that Troft soldiers don't go in for random killing. We have no idea whether the Qasamans will be that restrained." He hissed out a sigh and stepped back to the door. "Let's dump this thing and get upstairs. Governor Treakness needs to hear about this as soon as possible."

"And no one else?" Lorne suggested.

"Absolutely no one else."

The trash bin behind the building was only half full, leaving plenty of room for the dead spiny. "So how long have you been with Treakness, anyway?" Lorne asked as he slid the carcass through the opening into the bin.

"Not long," Poole said. "Don't know how much longer I'll be with him, either. He's ... difficult sometimes."

"Or some might say criminally abusive," Lorne said bluntly. "I'm surprised you didn't walk out your first day on the job."

"Governor Treakness has his own way of doing things," Poole said diplomatically. "You just have to understand him." He shrugged. "And as you know, sometimes you have to put up with something you don't like in order to get something you want."

Lorne cocked an eyebrow at him. "Are you talking about Treakness? Or about you?"

"Maybe a little bit of both." Poole lowered the lid on the bin. "Come on, we need to get back."

Koshevski had said he would leave the apartment door open. What Lorne hadn't counted on was that every other door on the fourth floor would also be open, and that every resident from behind those doors would be standing in the hallway, gazing at the visitors in silent pleading. "What's going on?" he asked as he and Poole eased gingerly through the silent throng to the doorway of 402 where Nissa was waiting, her face troubled as she surveyed the crowd.

"The word spread," she said quietly. "They're asking if we'll take all of them across to the Trofts' safe zone, too."

Lorne winced. "What does the boss say?"

"Governor Treakness is against the idea." She smiled wanly at Lorne's expression. "Don't worry, they've all already recognized him." Her smile faded. "Which is another problem. That Troft announcement a few minutes ago, the one we couldn't understand? It said that Governor Treakness had missed the meeting at the Dome and announced a bounty for his capture."

"Terrific," Lorne growled. "Same one they've put on the Cobras?"

"Better, actually," Nissa said. "Two weeks' worth of free food instead of just one."

"That's stupid," Poole murmured. His face had gone rigid as he, too, eyed the silent crowd. "Cobras are far more dangerous to them than politicians."

"Your boss might think otherwise," Lorne said.

"Especially when that boss has important work to do," Treakness's voice called from inside the apartment. "You three, stop jabbering and get in here."

They found Treakness standing in the middle of the living room talking quietly with Koshevski and a somewhat younger man with a distinct family resemblance. Seated on a chair to one side was a woman with a lined, strained face and the slight trembling in her legs that was the sign of Jarvvi's Disease. Three teenagers—two girls and a boy—stood behind her. All four were listening closely to the conversation, their faces taut and nervous. "This is Mr. Koshevski the Younger and his family." Treakness introduced them briefly as Lorne and the others came up. "They're packed and ready to go."

"What about the people out there?" Lorne asked.

"What about them?" Treakness asked. "The deal was for Mr. Koshevski's family."

"I'm not talking about the deal," Lorne said. "I'm talking about basic humanity."

Treakness shook his head. "Sorry, but humanity doesn't enter into any of this."

"Maybe not to you it doesn't," Lorne said, feeling the first stirrings of anger. "But it does to me. I'm a guardian of the people of Aventine—the oath I took specifically used that word."

"So did mine," Treakness agreed. "We also took an oath to obey orders given to us by our superiors, in this case Governor-General Chintawa himself."

"But we can help them," Lorne said.

"We can help them more by completing our mission," Treakness said firmly. "We can't do that unless we can get out of here without attracting Troft attention." He waved a hand in dismissal. "Discussion closed. Now, the nearest fenced street appears to be three blocks to the north. If we go with Ms. Gendreves's building-hopping idea, that means we'll have three streets to cross—"

"The discussion is *not* closed," Lorne interrupted. "We can't just walk away and leave them here."

For a moment Treakness eyed him coolly. "Fine, I'm listening," he said at last. "But tell me first where you propose to draw the line."

"What do you mean?"

"I mean do we take just the people on this floor?" Treakness asked. "Or do we open the invitation to everyone in the building? And if the whole building, why not the whole neighborhood?"

"If they can be ready in the next five minutes, why not?" Lorne countered.

"I'll tell you why not," Treakness said. "Because there will be Troft soldiers walking the safe-zone fences, and probably some sort of air surveillance. Even if we avoid the actual streets by going through buildings, odds are we'll be spotted before we reach the fence."

"So they spot us," Lorne said impatiently. "So what?"

"So remember why they created all these spine leopard-infested areas in the first place," Treakness said. "Do you really think the Troft who spots a crowd that size will assume all those people simultaneously decided to make a break for it on their own?"

Lorne frowned. "I don't understand."

"He's saying *one* family might be crazy enough to do something like this without a Cobra escort," Poole said quietly. "But not five or six or ten of them."

"*I'll* decide what I'm saying, if you don't mind," Treakness growled, glaring briefly at his aide. "But in this case, Broom, he's right. If the Trofts spot the kind of train you're talking about, they're going to damn well know there's a Cobra in there with them. And if the train attracts a spine leopard and you have to kill it, they'll even know which one of us you are."

Lorne grimaced. He was right, of course. On all of it. "I suppose," he said reluctantly.

"Glad you agree," Treakness said acidly. "Now, let's focus on the topic at hand: getting Mr. Koshevski's family out so we can get back on our way."

"That way ultimately being to Crystal Lake," Koshevski put in, tapping his brother on the arm, "which we still haven't quite figured out. I can get him to Ridgeline, but I'm stuck on how to get him past that. You have any ideas?"

"There's a bunch of warehousing and light industry just west of there," the younger Koshevski said doubtfully. "Plenty of cover. But *getting* them that far will be tricky..."

Lorne moved away from the discussion, his mind still snarled in frustration, and crossed to the room's wide, north-facing window. Directly below him was the street they'd just come in from, lined on the other side by apartment buildings. Through the small gaps between the buildings, he could see that the block was a narrow one, and that the buildings there went straight through to face onto the next street. One more street after that, according to Treakness, and they would reach one of the buildings facing into the Trofts' fenced-in safety zone.

Even that short a journey through spiny territory would be dangerous for a group of civilians. With a Cobra along, though, it would be nearly as safe as a walk through Calay Park.

But surely the Trofts knew that, he realized suddenly. In fact, wouldn't their automatic assumption be that *any* group, of *any* size, would only venture out under Cobra protection?

In which case, Treakness's argument for limiting the break to Koshevski's family was exactly backwards. A smaller group would merely make it easier for the Trofts to intercept and corral them, and probably ferret out Treakness's identity along with it. What they actually needed was as large a group as feasible, a mob that Treakness could more easily lose himself in.

And if they could throw a little extra confusion and chaos into the mix...

He leaned close to the window and looked as far as he could to both sides. Due west, seven or eight blocks away, was another of the Trofts' narrow warships, towering over the buildings immediately around it. To the northeast, another of the ships was visible, this one probably ten blocks away. The first ship was pointing south, the second east, but with their main weaponry mounted on swivels on the fore and aft wings, the alignment of the ships themselves was mostly irrelevant. Any trouble here, and both ships' arsenals would be locked onto him in seconds.

Or rather, they would be if he was four stories up, the way he was right now. At street level, the weapons would be blocked by the neighborhood's other buildings.

Would the Trofts be willing to destroy one or more of those buildings just to get at a Cobra they knew was lurking behind it? Lorne had no way of knowing for sure, but at this point it was probably a fair assumption that they wouldn't. The invasion was less than half a day old, and as far as he knew the Cobras hadn't yet started making a nuisance of themselves. The Trofts could probably afford to wait for easier pickings, and save the escalation to scorched-ground level until they needed it.

Still, with a little careful nudging, Lorne could probably persuade them to add the extra confusion of gunfire to the plan that was rapidly forming in his mind.

The only trick then would be living through it.

The conversation behind him had switched to Sunset Avenue and roadside culverts when he took a deep breath and turned around to face them. "I can do it," he announced.

The discussion broke off in mid-sentence. "You can do what?" Treakness asked suspiciously.

Lorne looked over the governor's shoulder and gestured to Nissa. "Tell the people out there they have five minutes to get ready," he said. "One backpack or less per person, and light enough that they can run with it for three blocks if they have to."

"Gendreves, don't move," Treakness ordered. "Broom, in case you've forgotten, we've already decided we're not taking a crowd."

"No, *you* decided we weren't taking a crowd," Lorne said. "And you were wrong. Nissa told me the Trofts are looking for you. You really think you'll be able to lose yourself in a group of ten people?"

"They have to spot us first," Treakness countered. "A group of forty will make that discovery inevitable."

"They're going to spot us no matter how many of us there are," Lorne said. "The trick is going to be to create so much confusion that we can slip into whatever group of civilians is on the other side of the fence before they can rope us all in and take us somewhere for a detailed look."

"And you think you can create that much confusion?"

"Yes," Lorne said flatly. "One way or another, I'll get us through."

"You'd bet your life on that?"

"I fully intend to."

For a long moment Treakness studied him. "I'll take that bet." He turned and nodded to Nissa. "Go ahead and tell them." He held up his hand, fingers splayed. "*Five* minutes."

Four minutes and thirty seconds later, Lorne, Treakness, and Poole were standing just inside the door they'd entered half an hour earlier, a long line of nervous civilians behind them. "What's your plan?" Treakness murmured as they peered outside.

"We start by getting across this street," Lorne said, leaning forward to look up and down the street. "Should be safe enough—I've killed the spiny who'd staked out this particular territory, and none of the others should have noticed it's empty and moved in yet. We'll head straight across to that apartment building over there, burn off the lock if necessary, and go through. Since the buildings over there face directly onto the next street, we won't have to worry about getting past any spine leopards that might be lurking in a back area or courtyard."

"But they'll be waiting for us in the street itself?"

"Probably," Lorne conceded. "And the next street will be even worse. From the level of crowd noise I heard when we first arrived, I'm guessing there are a lot of people out in the streets inside the Troft barriers."

Treakness grunted. "Yes, I heard it, too. They're probably mobbing the stores, panic-buying food and other supplies."

"The point is that a high concentration of potential prey always draws large numbers of spinies," Lorne said. "That's because it shrinks the viable territories—"

"The technical reasons aren't important," Treakness cut him off. "The point, it seems to me, is that next to the fence is also where the Trofts are most likely to see you kill one of them."

"True," Lorne said. "But I think I can turn that attention away from you and the others and give you a chance to melt into the rest of the crowds across the fence."

"By drawing all that attention onto you?" Poole asked.

"Hopefully, not for long." Lorne looked over his shoulder. "Nissa?" he called.

"We're ready," her voice called faintly back.

"Okay," Lorne called, grimacing as he turned to the door again. He hadn't wanted to put Nissa in the rear of the group this way, but Treakness had insisted that one of their party be back there to guard against stragglers, stating that if they were going to do this they were going to do it right. Since Lorne and Treakness needed to be in front to lead, and since Treakness had made it clear he didn't trust Poole not to botch the job, the task had fallen to Nissa.

At least Koshevski and his brother would be back there with her to help in case of trouble. Both men had insisted on taking that much of the risk on themselves. "Everyone stay close together," Lorne called. "Here we go." Pulling open the door, he strode out into the late morning sunlight, Treakness and Poole right behind him.

He'd expected the group to get across the street without difficulty, and he was right. What he hadn't anticipated was that some of the target building's residents had spotted the exit from the storm drain system, including the obvious fact that Lorne was a Cobra, and that the word had spread quickly enough for them all to be prepared to join in the mass escape.

"Was this part of the plan, too?" Treakness grumbled to Lorne after the group waiting in the lower lobby area had made their request.

"You're the one who suggested we bring the whole neighborhood," Lorne reminded him. "Anybody been keeping tabs on the street to the north?"

"I have," one of the residents spoke up. "There are at least two spine leopards out there."

"One of them killed and ate a squintal from one of the trees," someone else offered. "Will that make it less hungry?"

"A little," Lorne said. "Not enough. Is the building straight across another apartment building?"

"No, that one's all commercial," the first person said. "A two-story restaurant downstairs, a couple of attorneys' offices upstairs. There's an apartment building just to the west of it, but its street door is usually locked."

"That won't be a problem," Treakness said.

"But we could get in faster and more conveniently if I didn't have to burn it," Lorne said, thinking hard. "Okay. I'm going to need a large piece of paper, or several small ones, and a big marker. And a second- or third-floor apartment that faces that building."

"I've got all of that in my place," a young woman spoke up. "I'll take you up."

"What do you want the rest of us to do?" Treakness asked.

"Just stay here," Lorne told him. "I'll be back in a minute."

The woman's apartment was small and crammed full of travel souvenirs and mementos from all over Aventine. "I teach a children's art class," she explained as she pulled a roll of banner paper and a marker from one of the shelves. "They like to draw murals. Are you stationed here in Capitalia?"

"DeVegas Province," Lorne told her as he opened the marker and began to write on the paper in large letters.

"Ah—Archway," she said, nodding. "I visited there once. The Braided Falls area to the north is beautiful."

"They're hoping to turn that into a resort someday," Lorne said.

"Do you know how the next couple of blocks to the north are laid out? Supposedly, we've got just one more street to go before we hit one of the Trofts' safe zones."

"That's right," the woman said. "I was up on the roof earlier for a look. Twentieth Street is all fenced off with some kind of tall mesh."

"That's the safe zone, all right," Lorne said. "Tell me all about it."

"I'll make you a sketch," the woman said, tearing another small sheet off the roll and picking up a pen.

By the time Lorne finished writing his message she was done. "Okay, we're here," she said, pointing to a square bordering one of the streets. "That apartment building, plus the one next to it and the two behind it, are part of a four-building complex with this play/gathering area in the middle."

"What does the gathering area look like?" Lorne asked. "Grass and play structures?"

"Over here, yes," the woman said, touching the western part of the open area. "This side has trees and a walking garden."

Lorne grimaced. Which undoubtedly was hosting a spine leopard or two at the moment. "Okay, so we get through the garden and past or through the next building north," he said. "What's this big building across the street?"

"That's Hendrezon's of Westport," the woman said. "It's the biggest store in the area—covers that whole half block, right through to Twentieth."

Which meant that going in from their side of the building would lead the refugee group straight into the fenced-in safe zone. "And it has a door on this side?"

"It has three of them," the woman said, adding their locations to her sketch. "Though under the circumstances, the ones on this side are probably locked."

"As Governor Treakness said, locks are the least of our problems," Lorne said. "Okay, looks like we've got a plan." He gestured to his own paper. "What do you think? Will it be legible from across the street?"

"'Need to get through,'" the woman read aloud. "'Please unlock front door.' Should be clear enough. *If* someone sees it."

"Someone will," Lorne promised, gathering up the paper. "Go open that window over there, will you?"

The woman complied, and Lorne stepped up beside her, centering himself in the open section and handing her one end of his banner. Keying his opticals to a medium telescopic setting, he focused on one of the other building's windows and fired a low-power burst from his sonic.

The window he was watching didn't even quiver. He notched up the power setting and tried again. Still nothing. "What are you doing?" the woman asked.

"Trying to get their attention," Lorne told her. He notched up the weapon and fired again.

This time, he saw the glass vibrate a little. He keyed the sonic up one final notch and lowered his opticals' enhancement back to normal. "Help me watch the windows," he told the woman. "Let me know when you spot someone." Trying to watch the whole side of the building at once, he fired three short bursts.

Nothing happened. He fired the triple burst again, then again, then again. Vibrating windows were a fairly subtle signal, he knew, but they were perfectly noticeable to anyone paying even a modicum of attention to their surroundings. Certainly anyone who'd spent any time in the expansion regions would know that vibrating windows were often an indication that Cobras were tackling spine leopards nearby.

"There!" the woman said suddenly. "Top floor, second in from the right."

Lorne found the window. An old man was standing there, peering down at the street. A moment later, a younger man joined him, also scanning the area below. Lorne gave another triple burst with his sonic, and this time the young man looked up. His body seemed to twitch, and he tapped the back of his hand against the older man's arm and pointed at Lorne's sign.

The other looked up, too, and for a long moment both of them just stood there, staring. Lorne pointed at the sign, then lifted his hands in silent question.

The younger man said something inaudible, his eyes still on the sign. The older answered, glancing at his friend and then looking back at the sign. The younger man said something else—

"They're going to betray you," the woman beside Lorne said suddenly. "They're talking about it right now."

Lorne frowned. "What makes you say that? Do you know them?"

"No, but I know that look," she said. "They heard the Trofts' offer, and they're going for it. They're just trying to figure out how to collect."

CHAPTER EIGHT

Lorne stared across the street at the two men, a cold feeling knotting itself into the pit of his stomach. If they'd been in DeVegas Province he would have told the woman she was imagining things. The people out there would never betray their guardians, no matter how much the Trofts offered them.

But they were in the city now. Here, Cobras weren't associated with safety, but with dress uniforms and governmental pomp and ceremony. And no one here had ever seen a spine leopard, much less had any idea of how to deal with it.

No, he realized, the Trofts had figured the psychology of the situation perfectly. For way too many people, the chance to escape deadly danger at the cost of someone they didn't even know would be an easy decision to make. Especially when they could rationalize it by telling themselves they were doing it for their children, or spouse, or parents.

"What are you going to do?" the woman asked.

"Not much I can do except keep going," Lorne told her. "I was already planning to make as much noise and chaos as I could anyway, to try to get you all through the store and into the crowds on the other side before the Trofts could identify you and gather you together for a closer look. Now, I'll just have to make sure that wherever I finish up at the end of that is far enough away that it'll be hard for anyone in our group to point me out."

"Sounds dangerous."

Lorne shrugged. "The original plan wasn't going to be a whole lot safer."

Across the street, the two men finished their conversation. The younger caught Lorne's eye, pointed to the message in the window, and gave a thumb's-up. He touched the older man's arm, and together they left their window.

"I guess we're on," Lorne said, gathering up the banner and folding it up.

"You're still going to go through with it?" the woman asked.

"It's either that, or we give up and settle down here," he pointed out. "Let's take another look at that map of yours."

They stepped over to her schematic of the street. "Okay, so this is Hendrezon's," Lorne said, indicating the long building. "How tall is it?"

"Four stories," the woman said.

"What about the buildings on either side?"

"The one to the east is—let's see—I think it's five stories," she said. "The one across Mitterly Street to the west is four, the same as Hendrezon's."

"What about the two to the west of that?" Lorne asked.

"The first is also four stories, and the next one is three," she said slowly. "I think. Yes, it's three."

"Are all three of the buildings on that block connected to each other?"

"No, there are service alleys separating them," she said. "Not very wide, maybe one normal street lane each."

"And the other side of that third building runs up to Ellis Avenue," Lorne said slowly, trying to visualize the area and fit the terrain into the modified plan forming in his mind. It would be tight, but it should work. "We'd better get downstairs now, before they wonder if we got lost." He turned and headed for the door.

"Wait a second," the woman said, crossing in front of him and angling over to a free-standing wardrobe beside the kitchen nook. "They say Trofts aren't very good at picking out human faces," she continued as she flipped through the clothes inside, "but even they can remember someone's clothes." She pulled out a long, brown coat and held it out to Lorne. "Here—put this on. Once you get away, you can slip it off and melt into the crowd."

"Thanks," Lorne said, frowning as he took the coat. "How do I get it back to you?"

"You don't, genius," she growled. "You kick it under a parked car and get the blazes out of there."

"Ah," Lorne said, eyeing her closely. "You sure you want to do this? If the Trofts catch you helping me, they're going to kick you right back into the spine leopard zone again."

"Let them," the woman said firmly. "No, I mean that. You Cobras are our best chance of getting them off our planet. Whatever we can do to help you, that's what we need to do. And whatever *you* need to do, you do that, too. Okay?"

"Okay," Lorne said, slipping on the coat. The bulk of his belt bag made the garment too tight around his waist to seal, and he had to settle for sealing it only from neck to stomach.

He looked back at the woman, feeling a fresh sense of determination. Whether or not those two men across the way were planning to betray him, there were still people in Capitalia worth fighting for. "Thanks," he said.

"Thank me by staying alive," she countered. "And by getting us out of this."

The crowd in the downstairs hallway had grown considerably in the time that Lorne and the woman had been away, the word of the mass escape apparently having spread to the entire building. The murmur of conversation stopped as Lorne appeared, the people melting away to either side as he headed toward the far end.

Treakness and Poole were waiting by the door when he arrived. "There are a couple of men inside the door over there," Treakness said, eyeing Lorne's new coat. "Looks like they're set to open it for us."

"Good," Lorne said. "Here's how it'll work. I'll lead us to about the middle of the street, then stop there and watch our flanks while you take everyone the rest of the way."

"What if a spine leopard attacks before we reach the middle?" Poole asked.

"Then he'll stop a little earlier," Treakness said acidly. "Sounds good." He turned to the crowd. "We're heading out," he called. "Here are the rules. You will not spread out—no more than three people abreast. You will walk—*walk*—as quickly as you can without stepping on the person in front of you. You will stay close together, and no matter what happens you will *not* run. Running leads to chaos and panic, and we will not put up with either."

"And keep as quiet as you can," Lorne added. "I need to be able to hear trouble coming."

"Right," Treakness said. "Everyone understand?"

There was a general murmur of agreement. Treakness turned back to Lorne and gave him a sharp nod. "Go."

Taking a deep breath, Lorne pulled the door open and once again headed into the sunlight.

He'd hoped to make it halfway across the street before stopping. He had in fact covered no more than half that distance when the spine leopard attacked.

It came from above, from the branches of one of the neatly trimmed trees lining both sides of the street. Unfortunately for it, Lorne had caught the quiet rustling of leaves as it prepared for its attack, and was already pivoting up onto his right foot as the animal leaped into sight. There was no time for a proper target lock, but he had his leg up in time to slash an antiarmor laser blast across the spiny's flank as it arrowed toward the line of people behind him.

The creature was already dead when it slammed limply into a man and woman a few meters behind Lorne, tumbling all of them onto the pavement.

"It's all right," Lorne barked over the bubbling of reflexive screams as the two would-be victims scrambled madly to get back up on their feet and away from the predator. "Don't worry—it's dead. Everyone keep calm and keep moving."

To his mild surprise, they obeyed. There were a few muffled sobs of released tension, but for the most part the long line of people continued quickly and silently on their way. A hint of movement on the other side of the column caught Lorne's eye, and he made a quick rolling leap over the crowd. But it turned out to be merely a large squintal loping across the street on its way from one tree to another. Lorne stayed on that side, alert for more trouble, until Nissa and the Koshevski brothers appeared, bringing up the end of the line. Lorne fell into step behind them, and a few seconds later they were all safely inside their target building.

The two men were still holding the door open. "Thanks for your help," Lorne said, nodding to them. As he did so, he activated his opticals' infrared, creating a patterned red haze across their faces. "Nice to know there are still people you can rely on."

"No problem," the younger man said. His infrared pattern changed subtly, indicating an increase in heat output that might have been merely the result of the extra blood flow to his facial muscles as he spoke.

But there was no such innocent explanation possible for the rush of heat into the older man's face. His heartbeat had suddenly increased, the irrefutable mark of either exertion or emotion. And given that he was just standing there, it clearly wasn't exertion.

The woman had been right, Lorne realized with a sinking feeling. The two men were indeed planning to betray him.

Unless, maybe, he preempted that treachery by offering them the most important part of the Trofts' bribe himself. "We're heading over to the safe zone," he continued, nodding toward the people crowded into the hallway. "You two want to tag along?"

"Yes," the older man said without hesitation. "Thank you."

The younger man gave him a startled look, and his lip twitched. "Yeah," he said, with considerably less enthusiasm. "Sure."

"Good," Lorne said. "You've got five minutes to get anything you want to take with you."

The hallway here was narrower and more tightly packed than the last one had been, but again the crowd managed to move aside enough to let Lorne pass. "That went well," he commented to Treakness as he arrived at the governor's side.

"If you liked that, you're going to love this," the governor said sourly, gesturing through the door toward the gathering area beyond it. "There are at least two spine leopards back there."

"Probably even more than that," Lorne agreed, keeping his voice calm as he peered out the door's window. There were several trees back there, a couple of stands of bushes, a reed-and-flower patch big enough for a couple of spinies to hide behind, plus several benches and a children's play apparatus. "I'm guessing a family's moved in there. I'll need a few minutes to clear them out."

"You need any help?" Poole asked.

"Like what?" Treakness growled. "You offering to be bait?"

Poole grimaced. "No."

"Just wait here," Lorne told them. "Keep everyone calm and ready to go."

Dealing with spine leopard families came with both plusses and minuses. The big minuses were that there could be up to ten of the predators in a comparatively small area, and that they would move against their prey with the kind of close coordination that a similarly sized group of individual spinies never achieved. The chief plus was that the pattern those coordinated attacks normally took was straightforward and well known.

In this case there were eight of them, stalking him from the trees, bushes, and benches. They attacked in the standard twos and threes, and as Lorne gradually but steadily wore down their numbers, the stalking time between attacks increased, requiring him to make a turn or two through the gathering area in order to persuade them to move out of their concealment.

The whole thing took nearly ten minutes. In the end, Lorne got them all.

He was standing in the middle of the gathering area, breathing heavily as he scanned the treetops with his infrareds just to be sure, when the glow of grav lifts drifted into sight from behind the line of buildings to the east.

He dropped into a crouch beside a bench, keying in his telescopics. The incoming aircraft was a civilian-style transport, the same type as the ones the Trofts were using to bring in their spine leopards. But this particular transport wasn't showing any of the brisk determination he'd seen in others that morning as they went about their tasks. On the contrary, it was just wandering lazily across the sky, as if it had nothing in particular to do.

Or as if it was looking for the source of noises that might have caught the attention of the Trofts two streets away. Like, perhaps, the screams of dying spine leopards.

Grimacing, keeping an eye on the hovering transport, Lorne hurried back to the apartment building.

"Interesting technique," Treakness commented as Lorne rejoined him inside. "Very different from the robot spine leopard and Troft battles they run trainees through at the Sun and MacDonald Centers."

"You should try seeing the full range of those tests sometime," Lorne said. "We need to get going. There's a transport wandering around that's clearly looking for something."

Treakness's lip twitched. "Did they spot you?"

"I don't think so," Lorne said. "If they had, there should be more than just one of them up there. I'm thinking someone in the safe zone either heard the dying spine leopards or caught a reflection of one of my laser shots."

"Understood," Treakness said. "I notice there's a good-sized gap between the buildings over there. Did you see whether it went all the way through to the street?"

"I never looked in that direction, but one way or another we'll get through," Lorne assured him. "It'll be risky, running straight out into the street that way. But it'll be faster than going through the building, and speed is what we need right now."

"Agreed," Treakness said. "Same marching plan as the last street?"

"With one difference," Lorne said. "As soon as you're all through, maybe a little before that, I'm going to head off and try to draw the Trofts' attention away from you."

"How?" Poole asked.

"Just as safely as I can," Lorne said. "Regardless, we're going to be split up. I suggest that once we're inside the safe zone we plan to meet up six blocks to the west, on the northeast corner."

"Six *blocks*?" Treakness demanded, his eyes widening.

"We need the rendezvous to be far enough away from the chaos I'm hoping to create," Lorne explained. "We'll touch that corner on the hour and the half hour until we link up again."

"But who's going to protect us while you're off making noise or whatever?" Treakness protested.

"You'll just have to make sure you stay out of trouble," Lorne said impatiently.

Treakness clamped his mouth shut. "Fine," he ground out. "Anything else?"

"Just pass the word on to Nissa for me," Lorne hesitated. "And if any of us hasn't made it to the rendezvous in two hours, the others need to go on without him or her."

"Understood," Treakness said grimly. "Well, if we're going to go, let's go."

"Right," Lorne said. "Good luck."

Pulling open the door, he headed across the gathering area at a dead run, quickly crossing it and ducking into the narrow passageway between the two buildings on the far side. At the other end of the walkway, he saw now, their exit was blocked by a short wrought-iron fence. He target-locked the tops and bottoms of four of the vertical bars as he ran, and at five paces away he fired eight quick bursts from his fingertip lasers. Three of the bars snapped and fell to the ground, the fourth managing to hang on until the impact of Lorne's shoulder broke it free.

On the far side of the fence a pair of two-meter-tall blueleaf bushes decorated the buildings' corners. Between them, Lorne could see the street, and beyond that the stonework façade of the Hendrezon's storefront. Bracing himself, he raced between the bushes and out into the street.

And squarely into the path of two spine leopards.

There was no time for subtlety. Lorne leaped aside out of the predators' paths, target-locking both as he hit the pavement and rolled over on his shoulder. As the animals landed and started to spin back toward him he fired a pair of laser shots that dropped them both.

He rolled back to his feet, doing a quick three-sixty as he did so. There were three more of the predators to the east, but they were over a block away, out of position to attack the refugees now streaming across the street. To the west, two more spine leopards appeared as they charged around the corner of the Hendrezon's building where they'd probably been hungrily eyeing the human prey passing so tantalizingly close on the far side of the Trofts' fence. A quick double target lock, two more antiarmor blasts, and both predators were dead.

"Broom!" Treakness shouted from the front of the line of refugees, now running openly as they crossed the street behind him. "The door!"

Lorne had forgotten that the door on this side would probably be locked against the spine leopard threat. Turning toward the door, he swung his leg around and blasted the lock. "Get them in and through," he shouted back to Treakness. He gave the street one final visual sweep, then raised his eyes to the sky above him.

The transport that had been wandering around up there wasn't wandering anymore. It was arrowing straight toward him, weaving between the buildings as it dropped toward the street like a hawk zeroing in on a large rodent.

Lorne had no way of knowing whether or not the Trofts had added extra armor plate to the spacecraft, though at this distance it was doubtful whether a Cobra antiarmor laser would be powerful enough to penetrate even an unarmored hull. But the transport was a civilian design, and Lorne had seen plenty of such vehicles over the years. Keying in his telescopics, he located and target-locked the transport's nose sensor array and poured a full second of laser fire into it. Without waiting to see the crew's reaction, he turned and made for the Hendrezon's storefront, sprinting past the line of running refugees. Five meters from the building, he bent his knees in midstride, and shoved off the pavement as hard as his servos could manage.

He hadn't done a wall jump like that since his first week in basic training. But the maneuver was part of his collection of programmed reflexes, and as he flew facefirst into the patterned stone, his computer took over, extending his arms to first absorb the impact and then curving his fingers into talons and locking them solidly into handholds on the uneven stone. Before he was even completely settled he pulled convulsively down with his arms, shoving himself farther up along the wall, his hooked fingers again scrabbling for and then finding grips. Three more repetitions, and he made it to the roof.

He headed across at a dead run, dodging the various vents and protrusions, counting on his reflexes to handle any problems with the uneven surface as he focused his main attention outward. The transport that he'd fired on was still in sight but was no longer trying to close the distance between them. Off to the north, two more sets of grav lifts had appeared, both sets heading his way at high speed.

And off to the west and northeast, the two warships that were within firing range of him loomed ominously over the buildings around them. Lorne felt his skin tingling as he ran, wondering if their heavy lasers and missile launchers were even now being swiveled to target him.

If they were, their commanders had apparently not yet been given permission to fire. Lorne reached the northern end of the roof and skidded to a halt, dropping down onto one knee and peering cautiously over the edge.

He'd speculated earlier that the safe zone between the Trofts' fences would be crowded with people trying to stock up on food and other necessities. But he'd had no idea that it would be *this* crowded. The street scene below looked like a parade route, except that the street itself was as packed as the walkways on either side. Parked in the center of each of the three intersections Lorne could see one of the armored vehicles he'd seen driving briskly down the street just before he and the others had taken to the underground drainage conduits. Each of the trucks had four or five Trofts perched on top, monitoring the activity of the crowds swirling along below them. Other Trofts stood sentry along various sections of the fence, the laser rifles held prominently across their chests guaranteeing that the mob would keep a respectful distance.

And every eye behind every one of those helmet visors was turned upward toward Lorne.

"Well, you wanted them all looking at you," he muttered under his breath. Throwing targeting locks on each of the five Trofts on the vehicle in the intersection to the west, he pushed back from the edge of the roof and headed in that direction at a quick zigzag run. A few laser bolts sizzled past him from the street, but he was far enough in from the edge that they did nothing but blow some chips from the stonework.

The big ships still waited silently. Either they were hoping the ground troops could capture this particular Cobra alive, or else they were simply waiting for an easier shot.

If it was the latter, Lorne reflected grimly, they were about to get their chance. The edge of the building and the wide street beyond were coming up fast. Eyeing the chasm, using his opticals' target-lock system to measure the distance, he made a final adjustment to his stride, and as he reached the end of the Hendrezon's building he jumped.

And an instant later he was soaring across the street in a flat arc, the absolutely best and easiest target any Troft gunner could ever hope for.

He had gambled that the Trofts wouldn't be ready for this stunt, and it was quickly clear that he'd been right. He was already past the midpoint of his jump before any of the Trofts below even recovered enough to start firing at him, and none of those shots came very close to their intended target. Either the invaders were unaware of the full range of Cobra abilities, or else they had badly underestimated the depths of Cobra audacity and recklessness.

For five of the Trofts, it was probably the last lesson they ever learned. Lorne was nearly to the other roof, the laser fire from below still running wide of its target, when he tucked his left leg behind him and sent five quick antiarmor bursts slashing across the Trofts he'd targeted half a minute ago from the rooftop's northern edge. There was a faint scream from somewhere, rage or pain or death.

Then he was safely across, his knees bending as his servos

absorbed the impact of his landing. He dropped into a partial crouch, then straightened both knees and body as he shoved off into a resumption of his zigzag run.

He'd gone five steps when the whole sky lit up in front of him.

Reflexively, he squeezed his eyes shut against the brilliant flash of blue, his arms flailing momentarily for balance as a blast of heat and a tornado wind slammed sideways across him, nearly knocking him off his feet. His nanocomputer took over, ducking him away from the heat and then twisting him back into his zigzag pattern. The warship's laser fired again, this shot coming close enough for Lorne to smell the acrid scent of ozone. He kept his eyes shut, using his opticals to find safe footing. He dodged around a protruding vent, turned again in time to avoid another shot. Ahead, the edge of the roof was rushing toward him, and he could see the five-meter gap of the service alley that separated him from the next building over. It was a much shorter distance, and therefore an even simpler jump, than the one he'd already performed in getting across Mitterly Street from the Hendrezon's building roof.

Only this time, he knew, that trick wouldn't work. The instant his feet left the rooftop he would once again be on a ballistic path which would allow no zigzagging or dodging or any of the maneuvering that was currently keeping him alive.

The Trofts hadn't been ready the last time he'd pulled that stunt. This time, they would be.

And it was becoming apparent that the Trofts had done the same calculation and come to the same conclusion. The massive ship-mounted laser ahead that had been firing uselessly at him had gone silent, its gunners waiting in anticipation of the moment when Lorne would have to either jump or else come to a sitting-duck halt at the edge of the roof. Whichever he chose, it would then take only a single clean shot to end it all.

Reaching the end of the roof, Lorne jumped.

But not up and over as he had the last time, with the goal of bridging the gap and landing on the next rooftop. Instead, he leaped *downward*, aiming for the side of the other building.

For the second time in two minutes, the Trofts were caught completely by surprise. Lorne's body was in the middle of its rotation when the ship-mounted laser slashed its fiery death over his head, squarely through the space where he would have been if he'd tried to jump the gap. A second shot slashed through the edge of the roof, vaporizing a groove through the tile and stone and steel and raining a shower of debris along the wall toward him.

But Lorne was no longer there. His nanocomputer had once again taken over, turning him just enough in midair so that he hit the far wall feetfirst. His knees took the impact, the friction of his feet against the wall fractionally slowing him down and starting to flip him over. Before he could simply bounce off the wall and fall straight down, his knees straightened again, sending him back toward the side of his original building in a heels-over-head flip that again brought him to a feetfirst impact on the other wall, a few meters lower than the point where he'd started. Again his knees bent and straightened, again slowing him down and sending him back across the alley. One more bounce-and-flip, and he reached the ground, his knees bending one final time as he hit the service alley pavement—

—Dead center into a group of three very startled spine leopards.

Fortunately, Lorne had no intention of staying long enough for them to recover from their surprise. His knees straightened convulsively as he launched himself into a rolling leap over the Trofts' fence into the safe zone beyond.

This time, he nearly bowled over a knot of spectators who had been in view of his building-hop and were still standing there, wide-eyed, as he landed in their midst. "Sorry," he apologized as he bumped hard into two of them before he could catch his balance, staggering them backwards into another group. He craned his neck over the crowds, trying to see whether or not Treakness and the other refugees had made it through the Hendrezon's building yet and were coming out onto the street.

"Hey!" someone shouted.

Lorne turned. But the man wasn't shouting to him. Instead, he was facing the Troft armored vehicle and soldiers half a block away, waving his hand urgently over the mass of people. "Hey! He's over here. Damn it, he's over—"

He was cut off in mid sentence as another man stepped forward and backhanded him hard across the face. "Shut up, you fool," the second man snarled as the first spun around with the impact and fell heavily onto the pavement. "You want them shooting at us?"

He jabbed a finger at Lorne. "You—get out of here," he bit out. "You hear me? *Go*. We've got enough trouble as it is."

But I can help you! Lorne wanted to say.

The words died in his throat...because the man was right. Lorne *couldn't* help them, at least not with the help they wanted. He couldn't get them food or shelter or safety. All he could do was run around and make trouble, and probably get someone killed.

He looked at the other people around him. On every one of those faces were expressions of fear or despair, anger or even hatred. Not a single person was looking at Lorne with respect, trust, or hope.

"I understand," he said quietly. "Good luck."

Without waiting for a reply, he ducked between two of them and threaded his way through the crowds that were doing their panicked best to hurry away from the burst of combat that had unexpectedly brought fire and death into their captivity.

Midway down the block, he slipped off the coat the woman had given him and tossed it against the side of the nearest building.

He let the crowd carry him another block, wondering what he should do. The arrangement with Treakness had been to rendezvous six blocks west of Hendrezon's, but now that Lorne was actually experiencing the barely controlled chaos he was wondering if the governor and the others were ever going to be able to make it that far on their own.

But going back to get them entailed its own set of risks. It had been several minutes since the exchange of laser fire, and the crowd was starting to settle down, but the general movement in Lorne's vicinity was still away from the site of the brief battle. Turning around would mean going upstream against the flow, posing additional risk to the civilians he would be pushing past, but also possibly attracting Troft attention. Worse, if any of the people who'd had a clear look at him were still in that area, he might even find himself being pointed out to the invaders.

The thought of being killed by aliens who had invaded his world was bad enough. The thought of being betrayed to those aliens by his own people was far worse.

He was still trying to figure out what to do when a hand abruptly grabbed his arm.

Reflexively, he twisted around, trying to break the grip. But instead of letting go, the hand tugged back, yanking him nearly off his feet and spinning him all the way around.

He found himself staring into the angry eyes of a medium-tall, heavyset man. "You stupid idiot," the man snarled, just barely loud enough for Lorne to hear. "What the *hell* do you think you're doing?"

"Who are you?" Lorne demanded. Or tried to demand, anyway. The words came out sounding more like a nervous plea than an order.

"Name's Emile," the man said. He glanced around, then gave Lorne's arm another tug, this one lifting him a couple of centimeters clear of the pavement, and started pulling him through the crowd toward the side of the street. "Come on. We need to talk."

CHAPTER NINE

With a start, Jody woke up from her nightmare—the third, by her slightly foggy count, of the long night.

For a minute or two she lay still, her brain trying to work through the horrifying images of the dream, her mouth working moisture into an unusually bad taste, her eyes gazing upward at the blackness of the tent roof above her, her ears sifting through the eerie and dangerous sounds of the Caelian night.

She had counted the muted growls of three different animals, the buzzing of probably five different types of insects, and the slow breathing of Geoff and Freylan beside her when she suddenly realized that there was one sound that she should have been hearing but wasn't.

Her father's breathing wasn't there.

She pushed off the cover of her sleep sack and sat up, being careful not to jostle the others. Her father, who had been sleeping beside her against the tent's door, was gone.

"Great," she muttered under her breath as she slid out of the sack and rolled up onto her knees. She stepped over her father's empty sleep sack to the tent's flap, opened it a few centimeters, and peered out.

The forest was nearly as dark as the inside of the tent, the brilliant starscape visible from the middle of Stronghold almost completely blocked off by the trees rising around them.

But there was enough light filtering in through the vegetation to show that the trip wire barrier her father had set up was still in place, as were the two stun sticks he'd hooked to them to give any intruder a good jolt. The small clearing in front of the tent also had enough light for her to see that her father wasn't out there, either.

She frowned. Had he heard the inconvenient midnight call, as her brother Lorne used to call it when they were children? But there were trees all over the place out there that he could use for that. Surely he wouldn't have chosen one that took him out of sight of the tent.

Steeling herself, she slipped outside into the narrow area between the tent and the trip wires, being very careful not to touch the latter. "Dad?" she called softly.

There was no answer. But as the sound of her voice faded away, it seemed to her that there was a noticeable dip in the volume of growls, chirps, and scurryings around her. The creatures of the Caelian night had been made freshly aware of her presence among them. Setting her teeth, trying to watch everywhere at once, she slowly bent down and disengaged one of the stun sticks from the barrier. Holding it well away from her body, she straightened up again—

"That's probably not a good idea," a calm voice said from behind her.

If she'd been fully awake, Jody reflected, she probably would have jumped straight over the trip-wire barrier in front of her from a standing start, and with half a meter's clearance. But with her brain and body still half numb with interrupted sleep, she didn't even twitch. Raising the stun stick higher, she turned toward the voice.

The man was perched on top of one of the sections of the log-and-sapling wall Jody's father had built around the tent yesterday when he'd been working off his frustration. She couldn't see much of the stranger's face in the dim light, but from his voice and overall silhouette she guessed he was young, probably in his mid-twenties.

And from the way he was sitting, with all of his weight on his rear and right leg and his left leg free to move in any direction, she guessed he was probably a Cobra. "Why not?" she asked, hefting the stun stick a little. "You don't think I know how to use it?"

"Pretty rollin' sure you don't," he said unapologetically. "You're Capitalia born and bred. Not much call for that kind of weapon back in civilization."

"What makes you think I'm from Capitalia?" Jody countered.

"One: your accent," he said, holding up fingers. "Two: the way you moved when you bent over to pick up the stun stick."

"Really," Jody said, impressed in spite of herself. "All that just from the way I picked up something?"

"Yeah," he said, and she caught a faint flicker of reflected starlight from his teeth as he grinned. "And number three: your father told us. Jody Broom, right?"

"Jody *Moreau* Broom," she corrected. "I imagine a good Cobra like you remembers that name."

"What makes you think I'm a Cobra?" he countered in turn. "Not everyone out here is, you know."

"One: because you're not looking around right now," she said. "That means you're relying on your hearing to let you know if anything's sneaking up on us, and only Cobra audios are up to that kind of work. Two: you sit like a Cobra, with your antiarmor laser available for a quick shot. And three: my father wouldn't have left us under the care of anyone else. Where is he, by the way?"

The man touched his fingertips to his forehead in a mock salute. "Touché, I think the term is," he said, sliding off the barrier and walking around to the front. "He's gone off to Stronghold to confer with Harli. Harli Uy, that is, the governor's son."

"He's gone *into* Stronghold?"

"No, just near it," the man corrected. "As far as I know, no one's gotten into or out of the town since the Trofts landed."

Jody looked around, taking in the darkness around her. Caelian's daytime horrors were bad enough, and the nighttime collection was even worse.

But she couldn't just sit here behind logs and stun sticks and Cobra guards while her father was out there in who knew what kind of danger. "I'd like to see him," she said. "Can I get someone to take me there?"

"Sure," the Cobra said. "You can get me. He said when he left that you'd probably wake up eventually and want to join the party. Name's Kemp, by the way."

"Nice to meet you, Kemp," Jody said, wondering uneasily just what kind of party he was talking about. Surely they weren't tackling the invading Trofts already, were they? "How far away is this party?"

"About a kilometer," Kemp said. "Nice evening stroll. Smitty? Can you watch things here?"

"No problem," a second voice called back from one of the trees at the edge of the small clearing. Jody peered in that direction, and was just able to make out the silhouette of another man sitting in the low branches. "You want me to call Tammling to give you a hand?"

"No, I can handle it," Kemp said. "Just keep an eye on the other two."

Jody looked at the tent. "Maybe we should bring them with us," she suggested.

"Might as well let them sleep," Kemp said. "Your father said they'd had a hard day, and there's not much of anything they can do, anyway. Really not much *we* can do, either, until the rest of the group shows up."

"So who *are* you?" Jody asked. "I mean, if you're not from Stronghold, where *are* you from?"

"We're the Aerie contingent," Kemp said. "We're assuming Essbend caught Governor Uy's interrupted warning and is also on the way here, but with the comm system down there's no way to know for sure. Harli was planning on giving them until tomorrow to show up."

"Wait a second," Jody said, feeling her eyes widen. Aerie was fifty kilometers away. "You walked all the way from *Aerie*?"

"Oh, no, we came on spookers," Kemp said. "Grav-lift cycles we use for fast travel through the forest."

"That would have been nice to have," Jody murmured, thinking about their long walk through the woods yesterday.

Kemp snorted. "You'd have run them into a tree inside the first minute," he said. "They're nothing for amateurs to fool around with." He gestured toward the stun stick still in Jody's hand. "Speaking of which, you should probably leave that here."

"That's okay," Jody said, putting the safety back on and clipping the weapon to her belt. "You said it's a party, and this is the closest thing I've got to a party outfit."

"Not a good idea," Kemp said firmly. "If you want a weapon, the group's probably got a spare shotgun or rifle."

"Never used one of those before," Jody said. "At least I've got a little experience with this."

"Yeah, I can guess," Kemp said dubiously. "Fine—whatever. Come on—Wonderland awaits."

"Wonderland?"

"Everything on Caelian outside the towns, which is pretty much most of it," Kemp explained. "You probably have a different name for it in Capitalia."

"People have lots of names for it," Jody admitted. "I like *Wonderland* better. So what's the plan? I lead, and you hang back a little on my right where you can protect us both?"

"Actually, I prefer hanging a little to your left," Kemp said. "Otherwise, yes, that's the marching order. You're a fast learner."

"Caelian's a good teacher," Jody said dryly. "We ready?"

Kemp gestured. "After you."

Kemp had been joking, Jody knew, about the trip to Stronghold being a nice evening stroll. For one thing, it was the dead of the night, not evening. For another, it had taken Jody's group most of the previous day to get through the first six kilometers of their journey, and that had been in broad daylight. Covering the final kilometer would probably take most—if not all—of the rest of the night. If, the morose thought occurred to her, they made it at all.

Only Kemp *hadn't* been joking.

It was, very literally, the difference between night and day. Jody's father had picked his way carefully along their trail, checking every stand of trees and patch of bushes for stinging insects, watching the plants themselves for thorns and adhesives and other surprises, and above all keeping a wary eye and ear out for predators of all shapes and sizes.

Kemp didn't do that. Any of it. He strode through the forest like he owned it, apparently in complete unconcern, his fingers nudging at the small of Jody's back in silent encouragement every time she tried to slow down the pace. Occasionally he would touch one of her shoulders or the other, pressing with his fingertips until she'd veered far enough to avoid some unseen obstacle, then easing off until the next course change.

And every few seconds the forest would vibrate with a deep boom from his sonic, or would light up with the flash of his fingertip lasers or arcthrower as he drove off, burned, or killed yet another attacking predator or startled a spine-equipped herbivore.

"You're good at this," she commented once as he deftly took out a saberclaw with two laser shots.

"Like you said, Caelian's a good teacher," he said. "Quiet, now—I have to listen."

They'd gone another hundred meters when Jody began to see a hint of blue flickers ahead of them. The flickers grew brighter, then became half-seen flashes through the foliage, and finally resolved into a group of perhaps a dozen men standing silently together beside a thick tree bole.

Jody peered uncertainly at them, trying to figure out if her father was somewhere in the group. But before she could come to any conclusions, one of the men near the middle stirred and turned around. "I thought that was probably you," Paul said heavily. "I wish sometimes you were more for sleeping in."

"Never can unless I'm in my own bed," Jody said, frowning as she stepped up to him. She could feel the sense of unwelcomeness around her, almost as thick as the darkness. "Is there a problem? I mean, aside from the obvious? Kemp said you'd invited me to this party."

"That was before I had a full grasp of the situation," Paul said. One of the other men half turned and fired his laser at something, and in the brief flash Jody saw that her father's face was as tense as his voice. "Maybe it would be best if Kemp took you back to the camp."

"Only if you *and* Kemp are looking for extra trouble," Jody warned, a creepy feeling settling in on the back of her neck. She'd never seen such a dark mood in her father before. "Tell me what's happened. Maybe there's something I can do to help."

"We appreciate the offer, Ms. Broom," the man her father had been talking to spoke up. "But this is war. No place for civilians."

"This is Harli Uy, Jody," Paul said, gesturing to the other man. "Currently in command of the Cobra forces on Caelian."

"Honored to meet you, Cobra Uy," Jody said, ducking her head politely. "May I respectfully point out that your father thought I could handle myself well enough to allow me to come to Caelian. Let me repeat: whatever's going on, I'd like to help."

"And what exactly is this help you're offering?" Harli asked.

"I don't know yet," Jody said evenly. "Tell me what you need, and I'll tell you what I can do." She hesitated, but this was no time for modesty. "For whatever it's worth, my family has a long history of being underestimated."

Harli snorted. "That's the Moreau side of the family talking, no doubt."

"Actually, she gets it from both sides," Paul said. "But she's right about one thing: you never know what someone can bring to the table until you ask. Besides, it's not like we have anything in particular to lose by postponing the test a few minutes. Why not give her the basics of the situation?"

Harli snorted again. "Fine," he growled, beckoning to one of the other men. "Matigo? Make it the quick version."

Reluctantly, Jody thought, the man he'd called stepped forward and dropped into a crouch. "Down here," he said brusquely, gesturing Jody to join him. "Can you see?"

"Just a second," Jody said, getting down beside him and pulling out her flashlight. She turned it to its faintest setting and switched it on. "Ready. What am I looking at?"

"Nothing, yet," Matigo growled as he brushed away the leaves and other ground cover with his hand, leaving a more or less clear patch of dirt in the center of Jody's faint glow. "Here's Stronghold," he said, drawing a quick circle with his finger. "Clear zone around here; landing field here." He added another narrow ring around the first circle, then a rectangle on the south side. "The two Troft ships are here"—he drew a short line in the dirt on the rectangle, paralleling the edge of the circle—"and here"—he added a second line on the opposite side of the circle, again lengthwise. "They're good-sized, probably thirty meters tall and sixty or seventy long, though only thirteen or fourteen meters wide."

"Makes for a narrow frontal target," someone murmured.

"If they were fighting in space, which they're not," Matigo retorted. "Weapons seem to be concentrated in pivoting clusters on two pairs of small wings near the top of each ship, fore and aft and starboard and port. Looks like heavy lasers and missiles both, though we haven't seen them in action yet." He paused. "At least, *we* haven't."

Jody swallowed as she caught his meaning. "But the people inside Stronghold have?"

"We think so," Paul said grimly. "Matigo spotted a lot of burns and fresh fire-grooves in the buildings and grounds inside the wall. There's also a fair amount of new scoring on the top of the wall itself."

"I didn't think Trofts went in for mass killing," Jody said.

"Maybe we were wrong about that," Matigo said.

"Or possibly the Cobras in the city mounted some sort of counterattack shortly after the Trofts landed," Paul said. "If so, it doesn't look like they got very far before they were pushed back."

"And at this point we have no way of learning any of those details, either," Harli added. "With the comm system down and our handful of short-range radio frequencies being blocked, we can't communicate with anyone inside the wall."

Jody nodded. No wonder her father had sounded so grim. "So what's this test you mentioned?"

"We need a look at their weapons' capabilities," Paul explained. "The lasers in particular. We need to see their general power output, recovery cycle time, targeting arrangements, and anything else we can dig out."

"How are you going to get all that?" Jody asked.

"How do you think?" Matigo growled. "We're going to shoot at them and try to get them to shoot back."

Jody felt her stomach tighten. "You're not serious."

"Yes, we're serious; and no, of course it's not what you're thinking," Harli said. "You think Caelian's got Cobras to waste on suicide work?"

"They're going to send some men into a few of the trees," Paul explained. "They'll fire antiarmor shots at the weapons clusters from behind the boles."

"What about return fire?" Jody asked.

"We're talking steelwood trees here," Harli said. "Big, thick, heavy ones, too. There are ways of taking them down, but laser fire isn't one of them."

Jody grimaced. Unless, of course, the Trofts' weapons were accurate enough to fire straight back at the attacking lasers, in which case, some of the Cobras were about to become instant amputees. But that probably wasn't something she should bring up. Especially since they'd all probably already thought of it on their own. "You think it's a good idea to let the Trofts know there are Cobras out here?" she asked instead.

"What, you think maybe they haven't noticed?" Matigo asked sarcastically. His head snapped around, and he fired a double fingertip laser burst at something in one of the nearby tree branches. "Unless they're blind, they know we're here."

"Yes, but—" Jody stopped at her father's touch on her arm.

"All right, then," Harli said briskly. "Cobras, to your stations."

The group broke up, all the men except her father heading off in Stronghold's general direction. Jody watched them go, her hands clenched painfully. "It'll be all right," Paul told her quietly. "I've seen them. *You've* seen them. They know what they're doing."

"Against the Caelian forest, sure," Jody said. "But against Trofts?"

Paul exhaled quietly. "Come on," he said, taking her arm. "I need to help with the observation."

The spot Harli had chosen for the test was at the northwest edge of Stronghold's fifty-meter-wide clear zone, about three hundred meters from the northernmost of the two enemy positions. By the time Jody and her father reached the stand of trees that Harli and four of the others had settled behind, Jody could hear the sound of rustling leaves as the Cobras who would be taking the brunt of the risk worked their respective ways up into their chosen firing positions.

And as Jody peeked out between the trees she got her first clear look at the Troft warship.

It was every bit as big and imposing as Kemp's description had suggested, looming silent and dark over the town, its hull gleaming faintly in the starlight, its stubby wings with their collections of weapons pods reminding her of fists stretched out over the townspeople in a twisted parody of a blessing.

It was probably an image that the Trofts hoped would inspire fear and despair. But to Jody's surprise, the predominant emotion stirring inside her was anger. Anger that these aliens would invade her worlds. Anger that they would frighten and kill her people.

And whether Harli or Matigo or any of the Cobras believed it or not, she was damn well going to help them throw the invaders out. Somehow.

"Everyone set?" Harli asked quietly.

There was no answer. But Harli nodded twice, and Jody realized that all the Cobras were simply responding in voices too soft for her to hear, with their audio enhancers turned up to hear them. "Acknowledged," Harli said. "On one. Three, two, *one*."

And abruptly the landscape blazed with a barrage of painfully bright laser fire as a half dozen Cobras opened fire on the Troft ship, the bursts focused on the wings.

Jody winced back, squinting at the sudden assault on night-accustomed eyes. The attack seemed to go on forever, though it was probably only a few seconds.

The Cobras were still firing when the Trofts finally replied.

The answering fire came in a single, massive salvo that flashed across the open air as abruptly as the Cobras' own fire had begun, and suddenly the forest was filled with the stuttering crackle of blasted tree trunks and the secondary sizzle as hundreds of splinters and wood fragments rained down through the leaves around them. Both barrages ended, and for a pair of heartbeats the forest was dark and silent once again.

And then, without warning, a single flash lit up the night sky.

Only this one wasn't from the Cobras or the nearby Troft ship. This one came from the other Troft ship, the one a kilometer away to the south.

And it wasn't splinters and burned wood that hit the ground this time. This time, it was a human body.

His name, Jody learned, had been Buckley.

No one said much as two of the Cobras moved the badly burned body deeper into the forest, away from the Troft ship, and wrapped it in one of the silliweave shelters. Matigo muttered something over and over under his breath as they worked, but whether it was a prayer or a curse Jody couldn't tell. Nor did she feel any inclination to ask.

Harli didn't say any more than any of the others. But the glimpses of his face that Jody caught in the reflected light of the group's sporadic but never-ending antipredator fire sent shivers up her back.

Finally, with the body as protected from scavengers as they could make it, Harli called the group together. "All right," he said, his voice glacially calm. "Either the old legends were wrong about the Trofts not engaging in unnecessary killing, or else this bunch doesn't play by those rules. So be it. They've made their point, that with the geometry of their ship placement a simple frontal assault won't work. Our next attack will just have to be clever."

Beside Jody, Paul cleared his throat. "You assume the killing wasn't necessary," he said. "What if the Trofts thought it was?"

"You trying to excuse them?" Matigo demanded.

"I'm trying to understand them," Paul corrected. "That's what this test was supposed to gain us, right? Information?"

"If you think—" Matigo began.

Harli stopped him with a gesture. "Explain," he said.

"Suppose our barrage did more damage than we thought," Paul said. "Something that really worried them. In that case, they would have to do something to discourage us from trying it again. The northern ship couldn't get to the attackers through the tree boles, so they had to use the southern ship's weapons, which had clear shots of everyone. In fact, in that scenario, killing only one of us could actually be considered restrained."

Someone swore. "Restrained. Right."

"He's right, Broom," Kemp seconded. "We'd already finished firing."

"But the Trofts didn't know that," Paul pointed out. "As far as they knew, we might just be taking a breather before launching another attack."

"It's an interesting theory," Harli said. "So what exactly is this damage we supposedly did to their ship?"

"I don't know," Paul admitted. "I didn't see anything that should have worried them very much. But just because I didn't see anything doesn't mean it wasn't there."

"Spotters?" Harli invited, looking around the circle. "Anyone?"

"We were burning something off the wing," one of the others spoke up. "I could see bits of smoke where the shots were hitting. But it didn't look like the hullmetal was even getting scratched."

"Yeah, I didn't see anything, either," another man spoke up. "Though I suppose it's possible we warped the missile tubes a little."

"They still looked pretty straight to me," a third man said doubtfully. "And I was specifically watching for that."

"Anyone else?" Harli asked.

No one spoke up. "So," Harli said. "The smoke was probably just us burning off some kind of anti-radar coating. Hardly important unless they're expecting a space battle sometime in the near future."

"Sure as hell not worth killing for," Matigo growled. "So what's next? We got a plan?"

"Maybe," Harli said slowly, scratching his chin. "They may have already made a big mistake. Anyone else notice how close that ship is parked to the edge of the clear zone?"

There was a chorus of affirmative murmurs. "That could be our ticket in," Harli continued. "Wonderland's already starting to reclaim the land, and you might also have noticed there are a couple of access doors on the corners of the bow. If we can hang on out here and give the vegetation a few days to grow, we may be able to sneak up on them."

"That assumes they can't fire that close to their ship," Paul pointed out.

"Rotating weapons systems are always restrained so that they can't accidentally fire on their own ship or vehicle," someone said.

"I agree that you'd want to avoid misfires," Paul said. "But a blanket statement like that makes me nervous. Especially when none of us has had a great deal of experience with such things."

"When you get the Trofts to hand over the technical specs of their ships, let me know," Harli said. "Until then, we'll just have to give it a shot and see what happens."

"Maybe not," Jody spoke up.

"Look, kid—" Matigo growled.

"What do you mean?" Paul asked.

"Let's see what they can do," Jody said, her mind racing as she tried to work through the details of the plan that had only now come to her. "We send something poking around one of those doors and see what they do about it."

"And how do we do that?" Harli asked. "You have some special rapport with Caelian's animals?"

"Not really," Jody said. "But I do have some rapport with their dining preferences."

In the faint starlight, she saw Harli's eyes narrow. "Continue," he said.

"First of all, we'll need some bait," Jody said, sifting rapidly through the mental encyclopedia of Caelian's flora and fauna that she'd crammed into her brain on the trip over from Aventine. "A fleeceback, maybe—they're easy to catch and will go practically anywhere for midlia fruit."

"Midlia fruit?" Matigo echoed, sounding puzzled.

"She means tardrops," Harli told him.

"Right—that's what I meant," Jody said, feeling her face warming. "We collect some tardrops, crack them open and throw them against the hull near one of the doors—I'm assuming you can throw things that far—then turn our captured fleeceback loose."

Harli threw a frown at Matigo. "Are you expecting the Trofts to panic when they see a fleeceback charging their ship?" he asked.

"Not at all," Jody said. "As I said before, the fleeceback is just the bait. Once it's busy licking tardrop husk off the door, we send a gigger in after it."

"And you're expecting the Trofts to panic when they see a *gigger* charging at their ship?" Harli said again, his patience starting to show signs of coming apart.

"Not the gigger itself, no," Jody said. "But when they see what we've attached to the gigger's mouth tusks, maybe." Reaching to her belt, she unhooked the stun stick. "This."

Harli stared at the weapon, his forehead furrowed in thought. Then, slowly, his forehead cleared, and to Jody's astonishment he actually smiled. It was a thin smile, cold and not particularly friendly. But it was a smile. "Nice," he said. "We rig the stun stick to go off when the gigger hits the hull with it."

"Making for a nice high-voltage light show," Matigo added. Unlike Harli, he wasn't smiling. But at least his tone wasn't as hostile as it usually was. "And there's no place on a fleeceback to tie the thing, which is why you're talking a three-stage operation. Cute."

"Might even work," Harli said. He gestured to Matigo. "Take a couple of men and go hunt us down a fleeceback. I saw a couple of tardrop bushes back a ways—pick up some of the fruit while you're at it. Tracker, you're in charge of finding us a gigger."

"That won't be necessary," Jody said. "We have a caged one back at our camp."

"You have a caged *gigger*?" Harli asked, sounding stunned.

"She's right," Kemp confirmed. "I saw it."

Harli held up his hands. "I'm not even going to ask. Fine. Kemp, take Tracker and go get it. The rest of us will head around the rim and look for a good staging area."

He gestured. "We're burning darkness, gentlemen. Let's get to it."

CHAPTER TEN

The plumbing supply store Emile half led, half dragged Lorne into wasn't as crowded as the street, but there were still plenty of people milling around inside, busily cleaning the place out of supplies. Some of Capitalia's residents, apparently, were taking the long view of the Troft occupation. Still holding onto Lorne's arm, Emile maneuvered them through the shoppers and into an unoccupied office in the back.

"All right," the bulky man said when he'd closed the door behind them. "You obviously didn't get the memo, so let me lay it out for you. We are not, repeat, *not* to attack, antagonize, or otherwise disturb the Trofts. Got that?"

Lorne stared at him. "You're joking."

"Do I *look* like I'm joking?" Emile countered, pointing both index fingers at his scowling face. "That's straight from Governor-General Chintawa and the Directorate. Everyone in government service is to stand down and wait for further instructions."

"Including the Cobras?"

"*Especially* the Cobras," Emile growled. "Whatever the hell you thought you were doing up there, I hope you had fun, because that was your last hurrah."

"Until when?" Lorne asked.

"Like I said, until further instructions," Emile said.

Lorne stared at him, a hazy numbness settling across his mind. So they were giving up? The whole planet was just giving up?

Or was this some sort of Troft trick? "You have any proof of this order?" he asked.

Emile snorted. "What, you want an official government document with time-stamp fibers?"

"That would be nice," Lorne said. "Let's start with where you got your information. Better yet, let's start with some proof of who you are."

Scowling, Emile lifted his left hand and fired a low-power laser blast from his little finger into the floor. "Emile Chun-Wei, Dome Security, Cobra contingent," he said formally. "And you're Lorne Broom, current assignment DeVegas Province." He gave Lorne a tight smile. "Don't look so surprised. *No one* gets into the Dome without being properly logged in. Not even an off-the-record visitor to the governor-general." The smile turned sour. "Not even when he's the son of the infamous Jin Moreau."

"Her name is *Jasmine* Moreau Broom," Lorne said stiffly. "Only family and friends get to call her Jin."

"Whatever," Emile growled. "The point is that while you were stomping around the sewers this morning, the rest of us Cobras were setting up talking posts all across the city." He smiled again, or maybe it was more of a smirk. "And yes, we know all about you and Governor Treakness making for Crystal Lake."

Lorne grimaced. "The white-haired man back in Wei Kei's," he said, nodding. "Yes, I assumed at the time he wasn't close enough to overhear us. But of course, I also assumed a Cobra would have come over and offered to help."

"Those assumptions will get you every time," Emile said. "Interesting thing about it is that Chintawa hasn't said anything about Treakness being on any special missions."

Lorne felt his throat tighten. Treakness had told him Chintawa had authorized this mission. But he'd never heard it from Chintawa himself. Was it possible Treakness had made the whole thing up? "Maybe Chintawa was worried that word of the mission would leak out," he said, keeping his voice casual. "You mentioned talking posts. What are they?"

Emile rolled his eyes. "They're a set of top-floor windows where we sit with lights and tap out Dida code to each other," he said with exaggerated patience. "Surely your brother or father told you about Dida code."

"They may have mentioned it," Lorne conceded, feeling like

an idiot. Of course he'd heard of Dida code. It was a semi-secret system of dots and dashes that Cobras on Aventinian big-city duty were taught at the beginning of their tenure, a fallback method for maintaining short- and medium-distance communication if the comm system ever failed.

Lorne's father presumably knew Dida, as did Lorne's brother Merrick, who'd been assigned to Capitalia two years ago. In fact, now that Lorne thought about it, he realized that Dida was probably what Merrick had been talking about way back then when he grumbled about the complexities of city duty. Lorne himself, with his own life and career still wrapped up in the expansion regions, had actually forgotten the system even existed. "Well, then, there's your answer," he told Emile. "Chintawa was afraid the Trofts would tap into your light show, so he didn't say anything."

"The Trofts don't know Dida code," Emile scoffed. But his tone nevertheless sounded a little less truculent.

"Doesn't mean they can't record what you send and decipher the messages later," Lorne pointed out.

"I suppose," Emile said. "Kinda moot now, though. Where's Treakness?"

"Why?" Lorne asked cautiously.

"Why do you think?" Emile growled. "So we can take him back to the Dome and get the Trofts off our backs about our missing governor."

Lorne stared at him. "You mean you're just going to hand him over to them?"

"Of course," Emile said. "Face it, Broom, there's nothing he can do flailing around out here on his own. The Trofts want him, and they're going to keep giving the whole city grief until they get him."

"Since when do we cave in to grief?" Lorne demanded. "What happened to the oaths we took as Cobras?"

"You mean our oath to defend the people of Aventine?" Emile countered. "The people who are going to be dumped on just because some cowardly politician feels like running instead of sticking around to face the music like everyone else? *Those* people?"

"Treakness isn't running," Lorne insisted. "He's on a mission."

"Again, who says?" Emile asked.

"Chintawa sent one of his aides to get me before the Trofts landed," Lorne said stubbornly. "Why would he do that if Treakness just made up this whole thing?"

"How should *I* know?" Emile asked impatiently. "He could have had a hundred reasons for wanting you in the Dome when the balloon went up. You seriously think Treakness isn't smart enough to spot an opportunity when it falls into his lap and grab it with both hands? Come on, kid, use your head. He's using you, pure and simple. Now, where is he?"

Lorne took a deep breath. "You're right, I don't know for sure what's going on," he said. "But I don't believe that Governor Treakness is lying to me. I also promised I'd do everything in my power to get him out of the city where he needs to go."

Emile shook his head. "You still don't get it, do you? You can't *get* him out. That's the point." He waved his hand. "You see this safe zone? It's an island. A completely enclosed chunk of civilization in the middle of a spiny-infested city. The rest of the safe zones are exactly the same: a few fenced-in streets centered around one or two of their sentry ships, completely isolated from all the others. Even if you had a car, you couldn't drive from one to another."

"What about the cars outside the safe zones?" Lorne suggested. "I could get Treakness out there and grab one of those."

"And you don't think the Trofts will notice you driving around?" Emile scoffed. "You think that just because they've seeded the area with a few spinies that they're ignoring those areas? Hardly. They have armored troop carriers driving around the spiny zones, *plus* a line of fresh transports coming in from orbit all the time that have orders to survey the territory on their way down, *plus* a bunch of observation drones flying around the city and countryside watching for unauthorized movement."

"Then I guess we'll just have to walk," Lorne said through clenched teeth.

"Oh, right—that'll work," Emile said sarcastically. "Just be sure the spinies leave enough of Treakness for the Trofts to identify afterward. Come on, we're wasting time."

"You're right, we are," Lorne agreed, bracing himself. "I'm leaving. You can help me or stay out of my way."

Emile barked a short laugh. "You really think—?"

And dropped to the floor like a heavy sack as the high-voltage current from Lorne's stunner arced through him.

For a long moment Lorne gazed down at the unconscious Cobra, his heart thudding painfully in his chest. If Emile was right—if Treakness had lied to Lorne about his mission and his instructions coming from Governor-General Chintawa...

But it was too late to worry about that now. Way too late. Taking a couple of deep breaths, he slipped out of the room.

He'd told Treakness he would rendezvous with the group six blocks west of the Hendrezon's building. Given the faster time Lorne had been making as he ran along the rooftops, he expected to be the first one to arrive. To his mild surprise, he reached the corner to find Poole and the elder Koshevski already waiting, the latter looking darkly around, the former with his arms crossed over his chest, his fingers tapping nervously against his rib cage.

"There you are," Poole said, sagging with relief as Lorne slipped through the crowd and came up to them. "I was afraid you'd been—I mean, after you left us, and then we got here—"

"Yeah, all of two minutes ago," Koshevski interrupted, eyeing Lorne. "Got to say, though, that was a damn good show."

"Glad you liked it," Lorne said, looking around. "Where are the others?"

"They stopped at one of the health stores down the block," Poole said, jerking his head back in the direction they'd come from. "Nissa thought some—" he lowered his voice conspiratorially "—some disguise materials were probably called for."

"Good idea," Lorne agreed, turning to Koshevski. "What's happening with your brother and his family?"

"They've got some friends down the street," Koshevski said. "They should be able to stay with them, at least for a while."

"What about you?" Lorne asked.

Koshevski shrugged. "I'll probably stick around. There's nothing back at my place I can't get here. Been wanting to spend more time with my nieces and nephew anyway." His lip twitched. "But first we've got to get you to Ridgeline."

Lorne frowned. After the man in the crowd who'd tried to sell him to the Trofts, and Emile's flat-out refusal to lift a finger to help them, he'd sort of expected Koshevski to bail on them, too. "You're still up for that?"

"A deal's a deal," Koshevski said with another shrug. "There's an access point behind an arbor bench a block over that we should be able to use without being spotted. Soon as the others get here, we'll head over and you can take a look."

"Sounds good." Lorne nodded toward an exotic foods shop

across the street. "Let's go look around in there while we wait. We're a bit conspicuous just standing around."

Most of the more popular foodstuffs had already been cleared off the shelves, with only a few of the more acquired-taste items remaining. Lorne kept an eye on the rendezvous corner as they browsed, and when he spotted Nissa and Treakness approaching he bought a package of cured Esquiline trihorn meat and ushered the others back outside.

The two groups reached the corner at the same time. "I see you're still alive," Treakness greeted Lorne shortly. "Good."

"Thanks for your concern," Lorne said stiffly. "You're looking interesting yourself."

Treakness snorted. "I look like a fool," he said bluntly, patting gingerly at the streaks of color Nissa had run through his hair. "Hair coloring, cheekbone highlighting, and whatever this stuff is she's got all over my face."

"It's tan-effect," Nissa said. "It darkens your skin."

"And it itches like crazy," Treakness growled. "We have a plan?"

"Access point's half block that way," Koshevski said, nodding in that direction. "We're ready when you are."

"Excellent," Treakness said. Apparently, the thought that Koshevski might quit now that he'd gotten what he wanted had never occurred to him. "Lead on."

The access point was as Koshevski had described, tucked away behind the bench and spread of miniature trees that formed the small pedestrian arbor area, and just inside the Trofts' fence. "This should do nicely," Treakness said, looking around as the group gathered together around the cover. "Whenever you're ready, Broom."

"In a second," Lorne said, keying in his enhancers and giving the sky above them a quick but careful scan. "I'm told the Trofts have observation drones flying over the city."

"Where'd you hear that?" Koshevski asked.

"From someone who should know," Lorne said. If the Trofts had any drones up there at the moment, though, they were too high for him to spot. "Get ready," he said, getting a grip on the access cover. "Koshevski, you're first."

A minute later, with their sequential disappearance having apparently gone unnoticed by the milling crowds, Lorne carefully settled the cover back into place above his head and made the dark descent into the drainage system. "Everyone okay?" he asked quietly when he reached the bottom.

"Everyone except my back," Treakness said sourly. "It's already aching in anticipation. You people don't really *walk* these conduits all the time, do you?"

"No, we have rolling platforms and kneepads," Koshevski said. "But that stuff is all kept in the substations, and there aren't any anywhere along our way."

"Of course there aren't," Treakness growled. "Fine. Let's get on with it."

"I need a quick word with Governor Treakness first," Lorne said. "The rest of you go on ahead. We'll catch up."

"Okay, but don't get too far behind," Koshevski warned. "There are a couple of tricky spots a few blocks ahead."

"We won't be that long," Lorne said. "Get going."

He and Treakness stood together in silence until the sound of the others' footsteps had faded away into the faint murmur of the crowds going by overhead. "So?" Treakness asked.

"The man who told me about the Trofts' observation drones was another Cobra," Lorne told him. "He also said—"

"You met another Cobra up there?" Treakness interrupted. "Why in hell's name didn't you invite him to join us? We can use all the help we can get."

"I *did* invite him," Lorne said. "He said Governor-General Chintawa never said a thing about this special mission of yours. To anyone."

For a long moment Treakness didn't answer. Lorne keyed in his light-amps, to find that the governor's expression was as unreadable as his silence. "In other words, he thinks I lied to you," Treakness said at last. "What do *you* think?"

"I'd like to think I can trust you," Lorne said. "But to be honest, I'm not sure I can. I've been thinking about this thing, and parts of it just don't add up."

"Such as?"

"For starters, if this mission is really so vital, why am I the only Cobra on the job?" Lorne asked. "There were other Cobras in your neighborhood—we saw them get slaughtered by the Trofts right after I arrived. And as you said, we could certainly use more help. So why weren't they brought in?"

"Probably because by the time Chintawa was ready to start

calling them the Trofts had the comm system shut down," Treakness said.

"He got through to me just fine," Lorne pointed out.

"Because you were the first one on his list," Treakness said. "Or rather, Ms. Gendreves was, with instructions to go get you. By the time he finished talking to the Tlossies at Creeksedge and a few other people, the Trofts had crashed the system."

"Which was apparently replaced fairly quickly by a Dida-code flash setup," Lorne said. "So even if he couldn't get more Cobras to us at the beginning, he could have sent some after us."

"Yes, he could," Treakness agreed. "And no, I don't know why he didn't. All I can suggest is that he was afraid letting more people into the secret than he had to would increase the risk of word leaking out to the Trofts."

Which was essentially the same excuse that Lorne himself had offered to Emile. It didn't sound nearly as convincing coming out of Treakness's mouth. "That's one theory," he said. "You also told me Chintawa insisted I accompany you, which is supposedly why you waited until I showed up before heading to Creeksedge. But if the Tlossies are really on our side, why didn't you ask them to send a shuttle to pick up both of us? If the invaders aren't bothering their freighter, they probably wouldn't have shot down one of their shuttles, either."

"An interesting question," Treakness said. "Let me ask you one in return. Would you be performing this same cross-examination if, say, you'd been asked to escort Governor Ellen Hoffman to Creeksedge instead of me?"

"Under the same circumstances?" Lorne asked. "Of course."

"Really?" Treakness asked. "Because I'm sure you're as familiar with Governor Hoffman's pro-Cobra stance as well as you are with my own somewhat less enthusiastic position."

"That has nothing to do with the case," Lorne said.

"I think it does," Treakness said. "In your mind, my position on the Cobras automatically colors every other perception you have of me, including your opinion of my integrity and my honesty. So I ask again: would you automatically assume Hoffman would lie to save her own skin, the way you're thinking I would?"

"I'm not accusing you of lying," Lorne insisted. But down deep, he realized he couldn't dismiss Treakness's accusations nearly that easily.

Because the governor was right. If it were Ellen Hoffman standing here, he would indeed have been more inclined to accept her story about a secret mission. He certainly would have been more willing to risk his life for her.

And then, Lorne felt his breath catch in his throat as a horrible suspicion flooded in on him. "Poole," he murmured.

"What?" Treakness asked, frowning.

"Poole," Lorne said, activating his infrared and gazing intently at the heat pattern of Treakness's face. If the governor lied now, he should be able to spot it. "It suddenly occurred to me why he's here."

Treakness's heat pattern darkened, subtly but noticeably. "What are you talking about?" he demanded.

"I'm talking about you and traveler's insurance," Lorne said. "That's the real reason he's with us, isn't it?"

Treakness's pattern darkened even more. "I have no idea what you're talking about," he said stiffly.

"I think you do," Lorne said, the sheer arrogance of the man turning his stomach. "You know how most Cobras feel about you and your policies. You know that any of us would accept an order to protect you, but that not many of us would put much enthusiasm into the job."

He waved down the conduit. "So you invited Poole along, a nice convenient innocent bystander, to guarantee I'd put some real effort into getting you out." He felt his eyes narrow as another thought occurred to him. "Is that why Nissa's along, too? Did Chintawa send her to get me instead of asking the Tlossies to pick us up so that I'd have one more innocent bystander to play guardian to?"

"The Tlossies wouldn't leave the spaceport," Treakness said, some of the fresh heat fading from his face. "As to the rest, you can believe whatever you want as long as you obey your orders."

Lorne snorted. "So that's the bottom line?"

"Obeying orders?" Treakness asked. "Yes. And if you're worth the Cobra name, you'll do the same."

With a supreme effort, Lorne choked back his anger and contempt. "As you wish, Governor," he said, pitching his voice parade-ground formal. "Don't worry, I'll get you to the spaceport."

Lorne moved a step closer to the other. "But understand that this isn't over," he added softly. "Once this is all over, however long it takes, I *will* petition the Directorate for a full investigation of everything that's happened here today."

"That's your right as a citizen of Aventine," Treakness said, his own voice going as neutral as Lorne's. "Was there anything else?"

The man was cool, all right. Way too cool for Lorne's taste. "No, I think we're done," he said. "For now."

"Then I suggest we catch up with the others," Treakness said, gesturing toward the conduit. "It would be rather embarrassing to admit at the trial that you lost half our party while you were busy browbeating me with worthless questions."

"I suppose it would," Lorne agreed, gesturing in turn. "After you."

If any of the party had hoped this leg of their underground journey would be easier than the previous one, they were quickly disillusioned. The conduits on the west side of Capitalia were every bit as cramped, slimy, and uncomfortable as the ones closer to the central city. That meant there were just as many slips as before, and the same number of stops along the way to relieve the strain on backs and knees.

Still, Lorne noticed there was less groaning and fewer under-the-breath complaints than there had been earlier. Possibly the brief aboveground break had given everyone's joints and muscles sufficient recovery time to ease the discomfort.

Or maybe it was the thought of armed Trofts and hungry spine leopards roaming the landscape above that had given them all a new perspective on the advantages of this mode of travel.

But the trip was still long and slow, and within the first hour they began to encounter additional complications as they reached a more modern section of the drainage system where many of the larger conduits had given way to smaller ones. Koshevski never got lost in the maze, but as the percentage of passable conduits steadily decreased, he was forced to lead them through extra turns and sometimes long detours in order to keep them moving westward.

It was three hours past sundown by Lorne's nanocomputer clock when Koshevski finally came to a halt in a T-junction chamber. "End of the line," he murmured, gesturing to his right and left. "The only passable routes that are left lead northeast and straight south, neither of which will get you any closer to Crystal Lake or any facility or resource that might help you get there."

"So where exactly are we?" Treakness asked. "What's around us right now?"

"Okay, this is Duell Street," Koshevski said, pointing straight up. "It's a residential area two blocks west of Ridgeline. About three blocks north is Estes Park, five or six blocks south and a couple east is the Indus Entertainment Center, and about seven blocks west you hit the edge of the Vandalio Industrial Park."

"What do they make there?" Poole asked.

"Vandalio is mostly light industry," Treakness told him. "Electronics and small consumer appliances."

"Right," Koshevski said. "If you need a drill or laser torch, that would be a good place to look."

"What about the spaceport?" Treakness asked. "Where's that, exactly?"

"It's ten, maybe eleven kilometers west and a little north of the industrial park," Koshevski said, pointing at the blank wall beside him where another westward conduit should have been. "You don't want to go there, though."

"Why not?" Nissa asked.

"Because the first thing a smart invasion force does is secure the local transportation centers," Koshevski said. "Here, that means Creeksedge."

"Understood," Treakness agreed, nodding. "We'll be sure to give the place a wide berth."

"Yeah, good luck with that," Koshevski said. "Good luck with the rest of it, too. I'm sorry I can't do more, but this really is as far as I can get you."

"No apologies needed," Treakness assured him, offering his hand. "We're most grateful for your help. Thank you."

"You're welcome," Koshevski said. He shook Treakness's hand briefly, then did the same with the others. "You going to be all right if I just leave you here?"

"We'll be fine," Treakness said. "You just worry about getting back to your family."

"No problem," Koshevski promised. "Again, good luck."

With that, he slipped past them and headed back down the conduit, the faint glow from his flashlight just bright enough to show the footing ahead. A minute later, the bobbing light vanished around a turn.

"So what *are* we going to do?" Poole asked hesitantly.

"Well, we're *not* giving the spaceport a wide berth, if that's what you were wondering," Treakness growled. "Broom? You're up. What's the plan?"

"First thing we need is a look outside," Lorne said, taking hold of the rungs and starting up the shaft. "Wait here, and be quiet."

He reached the top of the shaft, and for a minute pressed his ear to the cover, his audios at full power. Nothing. Balancing his feet on the rungs, he eased the cover up a few centimeters and looked out.

Somewhere along the way they'd moved from Capitalia's central section, with its taller buildings and denser population, into one of the more spread-out suburban areas. Lining both sides of the street, set back behind trees, walkways, and softly glowing streetlights, were rows of single-family houses, each surrounded by a modest lawn of blueblade or curly-grass.

None of the houses showed any lights, and Lorne's first thought was that the residents had already fled to one of the safe zones. But his infrareds showed that all the houses were indeed inhabited, most of them by several people. Apparently, the occupants had decided to leave their lights off as a way of keeping a low profile.

It wasn't hard to figure out why. Lorne could see a half-dozen spine leopards from where he stood, moving about like shadows among the houses and shrubbery as they hunted for prey. Three blocks to the north, probably settled into the middle of the park Koshevski had mentioned, one of the Trofts' tall sentry ships towered over the neighborhood.

And drifting across the night sky were a handful of small grav lifts. Not transports—they were too small for that—which meant they were probably the observation drones Emile had told him about.

For a moment Lorne watched them meandering their lazy circles, a sour taste in his mouth. Through the long walk through the drainage system he'd come up with a plan for getting Treakness and the others at least to the vicinity of the spaceport, though if the Trofts had the whole place locked down, getting them the rest of the way to the waiting freighter might prove to be tricky.

But even the first part of Lorne's plan assumed that the Troft drones were only watching for moving cars and other powered equipment. If they were programmed to watch for *all* movement, pedestrian as well as vehicular, they probably wouldn't even get as far as the industrial park, let alone all the way to Creeksedge.

What he needed was a technical readout or spec sheet for those drones. Would the Tlossies at the spaceport have such data, or at least an idea of the invaders' capabilities?

Probably. But with the comm system still down, he had no way of putting that question to them. Even if the system was back in service, he couldn't trust it not to have Troft eavesdropping computers monitoring all of the planet's conversations.

Somewhere in the distance, a hint of a deep throbbing sound caught his attention. He keyed up his audios, and the sound resolved into the soft, throaty growl of a heavy engine. Some Troft vehicle, obviously, probably one of the armored troop carriers he'd seen back in the safe zone.

And as Lorne listened to the approaching vehicle, it occurred to him that he might not have to bother the Tlossies with this one after all.

Lowering the cover back in place, he climbed quickly down to the others. "Well?" Treakness asked.

"I'm going to have to go out for a while," Lorne told him. "All of you need to stay put until I get back." Reversing direction, he started back up again.

"Wait a minute," Treakness said. "Going out where?"

"If I'm lucky, I'll be back in an hour," Lorne told him. "But it could be two, or possibly three."

"What if you don't come back at all?" Treakness demanded harshly. "How will we know if you've been killed?"

"Just listen for laser fire and screaming Trofts," Lorne said impatiently. "That's usually a good clue. Just keep quiet—this is going to be tricky enough as it is."

He reached the top of the shaft and again carefully lifted the cover. The rumble of the troop carrier was definitely getting closer, and he could now see the faint sheen of headlights flicking across the landscape to the south as the vehicle approached. If it was heading back toward the ship three blocks north, it ought to be turning onto Lorne's street any time now...

And then, the headlights sharpened, and a large vehicle rolled into sight two blocks away. Lorne got just a glimpse of the vehicle's dark bulk before it finished its turn and the glare of the headlights washed out any hope of seeing anything more behind them.

But the brief look was enough to show him that it was indeed one of the armored carriers. More importantly, it had also showed the top of the vehicle's silhouette to be smooth, with no sign of Troft soldiers sitting on top as they had been back in the safe zone.

Which made perfect sense, of course. No sane soldier, no matter how good his body armor, would voluntarily expose himself to spine leopard attacks. Not when he could ride in safety and comfort inside an armored vehicle.

Quickly, Lorne lowered the cover back into place. The Trofts inside the carrier weren't likely to notice something as subtle as an askew drainage system cover, but there was no need to take that risk. Again pressing his ear against the metal plate, Lorne listened as the vehicle drew steadily nearer.

And as the leading edge passed over him, he pushed up on the cover, extended the little finger of his right hand through the opening, and fired his arcthrower.

The world around Lorne lit up briefly as the high-voltage arc slammed into the underside of the carrier. He fired again and again, aiming at the general area where the engine rumbling seemed to be loudest, trying to hit a vulnerable spot.

He was starting to wonder if the carrier even *had* any vulnerable spots when the engine abruptly died and the vehicle rolled to a halt.

Lorne took a deep breath, easing the cover all the way up and looking around. Most of the carrier had already passed him by, but the vehicle was long enough that its bulk still completely covered him. Equally important, the vehicle's designers had given it nearly half a meter of ground clearance, probably with the curbs and medians of a modern city in mind. There was plenty of room for Lorne to slide out of the shaft and get a grip on whatever convenient handholds the vehicle's underside presented him with.

Only to his surprise and consternation, there weren't any.

Frowning, he keyed his light-amps up a notch and looked again. No mistake: the long expanse of metal stretched out overhead was as solid as a family promise. There were a few small bulges and depressions, but no hooks, grilles, intakes, or knobs. Nothing that even servo-assisted fingers could get a solid hold on.

Something caught the corner of his eye, and he turned to see a new set of headlights coming toward him from the north. Apparently, the Trofts in the stalled vehicle had called for assistance, and that assistance was on its way.

Lorne slipped back down into the shaft, pulling the cover into place above him, and climbed down three steps. Again straddling the rungs, he got a grip on the topmost rung on one side with his left hand, pointed his right little finger at the spot where the curved metal joined the shaft, and fired his laser.

The shaft lit up with blue light, the metal sizzling as it disintegrated under the laser's heat. Droplets of metal scattered across his hands, and Lorne winced against the pinpricks of pain. A few seconds later the laser finished its work, and he shifted its aim to the other end of the rung. More sizzling, more tiny burns, and the rung came free in his hand. Tucking it under his arm, he got to work on the next rung down.

Half a minute later, with both rungs free, he again eased the cover off and looked out. The second vehicle had come alongside the stalled carrier, and Lorne could hear snatches of cattertalk over the rumbling of the newcomer's engine as the Trofts discussed both the unexpected engine trouble and the question of how best to get the disabled vehicle back to the ship. Sliding out onto the pavement, Lorne set the cover back in place over the shaft and rolled onto his back. He was taking a risk, he knew—if the Trofts decided to examine the dead carrier's engine out here, they would surely realize that it was no mere malfunction, but deliberate sabotage. If any of them then took the obvious step of looking underneath the carrier, this whole thing would come to an abrupt and violent end.

But chances were that none of them would want to linger in spiny-infested territory any longer than they had to. Listening to the ongoing conversation with half an ear, he set one of the rungs against the underside of the carrier and set to work.

By the time the conversation ended and the second vehicle began maneuvering itself into pushing position behind the first, he had both rungs spot-welded to the featureless metal at the right locations to serve as hand- and footholds. A minute later, as he pulled himself up as close to the undercarriage as he could, there was a sudden lurch and the stalled vehicle was once again in motion. Gazing out at his truncated view of the pavement, walkways, and lower parts of trees, streetlights, and houses, Lorne wondered if this plan was really as insane as it seemed, or whether it was even more so.

Two minutes later, they were there.

Lorne hadn't had a chance earlier to see any of the Troft ships unload its complement of ground vehicles, but he'd assumed that they were housed on the lowest level and simply rolled out once the proper hatches were opened. He was, he now discovered, half right. As they approached the ship, he saw a long ramp swing down from the narrow end, leading up to a hatchway that wasn't in the ship's lowest section, but instead was a good two or three decks above it. The two vehicles angled up onto the ramp, the second carrier's engine straining with the double load, and Lorne could see the faint glow of standard dark-orange Troft nighttime lighting coming from the wide opening ahead. The two vehicles reached the top of the ramp and leveled out, traveling perhaps another twenty meters through some sort of equipment bay before grinding to a final halt. There was another subtle change in the engine tone, and Lorne watched as the second carrier reversed direction and backed out and down the ramp, apparently heading out to continue the rest of the stalled carrier's patrol. As the engine sounds faded away, Lorne could hear the faint straining of other, quieter motors as the ramp was pulled back up again into closed position. The last hint of city light faded away into the gloomy orange, and with a hiss of pressure locks the ramp sealed itself into place.

And Lorne was alone. Inside an enemy ship.

Surrounded by enemy soldiers.

CHAPTER ELEVEN

Carefully, he took a deep breath. *I planned this,* he reminded himself. *This was my idea, and it's working perfectly.*

So far.

Above him, he heard a pair of dull thuds as the carrier's rear doors were opened and felt the slight rocking as the Trofts inside climbed out, their conversation revolving around the annoying engine trouble that had forced them to cut short their patrol. There were also several contemptuous comments about the lack of fighting spirit among Aventine's humans. Lorne watched their armored feet as the soldiers made their way across a floor crammed with machinery and other vehicles. They disappeared through a heavy door and headed one by one up a stairway. There was the sound of a hatch closing.

And then, silence.

Disengaging from his hand- and footholds, Lorne eased himself down onto his back on the deck, keying his audios to full power. The cold metal beneath him was an excellent conductor of sound, and he could hear a whole range of soft noises coming from deep inside the ship, everything from the hum of engines and ventilation fans to murmurs of distant conversation. But the vehicle bay itself appeared to be deserted. Fingertip lasers at the ready, he eased out from under the carrier and got to his feet.

The bay, as he'd already noted, was crammed with equipment

and vehicles, including several one-man floatcycles, two more
troop carriers like the one he'd disabled, and an even more
heavily armored vehicle that was probably the Troft version of a
compact urban battle tank. There were also racks of extra guns,
wheels, and other large replacement parts. At the far end of the
bay, across from the hatch and ramp, was a doorway leading into
what appeared to be a long, well-equipped machine shop. Also
at the far end of the bay, near the entrance to the shop, were a
pair of doors on opposite sides. The one on the left was the one
all of the departing Troft soldiers had taken on their way out,
with the other door directly across the bay from it.

Lorne looked around the bay again. Everything here was ground
vehicles, with no sign of the observation drones that he'd seen
flying over the city. Assuming that they were based from these
sentry ships, they must operate from a different deck.

He turned back to the hatchways on the bay's two sides, keying
in his telescopics and light-amps to try to read the markings on
them. Unfortunately, all they said were DECK 6-A and DECK 6-B, with
no indication as to the rooms or departments they connected to.

Still, the soldiers had taken the left exit, presumably heading
to their quarters or to check in with a duty officer. Either way,
that was definitely not a direction Lorne wanted to go. Mentally
crossing his fingers, he headed to the right.

Pressing his ear to the door again gained him nothing but
another set of faint sounds. He pushed open the heavy door, a
much quieter operation than he'd feared it would be, and found
himself looking into a narrow staircase that switchbacked its way
both up and down. Stepping onto the landing, he looked up.

The stairs weren't solid, but were made of the same weight-
saving metal gridwork used in the Cobra Worlds' own modest
collection of starships. The interference between the sections of
mesh kept Lorne from seeing more than about two floors up or
down, but that plus his hearing was enough to show that the
stairway was as deserted as the vehicle bay. On the assumption
that flying equipment like observation drones would be located
higher in the ship than ground vehicles, he started up, his ears
straining, his fingertip lasers ready.

And his heart pounding painfully hard in his chest. It was
nerve-wracking enough to be wandering around a warship full of
enemy soldiers. It was even more ominous when those soldiers

inexplicably seemed to have vanished. Could they really all have retired to their quarters or wardrooms for the night? *All* of them?

He was midway up the first flight of steps when it occurred to him that, yes, they really *could* have done that. The dawn landing had required everyone to be up early, and the invasion had been followed by a busy day of fence-building, negotiating, and spiny-unloading. Trofts could push themselves as hard as humans when they had to, but heavy physical labor took as much of a toll on them as it did on anyone else.

And it wasn't as if they were facing any serious resistance out there. From the comments Lorne had overheard, it was clear that Emile had been telling the truth about Chintawa and the Directorate having essentially capitulated. The government was cooperating with the invaders, the Cobras and patrollers had been ordered to stand down, and the average citizens were either cowering in their homes or scrambling to grab extra food and supplies with no interest or energy to spare for making trouble. Why *not* simply give the bulk of the invasion force the night off to rest, safe inside their warships, and leave the dull task of monitoring the night to the roving carrier patrols, the flying drones, and the spine leopards? In their position, a human commander would probably do the same.

He reached the first landing and eased the door open a crack. Beyond was a long corridor, again bathed in the nighttime orange, that seemed to stretch the entire width of the ship. There were several doors leading off in both directions, but none of them were open and he could hear no sounds of activity nearby. Closing the door again, he continued up.

He'd made it another half flight of steps, and was nearly to the midway landing, when the door one deck above him opened with a soft clang. A pair of Trofts, talking together in low voices, strode onto the landing and started down.

Frantically, Lorne reversed direction, heading back down toward the landing and the door below. But before he'd taken more than a couple of steps he knew he'd never make it in time, certainly not silently, certainly not without the approaching Trofts spotting his movement through the grillwork of the steps. The only way he was going to avoid being caught was to hide.

And in a bare stairwell, there was only one possible place to do that.

Pressing against the guardrail, he crouched motionlessly as he watched the Trofts come down the section of stairway above and to his right, heading toward the landing he'd just retreated from. He waited until they were two steps from the landing, then leaped up to the underside of their part of the stairway. His reaching fingers slipped into the grillwork they had just passed, getting a firm grip on the mesh. He pulled his body up beneath the stairs and swung his legs up and wedged his feet against the supports on either side of the steps. Pressing as close as he could to the underside of the steps, he froze.

The Trofts, their attention focused on their footing and conversation, never saw a thing. As Lorne held his breath, they made the turn around the landing and started down the steps beside him, the winglike radiator membranes on the backs of their arms brushing past barely half a meter from Lorne's own shoulder. He watched as they passed the vehicle bay door and continued one deck farther down before leaving the stairway and heading though the door back into the main part of the ship.

Lorne waited until the faint reverberations of the closing door had faded away and silence again filled the stairwell. Then, with a sigh of relief, he released his feet from their perch, got them back on the guardrail, and let himself back onto the other section of switchback. Wiping some of the sweat off his forehead, he continued on up to the door from which the two Trofts had entered the stairway.

The corridor beyond the door looked a lot like the one Lorne had seen one deck lower. With one difference: midway along this one was an open door. Notching up his audios, Lorne picked up the sound of low voices and the hum of machinery coming from that direction. He glanced up and down the stairway one final time and slipped into the corridor. Moving silently to the open door, he eased an eye around the jamb.

The room was a long one, nearly as long as the vehicle bay downstairs, though about a quarter of the way back it was cut into two sections by a thick transparent glass or plastic partition. On Lorne's side, in the smaller part, were three sets of curved monitor banks, each with twenty displays, each bank also including a full panel of controls. One of the panels was positioned straight back from the door, with the other two angled off to either side. The two Trofts he'd heard were sitting at the central and right-hand banks. Between them was a rolling heat cart on which sat a pot of simmering light-brown liquid that gave off a warm, spicy aroma.

In the larger part of the room, beyond the partition, were a pair of repair and fueling stations and two racks of two-meter-long, armored, dartlike machines equipped with floatwings and oversized sensor arrays.

Lorne took a deep breath. Perfect. Now if he could just get a good look at the monitor displays and figure out what exactly the observation drones were set to look for, he could start finding a way out of this place.

He was starting to ramp up his telescopics when, behind him, he heard the sound of the stairwell door starting to open.

There was no time to think, and only one place to go. Slipping around the doorjamb into the monitor room, he took a long step to his left and dropped into a crouch beside the couch of the unoccupied console, pulling the couch as much in front of him as he could.

The footsteps were coming closer. Lorne froze in place, hoping that the newcomer would continue on past and go off somewhere else on his errand.

With a rustle of radiator membranes, a Troft carrying a covered tray walked into the room.

The Troft tech at the central console swiveled around. [The time, it is overripe,] he said in cattertalk as he impatiently beckoned the newcomer toward him. [The view, was it sufficiently rewarding?]

[The meal, it was the only view I saw,] the newcomer countered stiffly. [The boredom out there, it is intense.]

[The boredom in here, it is likewise,] the tech at the other console said, also turning to face the newcomer. [The humans, they are hardly the danger we were warned of.]

[The other humans, perhaps it is they to whom the legends refer,] the newcomer suggested as the three Trofts busied themselves with the contents of the tray, which seemed to consist of some sort of small snack cakes. [Our strength, we waste it here.]

Keeping half an eye on them, Lorne rose a little higher from behind the couch and keyed in his telescopics.

The views on the monitors seemed to be of three types. One group, consisting of only a handful of displays, were set at a relatively low altitude and were stationary. Another, slightly larger group were ground-level and moving. The third group, which included the majority, were high-altitude and also moving. Another group of monitors were black, possibly the readouts from sensors that were only useful in space or atmospheric travel.

The first set of images, Lorne realized after a moment, were giving the view from the upper parts of the ship itself, probably from the weapon cluster wings, guarding the approaches to the Trofts' mobile fortress. The second group were more obvious: they were coming from the transport patrols as they wended their way through the ship's assigned territory. The third set were from the drones.

Lorne studied that last group, trying to figure out exactly what he was seeing. He could see the landscape stretching out across the displays, complete with houses, streets, trees, streetlights, industrial buildings, and some of the streams that fed into Crystal Lake to the west. The views seemed to overlap for a complete medium-altitude coverage, and on some of them he could see a bright mark or two that he tentatively identified as the roving Troft carriers.

And that was it. There were no individual heat signatures, no small-scale movement readings, not even any overall location patterns or flow data. Nothing that would give the invaders any hint that four humans were making a surreptitious journey across their freshly conquered land.

[—replace, and my post, I will return to it.]

Lorne snapped his attention back to the Troft conversation, and the sudden realization that he'd pushed his luck too far. The Troft who had brought in the tray had shifted his footing, and while his attention was still on the two at their consoles it was clear he was about to turn back to the door.

At which point he would be looking straight at Lorne.

Kill them! the frantic thought shot across Lorne's mind, the words as startling as they were appalling. Never in his life had he been angry enough or frightened enough to even consider killing someone, not even an alien.

But even as the fear of discovery flooded through him, the cold logic of the situation came in right on top of it. Even if none of the Trofts managed to cry out before they died, killing them would send bodies flying or falling all over the place, and he'd already noted how well these metal decks conducted sound.

Even if no one heard and came running, someone would eventually come to relieve these posts, and the resulting outcry and manhunt would eliminate any chance of getting Treakness to the spaceport. Lorne's only hope was to escape from the room and from the ship without being seen, and the only way to do that now would be to create a distraction.

His eyes fell on the rolling heat cart and the pot of simmering brown liquid.

There was no time to come up with anything better. Aiming his torso toward the pot, he activated his sonic.

The Troft with the tray had finished his conversation and had turned nearly to face Lorne when the pot shattered.

The three Trofts screeched in unison as they scrambled to get out of the way of the shards of glass and the hot brown liquid flying everywhere. With the aliens' full attention now turned in that direction, Lorne slipped out of the room, and a few seconds later was back in the relative safety of the stairway.

Earlier that day, outside Treakness's apartment building, he'd noted that the Troft ships had small ground-level doors at the bow. If he could get down there without being caught, maybe he could exit through one of them.

Of course, at that point he would still be in view of the weapon cluster cameras. But with the Trofts in the monitor room busy cleaning up the shattered pot, he could hopefully get clear before they were in any condition to take notice of his departure.

But even with the aliens' obvious contempt for the people they'd just conquered, they weren't being stupid about it. As Lorne pressed his ear to the lowest stairway door, he heard at least four different voices chatting casually to each other. The Trofts might not have sentries standing guard in the middle of spiny territory, but they were cautious enough to have those soldiers in position to act should something out there require it. Unless Lorne was willing to take on the whole bunch of them, he wasn't getting out this way. Grimacing, he retraced his steps up the stairway and returned to the vehicle bay.

The room was still deserted, whoever was in charge having apparently decided that repairs on the damaged carrier could wait until morning. Keeping an ear cocked for the sound of unexpected arrivals, Lorne made his way through the equipment and vehicles to the end where he'd entered. If he could find the controls to lower the ramp, he might still have time to get away before the Trofts upstairs finished their cleanup duty.

He'd found the board and was trying to figure out the controls when there was the sudden whine of motors and the ramp began lowering all by itself. The cool outside air flooded over him, and as it did the whine of the ramp's motors was joined by the rumble of a larger, heavier engine.

One of the Troft carriers was coming home.

Once again, there was no time to think it through. The ramp had already swiveled a third of the way down. A few more seconds, and the carrier would be on its way up. Half a minute after that, there would be Trofts stomping all around the bay. Lorne either had to hide, or he had to find a way to take advantage of the narrow window he'd been given.

And as he stepped to the edge of the hatchway, it suddenly occurred to him that the window was narrower than he'd first realized. The carrier's headlights aimed mostly forward and down, he'd noted earlier, and as long as the vehicle was on the street, the top of the ramp was mostly out of their range.

But the minute those front wheels hit the ramp and angled up, the headlights would be aimed squarely into the bay. If Lorne wasn't out of sight by then, he would be nailed like a gan fly against a white wall.

Clenching his teeth, wondering distantly if warfare was always this reckless and unplanned, he crouched down inside the bay with his back to the edge of the ramp, and as the far end of the ramp thudded onto the street, he frog-hopped a meter out onto the near end, then gave a second hop backwards that took him off the edge of the ramp into empty space. As he started to fall, he grabbed the edge with both hands, holding on just long enough for his body to rotate around the pivot points and swing underneath the ramp. At the inwardmost part of the swing, he let go and dropped to the pavement five meters below. His knee and ankle servos absorbed the impact, and for the moment he was safe.

But only for the moment. Right now he was out of sight of both the carrier's driver and the ship-mounted cameras, but as soon as the carrier reached the bay and the ramp swung up again he would be right back to the fly/wall predicament. His only hope was to take off right now and assume the Trofts in the monitor room would be focusing so much of their attention on the incoming vehicle that they wouldn't pay attention to any other movement.

It wasn't a good plan, and he knew it. The Trofts up there might be bored, but it was pretty unlikely they would be so inattentive that they could fail to see a human running madly away from the vicinity of their ship. But it was all he had, and waiting until the carrier was gone and the ramp was back in place would be even worse.

He was bracing himself for an all-or-nothing sprint when he heard a soft sound behind him.

And as his nanocomputer took over his servos and threw him to the side a spine leopard leaped past, its extended leg spines coming close enough to brush through the hair at the side of his head.

Reflexively, Lorne swiveled around on his hip, bringing his antiarmor laser to bear as he flicked a target lock onto the predator's head. The spine leopard braked to a halt and spun around, its eyes glittering eerily in the shadow of the ramp angling down above it. Its jaws opened halfway, and it lowered itself in preparation for another try.

And with a sudden rush of adrenaline, Lorne realized that maybe he had his ticket out of here.

He froze in place, half sitting and half lying as he waited for the spiny to make its move. The predator, perhaps sensing something was wrong, also hesitated, its eyes boring into Lorne's. Then, opening its jaws the rest of the way, it leaped.

Lorne waited until it was nearly to him before triggering his antiarmor laser. His leg swung up and there was a brief flash of blue just as the spiny slammed into his foot, the impact shoving Lorne half a meter backward along the pavement. The animal dropped with a thud to the ground, and as it did so Lorne heard the engine noise from the carrier above him change pitch as the vehicle finished its climb and rolled into the equipment bay. Jumping back to his feet, Lorne grabbed the dead spiny's front legs, being careful not to impale his hands on the spines, and flung the carcass across his shoulders like a heavy backpack.

And as the ramp began to swing up again, he bent over at the waist, crouched down as far as he could, and took off.

The first fifty meters were the hardest. He ran it in a terrified cold sweat, his feet trying to match the lope of a running spine leopard, his brain screaming the fact that his imitation wasn't even close, his back crawling with anticipation of the heavy laser that would surely cut through any second now, wiping him out of existence before any of his senses could even register the attack.

But the attack didn't come. He reached the side of the street and ran up onto the nearest lawn, crossing it and darting between two of the houses. Reaching the rear, he leaped over a fence the way a spiny would and no non-Cobra could hope to accomplish. He passed through another row of houses and loped onto and across the next street, angling a little to cut behind a row of trees that would momentarily shield him from the Troft cameras and lasers. Once behind the trees, he changed direction again, staying in their shadow as he angled toward the next row of houses.

Only then, as the fear-induced sweat began to dry, did he finally begin slowing his pace a little to something less frenetic. Whether the Trofts had missed the reflection of his brief laser flash in the glare of the carrier's headlights, or whether they'd seen it and attributed the flicker to something else, it was clear that they'd been completely taken in by Lorne's sheep's-clothing ruse.

The tension had almost faded, and Lorne was starting to congratulate himself on his cleverness and his luck, when two spine leopards appeared out of nowhere and jumped him.

He managed to discourage them without using his lasers, dodging their attacks and throwing servo-powered punches and kicks in return until they both gave up and left in search of easier prey. He wasn't so lucky with the next attack, though, and was forced to use his fingertip lasers and even a short arcthrower burst to finally put the spine leopards down. Again, while it seemed impossible that the Trofts hadn't spotted the brief battle, there wasn't any obvious response.

He'd made it halfway through another block of darkened houses when it belatedly occurred to him that the lack of *obvious* response didn't necessarily mean the lack of response.

Ahead was a sculpted bush. He dropped down beside it, freezing in place and keying his opticals and audios to full power. In the near distance he could hear the sounds of a pair of Troft transports, much softer than he'd usually heard them, as if they had been put on some kind of stealth mode. It was hard to tell, but they seemed to be coming up on both sides of him, working their way toward the area where he'd last fired his arcthrower.

He tilted his head back and studied the sky above him. One of the observation drones was hovering nearly overhead, while two more were moving into the area from opposite directions.

"Damn," he muttered under his breath. His plan had been to make his way to the industrial park Koshevski had mentioned and try to cobble together something that he could use to protect Treakness and the others from spine leopard attacks during the long walk the rest of the way to the spaceport.

But it was clear the Trofts knew or at least suspected a Cobra was working the neighborhood. The drones up there might not be programmed to watch for movement, but they clearly knew laser and arcthrower blasts when they saw them. And if there was one thing certain, Lorne would never make it to the industrial park without having to use at least one of those weapons again. Whatever he was going to put together, he was going to have to do it right here in this neighborhood, with whatever resources he could find.

Or rather, not in *this* neighborhood, but whichever neighborhood he could find to escape to. Mentally marking the locations of the two approaching carriers, he slipped away from the concealing bush and turned back toward the Troft sentry ship.

The dead spine leopard he'd used as camouflage was right where he'd dropped it during that first predator attack. Slinging it on his back again, he headed north, moving as casually as he could. The dead spine leopard's residual heat profile should help protect him from whatever infrared sensors the Trofts in the carriers were using, but rapid, panicky movement was even more eye-catching than heat profiles, and the last thing he could afford right now was to catch any of the Trofts' eyes.

Fortunately, the two carriers were still well to the south of him as the Trofts apparently worked on bracketing his last known position. Possibly they assumed he had gone to ground at their approach, and Lorne winced at the thought of the house-to-house search that was probably next on their agenda. Briefly, he wondered why they weren't bringing in reinforcements, a question that was answered a moment later as he got a glimpse of the sentry ship through the houses and saw the vehicle ramp starting down again. Grimacing, concentrating on looking inconspicuous, he kept going.

He was six blocks north of the ship, with no sign of alien

forces gathering around him, before he finally began to breathe easy again. He gave it one more block, and then turned eastward back toward the central city. According to Koshevski, the accessible part of the drainage conduit system angled northeast. Lorne had to find an access point into that section and get back to the others before they concluded he'd been taken and Treakness decided to do something stupid.

And once he'd done all *that*, he still had to figure out how to get them across the rest of the spine leopard territory to the spaceport.

He was passing one of the darkened houses when he spotted exactly what he needed.

He was still two blocks away from the group huddled in the underground chamber when he began to hear their worried whispered conversation. He was a block away when he was able to see them with his light-amplifiers.

They didn't see or hear him until he was ten meters away and turned his flashlight on his own face.

To their credit, the loudest reaction he heard was a gasped curse. "What the *hell* are you doing coming in from there?" Treakness demanded as Lorne reached the end of the conduit and joined the others in the narrow chamber. "I thought you were going to come back that way." He jabbed a finger upwards.

"Change of plans," Lorne said. "We need to head north. And keep your voices down—the Trofts are on the move out there."

"Looking for you, I assume?"

"More or less," Lorne said. "The good news is that the observation drones aren't keyed to look for individuals on foot. Not all that surprising, I guess, since any kind of motion sensors would keep getting triggered by the roving spinies."

"Aren't their infrareds good enough to distinguish between spine leopards and humans?" Nissa asked, frowning.

"You can't get fine-tuned infrared profiles from a grav-lift craft that small," Poole said. "The grav lifts cause too much interference with the readings. You can distinguish a human or large animal from, say, a car engine, but not two animals of about the same size."

"Been spending our weekends with the Dome's tech manuals, have we?" Treakness asked acidly.

Poole ducked his head. "Sorry, sir."

"But he's right, isn't he?" Nissa asked.

"*Yes*, he's right," Treakness growled. "Fine, so they can't pick us up from the air. But that won't stop them from picking us up on the ground. You have an answer for that one, Broom?"

"Actually, from what I saw the Trofts should only be a minor problem," Lorne said, studying the other's face with his infrareds. Poole's unsolicited comment had sparked way more heat in Treakness than Lorne had expected, even from him. He hoped the governor wasn't starting to come apart. "They seem to be relying on the spine leopards to do most of the patrolling in this part of the city, which means they have only token forces of their own on the streets."

"If that hasn't changed now that they know you're out there," Treakness pointed out.

"True," Lorne conceded. "But I'm expecting them to concentrate on the neighborhood where I killed a couple of spinies, which we won't be going anywhere near. The spinies are going to be the big problem, and I'm pretty sure the Trofts know it. If I use my lasers, the drones will spot it in an instant and send the troops straight to wherever we are. If I *don't* use my weapons, the spinies will eventually nail us."

"I trust you have a solution to that problem?" Treakness asked

"I think so, yes," Lorne said. He bent over at the waist and headed back into the conduit. "Come and take a look."

Traveling this part of the drainage system was every bit as unpleasant and backbreaking as all the earlier parts had been. But for Lorne, at least, it was worth all the trouble just to see Treakness's expression when the governor raised his head through the access point opening and got his first look at what Lorne had brought for them. "What in the name of hell is *that*?" he demanded.

"It's a garden shed," Lorne said, gesturing toward the squat, three-meter-square structure he'd borrowed from one of the homes down the block. "I know you don't see any of them in the city, but I'm sure you use things like this at your country estate—"

"I *know* what it is," Treakness growled. "What are you expecting us to do with it?"

"Walk to the spaceport, of course," Lorne said, beckoning. "If you'd step out of there, please, and let the others come up?"

"What, inside *that*?" Treakness demanded, making no attempt to move out of the others' way. "Don't be ridiculous—it's nothing but stamped sheet metal. It won't even stop a target slug, let alone a Troft laser."

"Technically, it's sheet metal over a ceramic grid foundation," Lorne corrected, giving the sky overhead a quick look. So far the drones still seemed to be concentrating on the area to the southwest where he'd given the Trofts the slip. "And as I told you before, if we pick our route properly the Trofts should never even notice us."

"So then why the—? Oh," Treakness interrupted himself, finally climbing the rest of the way out of the shaft. "It's supposed to keep the spine leopards away from us."

"Exactly," Lorne said as Nissa popped into view behind the governor. "And we're wasting time."

"Ah—a portable bunker," Poole said approvingly as he climbed out of the shaft behind Nissa. "And all the metal will even help diffuse our heat signatures for any roving Troft patrols. Very nice."

"Only if the spine leopards aren't able to bite through it," Treakness warned, tapping his fingertips against the metal. "This isn't very thick, you know."

"It doesn't have to be," Lorne assured him. "The first time a spiny starts nosing around I set the shed down onto its ceramic supports—you can see they stretch a few centimeters below the metal—and run a little current from my arcthrower into the appropriate spot. The spiny gets enough of a shock to discourage further investigation, but the Trofts don't see any of the big flashes their drones are looking for."

"Maybe," Treakness said doubtfully. "Too bad we can't give it a field test first."

"We can," Lorne said, "and I have. Twice, in fact, on the way over here. Everyone inside, please. We still have a long way to go."

After everything that had gone before, the walk to the spaceport ended up being refreshingly anticlimactic. The shed weighed over eighty kilos, a daunting challenge for human muscles but a casual load for Cobra servos and laminated bones. Lorne held the structure up by its center, keeping it high enough for general ground clearance but low enough that a roving spine leopard wouldn't be able to poke its snout underneath for a quick bite.

Nissa walked directly in front of him, peering through one of the under-eave ventilation slits where she could murmur warnings about curbs, bushes, houses, and other obstructions. Treakness and Poole walked at Lorne's right and left, watching for trouble through other slots and making sure they kept clear of the Troft sentry ships dotting the area.

Several times along the way Lorne had to set the shed down and deliver a mild shock to a persistent spine leopard. Twice during the trip they ended up sitting in one spot for several minutes while he drove off an entire family group that refused to take no for an answer.

But that was the worst of it. The sporadic Troft patrols themselves caused no trouble at all, since the rumble of their carriers' engines always announced their imminent appearance. That gave Lorne plenty of time to get the shed to an innocent-looking landing place beside someone's house or driveway, where it looked perfectly at home to anyone who didn't know the area.

Once, as the sound of the carrier began to fade away, Lorne noticed the twitch of a curtain in the house beside their mobile bunker, and his mind flashed back to the hostile crowd he'd had to face in the Twentieth Street safe zone. But either the homeowner didn't grasp the significance of the shed that had magically appeared beside his house in the middle of the night, or else he wasn't yet ready to betray his people to the occupiers.

Still, for the next two kilometers Lorne paid extra attention to the stray noises around them.

Two hours before dawn, they arrived at the Creeksedge Spaceport.

Lorne had expected it to be bad. It was worse.

"God," Nissa murmured as the four of them crouched beside one of the squat guidance beacons a kilometer from the spaceport's edge.

"And then some," Poole said soberly.

Lorne nodded in silent agreement as he gazed across the open ground. At the edges of the field, marking the four points of the compass, the invaders had placed four warships, bigger ones than the sentry ships they'd sent to guard Capitalia's intersections. Clustered around them like chicks around a mother hen were a dozen or more of the smaller transports that they'd used to bring in all the Qasaman spine leopards. In and amidst it all were dozens of Troft soldiers, some walking guard patrols, others driving carts laden with supplies into the spaceport's terminal and storage buildings or running hoses from the big fueling stations out to some of the transports.

"An interesting challenge," Treakness said calmly. "I trust you have a plan, Broom?"

Lorne grimaced, keying up his opticals a little as he gave the area a second, more careful look. Aside from the close-in foot patrols, there were also several of the armored carriers that had been set up in guard positions outside the cluster of ships, their roof-mounted swivel guns pointed outward. Still farther out, other carriers were tracing an outer sentry circle that, judging from the fresh ruts he could see in the ground, were coming no more than halfway to the beacon where their group was huddled.

But while the roving patrols weren't coming anywhere near their current position, Lorne noticed suddenly, they were coming right to the edge of the line of posts marking the banks of Tyler's Creek. "Which one is the Tlossie freighter?" he asked Treakness. "Do we know?"

"It should be that one right there," the governor said, pointing. "The one with the blue running lights."

Lorne grimaced. The transport was the ship currently nearest them, probably by the Tlossies' deliberate design. And that would have been very handy if the refugees could head directly there. Unfortunately, it was a quarter of the field away from the creek's closest approach, with two of the invaders' own ships between them.

But they would just have to deal with that. "Okay, here's the plan," he said. "We go back, head south, and get into Tyler's Creek. We'll head along it—"

"Wait a minute," Treakness interrupted him. "Did you say we get *into* the creek?"

"Afraid so," Lorne said. "The cut's pretty deep along there, but I doubt there's enough room on the edge above the water level for us to stay out of the big ships' sensor range. And unfortunately, the creek's the only way we're going to get in close enough without being spotted."

"But that water is *cold*," Treakness protested. "We'll die of hypothermia before we even get that far."

"It's not *that* cold," Lorne growled.

"Actually, lowering our body temperatures a bit will make us harder to identify," Poole murmured helpfully.

Treakness turned to him—

"I'm open to other suggestions," Lorne put in before the governor could get out whatever retort he was planning. "I just don't think there are any."

For a minute Treakness glared in silence across the distance, the light from the roving troop carriers glinting off his eyes. "We'll still need a way to attract the Tlossies' attention," he said at last. "They may possibly be willing to come out a ways and pick us up, but they're definitely not going to park by the creek and wait."

"I've got a couple of ideas," Lorne assured him. "With luck, we won't have to impose too far on their diplomatic immunity."

"Glad to hear it," Treakness said grimly. "Because I'm not at all sure how far that immunity extends." He exhaled a hissing sigh. "No point in putting it off, I suppose. I think the Chino Park picnic area will probably be the best place to get into the creek."

"Sounds good," Lorne said. "Let's get to it."

CHAPTER TWELVE

Fleecebacks, as Jody had already noted, were easy enough to catch. For Cobras, apparently, they were even easier, because the team that had been sent out to find one returned only minutes after Harli finally decided on the site for the test's staging area.

"I hope Freylan won't have a problem sending Snouts on a suicide mission," Paul commented to Jody as they sat on the ground a bit apart from the others.

"I'm sure he won't," Jody assured him. "It's not like they've had a long and rewarding relationship together. Remember, Freylan's the guy who used to name his lab equipment."

"Right." Paul paused. "This is a good plan, Jody," he continued. "I just wanted you to know that."

"Thanks," Jody said dryly. "But you'd better save the accolades until we see if it works."

"Success or failure doesn't change the quality of the plan," Paul said. "It only defines whether a good plan is also a *successful* good plan."

"Right. Important distinction."

"Actually, it is," Paul said, lowering his voice. "Harli's plan, for example, didn't work as well as we'd all hoped it would. But it was still a good plan, which is what made it worth trying."

Jody looked over at the other Cobras. Harli's back was to them, and she could see no sign that he'd heard her father's comment.

But she knew he probably had. "What's your definition of not working?" she asked quietly. "Because Buckley got killed?"

"That's part of it," her father said. "But mostly it didn't work because we didn't really learn anything."

"What do you mean?" Jody asked, frowning. "They shot back. We must have gotten *something* out of that."

"We saw the power levels they used against us, but we don't know if that was their full power or not," Paul said. "We saw their targeting capabilities, but they waited long enough to begin firing back that we don't know if the lasers were sensor-locked or manually aimed." He grimaced. "And as we've already discussed, we don't know whether Buckley's death was because our attack got too close to something important, or whether it was simply the Trofts sending a message."

"Yes, I see," Jody murmured, peering through the trees. A bit of Stronghold's wall was visible, a sliver of dull metallic sheen in the starlight. "Maybe *we* didn't learn anything, but if Matigo is right about the Cobras in the town launching an attack earlier, someone in *there* must have some better data on the Trofts' weapons."

"Which, even if true, is irrelevant," Harli spoke up, his back still to them. "We can't talk to them, they can't talk to us, and if the Trofts are smart they'll keep it that way." He half turned. "They're coming."

Jody tensed. "The Trofts?"

"Kemp and the others," Paul told her. He cocked his head. "And it sounds like Freylan and Geoff are with them."

He was right. Half a minute later, with soft footsteps through the leaves on the part of the Cobras and much louder ones on the part of Geoff and Freylan, the group arrived.

"Good morning, gentlemen," Paul said, nodding greetings at Jody's teammates. "I'm a bit surprised to see you here."

"We're a little surprised to be here," Geoff agreed, looking around. "A bit surprised at the company, too. You guys really made it all the way from Aerie? That's amazing."

"We're good at what we do," Harli said, stepping forward and peering into the cage swinging from the two Aventinians' shoulders. "Apparently, so are you. Most caged giggers I've seen tear themselves apart trying to break out. This one looks completely intact."

"Actually, the cage is Jody's—Ms. Broom's—design," Geoff told him.

"I see." Harli looked at Jody. "Did you also have a plan for rigging the stun stick to its mouth tusks?"

"Wait a minute," Freylan said before Jody could answer. "Stun stick? Kemp didn't say anything about a stun stick."

"We have to use Snouts against the Trofts," Jody said, wincing. She'd assured her father that Freylan wasn't attached to the animal, but seeing the intensity in his face she suddenly wasn't so sure about that. "I'm sorry."

"Never mind the gigger," Freylan said. "I'm talking about you. You and stun sticks don't exactly work well together."

"Don't worry. Jody's just going to describe the positioning," Paul told him. "We'll let one of the Caelians do the actual attachment."

"Oh," Freylan said, and to Jody's surprise the intensity and concern faded from his face. Apparently, he really *hadn't* been worried about Snouts. "I—yeah. Okay."

Paul looked at Jody, and even in the faint light she could swear she saw an amused smile tugging at his mouth. "I believe Cobra Uy asked you a question, Jody?" he said.

It took Jody a second to backtrack her memory that far. "I was thinking we could fasten it between the tusks, pointing forward, then rig it so that it would go off on impact. It would then fire when the tusks hit the fleeceback, which would presumably be right beside the ship. If everything goes right, that should kick up a show the Trofts won't be able to ignore."

"Things going right doesn't seem to be the pattern tonight," Harli growled. "But it sounds reasonable. You won't need a trigger, though—stun sticks have an on-contact activation setting."

"Really?" Jody said, feeling heat rise in her cheeks. "I guess I skipped that page in the manual."

"Not that we had much time for reading," Freylan put in.

"One reason we don't like visitors playing with Caelian gadgets," Harli said. "Any volunteers for belling the cat?"

"I'll do it," Kemp said, producing a small coil of tie wire as he stepped to the side of the cage. "Lower it down a bit, please. Not too much—I don't want its feet touching the ground. Ms. Broom?"

Jody handed him her stun stick, then took a long step back to watch.

She'd dealt with giggers and their rotten dispositions a couple of times during their brief stay on Caelian, and fully expected the operation to be, at the very least, noisy and, at the very most, draw a little of Kemp's blood. Fortunately, neither prediction came true. Kemp snapped a hand into the cage and got a grip on the back of Snouts's head, transferred the animal's neck into an armlock that pinned the struggling predator firmly in place, then braided the stun stick into position with the tie wire.

"Looks good," Harli said, nodding as he leaned in for a closer look. "Spotters, get to your positions. Remember that we want to see not only if the Trofts can hit a target right beside their hull, but also which lasers they use and what kinds of adjustments, if any, it looks like they have to make. Kemp, you stay with the gigger—release it on my signal. Tracker, Matigo, you're on fruit and fleeceback delivery. The rest of you, make a rearguard circle—I don't want something sneaking up on us while we're busy looking the other way. One minute."

Paul took Jody's arm. "Come on—you're with me," he said, and headed off to the right. Geoff and Freylan, Jody noted, were close behind.

Exactly one minute later, as they all watched through the trees, there was a sudden swishing of leaves and three small, dark objects arced through the darkness. Jody listened hard, and a couple of seconds later she heard the faint multiple thud as the tardrops splattered against the Troft ship. A few seconds later, with another flurry of movement and crinkled leaves, the fleece-back appeared. Sniffling audibly, it made a zigzag line toward the aroma Jody assumed was now wafting across the open ground of the clear zone.

"If nothing else, they might at least get some scratches on their nice clean spaceship," Geoff murmured.

Jody nodded, her fingertips tingling with memory. Despite the encyclopedia's warning that "fleeceback" was more sarcastic than descriptive, the first time she'd encountered one she'd nevertheless given in to the urge to touch the feathery soft-looking fur. The multiple finger prickings she'd received from something more akin to steel wool than the actual thing had dismayed her, amused Geoff, and worried Freylan.

The fleeceback had apparently spotted the dripping fruit now, and the zigzags changed into a straight-in run. So far, there was no visible response from the Trofts. The fleeceback trotted to a halt, gave a quick look around for trouble, then settled in to licking up the thick juice.

And with a final crackling of leaves, Kemp released Snouts.

Jody had never seen a gigger hunt before, though she knew that the encyclopedia listed the species as one of the least subtle predators on Caelian. Once again, the book proved correct. Snouts took off across the clear zone, arrowing straight for the fleeceback without the slightest attempt at silence or cover. Jody held her breath as it lowered its tusks and rammed into the fleeceback's side—

The lower front of the Troft ship exploded into a flickering crackle of blue-white light as the stun stick went off, pouring four hundred thousand volts of stored power into the fleeceback and the metal hull beyond. Through the flash and sizzle Jody saw Snouts jerk with surprise and pain as its own body caught the edge of the current flow.

The stun stick was still spitting out its fire when the forest lit up with the brilliant flash and thundercrack of a Troft heavy laser.

Jody still had her eyes squeezed tightly shut, the afterimage throbbing through her brain, when she felt her father's hand around her wrist. "Come on," he murmured in her ear. "Time to go."

"So that's that," Harli said, his voice dark and bitter. "They can fire right at the edge of their ship. Which means we're out of luck."

"Not necessarily," Paul said. "The Trofts had plenty of time to see the parade coming at them and figure out we were up to something. It may still be that their lasers are normally geared to avoid the hull, and that they had to do some kind of manual override to hit the gigger."

"So what?" Matigo countered. "Even if you're right about an override, it obviously only took them a few seconds to work it. That's not nearly long enough for us to get through that door."

"Unless we can figure out a way to make that work for us," Kemp suggested thoughtfully.

"Meaning?" Harli asked.

"I was just thinking that if they can fire on a gigger beside the door, maybe they can fire on the door itself," Kemp said. "If so, maybe we can trick them into blasting it open for us."

"Right," someone scoffed. "How stupid do you think they are?"

"Stupidity isn't the issue," Paul said. "The middle of a battle is a loud, tense, nerve-wracking thing, the kind of place where people can easily make mistakes."

"That may be how it is in the simulation room," Matigo said. "Not so sure about the real thing."

"The real thing is even worse," Paul told him firmly. "Trust me. I've heard my wife talk about the small battles she was in on Qasama. At times like that people tend to react without thinking. The trick is to get them to react the way you want them to."

"Maybe people are like that," Matigo said. "Trofts might be a little cooler under fire."

"That's possible," Paul conceded. "Jin never fought actual Troft soldiers, only armed merchantmen. But my guess is even Troft soldiers get rattled if you shake them hard enough."

"Which we don't know how to do," Matigo said.

"No, *we* don't," Harli agreed darkly. "But Stronghold took them on. Maybe they do." He swore viciously. "Damn it, we have *got* to find out what went down yesterday."

Jody took a careful breath. "Someone's going to have to go in there," she said. "Someone who can find out what happened and get that information back out here to you."

"How?" Matigo retorted. "Have someone write messages on paper aircars and send them over the wall?"

"I was thinking more about sending the data out via Dida code," Jody told him. "All that takes is a flashlight and a clear view over the wall."

"What's Dida code?" Geoff asked.

"It's a secret blink-code system that civilians like you two aren't supposed to know about," Paul said, an edge to his voice. "Thanks so much, Jody, for bringing that up."

"You're welcome," Jody said tartly. "So what's wrong with the idea?"

"Because like most games, Dida takes two to play," her father said patiently. "Unless I'm mistaken, I'm the only one here who ever served patroller duty in an Aventinian city. Cobra Uy?"

"You're right," Harli said. "As far as I know, every Cobra on Caelian came here directly from the academy, without even interning in the Aventinian expansion regions first." He cocked his head to the side. "But we're fast learners."

"I doubt you're fast enough," Paul said heavily. "Dida was deliberately designed to be as obtuse and hard to decipher as possible. When I served in Capitalia it took us two weeks to learn the system. I doubt you could learn it any faster."

"Fine, so it takes two weeks," Harli said. "I don't think the Trofts are going anywhere."

Jody braced herself. This was going to be awkward. "Or, even simpler, you could just send me in," she said. "I already know it."

It was, she reflected, probably just as well that she couldn't see her father's expression. "You *what*?" he asked, sounding as stunned as Jody had ever heard him. "How?"

"How do you think?" she said. "Back when Merrick was learning the system he needed someone to practice with." She lifted her hands, palms upward. "He was lousy at it. I was good at it. What can I say?"

"What can you *say*?" Paul echoed, his famous patience teetering on the edge. "What were you *thinking*? What was *he* thinking?"

"Yes, I know," Jody said, her own far-less-than-famous patience even closer to the crumbling point. "If it helps, we both feel terrible about it. The point is that I've got the skill, and we need it, and the thought of a D-class felony charge doesn't seem all that important out here with saberclaws and Trofts trying to kill us."

For a long minute no one spoke. Then, Paul stirred. "You have your flashlight?"

"Right here," Jody said, pulling it out.

"Lowest setting," her father ordered. "Tell me you honor and respect me, that I'm thirty point two times as experienced as you are, and that you'll never break a twenty-second-degree, hullmetal-clad rule again."

Swallowing, Jody keyed the flashlight for touch operation and set to work.

The Dida code was every bit as complex as Paul had told Harli, and Jody had nearly forgotten how long it took to send anything with any detail to it. Three minutes later, she finally finished. "That it?" her father asked.

"Yes," Jody said, refraining from pointing out that he already knew that. The close-off was, after all, an important part of any coded message.

"How'd she do?" Freylan asked. "Did she get it right?"

"Letter-perfect, actually," Paul told him. "She even got the numbers right, which is the trickiest part of the code." He looked at Harli. "I think we're in business. How do you want to work this?"

"Well, there's no point in trying to sneak in," Harli said. Jody couldn't see his expression, but his voice suddenly sounded a lot more respectful than it ever had before, at least when he was talking to her. "With the clear zone, and the way the two ships are positioned, there aren't any blind spots where she could even get to the wall without being spotted."

"Let alone over it," Paul agreed.

"Right," Harli said. "So it seems to me that the best approach is for her to have been outside the city when the Trofts landed—which the city records will show she genuinely was—and only now is coming back."

"She was out taking samples," Geoff suggested. "I mean, that's what we were doing anyway."

"You mean *we* were out taking samples," Freylan said firmly.

"Yeah, I said that," Geoff said, sounding puzzled.

"I mean we, as in all three of us are going back in together," Freylan said.

"Out of the question," Harli said firmly before Geoff could answer. "You two are staying here with us."

"And letting Jody go in alone?" Freylan shook his head. "No." He leveled a finger at Geoff. "*You*, of all people, ought to be telling them that. You're the one who—"

"May I have a moment alone with my colleague?" Jody jumped in, grabbing Freylan's arm. "Thank you. Come on, Freylan."

"But—"

"Come *on*," Jody said, pulling him outside the circle. "The rest of you, a little privacy, please?"

"Make it fast," Harli growled.

Jody nodded and kept going, pulling Freylan as far away from the others and the safety of their weapons as she dared. "Look, Freylan, I appreciate your concern," she murmured. "But they're right. You're safer out here with them than you are in there with me."

"All the more reason for someone to go in with you," Freylan said stubbornly. "If Geoff isn't going to volunteer, it's up to me."

"I appreciate the offer," Jody said. "But you're making it for the wrong reason."

"What reason is that?"

"You're being all brave and noble because you think I'm not here because of my degrees in animal physiology and management," she said. "You think Geoff invited me to join the team for some other reason entirely."

Freylan sighed. "So you know," he said heavily. "I'm sorry. I should have stood up to him right from the beginning. But"—he waved a hand helplessly—"he can talk me into anything. He can talk *anyone* into anything. That's how we got our funding in the first place."

"Which is why he's so valuable to the team," Jody said. "But you still don't get it. His reason for inviting me isn't what you think."

"Of course it is," Freylan said, and Jody could hear the embarrassment in his voice. "I was *there*, Jody. I saw how he looked at your picture on the registry. His eyes just—you know—kind of... you know."

In the darkness, Jody didn't even bother to suppress her sudden smile. Freylan was so *earnest* sometimes. Like a big, earnest, awkward dog. "He wasn't looking at my picture, Freylan," she said gently. "He was looking at my family affiliations, which are on that same registry page. *That's* what he was drooling over, not my face or my body or anything else."

She could sense Freylan's frown in the darkness. "I don't get it."

Jody sighed. Big, earnest, awkward, and innocent. "He saw that my father and brothers were all Cobras," she said. "He figured that if he got me to Caelian, one of them would probably volunteer to come along, thereby saving the team the expense of hiring someone to guard us while we were out in the wilderness collecting our samples."

Freylan seemed to digest that. "You mean he didn't—?"

"Of course not," Jody said, putting a little additional steel into her voice. "And if I'd even suspected he wanted me along for any sort of recreational purposes, I'd have turned him down flat."

"But—" Freylan shook his head. "And all this time I thought... he's crazy, you know."

"He's driven by thoughts of fame and fortune," Jody said dryly. "When a person like Geoff gets that taste in his mouth, everything else pretty much goes by the boards."

"I see." Freylan straightened up. "Thank you for clearing that up. I guess I've misjudged him." He hesitated. "And you, too. I'm sorry."

"No apology needed," Jody assured him. "Meanwhile, we *are* keeping everyone else waiting."

"Right." Freylan gestured. "After you."

They returned to the group. "Everything settled?" Paul asked, his tone suggesting that he'd probably heard more than Jody would have liked.

"Yes," Freylan said firmly. "We're both going."

Jody felt her jaw drop. "Freylan, I just got done explaining—"

"I'm not going because I feel obligated on behalf of the team to protect you," Freylan said. "If the Trofts bother to look at the records, they'll see that *four* of us left in that aircar. We might be able to explain splitting into groups of two, but we're never going to convince them that three of us stayed together and sent one back alone."

"He has a point," Harli said reluctantly. "The first rule of Caelian travel is to never do it alone."

"So I go with you," Freylan concluded. "Meanwhile, your father will be here with the rest of the Cobras, where he can assist wherever they need him. If they need to trap more animals for an attack on the ships, they'll have Geoff here, too."

Jody glared through the darkness at him. But his logic was unassailable, and he knew it. So did everyone else.

And even if all he could do was give her moral support, she had to admit such support would be more than welcome. "I give up," she said with a sigh. "So do we head out tonight or wait until morning?"

"Both," Harli said. "You leave from here right now, but you don't head back to Stronghold until morning. You can't plausibly leave from where you landed and pretend you didn't know the Trofts had invaded. Your site was way too close for that."

"True," Paul agreed. "Not only did we see them come in, but we also heard the explosions when they demolished the comm towers."

"And you'd be hard pressed to explain why you came strolling back to a city you knew had been occupied by an enemy force," Harli said. "So we're going to spend the rest of the night getting you and the aircar as far out into Wonderland as we can, so that you can innocently blunder into an occupied city all shocked and stunned by the situation."

"What if they spot us lifting the aircar out of the forest?" Freylan asked.

"They won't, because we're not going to," Harli told him. "We're going to turn the thing up on its side, strap five or six of our spookers to it, and haul it out through the woods."

Jody blinked. "Oh."

"Unless there are objections," Harli continued, in a tone that said there had better not be, "let's get to it. The six of you on transport duty, get to your spookers. The rest of you, gather around. We've got some thinking to do."

Jody had never ridden any kind of grav cycle before, not even the sporty little ones she'd seen scooting around Capitalia's streets. The Caelian spookers, which were at least twice those scooters' size and rigged with clusters of spines and rim guards to keep away opportunistic predators, were intimidating to the point of borderline panic.

But given that the other option was to walk the Caelian gauntlet, Jody didn't argue.

At least Kemp seemed to be a competent enough driver. She rode behind him on his spooker, holding tightly to the grip bar in front of her, torn between the urge to look over his shoulder and see what dangers might be lying ahead of them, and the equally powerful urge to just press her forehead against his back, keep her eyes shut, and not know.

From the glimpses she got of Freylan, hunched over behind Tracker, he wasn't doing much better than she was.

Jody hadn't expected six Cobras to have any trouble turning an aircar up on its side, and they didn't. Fifteen minutes after reaching the camp, they were off again.

It was nearly dawn by the time they reached the spot Kemp had chosen. "That's the Jakjo River," he said, pointing down the slope as the other Cobras unfastened the aircar and turned it upright again. "The place has a crazy ecology, probably because there's something in the water that supports a rollin' big number of pantra shrubs and kokkok vines. Perfect place for visiting animal researchers."

"Sounds good," Jody agreed, feeling her pulse thudding in her throat. Up to this point most of her attention had been focused on the dangers of Caelian itself. Now, suddenly, the full magnitude of the job she'd volunteered for was looming in front of her. "Are you and the others heading back to Stronghold?"

"Right," Kemp said. "Just as soon—" He broke off, swiveling around and snapping his leg up to send a laser shot into a saberclaw that had just been starting its leap. "As soon as you're in the air," he finished. "Oh, and once you're inside, make sure you put everything back in place. The Trofts'll find it pretty strange if they check out the aircar and find all the loose gear piled up along one side."

"We'll do that," Jody promised.

Kemp peered closely at her. "You ready for this?"

"No idea," Jody said honestly. "But whether I am or not, I'm doing it." She reached down and squeezed his hand. "Thanks for everything."

"No problem," Kemp said, squeezing rather shyly back. "Watch yourselves, okay?"

"You, too," Jody said. "Tell Cobra Harli that when I have something to report I'll try to find a place where I can signal due west."

"We'll watch for you," Kemp promised. "Good luck."

The trip through the forest by spooker had been a long, tedious, dangerous affair. The flight over the forest by aircar was considerably faster, and a whole lot safer. Within a few minutes, it seemed, Jody was able to see the sheen of Stronghold's wall in the sunlight now peeking over the forest to the east. "You ready?" she asked Freylan.

"Yes," he said, his voice shaking slightly. "You want me to do the talking?"

"No, that's okay," Jody said. It was probably a toss-up as to which of them was more nervous, but he *sounded* more nervous, and that could make all the difference. "I'll handle it."

The laser burn marks her father had told them about weren't visible right away, certainly not until after the Troft ships themselves came into view. But as Jody headed down toward their rental house she finally spotted them: small, crisply-defined black grooves in various places on the ground and several of the houses, all of them angling back toward one or the other of the warships' wing-mounted weapons.

She was searching the wall for signs of the scoring Paul had also mentioned when a two-meter-long, dartlike device suddenly appeared by her side mirror. "Whoa!" she gasped, jerking in reaction. She started to twitch the aircar away from the thing—

"Careful—there's one over here, too," Freylan warned.

Jody leaned forward and looked past him. The Trofts had the aircar flanked, all right. "Any idea what they want?"

As if in answer, the machine on Freylan's side edged over and nudged the aircar to the left. Jody tweaked her own controls that direction in response, then repeated the adjustment twice more as the dart continued its nudging. By the time it finally pulled back to its original escort position she was pointed at a spot just inside the wall and right by the northernmost Troft ship.

And as she headed for the ground Jody saw a group of armed Trofts emerge from one of the buildings beside her new landing site. They formed a semicircle around the open area, their heads and lasers pointed toward her. Keeping one eye on the lasers, Jody put the aircar down squarely in the middle of their semicircle.

"What's going on?" she called toward them as she and Freylan opened their doors and climbed out. Now that they were closer, she could see that, along with being armed, the Trofts were also wearing helmets and armored leotards. "What's wrong," she called again. "Did some screech tigers get in?"

"Identify yourselves," a flat translator-type voice came from somewhere in the group.

"I'm Jody Broom," Jody said. "This is Freylan Sonderby. Didn't we fill out the paperwork right?"

"Empty your pockets," the Troft ordered. "Everything on the ground. Now."

Grimacing, Jody obeyed, making a small pile of her comm, pen and notebook, aircar keys, multitool, wallet, and flashlight. Beside her, Freylan was doing the same. "What's going on?" she asked again as she straightened up.

Two of the Trofts left the group, their weapons leveled, and strode toward Jody and Freylan. "You will come with us," one of them said.

"Why?" Jody asked. The flat, translator voices, she could tell now, were emanating from round pins that each of the aliens had fastened to his left shoulder. "Come on, this is crazy. What's going on, anyway?"

One of the two Trofts marched straight up to her and pressed the muzzle of his laser against her chest. "You foolish humans," he intoned. "Do you think we are foolish, too?"

Jody heard a sharp intake of air, and out of the corner of her eye she saw Freylan stir, then freeze as the second Troft also jabbed his laser into his new prisoner's chest. "I don't understand," she said, a sinking feeling in the pit of her stomach.

"Did you think we would not see that you were outside the wall with the *koubrah*-soldiers?" the Troft demanded. "Now you return to the settlement as spies."

"That's crazy," Jody insisted, knowing it was hopeless but also knowing she had to try. "We've been up by the Jakjo River since yesterday morning."

"You will learn now the fate of all enemies of the Drim'hco'plai Demesne." The Troft jabbed her again with his laser muzzle. "Turn around, and walk."

CHAPTER THIRTEEN

The water in Tyler's Creek was swift, noisy, and every bit as cold as Treakness had warned it would be. Before the group had gone even fifty meters Lorne's feet and legs were numb, and before they'd gone fifty meters more his whole body was starting to shiver violently enough that he was making little splashes in the water. The other three weren't doing any better.

In fact, as Lorne studied them, he realized they were doing considerably worse. Their breathing was shaky as they waded through the water, and their infrared signatures were slowly but steadily fading as they lost body heat. The water only came up to their waists, which meant that their torsos should be out of the direct effects of the chill, but that small advantage was effectively nullified as, one by one, they lost their footing in the current pushing against them from behind and fell full length into the creek. Before they'd made it even halfway, all four of them were soaked to the skin.

They were still a good hundred meters from Lorne's exit point when Nissa had finally had enough.

"It's no good," she gasped, her teeth chattering violently as she staggered like a drunk against Lorne's side. "The governor—this is killing him. It's going to stop his heart. We can't do this."

Lorne looked at Treakness. The older man was staggering as badly as Nissa was, his infrared signature ominously low. He was losing heat fast, and whether he had heart problems or not was no longer the point. "You're right," Lorne conceded, trying desperately to think. He'd started this trip with a plan, and his cold-numbed brain still remembered what that plan was. But at this point, with his synapses frozen together like window frost patterns, he couldn't begin to come up with a rational alternative. Maybe if they climbed up onto the slope of the cut, staying out of the water but below the level of the landing field, they could crawl their way to the exit point without being seen.

But even if they did that, wouldn't their soaked clothes be just as cold in the air as in the water? Lorne tried to reason it out, but he couldn't seem to come up with the right answer.

"No," Treakness murmured.

Lorne frowned, focusing on the governor, wondering if he was imagining things. Treakness was still barely in control of his legs, and was clutching onto Poole for support as the two of them stumbled together through the water. But even through the shivering and the chattering teeth Lorne could see the determination in the man's face. "We go on," Treakness told him. "We have to. If we don't—" Another violent shiver ran through him, and as his hands slipped from their deadened grip on Poole's shoulder he fell to his knees in the creek, his head bowed with fatigue and cold.

Lorne felt his own frozen lips curl back in a silent snarl. Nissa was right—this was insanity. But Treakness was also right—if they quit now, they might as well just turn themselves in to the Trofts.

And if a Cobra-hating governor had the strength of will to go on, Lorne was damned if he would be the one to call a halt.

"We go on," he told Nissa. Wading over to Treakness, he pulled the kneeling governor back up onto his feet. Then, stepping between him and Poole, he got an arm around each man's waist and locked his elbow servos to keep them upright. "Nissa?" he called, nodding her toward him. "Behind me—arms around my neck."

For a moment she just stared blankly at him. Then, she seemed to get it. Sloshing up behind him, she raised her arms and dropped them limply across his shoulders. Lorne turned his head to his left, pinning her left arm to his shoulder. Hardly an ideal situation, but it was the best he could come up with. "Okay," he said. "Let's go."

"Lorne?"

Lorne blinked, some of the fog that had wrapped itself around his brain clearing away. He was still supporting Treakness's and Poole's sagging bodies, but Nissa was no longer hanging onto his neck from behind him. Instead, she had somehow gotten in front of him and was slapping his cheek. "Lorne!" she repeated. "We're here. Lorne?"

Lorne blinked at her ... and then, through his mental sluggishness he heard the rumble of an approaching Troft armored carrier.

Abruptly the rest of the fog vanished. "Yeah, I'm on it," he said. "Here—hold him," he added, shrugging his shoulder and shoving Poole into Nissa's arms. Shifting his other hand from Treakness's waist to his arm, he slogged over to the spaceport edge of the creek and started climbing the bank.

He had gotten one arm up onto the grass and was hanging there, shivering and gasping for breath, when the headlights from the carrier flared like twin suns squarely in his face. There was a sudden surge of its engines as the vehicle leaped forward, the glare intensifying to a painful level. Lorne turned his face away, his eyes squeezed tightly shut, and a few seconds later the engine's surge abruptly dropped back to a rumbling idle as the carrier braked to a halt. There was a sound of metal doors being flung open—

"Over here," Lorne gasped, not trying to suppress any of the trembling in his voice. His brain still wasn't working at full power, but he remembered enough about his plan to know that the more helpless the Trofts thought he and the others were, the better. "Please—he's dying. Please."

"Identify yourselves," a flat translator voice demanded.

"Carl DeVille," Lorne said. The carrier's headlights were still blazing into his face, but with his opticals he could see that the vehicle had stopped only seven or eight meters away from him. Two of the Trofts were striding in his direction, their weapons pointed at him, while two more stood back beside the carrier in covering positions. Behind them, he saw, the rear of the vehicle was still disgorging alien soldiers. "I'm an aide to Senior Governor Tomo Treakness," he continued. "I've got the governor here with me. Please—the cold—he's going to die if we don't get him out of the water."

One of the approaching Trofts lifted a hand to cover something on his shoulder, and Lorne keyed up his audios in hopes of catching whatever the Troft was saying to his superiors. But between the distance, the blockage of the Troft's faceplate, and the background noises of the carrier and the creek he couldn't hear anything.

Only then did it occur to him that if the Trofts wanted the missing governor dead and not captured, Lorne had just effectively abetted in the man's murder.

But even before that horrible thought was fully formed the Troft lowered his hand, slung his laser rifle over his shoulder, and squatted down at the edge of the creek a meter to Lorne's left. He spotted Treakness, hanging limply half in and half out of the water, then nimbly hopped down into the creek. Wrapping his arms around the governor's waist, he pulled him free of Lorne's grip and started up the slope. By the time he was halfway to the top, two more of the aliens had joined him, and together they pulled Treakness up onto the bank. The first Troft slid back down into the creek and repeated the operation with Poole.

They were pulling Nissa up onto the bank when a pair of armored hands closed around Lorne's forearms and pulled him the rest of the way up onto the grass. His rescuers turned him over onto his stomach, maintaining their grip on his arms, as a third moved toward them, the glint of wrist shackles in his hand.

And in that instant, Lorne made his move.

He heaved upward against the hands holding his arms, pulling himself off the ground and up into a kneeling position. Swinging his arms around and forward, he wrenched them out of the startled Trofts' grips, then continued the swinging motion up and back and slammed the backs of his fists into the sides of the Trofts' helmets. As their grips vanished and they toppled sideways away from him, he curved his right hand, little finger pointed at the soldier with the wrist shackles, and fired his stunner.

The Troft twitched violently as the current slammed through him and fell flat on his back. Six meters behind him, the group of Trofts who'd taken up backup positions swung their lasers around toward Lorne, only to stagger back as a double blast from the Cobra's sonic rocked them off balance. To Lorne's left, the three aliens who had pulled the rest of the shivering humans from the creek made a desperate scramble for their own weapons, then fell to the ground as three more lightning bolts from Lorne's stunner took them out. Surging all the way up onto his feet, Lorne charged into the group of sonic-staggered aliens, his stunner and servo-enhanced hands systematically laying them out.

The driver had thrown the carrier into reverse and was trying frantically to get out of there when Lorne ran behind the vehicle, ducked inside through the still-open rear doors, and nailed him with a final stunner blast.

The carrier was still moving backwards. Lorne ran forward to the cab, hauled the unconscious driver out of his seat, then dropped onto it himself. The controls were laid out differently from those of other Troft vehicles he'd seen, but they were easy enough to figure out. Bringing the carrier to a halt, he reversed direction and drove back to where he'd left the others, turning the vehicle sharply in toward the landing field as he stopped. Climbing out of the seat, he ran back to the rear and jumped out.

Treakness, Poole, and Nissa were still sitting on the ground, huddled together for warmth, looking around in confusion and disbelief at the unconscious Trofts scattered all around them. "Up, up, up," Lorne ordered, grabbing Treakness's and Poole's forearms and hauling them up onto their feet. "Move it, before they decide to start shooting."

"We're up," Treakness said, his voice slurred but his eyes starting to come back to full awareness. Weakly, he twisted his arm free of Lorne's grip and took hold of Poole's and Nissa's. "Go get it started," he told Lorne, staggering a little as he pulled the others toward the carrier. "Go on—we're coming."

"I'll be right there," Lorne said. Stepping over to the nearest group of unconscious Trofts, he loaded two of them over his shoulders, jogged past Treakness and the others to the carrier, and dumped the two aliens inside the back. By the time the three shivering humans reached the vehicle he had added four more to the pile.

"What are you doing that for?" Treakness huffed as Lorne pulled him inside and sat him down beside one of the crew couches.

"Insurance," Lorne said as he hauled Poole and Nissa inside and closed the doors behind them. "I'm hoping they'll be less likely to shoot at us if some of their own people are aboard. Everyone sit down and hold onto one of the benches." He pulled off one of the unconscious Trofts' helmets and headed forward toward the carrier's cab, jamming the helmet over his own head as he did so.

[—report, it will be submitted at once,] a stern Troft voice ordered into Lorne's ear. [The prisoners' status, it is what?]

[The prisoners, they have broken free,] Lorne called back in cattertalk, putting an edge of urgency into his voice. The driver was still lying limply on the floor; hauling him up, Lorne maneuvered them both onto the driver's seat, positioning the Troft so that he was between Lorne and any laser fire that might come through the windshield or side windows. [The remaining soldiers, they are attempting to subdue,] he added, and jammed his foot down hard on the accelerator.

The carrier leaped forward with considerably more acceleration than Lorne had expected. [The soldiers, they cannot hold them,] he continued into his borrowed helmet's microphone, letting his earlier urgency edge toward panic. A small part of his still sluggish mind wondered if Troft solders ever actually panicked, but he also knew that putting too much calmness into his masquerade wouldn't get him what he needed.

[The soldiers, they are to shoot to kill,] the controller's voice said grimly. [Group Leader Paeyrdosi, you will respond.]

[Group Leader Paeyrdosi, he is down,] Lorne said, turning the carrier toward a group of storage and fuel outbuildings a hundred meters to the right of one of the big Troft warships. Behind the outbuildings he could see one of the invaders' transports; behind it, though not visible from his position, should be the Tlossie freighter that was their goal. If he could keep the charade and the Trofts' uncertainty going for two or three more minutes, they might just make it.

But even in the dark, foggy hour before dawn the Trofts weren't *that* gullible. [To me, who is this who speaks?] the voice in Lorne's ear demanded. [One of the humans, are you he?]

Lorne grimaced. [Understanding, I have not,] he gave it a final try. [The prisoners, this vehicle they now command. The vehicle, they have ordered—]

"Yes, one of the humans I am," Treakness's voice cut in.

Lorne twisted his head around. Treakness, holding tightly onto one of the benches beside Poole and Nissa as the carrier bounced along the landing field, had appropriated another of the Troft helmets and had it over his head. "This is Senior Governor Tomo Treakness," he continued, the words coming out proud and stern despite his still shaking voice. "I'm in control of this vehicle and this spaceport. Do as I say, or suffer a level of death and destruction the likes of which your demesne-lords have never dreamed of."

[This destruction, you yourself will unleash it?] the Troft scoffed.

"This destruction, it is already prepared," Treakness ground out. "Did your demesne-lords really think that the people foresighted enough to create Cobra warriors wouldn't know that a day of invasion would someday come to us? The entire Creeksedge area has been carefully mined with explosives, many of them directly beneath your warships, all of them now armed and with operators standing ready to ignite them."

The Troft snarled something Lorne couldn't translate. [A bluff, you make it,] the alien accused.

"You can believe that if you choose," Treakness said. "And I certainly wouldn't order the destruction of our own facility unless absolutely necessary. But even leaving that aside, you can't deny that we have several of your soldiers with us inside this vehicle. Their lives, at least, rest on your balance pin."

[Foolishness, you speak it,] the Troft said contemptuously. [The suppressor's crew, their lives you think so valuable that concessions, you expect us to make them?]

"Well-trained soldiers are a valuable commodity," Treakness said. "A wise commander doesn't simply discard them for no reason. Especially since all I want in exchange for their lives is to borrow that transport we're heading toward, the one just past the fueling station."

[The planet, you cannot be permitted to leave it,] the Troft insisted.

"I have no intention of leaving Aventine," Treakness said stiffly. "My government-in-exile will dedicate itself to continuing the fight until every last one of you has been thrown off our world."

There was a brief silence. Lorne kept going, pushing the carrier for all it was worth, trying to watch everywhere at once. A small part of his mind wondered if the Tlossie freighter might have given up and left Aventine while they were nearly killing themselves wading through the creek, and wondered what he and the others would do if that were the case.

[The transport, you may go to it,] the Troft said suddenly.

"And you'll keep your people strictly away," Treakness warned. "Remember, we'll be able to see it the whole rest of the way. If anyone approaches it—*anyone*—I'll order the destruction to begin."

[The transport, no one will approach it,] the Troft promised. [In peace, you may board it and your departure, you may make it.]

Out of the corner of his eye, Lorne saw Treakness step from the rear into the carrier's cab and crouch down beside him, the helmet he'd been wearing no longer over his head. "What do you think?" he asked quietly.

"I don't like it," Lorne said, shaking his head. "They gave in way too easy."

"Agreed," Treakness said. "Fortunately, whatever they're planning to do once we're inside the transport is irrelevant. When you reach it, just circle around it and head for the Tlossie freighter."

"What if the Trofts decide to take us out before then?"

"How?" Treakness countered, waving a hand around them. "The armor on this thing is damn thick, probably thick enough to take a few shots from even ship-based lasers."

"Except for the windshield."

"Which is already at too low an angle for all but maybe one of the ships to hit it." Treakness pointed at the unconscious Troft sharing the driver's seat with Lorne. "Besides, you've cleverly set it up so that killing you would mean killing him, too. If Trofts hesitate to kill conquered peoples without reason, they certainly ought to hesitate even more before killing one of their own. Not until they're desperate."

"I hope you're right." The cluster of outbuildings was looming ahead on their left, and Lorne turned slightly to the right to give them an extra-wide berth. He didn't really think the Troft commander would have a group of soldiers lurking among the buildings ready to leap onto the captured carrier and try to force their way inside, but he had no interest in finding out the hard way. "I still think they've got something in the works," he added. Out of the corner of his eye he saw a brilliant flicker of blue light out the side window—

And with a blast of billowing blue-yellow fire, the cluster of outbuildings exploded.

The carrier caught the full brunt of the shock wave, skidding violently sideways for a few meters before toppling over onto its right side. Lorne, wedged in place between the seat and the unconscious Troft's rigid body armor, stayed in place just long enough for him to grab the edge of the seat before he and his living shield came loose and tumbled out to fall the full width of the carrier. The Troft fell straight down, landing with a sickening thud on his shoulder and back, while Lorne was able to hang onto the seat long enough to turn himself vertical and land instead on his feet.

For a moment he crouched there, his brain spinning with the aftereffects of the explosion. Behind him in the carrier's main section, Poole and Nissa were struggling to extricate themselves from the limp Troft bodies that had been thrown all around them when the vehicle was pushed over. Straight above him, through the driver's side window, he could see yellow flame and roiling clouds of smoke from the burning fuel station and other buildings.

And at his feet, twitching like an injured insect, was Treakness.

Blood running down the side of his head.

"Poole!" Lorne snapped as he dropped down beside the governor, his fingers probing gently at the blood flow. The cut didn't seem too wide, but he could feel the skin around it starting to swell. He must have hit his head when the carrier was blown over. "Poole!" he called again. "Nissa! Damn it, somebody get over here."

"What is it?" Nissa asked, her voice shaky as she worked her way to her feet. "What happened?"

"The governor's hurt," Lorne gritted out, pulling open his belt bag and hunting through it for his share of the group's medical supplies. "Looks like he hit his head."

"They *fired* on us?" Nissa said incredulously.

"On the fueling station," Lorne corrected tightly. "Probably figured the soldiers we were holding were armored and we weren't. Worth the gamble." He found a package of compression bandages and tore off the wrapping. "Here—lift his head for me."

"No, don't," Poole said as he came up unsteadily behind Nissa. "It's dangerous to move a head-injury patient unless you know what you're doing."

"You want to just leave him here?" Lorne demanded, glaring at him.

"The Trofts will take care of him," Poole said. "They want the governors and syndics as hostages or figureheads, not corpses."

"I don't care what the Trofts want," Lorne bit out. "If he doesn't get on that Tlossie freighter, the rest of us might as well not go, either."

"Leave me."

Lorne looked down. Treakness's eyes were open, gazing up at Lorne and the others with determination. "Hold still," Lorne ordered, unfolding the bandage and easing it into place over the wound as best he could without moving Treakness's head. "Don't worry, we'll get you out of here."

"Are you deaf?" Treakness continued. "I said *go*. Take Poole and Ms. Gendreves and get *out*."

"You don't understand," Lorne said, looking around for something they could use to immobilize his head in case Treakness had also suffered neck injuries. The benches fastened to the floor—the wall, now—were pretty narrow, but they were the best he was going to get. He started to stand up.

And stopped as Treakness reached up and grabbed his arm in a weak but determined grip. "I gave you an order, Cobra Broom," he wheezed out. "The Trofts could be here any time. Leave me and go."

"He's right," Poole said quietly. "We have to go."

Lorne twisted around to look at him. In the few seconds he'd been concentrating on Treakness, the nervous, mousy Poole they'd all spent the day with had vanished. In his place was a new Poole, a Poole who wore a quiet confidence and professionalism that Lorne hadn't even guessed might be lurking beneath the surface.

He turned back to Treakness. "What the hell is going on?" he asked quietly.

"I lied to you, Broom," Treakness said. He let go of Lorne's arm and touched the bandage on his head, wincing as his fingers brushed the injured skin. "Poole's the one who has to get on that Tlossie freighter, not me." A faint smile touched his lips. "I'm just the camouflage."

"I'll explain later," Poole added, his eyes aching as he gazed down at Treakness. "The question is whether we can get to the Tlossies before the other Trofts get here."

"I don't know," Lorne said. "Look, I don't care what you say. *Either* of you. We can't just leave him here."

"I'll stay with him," Nissa volunteered, her voice shaking.

"No," Treakness said. "If you're caught..." He gestured weakly toward her. "You're the new camouflage, Nissa Gendreves. As the highest-ranking Dome official still known to be free, I hereby grant you full authority of negotiation and treaty. You're the Cobra Worlds' representative to the universe at large." He shifted his pointing finger toward Lorne. "Remember that," he added. "If you're caught, she's the one you were trying to get off Aventine.

Not Poole. Her." His finger flicked toward the carrier's rear doors. "Now go," he said. "If I'm to die, don't let me die having failed in my last attempt to serve my world."

Lorne felt his throat tighten. He still had no idea what was going on, but Treakness was right. Whatever was at stake here, if they stayed they would lose by default. "Promise to be a rotten prisoner for them," he told Treakness, and got to his feet. "You two, come on."

The rear doors hadn't been damaged or even bent out of true by the carrier's crash. Lorne popped them without trouble, letting in a cloud of acrid black smoke as the lower door dropped to the ground with a thud. "Close your eyes," he ordered Poole and Nissa as he squeezed his own eyes shut and keyed in his opticals. Grabbing them around their waists, he headed out.

The smoke was even more intense outside, burning into his nose and lungs, and the angry crackle of the flames drowned out every other sound around him. Clutching his companions close to his sides, he led the group around the rear of the carrier and toward its front. The air was churning violently as the fire sucked in air from everywhere around it, and Lorne could feel the heat of the flames prickling at his skin. So far the carrier was blocking the worst of the heat, but that protection was about to end. Through the smoke, his infrareds could pick out the transport fifty meters ahead, the vehicle Treakness had theoretically bargained away from the Trofts.

He could also see the shadowy figures of Troft soldiers hurrying toward it, moving under cover of the smoke to prepare an ambush for the arrogant humans should they somehow manage to survive the crash and the fire.

Lorne grimaced, the smoke burning his lungs now starting to seep in around his tightly closed eyelids. In theory, the Trofts may very well have outsmarted themselves, with the smoke from their fire hiding their quarry from unaided eyes and the fire itself blanketing even their infrared signatures. In actual practice, though, the path in front of them was a horrendously daunting one. They would need to get away from the fire without succumbing to either the heat or the smoke, then get past the transport and the ambush the Trofts were setting up, and finally cover however much open ground remained before they reached the Tlossie freighter. If, indeed, the freighter was even still there.

He was still crouched by the front of the carrier, still trying to find a way to get his charges through all of that, when something large lifted into view above the Troft transport.

It was the Tlossie freighter.

And it was leaving.

Lorne's heart seemed to seize up. *No!* he shouted silently toward it. *We're here! Come back!*

And then, even as he stared helplessly at the departing freighter, it came around in a sharp right turn and headed straight toward the three humans hunched beside the downed carrier.

Lorne stiffened, the heat and smoke abruptly forgotten in a rush of hope and apprehension. The Tlossies were coming to them, all right—there was no reason for them to pass so close to the fire otherwise. But diplomatic immunity or not, they surely weren't going to be so brazen as to land under the invaders' guns. Did they have a plan? Or were they expecting their would-be passengers to come up with one?

Lorne was staring at the incoming craft, trying to come up with something, when the freighter's starboard bow hatchway ramp flipped down and what appeared to be a weighted cargo net rolled out.

The Tlossies had a plan, all right. The question was, would it work?

"Get ready," he shouted over the roaring of the fire, his opticals counting down the distance to the fluttering net, his brain whirring with the logistics. Nissa, the lighter of the two, would have to go first. "Nissa, I'm going to throw you into the air toward a hanging net," he told the young woman. "When I shout *open*, you open your eyes so that you can see to grab it. Got that?"

"What do—?" Nissa began, breaking off in a fit of coughing.

"I said *got that*?" Lorne snapped, his own lungs feeling like they were rapidly becoming coated with tar.

Still coughing, she nodded.

"Poole, you'll be next," Lorne said, letting go of Poole's waist and getting a two-handed grip on Nissa's belt and left leg. "Same deal. Ready?"

"Ready," Poole said.

The freighter and net were still coming. Lorne braced himself, tightening his grip on Nissa as he gauged the distance. Nearly in position...

And with a surge of servo-powered strength, he hurled her upward.

She might have gasped something, but with the roar of the fire he couldn't be sure. Turning to Poole, he got the same grip on his belt and leg as he watched Nissa hit the top of her arc and start down again. "Open!" he shouted.

There was no way to tell if she had actually opened her eyes or, if she had, whether she could even see the net sweeping toward her amid all the smoke. Lorne held his breath as the mesh slammed into her, slapping out of her ballistic path. Her hands scrambled wildly for purchase, and then her fingers slipped into the net and she was hanging on for dear life, her body bouncing wildly in the wind. An instant later Poole was flying through the air after her, and half a second later he also had grabbed solidly onto the mesh.

And as the freighter and net shot past overhead, Lorne turned and charged after them, driving his leg servos as hard and as fast as he could. Five seconds later he'd closed the gap enough to make a leap of his own for the netting. He caught the edge of the mesh, wincing as the full blast of heat from the fire burned momentarily into his skin. The freighter cut sharply to the left and angled up toward the sky, and as he again squeezed his eyes tight against the sudden roar of wind he felt the vibration of the net being reeled in. He held on tightly, watching Nissa and Poole, wondering if either of them would lose their grip as they were buffeted around and wondering what he could do if that happened.

But they didn't, and he didn't, and a handful of long, terrifying, agonizing seconds later they were hauled up onto the ramp and through the hatchway into a large airlock vestibule. As they sprawled on the deck, the hatchway closed behind them, and they were safely aboard.

"Lorne?" Nissa breathed, her reddened, squinting eyes staring at something behind him. Blinking some moisture into his own smoke-burned eyes, Lorne turned to look.

Behind them stood a semicircle of silent Trofts, each armed with a hand-and-a-half laser.

All of them leveled and pointed at the three humans.

[Your hands, you will raise them,] the Troft in the middle ordered sternly.

"I don't think that will be necessary," Poole said calmly. "It certainly won't be very effective."

For a moment the Troft eyed him. Then, gesturing to the others, he raised the muzzle of his laser to point at the ceiling. [The *koubrah*-soldier, you are he?] he asked Poole.

"No, *this* is the Cobra," Poole said, pointing to Lorne. "Cobra Lorne Moreau Broom, as your shipmaster requested."

[The *koubrah*-soldier Lorne Moreau Broom, you are he?] a new voice asked.

Lorne turned around again. Another Troft had stepped into the vestibule from the door leading forward toward the freighter's bridge and control areas. The newcomer was clothed in the same style of leotard as the others, but wrapped around his abdomen was the distinctive red sash of an heir of the Tlossie demesne-lord. [Lorne Moreau Broom, I am he,] Lorne confirmed in his best cattertalk as he climbed to his feet. The task was harder than he'd expected, and he had to use his servos to keep from dropping back to the deck halfway up. Clearly, the ordeal of fire and water had drained him more than he'd realized. [My deep and humble thanks for this rescue, to whom do I owe it?] he asked.

The Troft inclined his head. [The language of the Trof'te, you speak it well,] he said approvingly. [Ingidi-inhiliziyo, second heir of the Tlos'khin'fahi Demesne, I am he.] He gave a sort of clicking laugh. [*Warrior*, instead you may call me,] he added. [My full and proper name, it is difficult for humans to pronounce.]

Lorne bowed, his servos once again keeping him from falling onto his face. [Graciousness, it is yours,] he said.

Warrior's gaze brushed past Poole and settled on Nissa. [Three passengers, there were to be,] he said. [But males, they were all to be.]

"There was a last-minute alteration in the plan," Poole said, his voice low and strained. Unlike Lorne, he and Nissa weren't even trying to stand up. "Senior Governor Treakness was unable to join us." He gestured to Nissa. "This is Nissa Gendreves, assistant to Governor-General Chintawa. In Governor Treakness's absence, he's given her full diplomatic authorization."

[Authorization, we know not for what,] Lorne put in. [This mystery, will you not explain it?]

Warrior gestured at Poole. [The explanation, Dr. Glas Croi will provide it.]

Lorne frowned at Poole. "Who?"

"Me," Poole said gravely. "I'm sorry, Broom, but I couldn't let you know my true identity. Neither of you," he added, nodding to Nissa. "We couldn't take the risk that the invaders would capture us and figure out who I was. That's why Governor Treakness and I came up with the plan for me to play the part of a kicked-around aide. We hoped that if we were caught they would concentrate on him and ignore me."

"How clever of you," Lorne growled. "It never occurred to you that it might be useful if the man who was supposed to be guarding you knew exactly who he was guarding?"

"It did, and we decided against it," Croi said evenly. "My life, in and of itself, wasn't important. What was important was that we delay my identification long enough for Ingidi-inhiliziyo and this freighter to get safely off Aventine."

Lorne looked at Warrior. "I thought you had diplomatic immunity."

[To a point only, my safety lies there,] Warrior said.

"And still does," Croi said. "Tell me, Broom, how long did it take the surgeons to turn you into a Cobra?"

Lorne frowned at the sudden change of subject. "What?"

"Your Cobra surgery," Croi repeated. "How long?"

"Same as everyone else's," Lorne said. "Two weeks."

"How much of that was actually spent on the operating table?"

"I don't really remember," Lorne said. "Something like ten hours a day for eleven of those fourteen days. Call it a hundred-ten hours, I guess."

"Actually, it's a hundred and twelve," Croi said. "How would you like to have had it all done in five days, and only forty hours on the table?"

"Not possible," Lorne said flatly. "They're tricky operations. Even experienced surgeons like those at the academy hospital can only work so fast."

"Agreed," Croi said. "But that assumes human beings doing the surgery."

Beside Lorne, Nissa inhaled sharply. "Isis," she breathed.

"What?" Lorne asked, frowning again.

"It was a reference in one of Governor-General Chintawa's reports," she said, staring wide-eyed at Croi. "It's an acronym for Integrated Structural Implantation System."

Lorne looked back at Croi, a strange feeling in the pit of his stomach. "What exactly are you saying?"

"What I'm saying is that we're sitting on a huge technological breakthrough," Croi said quietly. He gestured past the circle of Trofts toward the freighter's stern. "Back there, tucked away in a hundred packing crates, is our brand-new prototype, Isis.

"The world's first fully automated Cobra factory."

CHAPTER FOURTEEN

For a long moment no one spoke. Lorne looked at Croi, then at Nissa, then at Warrior, then back at Croi. "You're not serious," he said at last.

"Deadly serious," Croi assured him grimly. "And you see now why it was vital that we get it off Aventine before the invaders caught wind of it. All of our Cobra equipment and weaponry, with no fail-safes or self-destructs in place, just waiting for someone to come along and take it apart until they learn everything about it and every single way to defeat you."

"Right," Lorne said, looking back at the circle of armed Trofts and putting a targeting lock on each of the aliens' foreheads. A probably useless gesture—an heir's ship would be teeming with Tlossie soldiers—but if this whole thing fell apart he would have to at least try. "No, we wouldn't want the Trofts getting hold of the stuff, would we?"

Croi snorted. "Relax, Broom. The reason Isis is aboard this ship is that Ingidi-inhiliziyo helped develop it."

"He *what*?" Lorne demanded. "Who authorized *that*?"

"I said *relax*," Croi said, starting to sound annoyed. "He hasn't been allowed to see or study any of the actual equipment. He just helped me create the robotics systems that Isis uses to implant it."

"He helped *you*," Lorne said catching the pronoun's significance. "So you're a robotics expert, too?"

"Hardly, though I do dabble a little," Croi said. "I'm actually a surgeon by training, which meant our areas of expertise intersected quite well."

"Handy when that happens," Lorne said, eyeing Warrior. [Your robotics expertise, it impresses me.]

[Surprises you, it in fact does,] Warrior corrected calmly. [Yet surprised, you should not be. A useless parasite, an heir is not one.]

[The truth, so it would seem,] Lorne said, turning back to Croi. "So that's the *what*. Let's hear the *why*."

"You mean why create Isis in the first place?" Croi asked. "Actually— and you're going to laugh—it was Governor Treakness's idea."

Lorne raised his eyebrows. "*Treakness*?"

"Governor Tomo Treakness of the loud rants against the whole Cobra project," Croi confirmed. "Now suggesting a new project costing even more money, at least at the outset. Ironic, isn't it?"

"I imagine he feels a bit differently about the Cobras now," Lorne murmured.

"Knowing the governor, I wouldn't bet on it," Croi said. "Regardless, Isis was an idea he and Governor Ellen Hoffman cooked up between them a few months ago. The prototype was supposed to be unveiled with all due pomp and ceremony sometime in the next day or two, then shipped out to Donyang Province for its trial run. The ultimate goal was to scatter these things all around the expansion areas and new worlds, where they would not only save costs but would also shift the center of Cobra operations completely away from Capitalia and putting them where most of the actual needs are."

"And where most of the recruits are coming from, anyway," Lorne said, a stray memory suddenly clicking. "Was that the ceremony Chintawa wanted my mother to come into town for?"

"Exactly," Croi said, nodding. "You know how politicians think: the woman who redefined the Cobra profile thirty years ago, on hand to offer a send-off to the next stage of Cobra redefinition, and all that."

Lorne grimaced. Except that no one in the Dome had allowed his mother's redefinition of the Cobra profile to stick, and moreover had actively concealed what she'd actually done for the Cobra Worlds. She would have been little more than a figurehead at Chintawa's big show, someone to extol and ignore at the same time. "Well, we're for sure not going to Donyang now," he said. "So what's the new plan?"

Croi's cheek twitched. "There's currently a lack of agreement on that point," he said. "Ingidi-inhiliziyo wants to head straight back to his demesne and bury Isis as fast and as deeply as possible."

"Really," Lorne said, flicking a target lock onto Warrior as well.

"Yes, really," Croi said. "And before you start leaping to paranoid conclusions again, Cobra gear won't work on Trofts. Their bone structure, the way their ligaments work and are attached, even the available body cavities—just trust me, they can't use the gear. Neither can any other Trofts."

[Yet as a way to destroy the Tlos'khin'fahi Demesne, it would serve well,] Warrior put in grimly. Behind him, the door leading to the control areas opened and another Troft strode quickly in and stepped to Warrior's side.

"What do you mean?" Lorne asked.

Warrior didn't answer, his full attention clearly on the newcomer murmuring in his ear. Lorne notched up his audios— [is here,] he caught the tail end of the Troft's words. [In person, do you wish to speak?]

[In person, I will,] Warrior agreed, his voice tight. Without even a glance at the three humans, he and the other Troft turned and walked quickly from the vestibule.

Lorne looked back at the ring of silent Troft soldiers, their weapons still pointed at the ceiling, then turned back to Croi. "Fine," he said. "I'll ask *you*, then. What did Warrior mean about someone using Isis to destroy the Tlossies?"

"Because its very existence is proof they collaborated with us," Croi said, frowning for a moment at the door where Warrior had disappeared. "In the past, their trading relationship with us has been a pretty good thing, for both sides. At the moment, though, all the political pressure is going the other direction."

"So I noticed," Lorne said. "Okay, Warrior wants to bury the project. What do *you* want to do with it?"

"Use it, of course," Croi said. "I think we should take Isis to Esquiline or Viminal, make a whole bunch of Cobras as fast as we can, then bring them back here to Aventine."

Nissa stirred. "You assume the Trofts haven't already landed on those worlds," she said, her voice limp with fatigue.

"You also assume you'll be able to convince enough psychologically qualified people to go under your robotic knife, knowing they're going to be thrown immediately into a war," Lorne added. "That may be harder than you think."

"The Dominion of Man had no trouble finding recruits a hundred years ago in *their* war with the Trofts," Croi pointed out.

Lorne shook his head. "Unfair comparison," he said. "The Dominion of Man had seventy worlds to draw from. We have five. *And* that still ignores Nissa's point that if the invaders have any brains at all they already have troops on *all* our worlds."

"I guess that's just something we're going to have to risk, isn't it?" Croi growled. "You have a better idea?"

A wave of sudden tiredness washed over Lorne's mind. "I can't even think five minutes ahead right now," he conceded.

Croi took a deep breath. "You're right, of course," he said. He took another breath and gestured to the soldiers. "Is there some place we can go and rest for a while? Maybe clean up a little, too?"

One of the Trofts gestured toward the door leading aft. [A place, it has been prepared for you,] he said. [Though the place, it was designed for three males.]

Lorne looked at Nissa. "It's all right," she said. "We'll manage." Gathering herself, she climbed to her feet.

"Fine," Croi said, doing likewise. He started to stumble, nodded his thanks as Lorne reached out a hand and steadied him.

They had all turned toward the aft door when Lorne heard the forward door open behind them. He looked over his shoulder to see the Troft who'd brought Warrior his mysterious message reenter the vestibule, his radiator membranes quivering with tension. [Your presence, Cobra Broom, the heir requests it,] he said.

A shiver ran up Lorne's back. Had the invaders spotted the surreptitious passenger pickup at Creeksedge and sent word ahead to stop the Tlossies? "Go ahead," he told Croi and Nissa. "I'll be there in a minute."

The Troft led him through a prep room, a narrow monitor and engineering station, and through a final door onto the bridge. Warrior was standing in the center of the room, gazing at a wraparound display showing the full three-hundred-sixty-degree view around them.

Lorne looked over his shoulder as he crossed the room to Warrior's side, grimacing as he spotted the ring of ships running a slow orbit above Aventine's equator. Not only did the invaders already have massive firepower on the ground, but they had extra backup waiting in the sky. Even if Croi was able to find enough recruits on Esquiline or Viminal, he would have the devil's own time getting them back onto Aventinian soil again.

[The approaching ship, do you see it?] Warrior asked.

Lorne shifted his attention forward. There was a flashing red ring superimposed on the image of a transport approaching from deep space. [The ship, I do,] Lorne confirmed. [The invaders, it is one of theirs?]

[The invaders, it is one of theirs,] Warrior confirmed. [Yet its occupants, Trofts they are not. Its occupants, humans they are.]

Lorne felt a sudden leap of hope. Had someone on Palatine or one of the smaller worlds managed to defeat the invaders, or at least push them back long enough to steal one of their transports?

And then, like a splash of cold water, the more likely explanation hit him. [Qasamans, they are?] he asked.

[Qasamans, they would appear to be,] Warrior confirmed.

Lorne took a deep breath. Croi had called it, all right, back when the two of them were dumping the dead spine leopard at Koshevski's brother's building. The invading Trofts and Qasamans had struck a deal, and the Qasamans were here to gloat. Or possibly to survey their new real estate. [Avoid them, we must,] he told Warrior urgently. [Your passengers, they must not identify us.]

[My passengers, they will not,] Warrior assured him. [Our sensors, far more advanced they are.]

Which made sense, Lorne realized. An heir's ship would have upgrades on pretty much everything, including the sensor array. [Avoid them, we must still do it,] he said.

[Speak with them, I must.] Warrior threw Lorne a stern look. [Silence, you will maintain it.]

[Silence, I will maintain it,] Lorne promised.

Warrior gestured to one of the Trofts, and a green circle appeared around the red-circled transport. Apparently, Warrior had decided to use a tight beam for his hail.

The seconds ticked by. Lorne looked around the other sections of the wraparound, noting the dozen or more transports moving inward toward Aventine. The second wave of Troft soldiers?

[The signal, it is acknowledged,] a voice came from the speaker. A woman's voice, Lorne decided, assuming Warrior had been right about the occupants being humans. Her cattertalk was far crisper and better enunciated than his, too, he noted with grudging admiration. [Assistance, how may we render it?]

[Your cargo bay, analysis shows it to be empty,] Warrior replied. [The predators, why have you none?]

Lorne grimaced. So it wasn't soldiers the transports were bringing in, but more spine leopards. Terrific.

[The predators, all died en route,] the woman in the transport said. [A disease, it was apparently brought aboard.]

[The message, it is understood.] Warrior hesitated, flashing an unreadable look at Lorne. [Jasmine Jin Moreau, is there word from her?]

Lorne felt his breath catch in his throat. *How in space had Warrior known that his mother had gone to Qasama?* He started to ask that question, stopped as Warrior lifted a warning hand. [Jasmine Jin Moreau, is there word from her?] he repeated.

And then, to Lorne's utter astonishment, a familiar, achingly missed voice came on. [Jasmine Jin Moreau, it is I.]

Again, Warrior lifted a warning hand. But this time, Lorne didn't have to be reminded to keep quiet. Whatever was going on over there, he had no intention of letting the occupants know that Jin Broom's son was listening in on the conversation. [The news from Qasama, what is it?] Warrior asked.

[The battle, it has been won,] Jin said, her voice cautious.

[Yet the war, it has been lost?] Warrior asked.

[The war, it is not yet over,] Jin corrected.

For a moment Warrior didn't speak. Lorne studied his face, sifting through his limited knowledge of Troft facial expressions and trying to figure out what the other was thinking and feeling. He was disturbed, certainly. That much was clear. But disturbed about what?

Warrior's radiator membranes fluttered. [Then our mission, it has failed,] he said, his voice tight and sad.

[Your pardon, I crave it,] Jin said. [Your mission, what is its purpose and meaning?]

Warrior looked at Lorne. [The mission, it is of no matter,] he said. [Its failure, that is all I need know.]

[The message, from *you* it came,] Jin said, her tone changing as if with a sudden revelation. [To Qasama, you wished me to go.]

Lorne felt a jolt run through him as the whole thing suddenly fell into place. The mysterious and unsigned note that had sent Jin and Merrick to Qasama in the first place—the collaboration with Treakness—Warrior taking the risk of staying put on

Aventine through the initial stage of the invasion in hopes of getting Croi and Isis off the planet. "You knew this was coming," he murmured, just loud enough for Warrior to hear. "You knew we were about to be invaded."

The other didn't reply. But the fluttering of his radiator membranes was all the answer Lorne needed.

[Your mission, I understand it now,] Jin's voice came again. [War with Aventine, your demesne-lord does not wish. Yet a stand against the attacking demesnes, he dare not take alone. A victory against them, one must first exist.]

[The truth, you speak it,] Warrior said. [A stand, other demesne-lords wish to make. But a stand against a victorious army, one cannot be made.]

[The reality, I understand it,] Jin said, her voice grim. [But hope, do not abandon it.]

Warrior looked at Lorne. [Understand, do you now?] he murmured.

Lorne inclined his head, hoping that would be taken as an assent. Certainly he understood what Warrior was attempting to imply about the situation and the Tlossies' involvement in it.

But there was another, darker possibility that made just as snug a fit around Lorne's limited collection of facts: the possibility that the Tlossies were in fact in league with the invaders. That they'd waited for Croi and Lorne, not to heroically smuggle them off Aventine, but so that they could deliver both Isis and its co-creator in a single, neatly-wrapped package. That they'd deliberately sent Jin and Merrick into a trap on Qasama, and that Lorne's mother was even now a prisoner on that transport.

But Lorne wasn't going to bring up any of those possibilities. Not until he had a better idea what part the Tlossies were playing in this drama. Certainly not here on the freighter's bridge, on ground of Warrior's choosing.

[Refueling, our transport needs,] Jin said into Lorne's musings. [Extra fuel, can you supply it?]

Warrior's membranes fluttered again. [To return to Qasama, enough exists,] he pointed out warily.

[The truth, you speak it,] Jin agreed. [But Qasama, we do not yet return there. Extra fuel, can you supply it?]

[This fuel, to what use?] Warrior asked.

[Victory against the attacking demesne-lords, its use will be,]

Jin said, and in his mind's eye Lorne could see a dark, tight smile on her face.

Warrior gestured, and the green circle around the distant transport began fluttering as the Troft at the communications board muted the transmitter. [Her purpose, what is it?] he asked Lorne.

[Her purpose, you heard it,] Lorne said, gesturing toward the comm board. [Victory against the invaders, she intends.]

[Such a purpose, she cannot possibly carry it out,] Warrior protested.

[Such a purpose, perhaps she cannot,] Lorne agreed. [But such a purpose, perhaps she can. My mother, others also have underestimated.]

Warrior looked back at the display . . . and as he gazed at the Troft's profile, Lorne suddenly realized how ridiculous his earlier suspicions had been. Of course the Tlossies weren't in league with the invaders. If they were, why go to all the trouble of running from Creeksedge instead of simply letting Lorne and Croi come aboard, gassing them in the airlock vestibule, and handing them over to their allies right there and then?

And why send Jin and Merrick to Qasama at all, where something unknown but obviously extremely interesting had apparently taken place?

Because his mother wasn't a prisoner aboard that transport, Lorne knew now. Even if the Qasamans had somehow been able to capture and restrain her, there was no way they could restrain her voice. Lorne had been analyzing his family's speech patterns all his life, and the tension level he'd heard in her voice had dropped when she figured out that Warrior was on the Cobra Worlds' side. That wouldn't have happened if she was a prisoner.

Warrior himself, though, was still staring at the transport's image, his expression still uncertain. Perhaps he was thinking through the stories of the young Jin Moreau's exploits on Qasama thirty years ago. Perhaps he was contemplating the ramifications of the older Jin Moreau Broom's presence aboard an enemy transport with a group of Qasamans.

Perhaps he simply knew he had no other choice but to hold onto hope.

He gestured again, and the green circle steadied. [Your course, you will hold it,] he told the transport. [To your side, we will come.]

[Our gratitude, you have it,] Jin said. [Your arrival, we will await it.]

Warrior gestured one final time, and the green transmission circle vanished. [The transport, journey to it,] he ordered. [A fuel download, prepare it.]

There were a pair of acknowledgments from two of the Trofts on the bridge. For a moment Warrior continued to gaze at the display, then turned again to Lorne. [Jasmine Jin Moreau Broom, to where does she intend to go?] he asked.

[The question, shall I ask it?] Lorne offered.

Warrior looked again at the display. [The question, you shall not ask it,] he said firmly. [Your presence here, she would question. The Isis, it must remain secret.]

[Wisdom, you speak it,] Lorne conceded. Sitting here while his mother's ship refueled alongside, knowing he was bare meters away from her without being able to find out what was going on, was going to kill him.

But while she was probably not the Qasamans' prisoner, he still had no idea of her actual status with them. Letting them know who and what was aboard the Tlossie freighter could be a very bad idea. Certainly not one they could afford to risk. [The question, if I may not ask, then the question, I cannot answer.]

[A new question, I then ask,] Warrior said. [Isis, what shall be done with it?]

Lorne grimaced. Terrific. The two people who actually knew the full capabilities of the damn thing had deadlocked, so they were bringing in an amateur to flip the coin for them.

And then, even as he wondered which one of them he least wanted mad at him, a sudden thought flashed through the fatigue coating his brain like the sludge in Capitalia's drainage tunnels. [To hide Isis, you wish it,] he told Warrior. [To employ Isis, Dr. Croi wishes it. Both ways, perhaps we can have them.]

For a moment Warrior eyed him. Then, with one final flutter, his radiator membranes settled back onto his upper arms. [Your statement, it intrigues me,] he said. [More, I would hear.]

"The tanks are nearly full," Ghofl Khatir reported from the transport's helm, craning his neck to look at his readouts one final time before swiveling around to face Jin. "A few more minutes, and we can be on our way."

"To Caelian," Carsh Zoshak muttered under his breath.

"Yes, to Caelian," Jin confirmed, eyeing him. "Have you a different option to suggest?"

The young Qasaman's lip twitched. "Nothing that would be better," he conceded. "It's just that I've been thinking about what you said about there being seven hundred Cobras on Caelian out of a total population of a little more than four thousand. One in six is an incredibly high number."

"I already explained that," Jin reminded him. "The planet is immensely and actively hostile toward the humans who live there. They need all those Cobras in order to survive."

"Yes, I remember," Zoshak said. "It also occurs to me that if the Cobras are that vital to the inhabitants' day-to-day lives, how do you intend to persuade any of them to come to Qasama with us?"

Jin grimaced. That was the crucial question, all right. Unfortunately, she still didn't have an answer to it. "We'll find a way," she said. "Certainly not all of them will come. Probably not even most of them. But enough will."

"Enough for what?" Siraj Akim put in. "Enough to actually throw back the next wave of Trofts who land on our world? Or merely enough to die alongside us in a blaze of glory?"

"I'm not particularly interested in death with glory, Siraj Akim," Jin said firmly. "For any of us: Cobra, Djinni, or civilian. My goals are life, victory, and freedom."

Beside Khatir, seated at the helm's second position, Rashida Vil stirred. "Tell us more about this Caelian," she said. "You speak of active attacks. How active are they?"

"The environmental pressure is pretty much constant," Jin told her, wincing. Up to now, with the Troft attack on Qasama, the discovery of her brain tumor, her son Merrick's wounding, and then this risky voyage to Aventine, she'd mostly succeeded in pushing Caelian to the back of her mind.

Now, though, all her thoughts and fears about what might be happening to her husband and daughter were coming back full force. "There are lots of predators, small, medium, and large," she told Rashida, "plus lots of herbivores with sharp spikes, poisoned tongues and quills, and other defenses. Organic plant life floats through the air and takes root on pretty much everything, which in turn draws insects and then the smaller predators."

Siraj snorted. "Sounds worse even than Qasaman village life."

"It does indeed," Rashida agreed soberly. "And I find myself agreeing with Carsh Zoshak's concerns. What can we say that will induce these Cobras to abandon their people to such attacks in order to help us?"

"That's not actually the proper question," Khatir said, running his fingers through his—unusual for a Qasaman—red hair. "The proper question is what can we offer them in trade."

"Are you suggesting we *buy* their assistance?" Siraj growled.

Khatir shrugged. "Be realistic, Siraj Akim. No one does anything except for a price."

"*We* do," Siraj insisted, slapping his chest in emphasis. "We serve the Shahni and the people of Qasama with no hope or expectation of any reward."

"Of course you expect something," Rashida said. "The price you've been paid—all three of you—is the right to call yourselves Djinn of Qasama."

"That's not the same thing," Siraj insisted.

"Actually, it is," Jin said. "Honor may not be a form of wealth, but it's a reward and a price just the same."

"Is that the price your leaders paid for you, too?" Siraj asked, a slight sneer in his voice.

"As a matter of fact, yes, it was," Jin said calmly. "We are very similar, Siraj Akim. More similar perhaps than you would like to admit."

Zoshak chuckled. "Now you're just being insulting," he said.

Abruptly, Siraj stood up. "Do you make humor at my expense?" he demanded.

The whole room seemed to freeze in place. Jin stared at Siraj, not moving, hardly daring to breathe. Both he and Zoshak were dressed in their Djinn combat suits, snug outfits of treated kriss-jaw hide stiffened by fiber meshwork, with strength-enhancing servos at the joints that keyed directly off the wearer's own nervous-system electrical impulses. Neither of them was wearing his helmet or the gloves that contained the Qasamans' version of Cobra fingertip lasers, but even without those weapons the suits made them into awesome fighting machines, in some ways even superior to Cobras. If they came to blows, it could be an extremely dangerous confrontation.

In the old days, Jin knew, clashes of honor on Qasama had taken the form of duels, some styles leading to death, others only wounding the loser's pride. With the cultural changes that had taken place over the past few decades, she had no idea what the current style of ritualized combat was. She was also not at all anxious to find out.

Fortunately, for now at least, she wouldn't have to. "My apologies, Ifrit Akim," Zoshak said formally. "No offense was intended."

For a moment Siraj continued to glare. Then, perhaps suddenly remembering that there were two non-Djinn outsiders present, both of them women, he let his shoulders relax. "Accepted, Djinni Zoshak," he said just as formally as he resumed his seat.

"So that's settled," Khatir said cheerfully into the lingering tension. "Excellent. According to the navigation data in the ship's computer, it should take no more than thirty-two hours to get to Caelian. Since we don't know whether the Cobras on Caelian will be willing to trade in the coin of honor and glory, I suggest we all spend those hours making lists of what we and the Shahni might offer for their assistance."

"What *we* might offer for their assistance," Siraj corrected firmly. "The Shahni are not here, and we cannot bind them to any agreements." He raised his eyebrows. "Cannot, and *will* not."

"No, of course not," Khatir said hastily. "I was merely suggesting that as the highest-ranking Djinni aboard you might be able to make tentative agreements, subject of course to later consideration and approval."

"We are warriors of the Shahni, Ghofl Khatir, not the Shahni themselves," Siraj ground out. "I will make no promise, and no bargain, that I personally cannot keep." He shifted his glare to Jin. "If that's not enough for the Cobras of Caelian, then we shall shake the dust of that world from our feet and return home."

"They'll come," Jin promised, a lump rising into her throat. "Enough of them will."

Siraj growled something under his breath. "I hope so, if only for the sake of my father," he said darkly. "*He* certainly believed in you." He shifted his gaze to the display, and the Troft freighter starting to move away from them. "But we shall see. We shall see."

The quarters Warrior had assigned his guests appeared to be a standard crew room, hastily and incompletely modified to accommodate human physiology. At one end of the room was a three-tiered bunk bed, at the other a compact shower/toilet/sink combination, with the walls between them occupied by a fold-down game table and a set of three lockers.

By the time Lorne dragged himself wearily through the door, Nissa had finished her shower and was fast asleep on the top bunk, dressed in one of a set of robes that the Trofts had left for them. Croi, in the midst of a cloud of steam behind the frosted glass, was busily scrubbing himself down.

Wearily, Lorne dropped onto the lowest bunk and pried off his shoes. He was sorely tempted to just roll over onto his side, close his eyes, and forget his own shower until after he'd gotten some desperately needed sleep. But he was filthy, his whole body ached with the day's activities, and a soothing shower would go a long way toward making him feel like a civilized human being again.

Besides, if he went to sleep now, it would probably be hours before he woke up. Croi had a right to hear about the decision Lorne and Warrior had come to sooner than then.

And he had a right to hear about it from Lorne.

Lorne had fallen into a light doze, still sitting up, when he was jarred awake by the gentle slapping of Croi's hand on his shoulder. "Broom?" the other said. "Shower's free."

Lorne blinked his eyes open, wincing at the sandlike grit beneath the lids. "Thanks," he said. "But we need to talk first."

"Not long, I hope," Croi said, sitting down on the edge of the bed beside him. "What are we talking about?"

Lorne hesitated, searching for the best way to say this. But he was too tired to even try to be diplomatic. "Warrior and I have decided where to take Isis," he said.

Croi's eyes narrowed. "*You* decided?"

"Yes," Lorne said. "We're taking it to Caelian."

Croi's jaw dropped. "*Caelian?*"

"Think about it," Lorne urged. "He wants it hidden? Fine—there are a hundred places on Caelian where we could put it where any invaders would literally kill themselves trying to get to it. You want to use it? Also fine—the people there are rough and tough, and heading to Aventine to fight a war would probably seem like a vacation compared to their life there."

"I don't know," Croi said, rubbing the bridge of his nose thoughtfully. But at least he wasn't yelling. "I'm not involved with the Cobra screening process myself, but the people who are say that the average Caelianite is borderline crazy."

"Because they prefer to stay put in their homes instead of moving to Viminal?"

"That's probably part of it," Croi said. "The point is that we may have trouble finding three hundred men who can pass the screening test."

"So open it up to women, too," Lorne suggested.

Something behind Croi's eyes seemed to suddenly turn to stone. "You're not serious."

"Why not?" Lorne countered. "You want to win this war and throw the Trofts off Aventine? Or are you more interested in playing by someone else's idea of what the proper rules of life ought to be?"

Croi snorted. "Look who's talking about playing by someone else's rules. Is that what this whole thing is about to you? Some bizarre way to justify your mother and your family?"

Lorne stared at him. "Are you even *listening* to yourself? Do you really think I had a plan involving stuff I didn't even know about until an hour ago?"

"It hardly matters what I think anymore, does it?" Croi shot back. "You and Ingidi-inhiliziyo have made your deal. The rest of us either can like it or live with it."

"Pretty much, yes," Lorne said, suddenly tired of this conversation. "And while you're deciding which you're going to do, I suggest you get some sleep. The whole thing will look a lot more reasonable in the morning."

"Which will be just about the time we'll be getting there, won't it?" Croi growled. "What is it, thirty hours to Caelian at a freighter's top speed?"

"From here, about thirty-one," Lorne said, standing up and starting to pull off his clothes. "I'm going to take a shower. Don't wait up."

Croi's only answer was another snort as he pulled his feet up onto the bunk, stretched out on his side, and pointedly rolled over to turn his back to Lorne and the universe at large. With a sigh, Lorne finished undressing, adding his torn, filthy, smoky clothing to the pile beside the door.

He was about to step into the shower when something made him turn around. Croi was still turned to the wall, but Nissa was lying facing out into the room. Her eyes were closed, and her breathing was slow and regular, but as Lorne keyed in his infrareds he saw that her heat signature was too high for that of a sleeping person.

Had she woken up during his argument with Croi? If so, how much had she heard? And what had she made of it all?

But his brain was too foggy to even consider such questions. Closing the shower door behind him, he turned on the water. His only goal right now was to clean himself off, get dressed, and climb up into the remaining bunk.

And to stay awake until he got there.

CHAPTER FIFTEEN

Given the way the Troft at the reception point had snarled at them, Jody spent the entire walk across Stronghold expecting to find an execution block waiting for her and Freylan at the other end. It was therefore with a mixture of relief and embarrassment that she discovered they were simply being escorted to the three-story Government Building near the center of town, where they were taken straight up to the governor's residence on the top floor.

They found Governor Uy standing in the living room, gazing out one of the north-facing windows, his hands clasped tightly behind his back. "Ms. Broom; Mr. Sonderby," he greeted them, looking surprised as he strode across the room toward them. "So that *was* your aircar I saw put down a few minutes ago. I was hoping it was."

"Yes, sir," Jody said as their Troft guard backed out of the apartment and closed the door. "We're very sorry for the intrusion."

"Don't be, my dear, dear young people," Uy said feelingly as he reached them.

And to Jody's astonishment he pulled both her and Freylan close to him, wrapping them in a tight group hug.

Which wasn't at all what it seemed. "Cameras and microphones in the living and dining room; microphones everywhere else," the governor whispered as he pressed their heads close to his. "Don't say anything you don't want them to hear. Understood?"

Jody nodded, a tiny movement in Uy's crushing embrace, and felt Freylan do likewise. Uy held the hug another second, then released them and stepped back. "You must be famished," he went on. "And badly in need of sleep, too, I warrant. An entire night spent out in Wonderland. My wife Elssa's in the other room—shall I ask her to fix you some food? Or would you prefer a place to rest first?"

"Both sound good," Jody said. "But before that, maybe you can tell us what in the Worlds happened here. I mean, we take off yesterday to get some samples, and come back to find armed Trofts in the streets."

"If it was a shock to you, I can assure you it was no less so to us," Uy said, gesturing to a conversation circle at the west end of the room. "The fact of the matter is that we appear to have been invaded."

"Incredible," Jody said as they all sat down, she and Freylan on one of the couches, Uy in an armchair facing them. "But that would certainly explain the laser slash marks we saw as we were coming in. They came in shooting?"

"Not exactly," Uy said. "I think they more or less expected us to simply and calmly accept their presence without making any trouble."

"And you didn't?" Freylan suggested.

Uy's throat tightened. "Not at all," he confirmed. "We were afraid that if we waited until they'd settled in and disembarked their troops it would put the civilians in greater danger than if we attacked before that happened. So we did. The Cobras targeted those little wings where most of the weapons seemed to be clustered and opened fire."

Jody winced. "Only even Cobra antiarmor lasers didn't do any good against them."

"No, they didn't," Uy said, his voice going bitter. "And then they fired back. We lost eighteen Cobras in that first salvo."

"Sending a message," Freylan murmured, his voice thoughtful. "The way they did last night."

Uy looked sharply at him, but Jody lifted a calming hand. It wasn't like the Trofts listening in didn't know all about last night's events, after all.

As Uy himself also quickly realized. "Yes, I woke up in time to catch the end of that show," he said. He hesitated, and Jody saw him brace himself. "You said they sent the same kind of message?"

"Their return fire killed a Cobra named Buckley," Jody said. "I think he was the only one."

"Buckley," Uy mused, and she saw him relax fractionally at the news that the Troft's violent response hadn't taken his own son. "Inevitable, I suppose, that it was him. You didn't know the man, but Joe was one of those who courted death on nearly a daily basis, yet always came cheerfully back for more."

"I'm sorry," Jody said, quietly. "So that brings the total to sixteen?"

"Oh, it brings it much higher than that," Uy said sourly. "We'd learned our lesson on that one, all right, but the day's seminars were hardly over. A few minutes after we gave up our assault, a ramp lowered from partway up the bow of each of the ships and a half dozen floatcycles came buzzing out and headed over the wall toward the gate. We took out three of them before the ship's lasers opened fire again. We lost five more on that one."

"I spotted what looked like the wreckage of a house at the south end of town," Freylan said. "Bad marksmanship on the Trofts' part? Or were some Cobras using it as a base?"

"Very perceptive," Uy said, nodding. "Yes, once the soldiers on the floatcycles got the gate open, the ship ramps went down all the way and a group of armored trucks came out and rolled into town. Six of the Cobras figured they would have a clear line of sight from the old Wymack place and decided to try a concentration of firepower on the windshield of the first truck in line."

"Did it work?" Jody asked.

Uy shrugged. "Better than anything else we'd tried, which isn't saying much. The volley stopped the tank, though the spotters said the windshield instantly blackened where the lasers hit, which blocked most of the blast and limited the damage. The Trofts' helmet faceplates work the same way, incidentally, which makes fingertip lasers useless against them. A close-in antiarmor shot will overwhelm that particular defense, though. We found that out later."

"Also the hard way, I expect," Freylan murmured.

"Very much so," Uy said. "As I said, the attack stopped the truck, though the spotters think the driver was still alive when they hauled him out and took him back to the ship. But before the Cobras could shift aim to the next truck in line, the northern ship decided to up the ante and fired a missile into the house. The blast not only killed all six Cobras, but also two civilians in the house next door."

Jody winced. "And after the trucks came in and started unloading soldiers, I take it you took a crack at them, too?"

"Of course," Uy said. "We had slightly better luck here. Hardly surprising, I suppose, since one-on-one ground warfare was what Cobras were originally designed for. Turns out their stunners work just fine straight through Troft armor, though you have to get within two or three meters for that kind of shot. The sonics and arcthrowers are good for a couple of meters more, and antiarmor lasers can nail them at about ten meters—twelve or thirteen if you aim for the faceplates. All told, we took out probably fifteen of them."

"At a cost of...?" Jody asked carefully.

Uy exhaled. "Fifteen more Cobras and five civilians. After that, the Trofts declared something they called martial stasis and ordered everyone to stay indoors under penalty of immediate execution."

Jody felt a shiver run up her back. Stronghold's original Cobra contingent had only numbered about a hundred and twenty. In a single day of facing down the Trofts—possibly even in just a few hours—they'd lost over a third of them. "What about food and water?" she asked. "Are the Trofts supplying those to the people?"

Uy shook his head. "They're apparently assuming we all have our own supplies—which we do, of course—and that we can make do until they decide the resistance has ended and that we can start coming out and shopping again."

For a moment no one spoke. "I didn't see any of the trucks you mentioned on our way in," Freylan said. "Did they pull them back into the ships?"

"I doubt it," Uy said. "I obviously haven't gotten any word from our spotters since we were all sent to our rooms, but my guess is that they're just hidden or camouflaged enough to make them hard to spot." He smiled tightly. "They know enough about Caelian to know there are a lot more Cobras here than the ones they've got pinned down in Stronghold. They aren't going to want to make it too easy for any fresh attackers to sniff them out."

And even Stronghold's remaining Cobras were probably not nearly as pinned down as the Trofts might think, Jody knew. But she knew better than to say that out loud.

"What I *do* know is that the Trofts have also instituted foot patrols," Uy continued. "I see them passing by as they roam the streets. We've had a couple of incidents nearby where they've fired shots, but whether they were shooting into the buildings or at someone outside I couldn't tell. I don't even know if anyone was killed or wounded. I've asked the soldiers outside to allow me to speak with one of their senior officers, but so far there's been no response."

He took a deep breath, his eyes locking on Jody's face. "So," he said, and stopped.

Jody grimaced. She knew what he wanted to ask: whether his son was all right, how many Cobras there were out there, and what they were planning.

And they both knew that she couldn't say a thing, about any of it.

"I have another question," Freylan spoke up. "You said the big ramp opened to let the floatcycles and trucks out. I also noticed two smaller hatchways on either side of the main ramp—horizontal ones, maybe three meters long and one high. Any idea what those are for?"

"You have sharp eyes," Uy complimented him. "Those are the access hatches for a bunch of dart-shaped flying things like the two they sent out to meet you a few minutes ago. Sensor drones, probably, since the first thing they did after the ships landed was to pop those hatches and send out a dozen of the things."

"A dozen from each ship, or a dozen between them?" Freylan asked.

"Six from each ship," Uy said. "More specifically, three from each of the hatches."

"Are they still out there?" Jody asked, her stomach tightening. If the Trofts had drones watching every move her father and the rest of the Cobras made...

"No, and they probably won't be sending more out any time soon," Uy said. "That was the other minor success of the day: we managed to nail seven of the drones—three that were hovering over Stronghold during our first attack, and another four when they were returning to their ships. As far as I know they didn't send any of them out again until the two that escorted you in."

His throat tightened. "All of that cost us another two Cobras."

"I'm sorry," Jody said quietly.

"As are we all," Uy said. "One other thing which may interest you. A couple of our spotters told me that, given the ship-mounted lasers' firing pattern, they think the weapons are automatically aimed but manually fired."

"Really," Jody said. "Yes, that *is* interesting. Do they have any ideas as to why the Trofts would set it up that way?"

"I assume it has to do with avoiding misfires," Uy said. "Or possibly sensor-locked fire controls are too easy to confuse or manipulate. I just thought it was curious, and that maybe you would, too."

"Yes, indeed," Jody said. And with that, she decided, she had enough to fill a preliminary report. Time to check in with her father on the other side of the wall. "I appreciate the information— I can't tell you how concerned Freylan and I were when we saw all those laser burns."

"I can imagine," Uy said, giving her a strained smile. "But enough talk. Can I now interest you in some food?"

"Yes, please," Jody said. She stood up.

And abruptly swayed, her knees buckling under her and sending her toppling toward the floor.

Both men lunged toward her. Uy was closer and got there first, catching her in a cradling embrace before she could hit the rug, pulling her in close to his chest. "Ms. Broom?" he asked anxiously.

Jody leaned in close to him. "West-facing bedroom," she whispered. "Any cameras?"

She felt the governor twitch as he realized that her collapse had been a fake. "No cameras," he whispered back. "At least one microphone."

"Sorry," she said aloud, breathing heavily into his neck as she pushed herself weakly away from him. "Sorry. That was embarrassing."

"Don't worry about it," Uy said, easing her around into a sitting position on the floor. Freylan had his own grip on her arm now, helping her down. "Are you feeling ill? Do you need to lie down?"

"I'm okay," Jody assured both of them. "But I think maybe I'd better lie down for a while. I guess I was more tired than I realized."

"Caelian can take a lot out of a person," Uy said. "Come on, let's get you to the guest room. Mr. Sonderby?"

The men each took an arm and helped Jody to her feet. Then, walking her like a toddler, they took her out of the living room, down a short hallway, and into a small but cheerfully furnished bedroom.

"Can I get you anything else?" Uy asked as they sat her down on the edge of the bed.

"No, this will be wonderful," Jody assured him. "Maybe Freylan can take you up on that offer of food."

"Actually, I think I'm too tired to eat yet, too," Freylan said. "It's not like either of us got much sleep out on the river."

"I suppose not," Jody said, putting a warning finger to her lips. He nodded, touching his ear to show he understood. "Maybe the governor could find someplace for you to lie down, too."

"I was thinking I could just stay here with you," he suggested. "I mean, not *with* you," he added, his face reddening. "I could sleep in that chair over there."

Jody frowned. *Trouble?* she mouthed silently.

You might need me, he mouthed back.

She hesitated, then nodded. "As long as you don't snore, sure, help yourself."

"I'll leave you two alone, then," Uy said, backing toward the door. "Whenever you're ready for food, just let me know." With a final nod at each of them, he left the room, closing the door behind him.

Now what? Freylan mouthed.

I need to find something to signal with, Jody mouthed back, looking around the room. The Trofts had taken her flashlight, and a quick check of the lamps showed that they were the multilevel type that would be useless for Dida signaling. Uy undoubtedly had a flashlight out there somewhere, but getting to it with Troft cameras watching could be tricky. "I meant what I said about the snoring," she said aloud as she went to the nightstand and pulled open the drawer. There was a pen and a pad of note paper inside, along with a small box of tissues, a small reader, and a set of book chips. No light. She started to close the drawer—

"You know, this bed really *is* big enough for two," Freylan said, coming up suddenly behind her and grabbing her hand. As she frowned at him, he reached into the drawer and pulled out the notepad. "I mean, I could sleep on one side and you could sleep on the other," he went on, stepping back and holding up the pad so that Jody was looking at its surface. He rotated it ninety degrees, turning the edge to her, then rotated it back up again. He repeated the operation, raising his eyebrows questioningly.

Jody smiled tightly, inclining her head to him. Providing her father and the other Cobras were paying attention, it should work. "Fine," she said, taking the pad from him and walking around the end of the bed toward the window. "Just be sure you *stay* on that side."

"I will," he promised, sitting down on the bed with a slight but audible creak from the frame.

Jody reached the other side of the bed and sat down facing the window. One of the trees beyond the wall had an odd look, and with a shiver she realized it was one of the ones that the Troft ship had blasted last night in an effort to kill the Cobra holding on behind it. Holding the pad up in front of her chest, she flipped it over and back five times. *Dit dit dit dit dit. Calling—anyone there?*

She repeated the signal, and again, and again, systematically checking out all the different trees she could see from her vantage point. Nothing. Were all Cobras positioned off to the side where they couldn't see her? Or could she be too far inside the window for even a Cobra to spot the flashing white of the paper?

And then, from one of the trees just to the left of the blasted one, she spotted a small, flickering light. *Dit dah dit dah dit dah. Received and understood—stand by.*

Taking a deep breath, she set the pad flat against her chest and waited. Two minutes later, the light began to flash again. *Dit dit dah dit dit dah. Ready—proceed.*

Squaring her shoulders, hoping her fatigued brain remembered everything Uy had told them, she began her report.

Paul finished his report, and for a minute the rest of the Cobras in the circle were silent. "Seems pretty obvious to me," Harli said at last. "The doorways at the base of the ship are easiest to get to, which means they're the ones that'll be the most heavily guarded. These upper ones, the big ramp and the little drone ports, are the ones they're not expecting trouble from. Ergo, those are our best bet."

"Except that all three are way too high for us to get to," Matigo pointed out. "Unless you know a way to rewire the spookers for more altitude?"

"No, but I wasn't really planning on a frontal assault," Harli said. "I was thinking more along the lines of delivering a package or two. Tracker, what's the explosives situation?"

"We've got enough to make a good-sized crater," Tracker confirmed. " 'Course, we're first gonna have to find a way to make the Trofts open up and say ah."

"I assume you're suggesting we throw a bomb in through one of the ports?" Paul asked.

"Exactly," Harli said, nodding. "If Dad's right about the lasers being fired manually, it should work. Actually, I should have figured that one out on my own—auto-fire is way too easy to manipulate. If we toss in a few mining explosives, there's a good chance they'll get in before the gunners spot the threat and take them out."

"We can't just use them as is, though," Tracker warned. "Right now, everything's got hard-wire triggers. We'll have to put together some timers or else rig up something wireless to set them off."

"That's okay—we've got time to work that out," Harli said. "Go grab everyone who's got explosives experience and get them working on delivery packages. Let's be optimistic and make four, one for each of the ports. Kemp, Matigo, you grab your spookers and head toward Essbend. They should have been here by now—maybe they missed that last message Dad was able to send out."

"Or they may be tied up with something else," Matigo suggested.

"In that case, untie them and tell them to gear their rears on over here," Harli said grimly. "They can leave a squad to guard the town, but everyone else is with us. We're going to need everyone we can get if we're going to take these bastards down."

"Got it." Matigo gestured to Kemp, and together they strode off into the woods.

Harli eyed Paul. "You got a brave little girl there, Broom," he said, almost grudgingly. "Don't worry—when the time comes, we'll get her back out."

"I know," Paul confirmed, feeling a familiar tightness in his chest. It was a tightness that had been with him almost continually during his long years of service to Aventine. It was the tightness that came of knowing that someone he cared about was in continual, deadly danger.

He'd mostly come to terms with that feeling as far as his two Cobra sons went. He'd never counted on having to feel that way about his daughter. Or his wife.

Caelian and Qasama, the two most dangerous places in the

known universe. And he'd sent members of his family to each of them.

With an effort, he pushed away the dark thoughts. Dark thoughts in the face of danger were a good way to get yourself killed. "What do you want me to tell her?" he asked.

"Tell her—" Harli broke off as he sent a flurry of fingertip laser fire at a group of doremis that had just launched themselves from low-hanging tree branches toward the two Cobras. "Tell her we'll contact her tomorrow morning," he said as the birds thudded into the carpet of dead leaves at their feet. "Let's make it right at nine-twenty. By then we should have the bombs ready and either have Essbend's group here or at least on the way."

"Right." Paul turned and started to climb back up his signaling tree.

"And if she can," Harli added, his voice sounding a little embarrassed, "have her tell my father that we're all right."

"I will," Paul promised.

And as he resumed his climb, he wondered distantly if Harli was also feeling that same tightness in his chest.

Jody had fallen into a light doze on the bed when she was startled awake by Freylan's hand tapping against her cheek. She opened her eyes, and was opening her mouth to speak when he touched a finger to her lips. Frowning at the unexpected intimacy, she reached up and started to push the finger aside.

And then the reality of their situation came roaring back through the fog, and she nodded both understanding and her thanks. *What is it?* she mouthed.

He pointed to the window. *Your dad's signaling.*

Jody sat up, blinking her eyes to focus again. *Dit dit dit dit dit*, she could see the small light flashing from the tree.

She picked up the pad. *Dit dit dah dit dit dah*, she sent.

Three minutes later, with a quiet sigh, she again laid the pad aside. *What is it?* Freylan mouthed.

More instructions tomorrow at nine-twenty, she told him. *Hang loose until then. Harli Uy's best to his father.*

Freylan grimaced. *Hang loose.*

Jody nodded. Like they were really going to relax here in the middle of an occupied city. *You hungry?*

Still more tired than hungry, he told her.

Me too. Pulling her feet up, she lay back down on the bed. Fifteen minutes, she promised herself, and then she would get up and go find food.

It was after noon when Governor Uy finally came in and woke them up with the news that lunch was ready. A few minutes later Jody dragged herself out of the room and headed toward the dining room, an equally bleary Freylan beside her.

It was, she decided, going to be a long, long day.

CHAPTER SIXTEEN

The next twenty-six hours were a flurry of work and preparation, with the added complication of continually having to shoot, stun, or beat back Caelian's assortment of deadly wildlife. For Paul, who'd already gone through one mostly sleepless night, the list of the day's activities promised to be an uphill climb.

Fortunately, Harli was a good enough leader to know better than to push his men too hard, especially with a Caelian Cobra's need for extra alertness. Despite his long to-do list, he made sure each member of the group got at least two four-hour sleep periods sometime during that long day and night. Paul, who knew nothing about explosives and was clearly considered by most of the others to be useless as a guard, got somewhat more.

Aside from the sleep and meal breaks, though, the group worked around the clock. By nine-fifteen the next morning, everything was ready.

Except that the Essbend Cobras still hadn't arrived.

"What the *hell* is keeping them?" Harli fumed as he glared westward, as if sheer force of will would enable him to see through a hundred thirty kilometers of wilderness to Caelian's second largest settlement.

"So do we wait?" Matigo asked.

Harli's jaw tightened. "No," he said. "Everyone's ready, and delay just gives the Trofts more time to spot the teams." He lifted a finger suddenly. "You know, come to think of it, maybe we can use this to our advantage. Broom?"

"Ready," Paul said.

"Okay," Harli said slowly, eyes narrowed in thought. "Send this to your daughter..."

With the remnants of her long day and short night having made for an early bedtime, Jody had woken up an hour before dawn, with a fresh plan of action for the day. Her father had told her during that last contact that he would be sending her information that she was in turn to leak to the listening Trofts. Jody had spent much of the previous day wondering how exactly she would do that without it *looking* like she was deliberately feeding it to them.

Now, with ten straight hours of sleep having finally cleared the dust and cobwebs from her brain, she'd figured out a plan. After all, an information slip would seem much more reasonable if the aliens thought *she* thought the governor's residence was no longer being monitored.

And so, with the rest of the household still asleep, she set about examining every square centimeter of the residence's public areas, searching for, finding, and destroying every hidden camera and buried microphone that the invaders had surreptitiously planted.

All of them...except one.

By the time Uy and his wife Elssa emerged from their room, she was able to report her success and give them a carefully edited version of what she and her father had discussed earlier from her guest room vantage point.

By the time the morning's message finally came through, Uy, Elssa, Freylan, and—hopefully—the listening Trofts were all ready and eager to hear it.

"It turns out your son didn't tell us everything when we were with him two nights ago," she told the group assembled in the living room. "The Cobras from Essbend hadn't shown up yet because they were working on something special to use against the Trofts. Apparently, they've finished it and are now on their way."

"Are we talking about a plan, or a device, or what?" Elssa asked. "I'm worried about the people of Stronghold."

"The biggest worry they have is regaining their freedom," Uy reminded her firmly. "Whatever Essbend's come up with, it's worth the risk to try it."

"Dad didn't say what exactly it is, Mrs. Uy," Jody said. "But from everything else we've seen on Caelian, I'm willing to bet it's going to be spectacular."

"I wonder which of the ships they'll target," Freylan mused, craning his neck to look out the window at the Troft warship looming against the forest backdrop to the north. "Be just our luck if they take out the south one and we don't get to watch."

"Well, you've got a fifty-fifty chance," Jody reminded him as she stood up. "Enjoy. Me, I need to get back in case they need to send us something else. I just wanted you all to have a heads-up."

"We appreciate that," Uy said, the crinkly lines around his eyes telling Jody that he was fully aware of the part he and the others were playing in her disinformation scheme. "Let me know if there's anything else they need me to do."

"I will," Jody said, and left the room.

And that was that, she thought, permitting herself a small smile as she once again settled herself and her notepad by the guest room window. If the Trofts had even a shred of military competence, not to mention a flicker of curiosity, they would be readying one or more of their drones to take to the air and head toward Essbend for a look at the Cobras' mysterious superweapon.

And when they did, they would be in for a surprise. Hopefully, a very loud, very violent surprise.

"That's it," Lorne said, nodding ahead at the dark planetary curve stretching out across much of the Tlossie freighter's wrap-around display. "That's Caelian."

[A place of lush greenery, it is,] Warrior commented from beside him. [A peaceful place, it appears from the sky.]

[A peaceful appearance, it is a lie,] Lorne told him, gazing at the thin blur of atmosphere at the edge of the dark disk, a queasy feeling in the pit of his stomach. There were reasons why people didn't usually come out of hyperspace this close to a planetary body, chief among them the fact that doing it wrong could easily get you killed. Apparently, Warrior had decided he would rather take those risks than give any enemy ships or probes in the area the time and distance for a long, lingering look at them.

Either he had a great deal of confidence in his crew, or else he had a reckless streak that Lorne hadn't previously been aware of. Or possibly both.

[A landing site, you will now provide one.]

"Working on it," Lorne told him, shifting his eyes from the main display to the false-color sensor image and trying to figure out just where over Caelian they were. If that was the edge of Southway they were coming up on, then the Whitebank River should be about eight hundred kilometers to the east. They could look along the river until they found the heat signature of Essbend, tucked between the water and the Banded Hills. After that, it would be a simple matter of going due east another hundred thirty kilometers until they found Stronghold.

[A radio challenge, it is given,] the Troft at the comm board reported. [Our identity, it is demanded.]

[Our identity, transmit it,] Warrior said calmly.

[Our identity, it is transmitted.]

Lorne took a deep breath. So the invaders *had* sent a force to Caelian. He had hoped fervently that they wouldn't bother.

Still, they *were* aboard an heir-ship of the Tlossie demesne. The invaders had honored that immunity once. They would surely do so again.

[A second craft, it has arrived at the planet,] the Troft at the sensors spoke up suddenly. [A radio challenge, the planet has also sent one.]

[The new craft, identify and locate it,] Warrior ordered. His voice was still calm, but Lorne could see that his radiator membranes were fluttering slightly against his arms.

[The craft, a medium-range transport it is,] the Troft reported. [Its location, at *var* by *yei* by *sist* it is.]

Lorne felt his stomach tighten. That vector put it slightly above and almost directly behind their own freighter. If someone was trying to box them in against the planet, he was doing a damn good job of it.

[Our immediate departure, the planetary authority demands,] the Troft at the comm board reported. [Our presence, it will not permit.]

[Our identity, again transmit it,] Warrior said. [Our business and presence, they must not be interfered with.]

[Our immediate departure, the authority insists upon it,] the Troft repeated. His radiator membranes were starting to flutter now, as well. [A landing, he will use force to prevent one.]

[Armaments, does this vessel possess them?] Lorne asked carefully.

[Armaments, it does not possess them,] Warrior said, an edge of anger coloring his voice. [A bluff, the authority makes one. An heir of the Tlos'khin'fahi Demesne, he will not attack him.]

[Our departure, the authority demands it,] the Troft at the comm said tensely. His membranes had now risen halfway up from his arms. [Our final warning, he states this is it.]

[Our course, continue it,] Warrior ordered. [A bluff, he makes one.]

[The order, I obey it.]

[If a bluff, he does not make one?] Lorne asked carefully.

[A bluff, he makes one,] Warrior said firmly. [A watch, you will keep it. A lesson, you will learn it.]

Or else he has a reckless streak, the thought ran through Lorne's mind again. Grimacing, he hunched his shoulders and settled in to watch.

Paul was staring with full telescopics at his assigned drone hatchway on the southern warship, waiting for the first sign that it was about to open, when the whole image suddenly spun and veered crazily. Jerking as a flash of vertigo slapped across his brain, he hastily keyed his opticals back to normal sight.

Just in time to see the southern Troft warship lift ponderously from the landing field. Leaning forward as large ships tended to do, it threw power to its grav lifts and rose into the sky, heading westward.

"What the *hell*?" Harli breathed from Paul's side.

"Looks like Jody convinced them, all right," Paul said grimly. "Only instead of sending out their drones, they decided to go check out Essbend for themselves."

"Well, *damn*," Harli said, turning around to gaze at the departing warship as it headed off into the distance.

"So what now?" Paul asked.

For a long moment Harli didn't answer. Paul watched as the Troft warship continued to climb and faded into the morning haze. "They want to play it that way?" Harli said. "Fine—we can play it that way, too. Everyone grab your bombs and come with me."

Without waiting for a response, he set off into the forest at a fast jog. "Where are we going?" Paul asked, hurrying to catch up.

Harli flashed him a tight grin. "Maybe the Trofts haven't thought about this part of it," he said, "but they've just taken fifty percent of their heavy firepower out of the picture."

He turned to face front again, his grin turning into a snarl. "Let's see if we can do something about the other fifty percent."

[The atmosphere, a ship has cleared it,] the Troft at the sensor board reported. [A course to our vessel, it has set one.]

[The type of craft, identify it,] Warrior ordered.

[A Drim'hco'plai Class II city sentry warship, it is one,] the Troft said. [The Aventine city sentries, of the same type it is.]

[Orders, I request them,] the helmsman spoke up.

[Our course, continue it,] Warrior said. [Our identity, again transmit it.]

[The warship's weapons, he has activated them,] the sensor Troft said, his membranes fully extended now.

[Orders, I request them,] the helmsman repeated more urgently. [Evasion, shall I initiate it?]

[Evasion, you shall not initiate it,] Warrior said.

Behind Lorne, the bridge door slid open, and he turned as Croi and Nissa hurried in. "What's going on?" Croi demanded, his eyes flicking over the displays. "Someone out there said we were under attack."

"Right now, we're just under observation," Lorne told them. "But the other is definitely waiting in the wings."

"Anything I can do?" Croi asked.

"I doubt it," Lorne said. "Surgeons are usually more useful after a fight than during it."

"Funny," Croi muttered. "I *can* fight, you know."

"So go get your biggest scalpel," Lorne said. "Something the size of a sword, if you have one."

"Broom—"

"If you haven't, I suggest you both go back to our quarters and wait," Lorne cut him off. "And if you hear laser fire, you'd better get all the rest of your scalpels ready."

"New blip," Khatir snapped, hunching over the transport's helm display. "Big one, coming up from the surface."

"Identification?" Jin asked.

"It's too far away for good resolution," Khatir said. "But from its overall size and shape, it could be one of the same kind of sentry ship we faced in the streets of Sollas."

Jin's hands curled into fists. She'd hoped against hope that the invaders would consider Caelian so useless and insignificant that they wouldn't even bother sending a force to occupy it.

And not only had they sent a force, they'd sent enough of one that they could spare a warship from their ground operation to come up here and check out an unexpected and uninvited intruder.

Or rather, *two* uninvited intruders. "Rashida Vil, can you confirm yet whether or not the freighter up there is the Tlossie who refueled us at Aventine?"

"What do you want me to say?" the young woman asked stiffly, throwing Jin a dark look. "We're too far away to see the hull markings, and we never had a transmitted ID signal from them."

"But who else could they be?" Siraj put in brusquely. "They're the only ones who knew who we were. They're the only ones who could have guessed where we were going." He shook his head. "The mission is over, Jasmine Moreau. I say we leave right now, before that warship gets within firing range."

"And return to Qasama empty-handed?" Jin asked. "That will hardly bring us honor."

"Better to arrive empty-handed than with no hands at all," Siraj countered. "If we linger, they'll take us all."

"We need allies," Jin insisted.

"There are none," Rashida said, her tone dark. "Your hope has failed, Jasmine Moreau. There are no friends for Qasama anywhere out here. There are only enemies."

"So you agree with Siraj Akim." Jin turned to Zoshak. "Carsh Zoshak?" she invited.

"I must also agree," Zoshak said. Unlike Siraj and Rashida, he sounded more disappointed than angry or bitter. "The freighter must have followed us here, coming out of hyperspace ahead of us so as to be able to give the alert to the other invaders. Why else would they be here?"

"I don't know," Jin said. "But the Tlossies aren't *other* invaders. They're not part of the group who've attacked our worlds."

"Yet here they are," Siraj pointed out, gesturing toward the forward display. "If they're not the invaders' allies, answer Carsh Zoshak's question. Why are they here?"

"Why did they allow us to escape Aventine instead of betraying us right then and there?" Jin countered. "Here, we still have a chance to escape. At Aventine, surrounded by warships, we would have had none at all."

"Perhaps they wished to see where we'd go next," Rashida suggested.

"According to Siraj Akim's reasoning, they already knew where we were going," Jin reminded her. "You can't have it both ways."

"We may not get it either way," Khatir put in, his voice suddenly odd. "The rising warship isn't heading toward us. It's heading toward the freighter."

"That's good, isn't it?" Rashida asked, looking at her own set of displays.

"Good for us," Khatir agreed. "Not so good for the Tlossies."

Siraj sniffed. "A meeting of allies."

"To what end?" Zoshak asked. "They can speak together just as well by comm."

"He's right," Jin said grimly. "The invaders are going in because they want a closer look at the freighter."

"As I said, not so good for the Tlossies," Khatir said. "Jasmine Moreau, do you wish me to go around them and try for the surface?"

Jin braced herself. "No," she said. "Transmit the clearance codes we got from the transport's pilot back at Qasama. Tell the warship that the Tlossies are with us."

Siraj's mouth dropped open. "*What*?"

"They risked their lives to help us back at Aventine," Jin said. "It's our turn now to help them."

"And if the Tlossies aren't as they appear?" Siraj demanded. "If they're allies of the invaders and are merely playing games with us?"

"They're not our enemies," Jin insisted. "They sent Merrick and me to Qasama to help you. They refueled us and got us away from Aventine. And they've been our trading partners for decades."

"Do you truly believe they're our friends?" Zoshak asked.

Jin looked him straight in the eye. "Yes."

Zoshak exhaled heavily. "Then I say we do it," he said. "Jasmine Moreau is our ally, Siraj Akim, and so far her instincts have proved to be good. I say we trust those instincts one more time."

"I too am willing," Rashida said.

Siraj snorted. "You're a woman."

"I'm translator and second pilot," Rashida said stiffly. "My opinion has a right to be heard and weighed."

Siraj glared at her a moment, then shifted the glare to Khatir. "And you, Ghofl Khatir?"

Khatir shrugged. "My opinion hardly matters," he pointed out. "You're the senior Djinni aboard. The decision is yours."

"But whatever you decide, it must be quick," Jin added.

Siraj locked eyes with her, his lips compressed into a thin, pale line. "What would you say to them?" he asked.

"We tell them we're from the Qasaman contingent," Jin said, thinking quickly. "Just in case the clearance codes are different between the different invasion groups. The Tlossies are a potential ally, and we were ordered to bring them here for a closer look at Caelian."

"Why would they want a look at a living death trap?" Siraj scoffed.

"Because there may be useful plants and animals down there," Khatir offered. "Or possibly mineral wealth."

"We'll go with the plants," Jin decided. "Especially their potential pharmaceutical uses. The Tlossies do a lot with that sort of thing."

Siraj gave a curt nod and shifted his eyes to Rashida. "Go ahead," he ordered her. "Be convincing."

Rashida turned around and keyed her board. [Your attention, we request it,] she said in cattertalk.

Jin listened with half an ear, watching the displays and trying to figure out what they would do if the invaders didn't go for their story. At the moment, the warship was far enough in, and their own transport far enough out, that they could duck back into hyperspace reasonably safely and get out of the system.

But that would mean abandoning the freighter to face the warship alone. Worse, by identifying themselves as the Tlossies' escort, Rashida had now effectively linked the two ships together. If the Qasamans made a run for it, or did anything else guilty-looking, that same level of guilt would automatically shift over to the freighter.

[—your course, you will hold it,] the Troft voice ordered, the words snapping Jin out of her thoughts. [Your orders, we will examine them.]

"Uh-oh," Khatir murmured.

Rashida turned around. "Jasmine Moreau?" she asked tightly. "What do I say?"

"What do I do?" Khatir added.

And suddenly, all eyes were on Jin. "Hold your course," she told them, her mouth going dry. "Just hold your course. I'll think of something."

❖   ❖   ❖

"Fire in three!" Harli shouted, his voice from half a kilometer away perfectly clear in Paul's enhanced hearing. "Audios down!"

Obediently, Paul keyed them back...and exactly three seconds later, the forest was rocked by a violent triple explosion. The echoes of the blast faded away.

And with a softer but even more horrendous crunching noise, the three huge steelwood trees that Harli's men had mined tilted over and fell, slamming with a rolling crunch against the top of the Troft warship.

The ship was big and massive. But so were the trees, and the ship's design had given it a dangerously narrow base...and as Paul watched in awe the ship tilted sideways and ponderously toppled over to slam into the city's outer wall. For a moment it balanced there, squeezed like the center of a sandwich between stainless steel wall below and Caelian steelwood tree above.

But the wall had never been designed for this kind of abuse. The rustling of branches from the fallen trees was still audible when the wall gave an abrupt screech of its own and collapsed beneath the warship's weight. With a final crunch of buildings and vehicles, the Troft ship came to rest on its side.

"Attack!" Paul heard Harli's distant shout. "All Cobras, attack!"

"We have no choice," Siraj said, his voice tight. "Do you hear me, Jasmine Moreau? We must leave. *Now.*"

"Ghofl Khatir?" Jin asked, her eyes flicking back and forth between the approaching warship's image and the rapidly decreasing distance indicator on the nav display.

"He may be right," Khatir said. "There's no way for us to know the range of its weapons."

"We will when they start firing," Siraj bit out. "You saw their power on Qasama, Jasmine Moreau. You know what they can do."

Jin grimaced. She knew, all right. And here they were, sitting in a transport designed for hauling people and cargo, with no extra armor anywhere on it.

Siraj was right. Staying here until they were blown out of the sky wouldn't gain either them or the Tlossies anything. All they could do was try to balance the line, to draw the warship as far from the freighter as they could before they ran, and hope the Tlossies would take the hint also and run for it.

"Wait a minute," Rashida said suddenly. "Ghofl Khatir? Am I reading this correctly?"

"You are," Khatir confirmed, sounding as puzzled as she did. "They're veering off. Hard. Heading... yes—heading back to the surface." He frowned at Jin. "Could they have been frightened off by something?"

"Are there any other spacecraft in the region?" Siraj asked.

"Nothing I can see," Khatir said.

"Unbelievable," Siraj murmured. "Why would they just leave that way?"

"They must have been called back," Jin said. "There must be some trouble in Stronghold that they need the warship there to deal with."

"God help those people," Zoshak murmured. "But if we still want to land, this is our chance."

Jin looked at Siraj. He hesitated, then nodded. "Take us in," he ordered. "Try to catch up with the freighter on the way. I'd very much like to know what he wants here, and I'd prefer to know it *before* we land."

"Acknowledged," Khatir said, and Jin felt herself being pressed back into her seat as he ran full power to the drive.

Jin took a deep breath. A brief respite at best, but maybe it would be enough. If they could get to the surface and into some kind of cover before the warship finished its other business and came back to look for them—

Her thoughts froze, a sudden chill running through her. *Before it finishes its business...* and whatever that business was, it almost certainly involved the killing or wounding of some of Stronghold's citizens. Human beings just like her.

And yet, until that moment not a single thought of their welfare had even crossed her mind.

A queasy feeling settled into her stomach. Was this what it was like to be a soldier? To become so focused on your own private corner of a battle or war that you had no attention left to spare for anyone else?

"We're gaining on them," Khatir announced. "Either that or they're deliberately holding back to let us catch—"

And then, without warning, the command room flared with a sudden blaze of light and the entire transport was jerked violently sideways.

Jin gasped as the scream of the depressurization alarm split the air, her mind flashing back to that horrible moment when the shuttle carrying her on her first trip to Qasama had also blazed with light and fury and tangled metal, and everyone except Jin herself had died a sudden, violent death. Her vision clouded over...

"Jasmine Moreau! Jasmine Moreau!"

Jin snapped her eyes open. Zoshak and Siraj were hunched over her, the latter anxiously and gingerly slapping at her cheek. "What happened?" she croaked.

"The warship apparently had second thoughts about us," Siraj said grimly. "Possibly they were bothered by our sudden change in velocity toward the freighter."

"They're coming back?" Jin asked, her heart seizing up as she checked her nanocomputer's clock.

But as best she could tell, she'd been unconscious for over ten minutes. If the warship had decided to come after them, it should surely have been here by now.

"No, they're still returning to the surface," Siraj said. "But they decided to take a parting shot at us."

Jin focused on the wall behind him. That whole side of the command room had turned the mottled, lumpy gray of emergency hull sealant. "Is it holding?" she asked.

"So far," Siraj said, glancing over his shoulder at the sealant. "But Ghofl Khatir says we've also taken some damage to the drive and grav lifts."

"How bad?"

"We'll make it to ground all right," Khatir said grimly from the helm. "But I don't know how close we'll make it to any of the towns."

Jin winced. On the ground, in the Caelian wilderness. This just got better and better. "Have you talked to the Tlossies?" she asked. "Is there anything they can do?"

"Yes, and yes," Zoshak said. "They're going to accompany us down, and then land with us whenever we have to."

"I told you they were our friends," Jin said, frowning at the two men still standing over her. All four Qasamans, she noticed belatedly, seemed to have come through the attack just fine. "What happened to me?" she asked.

Zoshak and Siraj exchanged looks. "We're not sure," Zoshak said. "You may have hyperventilated, or possibly something struck you. We didn't see anything, but we *were* all preoccupied with other matters at the time."

Jin felt a tightening in her chest. "Or else it's my brain tumor starting to cause trouble again. Is that what you're thinking?"

A shadow crossed Zoshak's face. "That was our other thought," he conceded. "I don't know what specific treatment the doctors gave you before we left, but I do know that all such techniques are only temporary. It may be that the weakness and blackouts you experienced on Qasama are beginning to come back."

"Is there anything we can get you?" Siraj asked.

Jin closed her eyes. Back on Qasama, Siraj's father Miron Akim had told her that she still had three months before the tumor in her brain killed her. Plenty of time, he'd assured her, for her and the others to gather whatever Cobras were willing to come to Qasama and return for her surgery.

Maybe he'd been wrong.

With an effort, she swallowed back the sudden fear. If he'd been wrong, then she was going to die, and there was nothing she or anyone else out here could do about it. At least she'd be able to see Paul and Jody one last time.

Provided, of course, that they made it to the surface alive. "Yes, there is," she told Siraj. "You can tell Ghofl Khatir and Rashida Vil to get us down in one piece. After everything we've been through, dying in a crash-landing would be just plain embarrassing."

Almost unwillingly, she thought, Siraj smiled. "That it would," he agreed. "Sit back and rest, Jasmine Moreau. We'll take it from here."

CHAPTER SEVENTEEN

With a horrible, incredible, utterly awesome crash, the Troft ship north of Stronghold toppled over onto the wall. It paused there for a second or two, then crunched through the stainless steel, smashing two homes and an aircar that happened to be directly beneath it, and slammed into the ground, one of the weapons wings on that side digging itself halfway into the plowed dirt of one of the town's vegetable gardens.

"Holy cats," Freylan muttered into the sudden silence.

"And you were afraid we were going to miss the show," Jody said, staring in disbelief at the downed warship. She'd read about how heavy steelwood was, but she would never have believed that three trees' worth of it could do *that*. Through the partially open window, she heard a distant shout.

And suddenly the forest beyond the ruined wall exploded with movement and the flashes of laser fire.

Harli's Cobras were attacking.

Instantly, Governor Uy was on his feet, charging to the window and throwing it wide open. "Cobras! Attack!" he shouted to the town below. "All Cobras—"

There was a flash of light, and with a choked-off gasp he fell backward and collapsed to the floor.

"Rom!" his wife Elssa gasped, jumping up from her chair and hurrying to her husband's side.

Jody got there first, knocking the older woman to the floor before she could reach the window. "No—keep down," Jody snapped as she helped Elssa back up onto her hands and knees. The window frame was flashing now with reflected laser fire, the town below them roaring with shouts and screams and the sound of breaking glass and heat-shattered building material. "Where's your medical kit?" Jody shouted over the din.

"Kitchen—cabinet beside the cooker," Elssa said as she crawled the rest of the way to Uy's side.

"Freylan?" Jody called.

"I'm on it," Freylan said, already running stooped-over toward the kitchen.

Jody looked down at Uy. His breathing was rapid and shallow, his face twisted with pain. Over his left lung, there was a small, char-edged hole in his jacket.

"What's happening out there?" Elssa asked, tears running down her face as she carefully lifted her husband's head off the floor. "Jody? What's happening?"

Jody's first thought was that the woman should be focusing her priorities on her husband, not her town. But a second later she understood: Elssa's son Harli was in the middle of the hell out there. "I'll check," she said, and crawled to the window. Bracing herself, she eased up beside it and looked out.

It was like a scene from a war movie, the whole thing strangely unreal while at the same time feeling closely, dangerously real. Below her, laser fire filled the streets, blasting chunks from buildings and shattering glass. The screaming she'd heard a moment ago was mostly gone now, replaced by shouts and grunts and the sounds of destruction. Across the city, the downed Troft ship's upper wings were spitting out rapid laser fire of their own, and Jody's throat tightened at the thought of her father and Harli and the other Cobras out there. The chaos seemed to rise over her like the edge of a wilderness dust storm, numbing her eyes and brain. A sudden impulse swept through her, an overwhelming urge to duck away from the fire and destruction and throw herself flat on the floor where she would be safe, or at least have the illusion of safety.

"What's happening?" Elssa asked again, her voice pleading.

Jody clenched her teeth hard enough to hurt, hard enough even to stop their fear-driven chattering, and with a supreme effort stayed by the window. *I'm a Moreau, and a Broom,* she reminded herself, *and I will damn it all not act like a terrified child.* Not in front of Uy and his wife; absolutely not in front of Freylan. *I'm also a scientist,* she added, *trained in observation. So get your mind in gear, kiddo, and observe.* Unclenching her jaw, transferring her internal tension instead into a death grip on the window sill, she once again peered outside.

The battle was still going strong, possibly even more devastating now in its noise and fury. But this time, as she forced herself to methodically scan the areas she could see, she noticed something she'd missed the first time.

All across the town, small groups of Trofts were heading north toward the damaged ship. The groups she could see had formed themselves into tight knots, their weapons turned outward from the centers as they fired continuously in all directions.

And with that, the seeming chaos blew away, exactly like the dust storm she'd just been comparing it to.

Because there was no chaos out there. Nor was there some horrible mass slaughter. The rapid-fire laser bolts were nothing more than cover fire, laid down by the Troft soldiers as they tried to retreat to their damaged warship.

She lifted her eyes to the ship itself. Its own heavy fire was the same thing, she saw: a desperate attempt to blanket the area around it with death to keep the Cobras from getting close enough to do any further damage.

"Jody?" Elssa asked.

"The Trofts are retreating toward the ship," Jody told her, daring to raise her head a little higher. A movement between two of the buildings caught her eye, and she saw one of the armored trucks similarly heading north. "Soldiers and vehicles both. Lot of firing going on, but I don't think they're actually hitting much."

She turned, her throat tightening as she realized what she'd just said. Uy, at least, had most definitely been hit. "How's he doing?" she asked, dropping back to her hands and knees and crawling over to them.

"I don't know," Elssa said tightly. She had moved around behind her husband and now had his head cradled on her lap. "His breathing is terrible, but he doesn't seem to be losing much blood."

Jody nodded. One of the few advantages of taking laser fire instead of a projectile shot was that laser wounds tended to cauterize, usually preventing the victim from bleeding out.

Unless, of course, all of the bleeding was going on inside. In that case, Uy was in just as much trouble as if he was bleeding into his shirt. Probably even more.

There was a movement at the corner of her eye, and Freylan skidded to a halt on his knees beside her, the emergency kit clutched in his hand. "Got it," he panted. "What do we do first?"

"Anti-shock," Elssa said, taking the kit from him and pulling it open. "Here—inject it into his thigh," she said, handing him a hypo.

Freylan grimaced, but took the hypo and pulled off the cap. "Internal wound sealant," Elssa continued, pulling out another hypo. "Jody, can you tear away his jacket?"

They had given Uy both hypos plus one containing a sedative and painkiller, and Elssa had the ventilator strapped over her husband's nose and mouth when a sudden peal of thunder roared across the city, rattling the windows. "Jody?" Elssa gasped.

"I'll check," Jody said, handing Freylan the hand pump half of the ventilator and scrambling back up onto her hands and knees. She moved over to the window and cautiously looked outside.

The second Troft warship had returned.

It was impossible, she knew, for a chunk of metal to look angry. Even so, for those first couple of heartbeats she could swear that the warship looked furious. It was hovering on its grav lifts directly above the downed ship like an avenging phoenix hawk standing over its fallen mate. Its own lasers had joined the massive firestorm, all four clusters spitting out a wide swath of destruction around the ship and the ground troops now clustered around it. This time, the circle of death not only carved through the forest but also across the northern end of the town itself. "The other ship's back," she told the others. "They're firing. A lot."

"Get away from the window," Freylan said, his voice tight. "And get back here. We need you."

The laser firestorm had slowed to mostly sporadic shots by the time they'd done everything they could for Uy. "It sounds like it might be safe enough out there to go get a doctor," Jody said, peering into Uy's sleeping face. His breathing was still labored, but it seemed reasonably stable. "Where's the nearest one?"

"Dr. MacClave's office is two blocks east," Elssa said hesitantly. "But I don't know if you should. Even if the Troft soldiers aren't back yet, the ship will still be able to see you between the buildings. I don't like sending you out into that."

"It'll be all right," Jody assured her, taking a deep breath and hand-ing the ventilator pump to Freylan. "I'll be back as soon as I can."

"No you won't," Freylan said, and to Jody's surprise he handed the pump back to her. "Mrs. Uy needs to stay here with her hus-band. You're the only one who can talk to the Cobras out there. That leaves me. I'll go."

But the Trofts might think you're a Cobra! "But—" Jody began.

She stopped. Jody, as a woman, the Trofts might question. Freylan, as a man, they might shoot down on sight. He knew all of that, of course.

But he was right. There was no one who could go but him. "Be careful," she said instead.

"Trust me," Freylan said, giving her a forced smile as he got to his feet. "Two blocks east, you said?"

Elssa nodded. "Thank you," she said quietly.

"No problem," he said. "We'll be back as quick as we can." Nodding at Jody, he hurried from the room.

"He's very brave," Elssa murmured, cradling her husband's head.

"Yes, he is," Jody said, staring at the spot from where Freylan had disappeared. Freylan Sonderby, the quiet, awkward, earnest one. Who would have thought he had that kind of strength under the surface?

"So are you," Elssa added.

Jody grimaced. *Right,* she thought sourly. *Like a big, fearsome fluffy rabbit I am.* "He'll be all right," she said. "So will Harli."

Elssa didn't answer. But then, Jody didn't believe it, either.

Sighing quietly, she fixed her eyes on Governor Uy's face and settled into a steady rhythm with the ventilator pump.

The transport had made it past the Whitebank River and was heading toward Stronghold when its damaged grav lifts finally gave up. Once again, as the ship slammed its violent, noisy way through the treetops, Jin had a terrifying flashback to that first crash landing on Qasama.

But once again, the present didn't repeat the past. Between them, Khatir and Rashida managed to bring the transport down with a minimum of buffeting and a maximum of intact hull.

"Any idea where we are?" Jin asked as they unstrapped from their seats.

"About seventy kilometers past the river and the village you said was there," Khatir said. "If your numbers are correct, that should put us about fifty kilometers from Stronghold."

Jin grimaced. Fifty kilometers, on foot, through the Caelian wilderness. That was not a pleasant thing to contemplate.

Unless perhaps they could hitch a ride with the Tlossies? But letting the freighter get too close to the invaders would also not be a good idea. Briefly, Jin wondered how good the enemy's sensors might be, and realized she didn't have the faintest idea.

But the Tlossies might. "Any idea where the freighter put down?" she asked.

"Sure—it's right behind us," Khatir said dryly. "We cut a pretty deep swathe through the trees on our way down."

"Shall I call them?" Rashida offered, turning to the comm board.

"No, we'd better just go back there and talk to them," Jin said. "We may be close enough to Stronghold for the invaders to pick up radio transmissions." She gestured to Siraj. "The three of you will want full gear, gloves and helmets both. Knowing Caelian, chances are there'll be something nasty waiting just outside the hatch."

Five minutes later, they were ready. "Okay," Jin said, taking a deep breath. "I'll go first. Rashida Vil, you might as well stay inside until we've talked to the Tlossies."

"Fine," Siraj said, slipping deftly in front of Jin. "Except that *I* will go first."

"Siraj Akim—"

"I'm senior Djinni, and you are ill," he cut her off. "There will be no argument."

Turning to face the hatch, he keyed the release and the hatch slid open as the ramp swung down to the ground. He stepped out, pausing at the top of the ramp to look around.

And abruptly spun a quarter turn to his left, his glove lasers spitting a double burst even as he twisted over hard at the waist. A large, tawny creature shot past, crashing with a heavy thud onto the ground at the other side of the ramp. "It's all right," Siraj called back inside. "I think I—"

He broke off, staggering as a burst of deep sound resonated through the open hatchway. A second later a figure dropped onto the ramp from the roof, batted Siraj's arms aside as he tried to bring his glove lasers around, and sent a second, more potent sonic burst rattling straight through the opening into the freighter.

But Jin's nanocomputer had already evaluated the danger and

thrown her onto her back on the deck, her palms pressed hard against her ears to minimize the weapon's effects. As the sound washed mostly harmlessly past her, she rolled her torso toward the open hatch, and as a second figure dropped off the transport's roof to join the first, she fired her own sonic.

Both figures staggered back, their arms waving madly as they fought for balance. Jin continued her roll onto her stomach, then shoved off the deck and bounced herself back up onto her feet. Three quick steps and she was on the ramp, grabbing one of the staggering men and locking her arms around his torso, pinning his arms to his sides. "Hold it!" she shouted.

"Identify yourself!" a voice ordered from somewhere in the forest around them.

"I'm a citizen of Aventine," Jin called back. "What in the name of hell do you think you're doing?"

There was a short pause. Then, with a soft rustle of leaves, a young man stepped out into the narrow clearing that the transport's violent passage through the trees had created. "Who's in there with you, citizen of Aventine?" he called.

Jin keyed her opticals for a closer look at his face. He still looked wary, but at least his hands and fingertip lasers were at his sides instead of pointed at Jin and Siraj.

Though of course there were probably other Cobras out there whose weapons *were* trained on her. "They're allies," she told the young man. "You attack everyone who comes to Caelian?"

"Everyone who comes here in Troft spaceships, yes," the young man said stiffly. "In case you didn't know, we're at war here. You have a name?"

"Jasmine Broom," Jin said. "You?"

The man's face seemed to tighten, and she saw the telltale twitch as he activated his own opticals. "Jasmine *Moreau* Broom?" he asked carefully.

"Yes," Jin said. "And you?"

"My name's Kemp," the other said. "I believe I've met your husband and daughter."

Jin felt her heart leap inside her. "They're all right?" she asked.

He hesitated, just a fraction of a second too long. "Last I knew, yes," he said.

"What's happened?" Jin demanded, her pulse starting to pound in her throat. "Something's happened. What is it?"

Kemp's lip twitched. "Who are these supposed allies you've brought with you?"

And then, to Jin's utter amazement, a familiar voice called distantly from the direction of the Tlossie freighter. "One of them is her son, Cobra Lorne Moreau Broom," Lorne shouted. "The lady asked you a question, Kemp."

Jin twisted her head to look in that direction, a flash of dizziness briefly touching her as the landscape rushed past in her telescopic vision. Lorne was pressed against the freighter's bow, his fingertip lasers pointed warningly across the distance at Kemp.

And in that brief moment of distraction, the man she was holding turned suddenly in her grip, forcing enough slack to slip partially out of her hold. He grabbed her arm and bent it up, completing his escape. Still clutching her arm, he spun back around toward her, bringing up his free hand and angling his torso once again toward her.

Only to topple backward and slam hard onto the ramp as the still kneeling Siraj slapped his legs out from under him.

"Enough!" Jin bellowed, a fresh wave of dizziness rolling over her. With a supreme effort, she fought it back. This was no time to look weak. "All of you, just *stop* it! You want to fight the Trofts, or each other?"

For a stunned moment no one moved or spoke, and Jin could feel their eyes boring into her. "Speaking as Jin Moreau's son, gentlemen," Lorne called, his voice deadly serious, "and as one who's heard that tone many times before, I can tell you right now that you ignore it at your peril."

Jin focused on Kemp. For another moment he stood as still as the trees around him. And then, to her surprise, he actually chuckled. "Point taken, Cobra Broom," he called. Lifting a hand, he gave a signal.

And with a general crunching of leaves, a semicircle of over twenty Cobras emerged warily from the forest. "We've now met your number one ally, Cobra Jasmine Broom," Kemp said. "Would you care to introduce the rest of your team?"

Jin braced herself. "I've brought four representatives of the planet Qasama," she said. "They seek your help, and offer theirs in return." She shot at look at the Troft freighter. "I believe we also have possible allies in a group of Trofts from the Tlos'khin'fahi Demesne."

One of the Cobras spat. "You expect us to trust *Trofts*?"

"The Tlossies have been our trading partners for over a generation," Jin reminded him.

"Maybe *you* trade with them," the Cobra countered. "You and Stronghold. We don't get much drop-in traffic out in Essbend."

"Well, you're making up for that today," Lorne put in. His voice was clear and even, Jin noted, but in her enhanced vision she could see the wariness in his own eyes as he gazed at Siraj in his scaled gray Djinn combat suit. "Not only do we have Qasamans and Tlossies, but we also have a representative from the Dome, as well as one of the surgeons who probably helped many of you become Cobras back on Aventine."

"Who?" one of the other Cobras asked suspiciously.

"Dr. Glas Croi," Lorne said. He paused, and Jin heard a murmur ripple through the Caelians. They knew that name, all right. "And for the record," Lorne continued, "the commander of this freighter isn't just some Troft merchant. He's Ingidi-inhiliziyo, second heir to the Tlossie demesne-lord."

Jin waited, expecting another murmur of amazement. But there was only silence. Apparently, these men weren't nearly as impressed by Troft demesne-heirs as they were by Cobra surgeons.

Fortunately, they were impressed enough. "It's pretty rollin' clear that this is going to take some time to sort out," Kemp said, giving another hand signal. "But we can't do it out here in the open. Your, uh, landing"—his eyes flicked pointedly to the transport's crumpled bow—"drove away a lot of the predators, but they're starting to come back."

"No point in doing it here anyway," one of the older Cobras added. "Harli's waiting for us at Stronghold."

"And whatever you have to say you'd just have to repeat it to him anyway," Kemp agreed. He locked eyes with Jin. "You trust these people?"

"I already have," Jin said firmly. "With my life. More importantly, with my son's life."

"Okay," Kemp said. He still didn't look particularly happy about the situation, but it was clear he knew that any further decisions rested with someone higher up the command structure than he was. "We'll bring in the spookers and load up. I hope you haven't got much you need to take—it's going to be tricky enough riding double with all our stuff as it is."

"We'll manage," Jin promised.

"But we can't just leave the freighter here out in the open," Lorne called, pointing at the vehicle behind him. "We need someplace to hide it in case the invaders spotted us coming in. A deep river or lake will do—Warrior says a few days' immersion in water won't hurt it any. Any ideas?"

Kemp looked around the group. "Gish? You're the expert on this part of Wonderland."

"There's the Octagon Cave complex," one of the Cobras said. "That would probably be proof against at least a casual sensor scan. You sure you want to let them out of our sight?"

"Don't worry, it won't be all of them," Lorne told him. "Warrior— that's Ingidi-inhiliziyo's more pronounceable name—has already told me he wants to be in on any discussions we might have."

"Oh, *does* he?" Gish growled.

"Yes, he does," Lorne said calmly. "And I think Nissa and Dr. Croi should come with us, too."

"At least Dr. Croi," Kemp agreed. "No offense, Broom, but his opinion regarding your Troft pals is going to carry a lot more weight here than yours."

"No offense taken," Lorne said. "If you'll send someone back here with the coordinates to those caves, I'll get the others ready to travel."

CHAPTER EIGHTEEN

For Lorne, the spooker ride turned out to be far and away the most terrifying part of his entire wartime experience so far. His Caelian driver, a Cobra named Fourdalay who was clearly a lunatic, pushed the cranked-up, spike-covered grav cycle like he was trying to burn out all of its thrusters in one massive overload.

Or possibly his death wish involved something more spectacular. A thundering high-speed crash, say, followed by a massive fireball. The way he shaved the tolerances between the corners of the spooker and Caelian's never-ending assortment of trees, thorn bushes, and rock outcroppings—that could very well have been his plan. Clutching the grip bar, Lorne decided that even facing down two Troft warships on the rooftops of Aventine hadn't been this frightening.

His only comfort, and it wasn't much of one, was that all the rest of the Cobras were driving with exactly the same degree of recklessness.

The ordeal seemed to last forever. But finally, Fourdalay eased back on the throttle, and a couple of minutes later they glided to a smooth halt beside a pair of other men. There was a brief, quiet conversation between them and Kemp that Lorne didn't even bother to eavesdrop on, and with clear reluctance the visitors were passed through and escorted a dozen meters farther to where Governor Uy's son Harli was waiting for them.

Lorne had expected Harli to be just as suspicious of the new-comers as Kemp and his crowd had been, or even more so. To his surprise, once the initial shock had faded away, the Cobras' leader welcomed them all with at least a measure of guarded civility. It was only later that it occurred to Lorne that perhaps Harli's brief acquaintance with Paul and Jody may have paved the way for him to trust Jin's judgment as to the trustworthiness of both the Qasamans and the Tlossies.

And a few minutes later, after the Essbend contingent had been sent to one of the equipment caches to unload their gear, and sentries had been posted against the ever-present predator threat, Harli sat them all down in a circle and the debriefing began.

The stories were many and varied, and even with obvious time-editing going on, it took nearly an hour for the Qasaman, Aventinian, and Caelian accounts to be laid out before the entire group.

Lorne didn't say much during that hour. Croi had made it clear before they left the freighter that he, not Lorne or Nissa, would tell their part of the story. He'd made it even more clear that none of them was to even hint at the existence of the precious cargo aboard the freighter that Warrior's crew had now hidden away in Gish's cave complex. Despite Jin's assurances, it was obvious he didn't trust the Qasamans any farther than he could spit them.

The Qasamans. Lorne studied them as Siraj Akim presented their part of the story to the rest of the gathering in fairly decent Anglic. The head of the three Djinn didn't trust any of them, and wasn't particularly happy to be here, an attitude abundantly clear from the tightness Lorne could see in his cheek and throat muscles. But he spoke calmly and fearlessly enough as he described the attack on Qasama and the reason he and the others had traveled with Lorne's mother to the Cobra Worlds.

His grasp of Anglic puzzled Lorne until he realized that the Djinn had probably been created as an answer to the Cobras, with the intent of fighting them toe-to-toe whenever the expected Cobra Worlds' invasion of Qasama began. Under that scenario, one of a Djinni's jobs would certainly be to learn the invaders' language.

The second Djinni, Carsh Zoshak, seemed a bit more comfort-able with the group as a whole. Reading between the lines of his part of the story, Lorne guessed that his greater acceptance was tied to the additional time he'd spent fighting alongside both Jin and Merrick back on Qasama. As with Harli, familiarity with members of the Broom family seemed to create a higher level of trust in their judgment.

Lorne did notice, though, that neither Siraj nor Zoshak seemed to be allowing Jin to add much to their rendition. More than once, he wondered if she'd been ordered to stay out of the discussion, just as he and Nissa had been ordered by Croi to do likewise.

The Qasaman woman, Rashida Vil, seemed nearly as nervous about the group as Siraj. But in addition, Lorne had the impression that she was trying very hard to make herself invisible, possibly trying to press herself into the massive tree trunk she was sitting against. She'd contributed virtually nothing to the conversation, and then only to answer direct questions posed to her by Harli or one of the other Caelians. Considering that she was not only the Qasaman's second pilot but also their primary Troft translator, Lorne could only assume that she'd received the same order of silence that his mother had.

The surprising one of the bunch was the third Djinni, Ghofl Khatir, who in contrast to the other Qasamans seemed completely at ease with his surroundings. Possibly more at ease, in fact, than even the Caelian Cobras. He had settled himself at the side of the circle beside Croi and Warrior, tossing in occasional comments wherever appropriate and smiling genially at everyone around him whenever he wasn't talking. Croi and Warrior, for their part, seemed to regard Khatir like a black-sheep distant cousin who'd unexpectedly showed up at a family reunion and who no one could quite figure out what to do with.

But the Qasamans weren't the real problem, at least not from Lorne's point of view. True, their government had once sworn eternal hatred against the Cobra Worlds, but that was all in the distant past. His mother had vouched for this particular group, and that was good enough for him.

What was bothering him was what his mother *wasn't* saying.

Because there was something she was holding deep inside her. Something tense and unpleasant. Lorne had always been able to detect one of his siblings' illnesses, usually before even the sibling was aware of it, and he could clearly see the signs of stress in his mother. He could see the extra tension around her eyes, well beyond even what their current situation warranted. He could hear the slight hesitation in her voice during her rare comments, her careful weighing of every word as if she was afraid she would slip and say something she shouldn't. He could see it in the way she'd been gripping her husband's hand ever since they'd all sat down together.

Even more significantly, he could see it in the Qasamans' faces. Though they were clearly trying to hide it, all four of them were paying close attention to her, their eyes flicking over to her for a quick evaluation every few seconds. Zoshak in particular seemed to be not quite settled on his patch of ground, as if he was expecting he might have to leap to her side at a second's notice.

Was there something important that she and the Qasamans were holding back? Something of the same caliber as the Aventinians' own Isis secret?

Or was it something more personal? She'd told them briefly about the injuries Merrick had suffered in the Qasamans' final attack on the invaders' occupation force. Had she been wounded, too, perhaps internally where it didn't show?

He didn't dare ask, not here in the middle of a war council. But he would find an opportunity to do so. And soon.

"Well," Harli commented when the last report was finished and the last question answered. "I guess I never really believed that Caelian was the whole focus of this whole Troft invasion. But I would never have believed how damn serious they were about the whole thing, either." He eyed Jin thoughtfully. "Though the reason why Warrior and his buddies would send you to Qasama still eludes me."

"Perhaps *because* you wouldn't otherwise have believed that the Qasamans had also been attacked," Jin suggested. "If Siraj Akim and the others had shown up here alone, would you have listened to them?"

Harli made a face. "Probably not," he conceded, looking over at Siraj. "I'm still not sure what you think we can do for you, but right now that's kind of a side issue. Our first job is to figure out how we're going to get these damn Trofts off Caelian." He threw a hooded look at Warrior. "No offense," he added.

[Offense, I do not take it,] the Tlossie assured him.

"So what exactly is the situation over there?" Lorne asked. "You said the one ship had fallen onto the town's outer wall?"

"Was pushed over onto it, yes," Harli said. "A good-sized section was crushed, which is going to be another rollin' problem pretty quick down the road. Anyway, the second ship has set up shop right behind it, and they've put a cordon of armored trucks and troops around both of them. Your sister's currently got the best vantage point of any of us, and her guess is that they're trying to take off the downed ship's grav lifts and reposition them so that they can get the thing stood upright again."

"They can't just turn the grav lifts around in place?" Croi asked.

"Apparently not," Paul told him.

[Such equipment, it is not usually moveable,] Warrior put in. [A situation like this, one does not often encounter it.]

"Warrior agrees," Paul translated. "They're going to have to physically take the grav lifts off."

Harli snorted. "Pretty stupid design for a warship, if you ask me."

"You wouldn't think that if you'd seen how they took over the streets of Capitalia," Lorne said grimly. "They're exactly the right design for dropping into the middle of city intersections as mobile command posts."

"Well, they don't make much sense *here*," Harli said. "The point is that right now we've got the advantage, but only until they get that first ship back up again. Any ideas?"

"There's a hatch on the upper hull near the stern," Jin said. "Any chance the Cobras in Stronghold can get to it?"

"Maybe, but it would be damn costly," Harli said. "Like I said, they've put out a ring of armored trucks and soldiers, including the part that's sticking into Stronghold. I don't doubt the other ship has most of its weapons tasked for defense, too."

"More than that, we've already lost over a third of Stronghold's Cobras," Kemp added. "Sending the rest in an open attack against a target everyone knows is obvious would be a pretty sure form of suicide."

"He's right," Harli said. "I won't order it except as an absolute last resort. Even then only if you can convince me it has a real chance of success."

"Why do you ask about that particular hatch?" a Cobra named Matigo asked. "Is it more vulnerable than any of the others?"

"I don't know," Jin said. "But that's the one I got a look at, and I know how the catches and seals are positioned. I also got a quick look at the room below it. If we can get a small group of Cobras inside they should be able to take that area and hold it."

A ripple ran though the group. "You saw *inside* one of their ships?" Kemp asked.

"Briefly, yes," Jin said. "Unfortunately, we didn't have the time or the manpower necessary to do anything more."

"Pity," Harli said. "But like I say, the downed ship is being watched like a sticker's nest, which is why I want us to find a way to hit the other one. If the Trofts have any brains at all, they won't be expecting our attack there."

"What about Caelian itself?" Siraj spoke up. "Even from our few hours here we've seen how dangerous and persistent its wildlife can be. Can we allow that wildlife to deal with the invaders?"

"Personally, I think it would be a rollin' kick to sit back and watch how badly a bunch of inexperienced Trofts do against Wonderland," Harli said. "Unfortunately, we can't afford the time. The floating organics and insects have started being trouble for them, but so far the big predators haven't seemed interested."

"Speaking of which, you're all going to need to shave your heads if you don't want your hair turning green," Matigo warned, gesturing toward the newcomers. "You'll have to learn how to scrape your clothes, too."

"That can wait," Harli said. "But the predator idea is still worth pursuing, even if only as a distraction. We've got a few men in the woods right now, collecting plants that should attract some of the bigger animals. That other friend of Jody's, Geoff Boulton, is helping fine-tune the selection."

"The problem being that we've already pulled that trick once," Paul put in. "Having now seen it, the Trofts will undoubtedly be watching for us to try it again."

"Those bow hatches will be tricky anyway," Lorne told him. "They've got troops sitting just inside waiting to shoot at anything non-Troft that barges in."

"What, *you* got to see inside one of their ships, too?" Matigo asked.

"I didn't see the guard spots themselves," Lorne said. "I was inside one of the stairways that run along the sides of the ship in that area. But I could hear the troops through the door."

"Wait a second," Paul said, frowning. "You got *inside* one of their ships?"

"For a few minutes, yes," Lorne said. "I hitched a ride underneath one of their armored trucks."

"You didn't tell us anything about that," Croi said, staring in disbelief at him. "No wonder the Trofts were so serious about hunting you down afterward."

"Oh, I don't think they ever knew I was there," Lorne assured him. "I only went in to try and find out how sophisticated their drones were."

"How sophisticated were they?" Paul asked.

"Near as I could tell, they were only running visual and large-engine heat signatures," Lorne said. "That means they shouldn't be able to distinguish us from any of the large predators out here. The shipboard sensors are probably better, though."

"They are," Harli said grimly. "Trust me. Did you happen to find a way to disable those trucks while you were hitching that ride, by the way?"

"A few arcthrower shots into the engine from underneath seemed to do the trick," Lorne said. "But I suspect the topside armor is more resilient."

"The soldiers themselves are tricky, too," Jin said. "The armor is pretty thick, and those faceplates blacken if you fire a fingertip laser at them, which blocks the shot. But sonics can still stun them, and antiarmors and arcthrowers still work, too. The lower-power stunner that most of you have will also get through the armor, though you have to be pretty close to use it."

"If we ever decide we just want to wound them, we'll let you know," Harli said sourly. He shifted his attention to the three gray-suited Qasamans. "What about you? Any special weapons in those—what did you say they were? krissjaw hide?—those krissjaw-hide suits?"

"We have small lasers in the gloves," Siraj said, indicating the slender tube running beneath the little finger of each of his glove. "They are similar to yours."

"Only more powerful," Jin added. "Theirs *can* punch straight through the Troft faceplates and kill them."

"We also have a version of your sonic stunner," Siraj continued, "though from what I've seen it is less versatile than yours. As far as I know, it was never directly used on the Trofts during their invasion of Qasama, so I do not know how effective it would be against them."

"Each of us also carries three small gas canisters with a quick-acting sleeping gas," Zoshak said, tapping his belt. "The same gas as was used in the Lodestar Hospital," he added, looking at Jin.

"How quick-acting was it?" Paul asked.

"Very," Jin confirmed. "As far as I know, the Trofts in the

building went down without ever firing a shot." She grimaced. "Unfortunately, it affects humans just as fast as it does Trofts."

"We have special filters permanently implanted in our nostrils to protect us," Zoshak said. "Unfortunately, we have nothing similar to offer you."

"Well, gas is a moot point until we're inside the ship, anyway," Paul said. "What about the Trofts' ground tactics? You have any insights to offer?"

"They're about what you'd expect," Jin told him. "They use their heavy weapons freely in fending off attacks and supporting their troops, but they do still seem reluctant to engage in mass killings, at least of civilians. The troops themselves sometimes have a tendency to bunch up, which helps protect the ones in back who then shoot over the shoulders of the ones in front. One way to take down that kind of formation is to first hit them with a sonic, then jump or run into the middle of the group and start taking them out with arcthrowers, antiarmors, or fists and feet."

"Is that last one theory, or did you actually do it?" Kemp asked.

"She actually did it," Zoshak said, an edge to his voice. "On top of one of those ships, in fact."

Kemp inclined his head. "I'm impressed," he said, and to Lorne's ears he sounded like he genuinely meant it.

"My grandfather was Jonny Moreau," Jin reminded him. "We've been fighting Trofts off and on for a long time."

"So it sounds like our best bet is to put the Djinn in near the front of any attack, where their glove lasers can nail the first line of soldiers," Paul said thoughtfully. "Supported by a full line of Cobras, of course."

"Maybe some of them up in trees where they can bring their antiarmors more fully into the fight," Jin added.

"Good idea," Paul said, nodding. "Possibly with some flash-bang or smoke grenades going off, too, if we can rig up something like that."

"None of which will make a shred of difference once they open up with those shipboard lasers," Harli said heavily. "We're going to need some way to either shield ourselves from them or else get them tied up shooting in some other direction."

"Why not just blind them?" Lorne suggested. "The cameras are right there on the wings along with the weapons. They ought to be easy enough to take out."

"How do you know about the cameras?" Matigo asked, frowning.

"I told you—I was in the ship's monitor room," Lorne said. "From the images I could see on the displays, it was pretty clear that's where the cameras were."

"I'll be damned," Harli murmured. "You were right, Broom. They didn't kill Buckley just to send a message. They really *were* reacting to a real, genuine threat."

"When was this?" Jin asked.

"When we were trying to evaluate their targeting capabilities by shooting at the weapons clusters," Paul said.

"You know, in that case we may just have a plan here," Harli said, the first hint of cautious excitement slipping into his voice. "We disable the cameras, and then hit them as hard and as fast as we can."

"I don't know," Matigo said doubtfully. "They're not going to just sit around being blind, you know. They have to have some backup system available."

"Of course they do," Harli said with a tight smile. "They've got those flying drones." He leveled a finger at Matigo. "Only the minute they open the hatches to send them out, we'll lob in a few bombs. Maybe some of the Qasamans' gas canisters, too."

"Won't do any good," Lorne told him. "The monitor room is part of the drone bay, but it's separated from that end by a big divider, glass or plastic, I'm not sure which. A bomb going off inside the hatch might damage a drone or two, but it'll be a pretty isolated effect. And gas won't do any good at all."

Harli swore under his breath. "But damn it all, the thing's a *hatch*," he growled. "A hatch they're going to just open up for us. There has to be a way to turn that to our advantage."

"Of course there is," Siraj said.

Everyone looked at him. "And?" Harli prompted.

"A bomb or a canister will not work," Siraj said calmly. "We must therefore send a man."

"That's a nice thought," Harli said. "Unfortunately, our spookers won't go that high, and it's too far for even Cobras to jump."

"Not so fast," Paul said, looking up at the trees towering over them. "What if we started the jump from halfway up a tree?"

"Too unstable a launch position," Matigo said. "Besides, any tree close enough to have a clear shot at the hatch will be visible from the ground. We'd never get high enough before we were spotted and shot."

"A tree is not necessary," Siraj said. "We—the Djinn—can throw him."

"You can *throw* him?" Harli echoed incredulously. "How strong are those suits of yours, anyway?"

"They're plenty strong," Jin said, frowning intently at Siraj. "But not *that* strong." She lifted a finger. "Unless their human payload does his full share of the work."

"Correct," Siraj said, nodding. "The two on the ground will throw the third upward. As he is being thrown, he will straighten his own leg servos to push off the others' hands."

"Adding in another pair of servos' worth of boost," Paul said, nodding slowly. "Tricky, but it might work."

"More than just tricky," Harli warned. "That sort of stunt takes serious timing to pull off, and as far as I know nothing like that is programmed into our nanocomputers."

"No, but we've got time to practice," Lorne said. "I assume we won't want to move until nightfall anyway."

"What, you saying *you're* going to go?" Harli shook his head. "Sorry. Matigo or Tracker can do it."

"Carsh Zoshak will do it," Siraj said firmly. "He has trained for such maneuvers."

"Good—I'll be happy to have the company," Lorne said. "But I'm the one who's actually been inside one of those things. Whoever else goes, I have to go, too."

Harli glared at him. Lorne returned his gaze calmly and evenly, waiting the other out, knowing he really didn't have any choice in the matter. "Speaking for ourselves," Siraj said into the taut silence, "we have fought alongside one son of Jasmine Moreau." He nodded gravely at Lorne. "We would welcome the chance to fight alongside another."

There was another brief silence. Then, Harli gave a noisy sigh. "Fine," he said. "Kemp, get some men together and take the Djinn and Broom somewhere where they can practice. Devole's Canyon, maybe. The rest of you, we've got a lot of work to do. And someone get Boulton back here—we'll want to pick his brain on all this."

"Right," Kemp said briskly, getting to his feet. "Broom? Djinn?"

The Qasamans stood up and followed Kemp as he headed back through the trees toward the spot where the Caelians had left their spookers. Bracing himself, Lorne stood up, too, and turned to his parents. "Gotta go," he said as casually as he could.

"We know," his mother said. Her face was pinched, and he could see a fresh layer of fear in her eyes. But she nevertheless forced a smile. "Be careful."

"I will." Lorne nodded at his father. "Keep an eye on her, okay? This place isn't exactly safe."

"I will," Paul promised, and Lorne could see him give Jin's hand an extra squeeze. "Have we mentioned lately how proud we are of you?"

"Thanks," Lorne said. "But it's not like I've got a choice. I'm a Moreau and a Broom. I've got a lot to live up to."

"You've already lived up to it," Paul assured him. "And you'll be adding even more to that legacy tonight." He gestured. "Now get going. You've got a busy day ahead of you."

Governor Uy shook his head. "They're insane," he murmured. "You realize that, don't you?"

"Probably," Jody agreed, keeping her voice down despite the fact that she'd long since destroyed all the Troft microphones in the governor's bedroom. "My family is, anyway. I can't speak for yours."

"Oh, no, Harli's as mad as they come," Uy assured her, a weak smile touching his lips. The smile disappeared into a fit of coughing, his face contorting in pain with each convulsion.

Jody winced, frustration simmering like bile in her stomach. The doctor had stabilized Uy as best she could. But it was going to require the equipment at the town's medical center to properly deal with his injury, and the center was within laser shot of the sentry ring the Trofts had thrown around their downed ship. Uy had flatly forbidden any of them to even approach the place, let alone try to get him there.

Jody didn't like it any better than any of the others did. But she could understand his reasoning. With the mood the Trofts were probably in right now, walking into their sights would not be a good idea.

But it meant that all she and Elssa could do was try to keep him comfortable, give him pain medication when he needed it, and watch him suffer.

And hope that Harli's plan actually worked.

The coughing ran its course, and for another minute Uy lay back against his pillows, refilling his lungs with short, panting breaths. "Well, mad or not, it sounds at least possible," he said when he had finally recovered enough to speak. "Did he say what he wanted me and the Stronghold Cobras to do?"

"I think his exact words were that you were to rest, recover, and stay out of the line of fire," Jody said. "He also sent his love."

"Yes," Uy murmured, and Jody again felt her stomach tightening as she saw in his face the recognition that this might be his son's last night alive.

Just as it might be the last night for Jody's own mother, father, and brother. Three of the four people she held most dear in all the universe could be taken from her before Caelian's next dawn.

At least they had preparations to help keep their minds off the danger ahead. Jody had nothing.

"Well, that's me," Uy said. "What about our Cobras? Does he want them to provide diversion or flanking or anything else?"

"I'm sure he'd love for them to do that," Jody said. "But since we're all stuck in our houses and can't properly communicate with them, he's decided he can't really give them any instructions."

"They won't need any," Uy said. "They'll know when to take action."

"Yes, he thought they might," Jody said. "I guess we'll just have to leave it to them to decide what to do."

"They'll do their job," Uy said. He paused, and Jody could see him making a conscious effort to push his fears away. "They'll be all right," he added quietly. "Your family will. They've survived Aventine's expansion regions, not to mention everything Caelian's been able to throw at them. They'll make it."

"I know," Jody said, forcing a smile she didn't feel. "So will Harli."

"I know," Uy said.

Jody took a deep breath. "Right," she said. "Meanwhile, it's time for your medicine."

She turned to the table beside the bed, blinking back tears. They were liars, of course. Both of them.

She just wasn't as good at it as he was.

CHAPTER NINETEEN

Night had fallen on Stronghold, and two hours of darkness had crawled slowly past. The sky was cloudless above the trees, the stars of Caelian blazing down on the town and the forest arrayed against it.

And all was finally ready.

Jin stood with Kemp and Matigo and the rest of the Cobras that Harli had dubbed the spearhead team, gazing through the trees at the ring of outward-facing floodlights the Trofts had set in front of their sentry line. Whether the lights were supposed to blind potential attackers or merely keep them from sneaking up on the ships unnoticed, Jin didn't know. All she knew was that she and her family were about to go into deadly danger.

Would any of them survive this night? There was no way to know. Even Jody, in the relative safety of Stronghold, wasn't immune to the fire and hell about to burst on the region like a volcanic eruption. Governor Uy's wounding earlier that morning clearly showed that much. By the time the Caelian wilderness was again dark and silent, everyone she held dear might be dead.

And there was nothing she could do to prevent it, except do her best.

She felt her throat tighten. She'd done her best back on Qasama, too. But that hadn't been enough to keep her eldest son Merrick from being critically wounded.

For a moment her thoughts flicked to him across the light-years. Was he recovering now under the care of the Qasaman doctors and their vast pharmacopoeia of healing drugs? Had he suffered a relapse, and was even now barely clinging to life?

Or had he already lost that final battle?

There was no way to know. There was also nothing to be gained by thinking that way. Nothing she could do, not even doing her best in the impending battle, could help him now. All she could do was hope they could win this battle, and that they could persuade some of the Caelian Cobras to return to Qasama with them. Only then would she finally be able to see Merrick again, and to learn what his fate had been.

Something brushed her arm, and she looked down to see a delicate insect with a wingspan the size of her fist nibbling away at her sleeve. With a grimace, she shook it off, encouraging its departure with a flick of her fingers. For the battle Harli had sent someone back to Aerie to get the Cobras' official operation suits, ceremoniously presented to them on graduation from the academy and stored away ever since their arrival on Caelian. The outfits were more comfortable and far better suited for combat than anything else available, but the fact that they were partially made of organic fibers meant that the Cobras were going to have to put up with all the annoyances of Caelian ecology while they fought against the Trofts.

It was only minor comfort to know that the Trofts were also having to deal with the floating spores and organics and the wide range of fauna ready, eager, and willing to come in for dinner.

"Gunners, ready," Harli's distant voice came in Jin's enhanced hearing, just barely audible over Caelian's night noises. "Fire in three; audios down."

Taking a deep breath, Jin keyed off her audios . . . and two heartbeats later the forest exploded with a crashing volley of shotgun fire. A heartbeat later came a second volley, this one slightly more spread out than the first, and then a third, this one easily discernable as six separate shots.

And as the thunder faded away, the night returned to relative silence. "Broom?" Kemp murmured from behind her.

Jin leaned a little to the side, giving herself a view of the standing warship's forward starboard wing through the tree branches. The berries Tracker and his team had just fired up into the weapons cluster showed up clearly on her telescopics, the sticky husks dotting the lasers and missile tubes, the viscous juice slowly and reluctantly moving across the metal.

"Here they come," someone murmured. "I can hear them."

Jin notched up her audios...and even as she caught the feathery rush of batting wings a swarm of mothlike insects burst into view. They flew to the weapons cluster, jostling each other as they vied for the sweet roseberry juice, creating a wide, dense cloud of wings and bodies in front of the Trofts' cameras.

A laser flared through the swarm, the intensity of the light jolting through Jin's enhanced vision like a slap across the face. Another shot blazed out, vaporizing another handful of moths, and then two more shots snapped out in rapid succession. Peripherally, Jin could see that all the other weapons clusters on the two ships were also firing blindly now as they attempted to drive the insects away.

But the moths' brains were far too small to realize that their fellows were being slaughtered by the bucketful, and they wouldn't have cared even if they had realized it. As each shot opened a pathway through the cloud it was instantly filled as moths on the periphery crowded in toward the alluring smell of the berries.

With a few handfuls of berries, and help from the relentless Caelian ecology, the Trofts inside the ship were now blind.

Jin took a deep breath. "Get ready," she said. "It won't be long now."

"There!" Jody said, jabbing a finger at the warship wings as she handed Uy's night binoculars to Freylan. "You can see the fluffers clouding in."

"Yeah, I see them," Freylan confirmed, pressing the binoculars to his eyes. "They must have used roseberries—there's nothing else that drives those things that crazy."

"Way to go, Geoff," Jody murmured, wincing as the ships' lasers suddenly flashed to life, blazing through the swarming insects. If the Trofts were able to kill enough of the fluffers or just drive them away...

Freylan snorted. "Like *that's* going to do any good," he said contemptuously. He handed the binoculars back to Jody and reached to the table beside them for the flare pistol Uy had found in his emergency kit. "Let me know when."

Jody nodded, her throat tight as she watched the Troft lasers still trying to drive the fluffers away. Any minute now...

Twenty meters up his assigned tree, holding tightly to the branches, Paul watched the Trofts' useless light show as they tried to drive the moths away from their monitor cameras. Any minute now...

"Perimeter team: fire," Harli's voice drifted over the mad fluttering of insect wings.

And all around the area, the ground and trees came alive with Cobra antiarmor laser fire.

Paul was right in there with them, pressing his left leg close to the tree trunk as he targeted and blasted the four floodlights of the Troft perimeter nearest his position. He had finished knocking out the last of them when a flurry of return fire slammed into his tree, blowing splinters and chunks of charred wood across his sight.

Instantly, he swung his leg back behind the trunk and let go his grip, dropping below the hail of laser fire to the next set of handholds he'd prepared. Glancing around the trunk, he targeted three of the Troft soldiers who were firing at his tree and again swung his leg around into position. Three quick shots, and then he pulled the leg back and dropped again. This time he was in position and scouting his next target when the return fire began hammering at the spot he'd just vacated.

Again he peered around the tree, ignoring the splinters raining down as he took stock of the situation. The duck-shoot phase, as Harli had dubbed it, was unfortunately over. The remaining ground troops were abandoning their exposed positions behind the ring of shattered floodlights and were scurrying as fast as they could for the cover of the armored trucks. The trucks themselves were rolling forward, coming to their troops' support—

There was a brilliant triple flash, and one entire side of the tree just above Paul vaporized as one of the trucks fired a cluster shot into the wood. Grimacing, Paul dropped another three meters, then shoved himself sideways off his branches and leaped to the next tree over.

Just in time. The truck's commander had decided Paul's first tree was definitely serving as enemy cover and was methodically firing shot after shot into it with the clear intent of bringing it down.

From somewhere to Paul's left another shotgun blast thundered across the crackling of wood and the hissing of laser fire. Having blinded the warships, the gunners were now trying to do the same to the trucks by sending roseberries into their windshields.

Only this time the shotguns' blasts were followed by the multiple crackle of small but deadly explosions.

Paul winced. Jin and the Qasamans had warned them about the small, self-homing antipersonnel missiles the Trofts had used against riflemen in Sollas, but he'd hoped that this group of Trofts had assumed they would be facing only Cobras and had therefore not bothered to deploy that particular weapon. Unfortunately, it was clear now that they had, and he could only hope the gunners were following Harli's orders to get clear of their positions the second they fired.

He looked around the tree again, keying in his opticals and studying the ground soldiers carefully. Most were carrying the standard hand-and-a-half laser rifles, but crouched beside one of the trucks he could see a soldier holding something considerably bigger. Flicking a target lock onto the weapon, Paul curved his leg around the tree and fired.

And instantly dropped down again, this time all the way to the ground, as another pair of trucks fired a withering hail of laser fire at him. Still, even as the tree shattered above him, he was able to take some satisfaction in the distant sound of a muffled explosion. One antipersonnel missile launcher, apparently, eliminated.

Only now he had some serious problems of his own. Someone had tagged this tree as being the hiding place of the Cobra who'd taken out their missile-tube operator, and that someone seemed to be taking it personally. Even as Paul huddled down behind the trunk, trying to squeeze himself into the smallest possible target, he could hear and feel the tree being literally taken apart above him. And not just the tree—the rapid fire was flanking the trunk on both sides, preventing him from going either direction. If the Trofts kept this up, sooner or later they would get him.

"Broom!" a voice called urgently from above and to his right.

Paul looked up. One of the Caelian Cobras was clinging to a tree about ten meters away, looking across at him. "Back it up ten meters," the Cobra called, jerking his head that direction. Shifting his attention back toward the battle line, he lifted his left leg and began some rapid fire of his own.

Paul tensed, waiting for the inevitable burst of killing enemy fire. But even as the laser blasts against his own tree faltered and started to shift to this new target, the Cobra hunched up, pressed his right leg and hand against the tree trunk, and shoved himself violently backwards away from the tree. As he soared through the branches he spun halfway around, turning a full hundred eighty degrees just as he reached another tree four meters behind him. He struck it off-center, catching the trunk with his right hand and pivoting around that grip to swing around to safety behind it. He took a second to settle himself, then repeated the hunch-and-shove maneuver, ending up behind a tree three meters farther back. "Broom!" he snapped.

With a start, Paul realized that he was still behind his smashed tree, and that the Trofts had shifted their attack over to the tree where the other Cobra had been twenty seconds earlier. Staying low, he backed away from his own tree, retreating to the one ten meters back that he'd been directed to.

The other Cobra was already there, crouched behind the tree and some associated bushes, when Paul slipped around to safety on the other side. "Thanks," he murmured.

"No problem," the other said. "You okay?"

Quickly, Paul took inventory. His leg was throbbing with a couple of minor burns, and there were probably a dozen wood splinters digging through his clothing in various places. Nothing serious. "Okay enough to get back in the game," he told the other. "We might want to try a different neighborhood, though."

"There's an empty spot over there," the Cobra said grimly, pointing to their left. "I'm pretty sure Yates and Colchak are both down."

Paul grimaced. "Okay," he said. "I'll take point."

They had made it about five meters when once again Paul heard Harli's voice lift above the noise of battle. "Kangaroos—go!"

"Kangaroos—"

Even before Harli finished giving the order, Zoshak was off, sprinting along the hardened, leaf-free path Lorne and the Qasamans had painstakingly cleared during the hour before sundown.

Lorne watched him go, his hands feeling unnaturally sweaty as he shifted his attention back and forth between Zoshak and the other two Djinn standing ready at the far end of the path. He'd learned the maneuver well enough, at least according to them, and in fact had nailed their last five practice throws perfectly.

But that had been out in the Caelian forest, in the middle of the afternoon and far removed from any Trofts with lasers. If this jump turned out to be the one Lorne botched, he was going to come tumbling down into the middle of an armed camp.

But there was no time to worry about that now. Zoshak reached the other two Qasamans and leaped up and forward toward them. Siraj and Khatir caught his feet in their gloved hands and hurled him upward and forward through the few light branches still between him and the clear zone. He arched upward across the night sky, heading toward the drone hatchway that was even now folding down from the side of the ship.

And now it was Lorne's turn.

He took off down the path, watching his footing, watching the two waiting Qasamans, adjusting his stride, trying to remember everything he'd learned, trying to forget the armed Trofts he would be flying helplessly over. He reached the jump-off point and leaped, tucking himself and bending his knees as he flew toward them. The Qasamans caught his feet, and as they shoved him up he also shoved himself downward with the full strength of his leg servos.

And with a brief slapping of branches across his face he found himself soaring high over the clear zone.

Over the battlefield.

It was like nothing Lorne had ever seen before, and even the brief glimpse was enough to turn his stomach. The blazing sizzle of blue laser light was everywhere, brilliant eye-hurting flashes from the armored trucks' swivel guns, somewhat dimmer ones from the Cobras lurking among the trees. The sound of splintering wood and shattered rock filled the night air, punctuated by gunshots, small explosions, and the grunts and screams of the injured and dying. Scattered across the clear zone, briefly lit by every laser flash that shot past, were the unmoving bodies of dead Trofts.

Resolutely, he tore his eyes away from the carnage, shifting them back to the ship now rushing toward him. Ahead, Zoshak finished his own journey by slamming into the hullmetal just above the drone hatch, the combat suit servos in his outstretched arms and legs absorbing the impact. Smoothly, almost gracefully, he slid neatly down the hull and disappeared through the opening.

It was only then that Lorne realized to his horror that his own jump was going to be short.

He tensed, keying his opticals for a quick range check. But there was no mistake. Instead of hitting the opening, or even hitting the hull above it as Zoshak had just done, he was going to hit below the open hatch.

There was only one chance. Stretching his arms as far as he could above his head, he curled his fingers into hooks and locked the servos into place.

He made it, but just barely. His fingers caught the edge of the hatch, his legs swinging around to slam shins-first against the hull below.

For a second the vibration of the impact threatened to slide the hooked fingers loose and send him tumbling to the ground below. He tried to get his thumbs up underneath, but the metal was too thick for them to reach. In desperation, he pulled himself up and jammed the top of his head against the underside of the hatch, wedging his fingers tightly in place and finally stopping their drift toward the edge. He gave himself another second to dampen out the motion, then reset his grip and pulled himself up onto the hatch, catching a hint of reflected laser light from inside as he rolled onto his side and slid sideways through the opening. Bouncing off the drone that had been moving up toward the opening when it was so rudely interrupted, he tumbled onto the bay deck.

To find himself in the middle of yet another battle zone.

Fortunately, so far the battle was only going one direction. Crouched on the deck beside a tall rack of drones, Zoshak was firing a barrage from his glove lasers, shooting through the glass partition at the Troft techs scrambling madly to get off their couches and into cover behind the consoles. He'd already nailed one of the aliens, and as Lorne scrambled back to his feet another one twitched and toppled limply to the ground.

"No visor blackening here," Zoshak called, his voice grimly pleased as he continued to fire.

"No need for it inside," Lorne called back, eyeing the tiny slagged holes in the glass where the Djinni's lasers had punched through the barrier. "Watch your fire—I'm going to see if I can get us through it."

He was halfway to the barrier, wincing a little as Zoshak's fire shot past him on both sides, when the door at the far end of the monitor room swung open and a half-dozen armored Troft soldiers appeared, charging through the doorway in two-by-two formation. Their lasers swiveled around as they spotted the intruders beyond the glass—

"Cover!" Lorne shouted back over his shoulder. He leaped up into the air, his left leg swinging around in a quick arc as he raked the soldiers with laser fire.

The blast caught the first two across their faceplates, and as their shots sizzled through the barrier and burned past Lorne's head they jerked back and fell. But as Lorne finished his sweep and swung his leg back to trace another arc across the ones next in line he realized that he'd made a fatal mistake. This second, lower sweep of his laser was catching the Trofts across their chests instead of their faceplates, and with the small but significant attenuation created by the glass he was shooting through even his antiarmor laser wasn't quite powerful enough for quick-kill shots through the aliens' armor.

And as the aliens staggered back, their torso armor spraying out smoke and bits of metal and ceramic, their lasers were now tracking toward him.

Desperately, he tried to bring his laser around for another pass. But the momentum was going the wrong way, and he was still flying through the air with no way to take cover. When those lasers finally lined up on him, he knew, he would be dead.

And then suddenly Zoshak was leaping across Lorne's line of sight, flying forward in a sideways arc like a Cobra executing the kind of wall jump Lorne had used to get off the rooftops back in Capitalia. The Djinni's feet hit the barrier with a resonating thud.

And to Lorne's astonishment, a jagged oval of glass popped out of the barrier and tumbled into the monitor room. "Take them!" Zoshak snapped, dropping flat on the deck out of Lorne's line of fire.

And with a section of the barrier out of the way, Lorne's laser *was* now capable of punching through the aliens' armor with a single shot.

The four remaining soldiers knew it, too. They were already on the move, giving up their chance to catch Lorne with a killing shot as they dove for cover behind the center console.

But Lorne's lasers weren't a Cobra's only weapons. Even as Lorne landed again on the deck, he raised his right hand, little finger pointed forward, and fired his arcthrower. With an ear-splitting thunderclap the lightning bolt flashed through the hole in the barrier and into the center console.

And with a thunderclap almost as loud as that of the arcthrower itself, the delicate electronics and control systems inside flash-vaporized, shattering the displays and blowing the cabinet apart.

The soldiers pressed against it never even had a chance. The blast slammed them backwards, staggering them once more out into the open.

They were once again trying to bring their weapons to bear when Lorne's antiarmor laser ended the battle for good.

"Well done," Zoshak said, jumping back to his feet.

"You, too," Lorne said, eyeing the hole in the glass. It was way too small to get through, which meant they were either going to have to see if their sonics could shatter it or else break through it with brute strength. Gingerly, he got a grip on one edge.

And watched, wide-eyed, as Zoshak casually kicked the area directly beneath the hole, breaking it free and leaving an opening that they *could* get through. "After you," the Djinni said, gesturing.

"How did you *do* that?" Lorne asked as he ducked down and slipped gingerly through into the monitor section.

"It was your laser shot," Zoshak said, sounding surprised that Lorne would even have to ask. "I noticed that as you shot at the Trofts you were also carving a circle in the glass, weakening it. I simply supplied the force necessary to break it free."

Lorne felt his cheeks warming. He'd noticed the effect Zoshak's own lasers were having on the glass, but the fact that he was doing exactly the same thing had missed him completely. "And that?" he asked, gesturing at the lower section.

"I used my glove lasers to weaken it while you were dealing with the soldiers," Zoshak said. "To the stairway?"

"To the stairway," Lorne confirmed. He crossed the room, stepping gingerly over the smoldering alien corpses, and eased his head out the door.

For the moment, the corridor was deserted. But he doubted the Trofts would leave it that way for very long. The stairway to the right was marginally closer; slipping outside, he headed that direction. If they could get down the stairway to the guardroom at the bottom, Zoshak should be able to lob one of his gas canisters in and take out the whole squad without any further fuss or bother. He reached the door and opened it a crack.

And flung it wide open as he caught a glimpse of two Troft soldiers a meter away charging across the landing toward him.

He gave them a quick burst from his sonic as he leaped forward, and as they staggered back he grabbed their lasers and wrenched the weapons away from them. "Above!" Zoshak shouted.

Lorne had just enough time to look up and see the crowd of armored figures clattering down the grillwork stairway toward him before Zoshak grabbed his arm and yanked hard, throwing him back through the door into the corridor. "Wait here!" the Qasaman shouted.

He was pulling one of the gas canisters from his belt as he grabbed the edge of the door and slammed it shut in Lorne's face.

"*Damn!*" Lorne snarled. Zoshak alone in there, even with that fancy Qasaman gas...

But it was too late to argue the point. Even if he thought he could hold his breath long enough to help Zoshak take out all those Trofts, opening the door now would let the gas dissipate out here into the corridor. Without that edge, taking on that number of enemy soldiers would probably get them both killed.

But if Zoshak thought Lorne was just going to stand here waiting for permission to rejoin the fight, he was badly mistaken. Throwing a final glare at the door, sending up a quick prayer for the Qasaman's safety, he turned and headed back toward the monitor room.

The lasers were still flashing, and the cold feeling that her younger son was dead was starting to settle into Jin's heart, when the standing warship's portside door abruptly swung open. "There!" she called loudly. "The door's open! It's open!" She started to stand up for a better look.

And was yanked back down again. "Easy," Kemp murmured. "I'm sure Harli heard you just fine. Don't make yourself a target, too."

Jin winced. He was right, of course.

But hunched close to the ground this way, she didn't have a clear view of that open door. There was no way to see if Lorne and Zoshak were both in there waiting for the spearhead team.

Or whether it was only Zoshak who was still alive.

"Damn," one of the other Cobras muttered.

Jin's heart skipped a beat. "What is it?"

"They've spotted the open door," the Cobra said tensely. "They're heading back toward it."

Jin stood straight up, shaking off Kemp's hand on her arm. Three groups of Troft soldiers were on the move, abandoning the relative safety of the armored trucks and running toward the warship, pouring laser fire through the open doorway as they went.

The other Cobras had spotted the sudden activity, too. All around Jin, the blue laser flashes intensified, their focus shifting from the trucks and the soldiers still huddled beside them to the groups converging on the open door.

But the Trofts were too far away for good shots, and many of the Cobras' lines of sight were blocked by the trucks, and the trucks themselves were stepping up their own fire in reply.

And as Jin watched helplessly, she saw that the desperate counterattack would fail. The Trofts would make it back to the ship, or enough of them would.

And whoever was waiting by the door, if her son was still alive, he wouldn't be alive much longer.

"It's open!" Freylan announced excitedly. "They did it. They got the ship's door open."

"I see," Jody said, a hard lump in her throat as she peered across the town. Yes, Lorne and the Qasaman who'd pulled off that human birdman stunt had indeed done it, fighting their way down to the bow door and getting it open.

But unless the Cobra assault force could get across the battlefield to it, the whole thing would be for nothing. And there were still a lot of soldiers, trucks, and gunfire between the edge of the forest and the warship.

And then, she saw something that froze her heart. Three groups of Troft soldiers had left the battle line and were charging back toward the open door, firing at it as accurately as they could while still running at top speed. "Freylan?" she asked.

"I see them," he said grimly. "Damn it all—I was hoping they wouldn't spot it so quickly."

"Can the Cobras out there stop them?"

"I don't know," Freylan said, sweeping the edge of the forest slowly with the binoculars. "I don't think so."

Jody took a deep breath. "In that case," she said, "it's time."

Picking up the flare pistol from her lap, she pointed it out the window in the direction of the Troft ship and fired.

The flare ignited, its red glow barely even registering amid the stuttering laser fire. Jody watched the running Trofts, waiting for something to happen.

But nothing did. Down in the town part of the invaders' sentry ring, one of the Trofts took a shot at the flare, the beam slicing through the sky beside it but missing both the parachute and the flare itself. From somewhere below came a high-pitched bellow, like a human voice trying to imitate the roar of a screech tiger.

And suddenly, the town exploded with laser fire. Some of it came from the houses and buildings, targeting the ring of Trofts inside the wall. Another group came from positions on top of the wall itself, that group cutting across the aliens racing toward the open warship door.

The Stronghold Cobras had joined the battle.

CHAPTER TWENTY

The distant screech echoed across the battlefield, and Paul had just enough time to wonder what it was when a fresh barrage of laser fire exploded from the top of Stronghold's wall.

And as he watched from his new treetop firing post he saw the Trofts racing for the warship stagger and twitch and fall.

One of the other Cobras nearby gave a war whoop. "Way to *roll*, Shingas," he called even as he sent another pair of laser bolts at the nearest Troft truck. The truck replied by swiveling its gun toward him and firing back.

Targeting the gun barrel, Paul fired a pair of shots of his own. The trucks were still holding up well against the Cobras' onslaught, but someone in Paul's group of fighters had come with the idea that if they could hit the gun barrels hard enough and often enough the metal might warp enough to ruin the lasers' alignment and render them useless.

So far the plan didn't seem to have yielded much in the way of results. But Paul had nothing better to offer. The truck was still firing at the other Cobra, shredding the other's tree, its gun barrel still presenting a perfect target to Paul's own position. Targeting it again, he sent two more bolts into the metal.

And gasped as an unexpected shot from somewhere else blazed across his sight and sliced a line of pain across his exposed left leg.

He didn't remember falling from his perch, but what seemed

like an instant later he found himself sprawled on the ground at the base of the tree, his eyes squeezed shut against a rain of charred wood and smoking branches, his entire leg throbbing. He groped a shaking hand toward it—

"Don't touch," a gruff voice said from above him.

Paul opened his eyes to slits. One of the other Cobras was kneeling over him, his body partially blocking the rain of debris, his face set in stone as he dug through his medical pack. "Never even saw it," Paul heard himself murmur, the small part of his brain that was still functioning amid the agony vaguely surprised at how calm his voice sounded.

"They had a backup truck all set," the Cobra said grimly. "Sent the first one out as bait, and then tried picking us off when we shot at it."

"And I fell for it." Fell for the trick, then fell out of the tree. Somehow, that struck him as incredibly funny. "How bad is it?"

"Bad enough," the Cobra said. "I've given you something for the pain and infection, but we're going to have to wrap it."

Paul nodded. The pain was starting to fade away, a strange lightheadedness moving in like a fogbank to take its place. "I'll do it," he said. "They need you out there." He reached to his throbbing leg.

To find that one entire side of it was missing. The Troft laser blast had burned out a line of skin and muscle and tendon that reached nearly all the way down to the ceramic-laminated bones.

"Get *away* from that," the Cobra ordered, slapping Paul's hand away from the injury. "Doesn't matter anyway. We're dead—we're all dead."

"No, we're not," Paul insisted through the gathering haze. "We can still do this."

"How?" the other demanded. "We've got nothing that can stop those damn trucks."

And as if on deliberate cue, a sudden thundering crash came from beyond the line of trees. "What the—?" the Cobra said, hopping to his feet and staring through the trees into the clear zone. Clenching his teeth, ignoring the remnants of pain in his leg, Paul forced himself up on his elbows and craned his neck to see over the low bushes in front of him.

One of the Troft trucks, either the one he'd been shooting at or the one that had shot at him, was spread out on the ground, its wheels splayed outward, its swivel gun bent uselessly, its entire roof caved in. Mashed across the crushed roof, having clearly descended at a very high rate of speed, was a mass of wrecked and unrecognizable machinery.

And then, even through the haze of the drug, Paul got it. Lifting his eyes, he peered up at the warship and the still-open drone hatch.

Just in time to see another drone float carefully out of the opening. It drifted away from the ship and moved slowly across the battlefield as if taking stock of the situation. Then, turning its nose downward, it dove at full speed toward the ground and slammed squarely into the top of a truck a hundred meters away.

And despite the pain and the knowledge that he would never walk properly again, Paul smiled. "What was that," he said to the other Cobra, "about having nothing that can stop the damn trucks?"

The last image on Lorne's monitor was that of an armored truck's roof rushing toward him. Then, abruptly, the monitor scrambled and went dark. A second later, through the hatch opening, he heard the distant boom of another Troft vehicle biting the dust.

Two trucks down. No idea, actually, of how many more to go.

But then, he didn't have to take out *all* of them. The eagle's-eye look he'd gotten of the battlefield with that second drone had shown that there were only three of the vehicles in position to attack the spearhead force preparing to cross the clear zone to the door Zoshak had opened for them. Those three—those two, now, actually—were the only ones he absolutely had to neutralize.

Assuming, of course, that Zoshak had in fact managed to get the door open. Both of Lorne's drones had necessarily had to start their attacks from a serious height, and he hadn't yet had a chance to float one of them lower to check out the door in person. But he'd seen a sample of Zoshak's work, and he had no reason to believe the Qasaman hadn't fully completed his job.

Time for Lorne to do likewise.

The display winked: the third drone was ready to launch. Keying over the control stick, Lorne activated the grav lifts and released the drone's rack restraints. Sooner or later, he knew, the Trofts still inside the ship with him would tumble to what he was doing and send someone in here to stop him.

Hopefully, he would finish clearing the way for his mother and her team before that happened.

One guard truck down. Two more to go. Concentrating on not banging the drone against the bay wall, he maneuvered the slender machine up and out through the hatchway.

Jin watched as a drone came for the third and final truck blocking their path to the ship. The Trofts inside the vehicle had figured out what was happening and were taking frantic steps to avoid it. The soldiers who'd earlier taken refuge inside it came boiling out through the rear doors, firing their lasers skyward as Lorne or Zoshak or whoever buzzed the drone high above their heads. The truck itself, meanwhile, had abandoned its post and was driving around in a sort of high-speed evasive course which, considering the situation, was nearly as useless as it was ludicrous.

But the soldiers weren't trained for that kind of straight-up shooting, and were moreover now within range of the Cobras in both the woods and the town. Even as they jerked and died the drone did its now familiar swan dive straight down into the desperately running truck. There was one final teeth-tingling grinding of metal on metal, and the truck slammed to a halt.

And with the final barrier down, the way was now open.

"That's it," Kemp snapped. "Let's go." He lunged up out of cover and sprinted at full speed across the clear zone toward the open warship door.

Jin had intended to be right behind him. But even as she straightened and started to run, she found herself in fourth place among the other twelve Cobras.

Mentally, she shook her head. She really *was* getting old.

And yet, even as she tried to emulate Kemp's evasive, broken-vector running style, she felt a surge of exhilaration run through her. *This* is how it should have been on her first trip to Qasama: not a lone Cobra facing danger, but a whole team of them working together to defeat an enemy. This was what she'd volunteered to become all those years ago. This, ultimately, was what she'd been created to do.

There was a close-in flash of laser light, and the Cobra running beside her gave a gasping choke and sprawled facefirst onto the ground.

Jin redoubled her pace, the adrenaline still pumping through her veins but the budding thrill of battle abruptly gone like dust in the wind. Ahead, Kemp had reached the warship door, and without even pausing to check for lurking danger he sprinted inside. Jin watched closely as the other Cobras ahead of her followed, waiting tensely for the sudden volley of laser fire from inside that would mean the open door had been a trap.

But no such enemy fire came. She reached the door, and with a final leaping step was temporarily safe. "Watch it," someone warned.

Jin keyed in her opticals, her own eyes still recovering from the dazzling display of laser fire outside. She was in a narrow room about seven meters long and three wide, with long benches along both sides and weapons racks on the walls above them, some of the clips still holding lasers and other weapons. The half-dozen Trofts who had apparently been manning the place were sprawled on the deck, dead or unconscious, Jin didn't know which. As she quickly picked her way through the bodies, she saw Zoshak and Kemp at the far end of the room, conversing in low voices beside a half-open door with a stairway visible beyond it.

"Do we seal up?" someone called from behind Jin, and she turned to see that the last member of their team had joined them inside.

Or rather, the last surviving member of the team. Four of the original thirteen, she saw, were no longer with them.

"No, leave it open," Kemp told him. "Some of the others might get a chance to join us. You stay here and watch—if the Trofts make a try for it instead, seal it up."

"The control box is on the wall to the right of the door," Zoshak added, pointing. "The red control should seal the door."

"The rest of you, we're heading up," Kemp said. "There are"—he grimaced as his eyes flicked over the group—"nine of us, so we'll run groups of three. Spread out, kill any Troft you run into—"

"Unless he surrenders," Jin put in. "We might want some of them kept alive for questioning."

"Unless he surrenders," Kemp confirmed, not looking especially happy about it but apparently accepting her logic. "Jasmine, Zoshak, you're with me. We'll take the top deck—the rest of you, group up and each take one of the lower decks."

"What about Lorne?" Jin asked.

"From the way those drones were hawk-diving out of the sky

out there, I'd guess he's in the drone control room," Kemp said. "That was Deck Four, Zoshak?"

"Yes, sixth door on the left," Zoshak confirmed. "Shall we go to assist him?"

"No, I want us to go find that upper hatch, the one Jasmine says she got a look into on Qasama," Kemp said. "Olwen, take two men up to Deck Four—give Lorne some backup. And everyone keep an eye out for anything that might be a fire-control room. If we can get control of those wing-mounted weapons, we'll be able to end this thing right here and now."

After the firestorm of laser bolts they'd had to fight through outside the ship, Jin had expected to face much the same level of resistance inside. To her surprise, not only was the stairway deserted, but so was the Deck One corridor when they arrived there a cautious minute later. "Where is everyone?" she murmured.

"Probably in there," Kemp said, nodding at the rows of closed doors lining the corridor. "I'm betting they started out the evening with most of their actual soldiers outside, and that Zoshak and Lorne have already taken care of a lot of the ones that weren't. Now that a whole bunch of us are in here, too, their only chance is to go to ground."

"This is the deck we want," Zoshak said firmly. "This is where all the important command centers are located."

"How do you know?" Kemp asked, frowning as he cocked his head to the side. "I don't hear anything."

"The room identification plaques," Zoshak said, stepping to the nearest door and pointing to a small discolored patch beside the nearest door. "They have all been removed." He tried the handle. "And the doors themselves are of course locked."

"Good call, Carsh Zoshak," Jin said approvingly. "So. Door to door?"

"Door to door," Kemp confirmed. "But let's see first if we can figure out which ones have actual Trofts cowering behind them. I'll take left; you take right."

Jin nodded and stepped to the nearest door on the right. Pressing her ear against it, she keyed in her audio enhancers.

The faint background noises of the ship leaped suddenly into sharp focus. Consciously, she pushed aside the various genera-tor, pump, and relay noises and tried to sort out the sounds of breathing, conversation, or flapping radiator membranes.

Nothing. Keying down her audios, she headed down the corridor toward the next door in line.

She had made it halfway when a sudden new sound cut through the background noise: a sharp, multiple snapping noise, coming from at least two directions. "Kemp?" she whispered.

"I hear them," Kemp said grimly. "Damn."

"What is it?" Zoshak demanded.

"High-energy capacitors discharging," Kemp told him. "Sounds like they've got the big lasers going again. The fluffers must have finished off the roseberries and cleared out."

And with the big weapons' targeting systems clear, the Cobras in both the town and the forest were now in deadly danger. "We have to shut them down," she said.

"No argument." Kemp waved a hand down the corridor. "Any guesses as to where they're firing them from?"

"No, but you and Carsh Zoshak are going to find out," Jin said, peering down the corridor. Midway to the other end was another corridor that bisected theirs. At the aft end of that corridor, if she was visualizing things correctly, would be the ready room attached to the topside hatch. "I'll go on top and see what I can do about them from outside."

"What?" Kemp demanded. "Wait a minute—"

"If you get control of the weapons, fire a burst high over the forest or town," Jin called over her shoulder as she ran toward the corridor. "Good luck, and watch yourselves."

The cross-corridor, thankfully, was also deserted. Jin headed aft, keeping her audios high enough to hear incautious footsteps. The corridor ended in yet another unmarked door; bracing herself, Jin tried the handle.

It was unlocked. Readying her sonic, she pushed it open a crack and looked inside.

The room was small and as deserted as the corridors. On its walls were more of the weapons racks she'd seen in the guardroom downstairs, except that these racks were all empty. Along with removing the room ID plaques, the techs up here had also taken the time to raid the local armory before locking themselves in their rooms.

In the center of the ceiling, at the top of a narrow stairway, was the hatch.

Seconds later she was up on top of the hull crest, the wind

whipping across her face and tugging at her green-flecked operation suit, her eyes and ears filling once again with the light and noise of the battle still raging on far below.

And as she stood there, getting her bearings, one of the wing lasers flared, flashing brilliance across the landscape as it blazed death and destruction somewhere inside the forest.

She took a deep breath. Kemp and Zoshak might find the weapons' control room in time. Having located it, they might figure out how to break in and fight their way through the Trofts inside without getting themselves killed.

But the odds were that they wouldn't. Not until a lot more Cobras out there had died.

Which meant it was up to her. Somehow, she had to come up with a way to disable the weapons from up here.

And she'd better come up with it fast.

Jody's experience with battles up to now had consisted of detailed descriptions in books, many of them accompanied by neat lines and arrows. Compared to that, the real-life battle raging across the town and clear zone around her was utter chaos.

Nevertheless, as near as she could tell, it had looked like the Cobras were going to pull it off. Certainly once her mother's group made it inside the warship, she had dared to hope that it was almost over.

But that was before the big wing-mounted lasers had unexpectedly sprung to life. Now, watching helplessly as the weapons blazed death and destruction across the human forces, slicing through trees and houses, her hopes were suddenly hanging by a thread.

"They'll make it," Freylan said, his hands gripping the binoculars tightly as he pressed them to his face. He'd taken over binocular duty a few minutes ago, when the violence and death had unexpectedly hit Jody's gag reflex and she couldn't bear to watch it close-up anymore. "They're probably just having to fight their way through a few leftover soldiers. They'll make it, and they'll get those lasers shut down."

"I know," Jody murmured. But she knew no such thing, and neither did he. The Trofts wouldn't have just a few leftover soldiers in there—the ones inside the ship would undoubtedly be their best. That was certainly how Jody would have arranged things, anyway. There was no guarantee that the Cobras would be able to fight through those soldiers and find their way to the weapons control room. Certainly not without taking serious casualties.

And Jody's mother was a fifty-two-year-old Cobra with arthritis and a bad knee. If any of the attack team was going to die, it would probably be her.

"Whoa!" Freylan said suddenly, leaning toward the window. "What the...? Jody, your mother's up on top of the ship!"

"*What*?" Jody snatched the binoculars from him and pressed them to her eyes. To her utter amazement, she found that he was right.

Her first reaction was a sigh of relief that Jin hadn't been killed fighting her way inside. But midway through the sigh, the realization of what her mother was doing up there suddenly flooded in on her. "Oh, no," she breathed. Shoving the binoculars back into Freylan's hands, she dashed toward the living room doorway, banging her knee against the couch in her haste. "Get away from the window," she snapped.

"What are you doing?" Freylan asked as he hastily climbed out of his chair and pressed himself against the wall.

"I have to let Dad know," she said, finding the light switch. "She's going to try to knock out the lasers from up there."

"By *herself*?"

"You see anyone else up there?" Jody shot back, her brain working furiously to compose a message she could send quickly. "Close your eyes or lose your night vision."

Squeezing her own eyes tightly shut, she began flipping the switch, on-off, on-off in Dida code. *Mom on top of ship—trying for lasers. Assist*?

"Tell him to contact Lorne," Freylan said suddenly. "If he hasn't used up all those drones yet, maybe he can throw some of them into the weapons clusters."

Jody nodded. "Right."

It was only as she was starting her third repeat of the message that it occurred to her that there might no longer be anyone out there capable of reading it.

"Broom? *Broom!*"

With a start, Paul snapped back to consciousness. A foggy, dreamy sort of consciousness, but consciousness just the same. "What is it?" he asked, his voice sounding oddly slurred.

"We got a message," the Cobra said as he grabbed Paul's chest under his arms and pulled him up into a sitting position. "There— the governor's residence."

"I see it," Paul said, blinking a couple of times to clear his vision and his brain. *Dit dah dah dah dit dah dit dit . . .*

"Well?"

"She says Jin's on top of the warship," Paul said, struggling to push himself higher. "I need to tell Lorne to fly his drones into the clusters." He took a deep breath.

And broke into a sudden fit of coughing.

"S'okay," the other Cobra said, lowering him to the ground again. "I got it."

He got Paul settled, then stood upright behind one of the trees and filled his lungs. "Lorne Broom," he bellowed. "Cobra skipper nest! Drones hoverbird feeding! Move it!"

"What was that?" one of the Cobras, a rough-looking man named Olwen, said suddenly.

"What was what?" Lorne asked, staring at his displays with a sinking heart as he waited for the ready light to come on. There were still two of those armored trucks out there, not counting whatever was still operational inside Stronghold, and he'd figured on taking them out with his last two drones.

Only now the game had suddenly changed. From the intensity of the laser fire outside, it was clear that the Trofts had the ship's main weapons clusters operational again.

"I heard someone call your name," Olwen said, ducking though the hole in the barrier and hurrying toward the open drone hatch. "Yes," he added, raising his voice as he crooked his ear toward the open drone hatch. "He's saying 'Lorne Broom . . . Cobra skipper nest . . . drones hoverbird feeding . . . move it.'"

Lorne stared at him. "*What?*"

"Skipper nests are at the very tops of trees," one of the other Cobras said. "Sounds like Kemp or one of the others made it up on top of the ship."

"And hoverbirds come up underneath hanging flowers to feed," the other Cobra added.

"I'm guessing that means they want you to ram the drones into the weapons clusters," Olwen concluded.

"Right," Lorne said, grimacing. Great plan.

Only there were four weapons clusters, and he only had two drones.

But he could at least take down two of them. "Let's give it a try," he said. "Olwen, stand clear."

Olwen nodded and took a couple of steps to the side. The forward starboard cluster first, Lorne decided as he popped the second-to-last drone from its rack and sent it drifting toward the hatchway. Not only was that the closest group, it was also the one with the widest field of fire into the area where most of Harli's Cobras were positioned. Resettling his grip on the control stick, he flew the drone past Olwen and out through the opening.

He'd gotten it maybe four meters outside the ship when the starboard lasers flared, and the indicators went crazy as the drone was shattered to scrap. The monitor blanked, the indicators went solid red, and even from the far side of the barrier Lorne had no difficulty hearing its remains crash to the ground.

"Well, *damn* it," one of the other Cobras muttered.

"Yeah," Lorne said. There were still four weapons clusters, and he only had one drone left. "Any ideas?"

There was a moment of silence. Then, through the barrier he heard Olwen snort. "Matter of fact, yeah, maybe I do," the Cobra said. "How good are you with that control stick?"

Lorne shrugged. "I nailed six out of six trucks, and three of them were trying to run. That good enough?"

"Should be, yeah," Olwen said. "Hang on."

He turned to the opening, and Lorne saw him fill his lungs. "Twist and whist!" he shouted. "Twist and whist, on the half-gigger!"

Frowning, Lorne looked at the other Cobras. They looked every bit as puzzled as he felt.

And then, their expressions cleared and understanding appeared. Still frowning, Lorne notched up his hearing a little, wondering what kind of response Olwen would get from below.

Apparently, they had understood the reference down there, too. "Twist and whist on the half-gigger," Harli's voice came drifting up to them. "Twist and whist on mark."

"We're on," Olwen announced, hurrying back through the barrier. "How fast can you get that last drone in the air?"

"It's running startup now," Lorne said. "Another ninety seconds."

"Good," Olwen said. "Here's what you're going to do..."

For a minute Jin crouched on the warship's crest, listening to the battle below as she tried to come up with a plan.

The list of options wasn't very long. Her fingertip lasers would be useless against the weapons clusters—they were far too heavily armored. Her antiarmor laser might make some headway at close range, but only if she could sit there and continue to pour fire into the things.

Only she couldn't do that. Back on Qasama, the Trofts had shown they could adjust the aiming of each cluster to fire above the other wing on its side. Once she climbed out onto any one of the wings, she would have minutes at the most before the Trofts at the controls were able to remove the safeties that prevented accidental misfires of that sort, target her, and fry her right where she sat.

She frowned suddenly, her ears pricking up. Had someone down there just called Lorne's name? She notched up her audios, her heart pounding suddenly in her throat, wondering if they were calling for a medic for him.

But it was just a group of strange words, probably some kind of code message being sent to him inside the drone control room. Keying her audios back down, she turned back to the immediate problem at hand.

Or tried to turn back to it. Her brain felt sluggish, the way it had at critical times back on Qasama. More evidence, if she'd needed it, that her brain tumor was starting to reassert itself.

But the tumor would kill her in weeks or months. The Trofts would kill her tonight, and everyone else with her, if she didn't get back on top of this. Shaking her head to try to clear it, she focused again on the options.

Her lasers were out. Her sonics were obviously out. Using her servos to physically rip the weapons out of the cluster was even more obviously out.

Which left her arcthrower.

Grimacing, she squatted down on the crest beside the aft-portside wing, keying her telescopics and peering forward at the bow-portside wing. There was at least one missile tube in there among the lasers, she knew, and while the missiles waiting inside were well protected from laser fire from below, she doubted its designers had anticipated that it would have to withstand a high-voltage current hitting it at this range.

The problem was that in order to do that she would have to climb out onto the wing, lean over the edge, and fire her arc-thrower straight down the missile tube at point-blank range.

She swallowed hard. There was no way it could work, she knew in the cold depths of her mind. The Trofts monitoring the weapons would spot her as she moved onto the wing, and either her target cluster's own lasers would get her while she was leaning over, or else the forward ones would shoot back and nail her before she got even that far.

But she had to try. Even if all she accomplished was to demonstrate the technique to the Cobras who would come after her, and to warn them of the risks, she still had to try. Taking a deep breath, still maintaining a low stance, she eased toward the aft wing.

And then, over the crest of the hull, she saw the diffuse reflected light of a sudden barrage of laser fire. She had just enough time to wonder what they were shooting at when the ones on her side of the ship also erupted in a massive firestorm. Not into the forest or town, but straight across the landscape.

She was staring at the blazing fury of the attack, wondering what in the Worlds was going on, when an object shot into view across the warship's bow, twisting and turning and jinking across her line of sight, staying about a quarter second ahead of the laser fire.

It was one of the drones, the kind that Lorne had dropped on several of the trucks earlier to clear the path for her team. Jin watched, waiting for it to do the same sort of nosedive, wondering which truck was in for it this time.

Or maybe he had something else in mind, she thought with a surge of hope. Maybe he was trying to get the drone clear so that he could drive it into one of the weapons clusters. If he could do that, maybe she wouldn't have to give up her life after all.

But the drone seemed to be making no attempt to attack the clusters. For that matter, it didn't seem to be doing anything at all. It just flew back and forth, staying ahead of the lasers, as if Lorne was daring the Troft gunners to take it down.

And then, through her foggy mind, Jin suddenly got it. This particular drone wasn't an attack, the way the Troft gunners obviously assumed.

This one was a diversion.

And even as Jin belatedly came to that realization, another group of laser bolts abruptly lit up the night sky.

But this fire wasn't coming from any of the ship's weapons. It was coming from the swivel guns of four of the trucks Lorne had earlier disabled and the Trofts had subsequently abandoned.

And all four of the lasers were firing at the forward weapons cluster on Jin's side.

The drone was instantly forgotten as the Troft gunners shifted their aim to the unexpected attack from below. But the trucks had been built to withstand such intense attacks, and even as all four trucks became enveloped by clouds of vaporized armor plating, their guns continued to fire. Jin held her breath...

And with a thunderous explosion, the weapons cluster erupted in a blaze of fire as its missile pack ignited. The blast sent debris shooting past Jin as the shock wave slammed into her, threatening to throw her off of her perch. She ducked lower, steadying herself, as the fireball faded away. Daring to hope, she peered through the spreading cloud of smoke.

To find that the attack had succeeded. The cluster was completely gone.

So was the wing the cluster had been attached to.

The mate to the wing that Jin was about to climb out onto.

There was nothing to be gained by thinking about it. Turning her eyes away from the jagged stump where the forward wing had once been, Jin jumped onto the aft wing beside her and dropped flat onto her belly. The warship's assault on the trucks had faltered, she noticed, the Trofts in fire control no doubt reeling from the unexpected loss of a full quarter of their weaponry. Jin had to do this now, before they got their mental balance back and spotted her up here.

If she died, she died. At least it would be quick.

Pulling herself forward, she leaned over the leading edge of the wing and aimed her little finger straight into one of the missile tubes. Taking a deep breath, she fired her arcthrower.

She never even heard the explosion that shattered the cluster and hurled her upward across the sky.

The four lasers lanced up from the ground beyond the wall, converging on the weapons beneath the warship's forward wing. The ship responded with an intense barrage of its own, and for a half-dozen agonizing seconds the duel raged on. Jody watched, holding her breath.

And then, with a brilliant flash, the forward cluster exploded, sending flaming debris flying in all directions and hurling the crumpled wing itself high into the air. It arced up and back down, and as the echoes of the explosion faded she distinctly heard the muffled thud as it landed somewhere inside Stronghold. "One down," she said with grim satisfaction. "Three more to go."

"Maybe just two," Freylan said. "If your mother can—oh, God."

"What is it?" Jody asked tensely.

"It's your mom," Freylan said, his voice rigid with horror. "She's on the aft wing. She's *on* the wing."

"*What?*" Jody gasped, her breath catching in her throat. "But didn't she see that—?"

"Of course she saw," Freylan said. "She's going to do it anyway."

"No," Jody breathed, her stomach churning as she watched the distant figure hunch forward on the small wing. "She can't."

But of course she could. And she would. Because there was danger, and war. And because Jin Moreau Broom was first and foremost a Cobra.

A Cobra.

It was a small chance. But it was the only one Jody had. Leaping to the window, she flung it all the way open. "Cobras!" she shouted as loudly as she could, knowing that there were still Trofts inside Stronghold's wall who might shoot at her and not giving a damn. "Cobra on the ship wing—needs assist and rescue!"

She was filling her lungs to repeat the message when the wing exploded.

"*No!*" she screamed, all of her pain and fear and rage compressed into that single word. The fireball was dissipating—

"There!" Freylan snapped. "There—way up there!"

Jody's eyes darted back and forth across the starry sky, her heart thudding in her throat.

And then, suddenly, she saw her mother, arcing high overhead, a piece of the wing soaring along beneath her as if flying in formation. She was tumbling slowly head over heels, her arms and legs splayed out limply, unconscious or injured.

Or dead.

Time seemed to stretch out. Helplessly, hopelessly, Jody watched as her mother reached the top of her arc and almost lazily curved over and started down again. She was still tumbling slowly, and a small, detached part of Jody's mind wondered how she would be turned when she hit the ground. Not that it probably even mattered. An impact from that height would probably kill her no matter how she landed. If she wasn't dead already.

She was picking up speed now, and Jody saw that she would land just inside the wall a little ways to the west, in an open area where Jody would be able to see her all the way to the end. If, that is, Jody had the courage to stay with her mother the whole way. Would she have that courage, or would she turn away, abandoning her mother to die alone, with no one even watching? A movement to her left caught her eye, and she shifted her eyes that direction—

To see a figure jump up onto the wall from somewhere outside and launch himself upward in a powerful Cobra leap aiming straight for Jody's mother.

Jody had barely enough time to tense up as the two arcing paths approached each other. The two figures intersected—

"He's got her," Freylan crowed. "He's got her!"

Jody nodded, not daring to speak, not daring to breathe. The Cobra's own upward arc had been flattened as he caught the falling body, and now both of them were falling back to earth. Jody watched, her hands tightened into fists, knowing that Cobra leg servos could absorb a lot of the force of the impending impact, but also knowing how easy it would be for her mother's rescuer to lose his balance and slam both of them facefirst onto the ground. Almost there...

And then they were down, the Cobra's knees bending hard with the impact, his legs simultaneously pumping as he tried to get his feet moving to catch up with his horizontal momentum.

But there was too much to be made up, and his legs were already busy trying to slow their descent, and as Jody watched she knew he wasn't going to make it. His body staggered off-balance and he started to pitch forward.

And then, suddenly, two more Cobras appeared out of nowhere, sprinting up behind the staggering figure and grabbing both him and Jin's limp body into their arms, locking the four of them together as they all ran, first stabilizing their group momentum, then braking to a fast but controlled halt.

"She's okay," Freylan said, his voice weak with relief as he handed Jody the binoculars. "I saw her blink, Jody. She's okay."

Jody pressed the binoculars to her eyes, almost afraid to hope. But he was right. Though her mother's face was flushed and burned, her eyelids were fluttering with slowly returning consciousness.

It was only then, as Jody let her eyes drift with relief and gratitude from her mother's face, that she saw that the arms still cradling Jin were clad in gloves and sleeves of scaled gray.

It wasn't one of the Cobras who had answered Jody's frantic call for help, who had raced across the battle zone, risking his own life, and leaped up from the wall to save the life of her mother.

It was one of the Qasamans.

Jody was still trying to wrap her mind around that when the forest once again lit up with laser fire.

She snapped her eyes back to the warship. The lasers from its remaining two weapons clusters were firing, all right.

But they were firing high above the forest, away from any of the Cobras.

[Soldiers of the Drim'hco'plai Demesne, I speak to them,] an amplified voice rolled across the suddenly quiet battlefield. [Our surrender, we have given it. Your surrender, you must also give it.]

"What's he saying?" Freylan asked.

Jody took a deep breath. "He's saying it's over," she said. "We've won."

For a moment Freylan seemed to ponder that. "No," he said quietly. "We may have won. But it's not over. Not by a long shot."

CHAPTER TWENTY-ONE

It took the rest of the night to collect the wounded and get them under the care of Stronghold's medical personnel; to gather, disarm, and contain the Troft prisoners; and to gather and seal the dead for proper burial.

To Lorne's way of thinking, there were far too many in all three categories.

The sun was rising over the eastern forest when the word came that Harli Uy had summoned him to the Government Building for a final council of war.

The main conference room was already crowded when Lorne arrived. Harli was there, seated in the chair at the head where his father would normally be. Occupying the three chairs on either side of him were six other Caelian Cobras: Matigo, Olwen, Kemp, Tracker, and two more from the Stronghold contingent whom Lorne didn't know. Beside them to Harli's right were Lorne's parents and sister, with an empty chair between his mother and Jody that was obviously being saved for him. Facing them on the opposite side were the four Qasamans and Warrior, the Troft looking joltingly out of place among the humans. Lined up around the walls were more Cobras and a few of Stronghold's ordinary citizens, plus Croi and Nissa, who were hovering nervously behind Warrior. Behind Jody, Lorne noticed as he sat down, were Freylan and Geoff, both of them looking even more lost than Croi and Nissa did.

Lorne was apparently the last of the invited group to arrive. Even as he took his seat, Harli stirred and rose from his. "Thank you all for coming," he said, nodding first at those around the table and then acknowledging the people lining the walls. "I know you're all dead tired, and I also know there's still a lot of work to do, so I'll make this as brief as possible." He gestured to the four Qasamans. "Some of you know, others of you may not, that we have four representatives from the planet Qasama among us."

From the complete lack of reaction at Harli's announcement, Lorne concluded that everyone in the room had indeed already heard that particular news. Probably everyone in Stronghold knew it by now. "And all four of them were highly instrumental in kicking the Trofts' collective butt," he added.

"Thank you, Broom, I *was* getting to that," Harli said, throwing a brief glower at Lorne. "As Cobra Lorne Broom says, they were indispensable members of our attack force. In fact, I'd go further. Without them, we would almost certainly have lost the battle. We would absolutely have lost a great many more Cobras."

Lorne glanced around, noting all the nodding heads. The people of Stronghold knew that, too.

"What you probably *don't* know," Harli continued, "is that Ifrit Siraj Akim and his people came to Caelian looking for help. Apparently the Trofts—*some* of the Trofts," he corrected, nodding a tacit apology to Warrior, "have decided they don't like sharing this part of space with us humans. Just as Caelian and Aventine have been attacked, so also was Qasama. Ifrit Akim has therefore come here looking for help."

He looked around the room again. "Specifically, he's looking for Cobras willing to go back to Qasama with them and fight."

Lorne had expected that one to generate at least a murmur, whether of disbelief, disapproval, or dismay. The silence that instead filled the room was far more ominous.

Matigo broke the silence first. "What does your father say?" he asked.

"The governor's still in emergency surgery," Harli said. "I didn't have time to brief him on their request before he went under."

Matigo nodded and shifted his attention to the Qasamans. "How many Cobras would you need?"

"As many as are willing to come," Siraj said. "As many as you can spare."

"And therein lies the problem," Harli said heavily. "As of three days ago, before the Trofts landed, we had around seven hundred Cobras on Caelian. Even with that we were barely holding our own." He waved a hand. "As of right now, we're down over three hundred from that number, including the dead and wounded. We also have a major part of the Stronghold wall to rebuild, nearly two hundred Troft prisoners to manage, plus all the rest of Caelian's challenges to deal with."

"In other words," Siraj said, his eyes boring into Harli's, "your answer is no."

"That's not fair," Jody spoke up fiercely. "We wouldn't even be sitting here if it wasn't for them. You said that yourself. You can't just say thank you and send them away."

"What do you suggest?" Harli countered. "You've seen what we have to deal with on Caelian. How many Cobras of our current four hundred do *you* think we can spare?"

"That's the wrong question," Jin said, her voice less agitated than her daughter's but no less firm. "It's not a matter of what the cost will be of sending Cobras to Qasama. The real question is what the cost will be if you don't."

"Seems to me that if we're going to send our Cobras anywhere it ought to be to Aventine," one of the men along the wall muttered, his eyes hard as he stared at the four Qasamans. "*They* haven't been running around for fifty years swearing to destroy us."

"The situation on Qasama has changed," Siraj said evenly. "The Shahni are willing to let go of the insults of the past."

The man by the wall snorted. "Big of them," he growled.

"The Qasamans are a proud people," Jin said. "They would never ask help from someone they considered enemies. The fact that they sent Ifrit Akim here is proof that the old animosities are gone, or at least faded enough for us to try to make a new start."

"Wait a minute," Nissa spoke up from behind Warrior. "Why are we even talking about more fighting? Warrior said that once we had a victory against the invaders the Tlossies and some of the other demesnes would be willing to help us."

Warrior's radiator membranes fluttered. [A victory, this is not a sufficient one,] he said.

"What did he say?" Harli asked.

"He said this wasn't a sufficient victory," Paul spoke up. "Unfortunately, he's right."

Matigo sent a hard look at the Troft. "In whose opinion?" he growled.

"In everyone's," Paul told him. Matigo turned to him— "Yes, I was there, too," Paul continued before the other could speak. "I saw what it cost." He waved at his heavily bandaged left leg. "I paid some of that cost myself, you know."

"The problem is that Caelian's too unimportant for anyone to care about," Harli said. "Is that what you're saying?"

"That, and the battle itself was too small for the Tlossies or anyone else to consider it genuinely significant," Paul said. "I'm sorry, but that's just how it is. A small group of humans taking down two ships' worth of Trofts could easily be considered a fluke. Especially since you had a fair amount of help from Caelian's own flora and fauna."

"What it boils down to is that there are only two places where a significant victory will be enough to get the Tlossies moving," Jin said. "Aventine and Qasama." She looked at Warrior. "Am I right?"

[A victory on either, it would be significant,] the Troft agreed.

"Well, Aventine's out," Lorne said. "Not only would we never get in past all the ships the invaders have in orbit, but the people and government there are pretty much useless."

"How *dare* you?" Nissa snapped. "Just because Governor-General Chintawa didn't go running out into the street with a gun you think he's *useless*?"

"No, I'm saying he's useless because he ordered the Cobras to stand down without even trying to fight," Lorne countered. "He also called the governors and syndics together so that he could call for a nice, neat surrender."

"He was buying time," Nissa retorted. "Buying *us* time, so that we could get off Aventine with—"

"I have a question," Croi spoke up suddenly from beside her. "Cobra Uy, you say you don't have enough Cobras to send to Qasama. What if we could get you some more?"

Matigo snorted. "As long as we're wishing, how about getting us a Dominion of Man naval squadron?"

"I'm serious," Croi insisted. "What if I could get you some fresh Cobras? Would you have enough then to send some of yours to Qasama?"

"How many extras are we talking about?" Harli asked.

"I can get you three hundred," Croi said.

"And how fast can you get them here?"

Croi hesitated, his eyes flicking around the room. "About five days."

"Five *days*?" Matigo echoed as a stunned murmur broke out among the observers.

"Relax, everyone," Harli said, raising his voice over the excited chatter. "He's talking about Viminal, which also means he's talking through his ear. Sorry to break this to you, Dr. Croi, but if the invaders bothered to hit Caelian, they certainly didn't forget about Viminal."

"I'm not talking about Viminal," Croi said, looking around the room again. "I just can't—here with all these people—"

And in that moment, the fog of fatigue around Lorne's mind seemed to part... and suddenly he knew what he had to do. "He's talking about Isis," he spoke up. "It's an automated—"

"Broom, shut your mouth!" Nissa snapped, stepping up to her side of the table.

"It's an automated Cobra factory currently aboard—"

"*Damn* you, Broom, shut *up*!" Nissa snarled, her face rigid with anger as she jabbed a finger at the men standing behind the Broom family. "You—Cobras—shut him up!"

"Hold," Harli said, his voice icy cold as he held up a restraining hand, his eyes locked on Lorne's. "I want to hear this."

"No," Nissa ground out. "Cobra Uy, if this man says another word—if you *listen* to another word—I swear I'll have you and everyone else in this room up on charges."

"On whose authority?" Paul asked mildly.

"On the authority given me by Senior Governor Tomo Treakness," she said, turning her glare on him. "Dr. Croi heard him, and so did Cobra Broom. He granted me full authority of negotiation and treaty, and named me the Cobra Worlds' representative to the universe at large."

"I don't think this is exactly what he had in mind," Croi said hesitantly.

"I don't care what he may or may not have had in mind," Nissa retorted. "What he *said* was that I have full Dome authority. I'm exercising that authority now."

For a long moment the room was silent. Then, Harli stirred. "Your authority and orders are noted," he said quietly. "I still want to hear it."

"Cobra Uy—"

"And if you persist in interrupting," he added, still quietly, "I'll have you removed from this room." He turned back to Lorne. "Cobra Broom?"

Lorne took a deep breath, his mind flashing back to the family dinner—was it only three weeks ago?—where they'd all discussed the ramifications of the urgent note his mother had received to go to Qasama. Even then, he remembered, the risk of treason charges had been mentioned. Somehow, he'd never really expected it to come down to that.

Apparently, it had.

"Isis is an experimental program," he said, keeping his attention fixed on Harli. Even out of the corner of his eye he could see the fury on Nissa's face. "It's a robotic system for creating Cobras, bypassing the human surgeons. I gather it's pretty much self-contained, and I'm told it'll shorten the time necessary for equipment implantation from two weeks to five days."

Harli looked at Croi. "Has it been tested?"

"It has," Croi said. "The prototype"—he glanced at Nissa, looked hurriedly away—"is in the cargo hold of Ingidi-inhiliziyo's freighter."

"And you say it has enough equipment to make three hundred Cobras?"

"Yes." Croi hunched his shoulders. "Fewer if there's some breakage, of course."

Matigo whistled softly. "Damn, but three hundred new Cobras would be nice to have."

"I'm sure they would." Lorne braced himself. "But I'm afraid you'll have to wait for the next one." He looked at Siraj. "This one's going to Qasama."

"*What?*" Matigo demanded, his voice barely audible over the sudden uproar from the room.

"It has to," Lorne insisted, raising his own voice as he tried to be heard. "Listen to me. Please—*listen* to me."

"Quiet," Uy ordered.

The governor's son hadn't even raised his voice, Lorne noted. But within a couple of seconds the room was quiet again. "Continue, Broom," he said into the rigid silence.

"We can't win this war by ourselves," Lorne said, keeping his voice as steady as he could. "That should be obvious to everyone in this room. The Cobra Worlds haven't got the numbers, the weapons, or the industrial capability. No matter how many Cobras we have, if we try to go head to head with the invaders, we *will* eventually lose." He gestured toward Warrior. "The only way to win will be to persuade the Tlossies and some of the other local demesnes onto our side."

"Who've already said they won't come aboard without a major victory," Jin murmured.

"Exactly," Lorne said. "As was already stated, it has to be Aventine, or Qasama."

"So take this Cobra factory to Aventine," Matigo said.

Lorne shook his head. "We already covered that," he said. "Aventine is out."

"Because the people won't fight?" Nissa demanded bitterly.

"Because they aren't ready for war," Lorne told her. "They don't have the weapons or the soldiers." He grimaced. "And from what little I saw, they don't really have the mind-set."

"But the Qasamans have all of that," Jin said. "And they have more." She looked at Harli. "Lorne's right, Cobra Uy. Humanity has just one chance to pull this off. That chance is Qasama."

"Let's suppose you're right," Harli said slowly. "Let's suppose you take this Isis thing to Qasama, and you win. What then?"

"What do you mean?" Jin asked, frowning.

"I mean the Qasamans will have Cobras," Harli said flatly, his eyes shifting to Siraj. "And new, milder tone or not, I don't think we can trust them not to turn around and send those Cobras straight back at us once this is over."

"I have already said the Shahni no longer see your worlds that way," Siraj reminded him.

"I understand," Harli said. "And for whatever it's worth, I think you're being sincere about that. The problem is that you're making promises for your government, and I frankly don't think you have the authority to do that."

Beside him, Khatir stirred. "No, he doesn't," he agreed. Reaching into his pocket, he pulled out a small, ornate disk and laid it quietly on the table in front of him. "But I do."

Siraj leaned forward for a closer look at the disk, his eyes widening. Lorne keyed in his infrareds, and there was no mistaking the utter surprise flowing across the other's face. "You're an *ambassador*?" he asked, looking with astonishment at Khatir.

"Yes," Khatir said. "Though only for the purposes of this mission, of course." He looked at Siraj and Zoshak. "That was why I was removed from that final battle in Sollas," he added. "I needed as much instruction as possible in the demands and parameters of my new position."

"I thought you came merely to serve as our pilot," Zoshak said, sounding as confused as Siraj.

Khatir shrugged. "Certainly I'm that as well," he said. "But Rashida Vil is far better qualified than I. No, *this* was my ultimate purpose in coming on this mission."

"Even though you don't even like us?" Jin murmured.

"My personal preferences are of no matter," Khatir said evenly. "But since you mention that, allow me to state that much of my animosity toward you in Sollas was based on my doubts about your abilities." He looked at Harli. "Having now seen you in true combat, those doubts have been put to rest."

"Mighty generous of you," Harli said dryly. He gestured at the disk. "I take it that's the sign of your diplomatic authority?"

"It is an ambassadorial signet," Siraj confirmed. He still looked flabbergasted, but his infrared pattern indicated he was starting to get back on balance again. "Such tokens are old and revered, and are given only to the highest of the Shahni's negotiators."

"And as such, I place the future of our peoples in your hands," Khatir said, visibly bracing himself. "Do you wish a full treaty of friendship with the Shahni? Do you wish merely a pact of nonaggression? Whatever your desire, you need only place it in writing, and I will sign it."

"I appreciate the offer," Harli said hesitantly. "Unfortunately, *I* don't have that kind of authority. Neither does my father."

"But there's someone here who does," Croi spoke up suddenly. "As Ms. Gendreves has already stated, she has full power of negotiation and treaty."

Nissa snorted. "Please," she said disdainfully. "If you think I'm going to hand these people Cobra capabilities in exchange for a worthless piece of paper, you're sadly mistaken."

"Why?" Jin asked. "Fine, so assume that Ghofl Khatir is lying, and that any treaty he signs is worthless. Even with Cobras, how could Qasama ever be a threat to the Cobra Worlds? *Why* would they be a threat? They don't need our land or resources—they have more than enough of their own."

"What about revenge?" Nissa countered.

"They don't even have space-flight capability," Jin argued. "How exactly would they go about invading us?"

"When this war is over, our full attention will be turned toward the rebuilding of our world," Khatir added. "Besides, revenge is for fools."

"The driving force behind the Qasamans' animosity hasn't been revenge," Jin continued. "It's been the fear of another incursion by us. If we have a nonaggression treaty, and they don't have to worry about that, whatever's left of those feelings are going to go away."

"Unless you're suggesting that *our* side of the treaty would be the worthless half," Lorne put in pointedly.

Nissa shook her head. "No," she said flatly.

"What if the Qasamans sweeten the deal?" Jody spoke up suddenly. "What if they offer us a peace treaty *plus* something we can't get anywhere else?"

Nissa snorted. "Such as?"

Jody leveled a finger across the table. "Look at their combat suits," she said. "*There aren't any organics on them.*"

And for the first time since the meeting started, a genuinely stunned silence filled the room. "That's impossible," Kemp said. "They must have scraped them."

"We have done nothing of the sort," Siraj said, frowning curiously as he gazed at his arm, turning it around to look at it from all directions.

"You people have been looking for something that'll keep the organics, spores, and insects off you for decades," Jody went on. "Well, somehow, the Qasamans have come up with one."

"Actually, it may be even better than that," Lorne added as a stray thought suddenly rose from his memory. "Out in Devole's Canyon, when we were practicing for our attack, the giggers and screech tigers were just as annoying and persistent as they apparently always are. But I don't think anything smaller even came near them."

"He is correct," Siraj confirmed. "I noticed that also, but it seemed of only minor importance at the time."

"What exactly is that material?" Freylan asked, leaving his place by the wall and circling around the end of the table to the Qasamans' side.

"Treated krissjaw hide," Siraj told him, pulling one of his gloves from his belt and handing it to Freylan for examination.

"We've tried treated predator hides," Matigo said. "They don't do a bit of good."

"Maybe it's something unique in the treatment process," Freylan suggested, kneading the material of the glove as he studied it. "Or something *inside* the material. What are all these fibrous things?"

"They are stiffeners," Siraj said. "They give extra strength to the material when the servos are operating, becoming rigid when a small current runs through them."

"I'll be damned," Geoff said softly.

Lorne turned in his chair to look at him. "What do you mean?"

"It's the current," Geoff said, his voice chagrinned, embarrassed, and excited all at the same time. "Why the hell didn't anyone see that before? The current in the Djinn combat suits—it creates the same kind of low-level electric field produced by the skin, muscles, and nervous systems of living creatures."

"Thereby fooling the organics and spores into thinking it's living animal tissue," Harli said, some of Geoff's excitement starting to creep into his voice. "You might be right. You rollin' well might be right."

"So what kept the predators away?" Kemp asked.

"Who cares?" Geoff said. "I mean, yes, that's important, and we'll need to figure that out. But the point is that with those suits, you've got ninety percent of the Caelian problem licked."

"More than that," Freylan added. "Remember, these things are at heart combat suits. They've got sonics and lasers built right into them. More than enough to handle giggers and probably even screech tigers." He held up the glove toward Harli, then waved it around the room. "Don't you see? With enough of these suits *Caelian won't need Cobras anymore.*"

"At least not the numbers you need now," Jin said. "But the point's well taken." She looked at Khatir. "Ghofl Khatir?"

"Add it to the treaty," Khatir said without hesitation. "As many suits as you need, once the war has concluded, plus peace between our worlds in exchange for the Isis facility."

Siraj leaned over and murmured something to him. "A correction," Khatir said. "The main combat suit delivery will still need to wait until after the war, but I am informed that there are two spare suits currently aboard our transport. You may have those immediately."

Jin turned to Nissa. "Well, Ms. Gendreves?"

"I don't care if they offer to cover every Cobra Worlds citizen with gold," Nissa said icily. "I will not sign any treaty with these people."

"That's all right," Paul spoke up unexpectedly. "I'll sign it."

Nissa drew back, her eyes running up and down him. "*You?* You have no authority to speak for the Dome."

Paul folded his arms across his chest. "Prove it."

For the first time, Nissa seemed actually at a loss for words. "You can't just sign for the governor-general," she insisted after a few seconds.

"The Dome could renounce it," Harli agreed quietly. "Probably would, in fact."

"Fine," Paul said. "But in the meantime, the Qasamans will have their Cobras." He looked at Khatir. "And with luck, we'll have our victory."

"This is insane," Nissa snapped. "Cobra Uy, I demand you stop this travesty at once."

For a long moment, Harli gazed at Paul's face. Then, slowly and deliberately, he sent the same gaze around the room. He gave a small nod, and finally looked back at Nissa. "I'm sorry, Ms. Gendreves," he said. "But I have no evidence that Cobra Paul Broom doesn't have the authority he claims. I therefore can't interfere with him."

Nissa actually sputtered. "This is lunacy!" she snarled. She spun to glare at Paul. "This is *treason.*"

"This is war," Harli said bluntly. "We do what we have to."

Nissa shot a look of her own around the room. Then, slowly, she straightened to her full height. "Fine," she said, her voice back under control. "You do your little treaty. I can't stop you. *But.*"

She leveled a finger at Paul. "If you do," she continued, her voice deadly, "I state right now, in front of all these witnesses, that you have committed high treason. And I *will* have you arrested and brought up on those charges."

"Understood," Paul said. "Understand in turn that if you're able to find a court at the Dome to file those charges with, it'll mean we've won the war. In that case, I'll consider any punishment I receive to be a small price to pay."

For a moment Nissa held his gaze. Then, without a word, she turned and stalked out of the room.

Paul took a deep breath. "Cobra Uy?" he asked. "Do you have someone trained in writing up official documents?"

"I'll get him on it right away," Harli promised. "In the meantime,

Matigo, perhaps you'd be good enough to gather a team to escort Warrior back to his ship and bring it here to Stronghold." He gave Khatir a strained smile. "I'd like to at least see this Isis thing before we all commit treason with it."

Twelve hours later, they were once again in space.

Lorne was sitting alone in the Troft freighter's cramped dining area, gazing out at the stars, when he heard soft footsteps approaching from behind him. From their rhythm... "Hi, Mom," he said, not turning around. "Dad gone to sleep yet?"

"Yes, just now," she said, coming over and sitting down beside him. "How are you doing?"

Lorne huffed. "How do I even answer that?" he asked. "Five days ago, I was standing in front of Governor-General Chintawa, listening to him rant and rave and demand that I drag you to Capitalia for some big overblown politically-charged ceremony. Since then I've fought my way through one war zone, fought my way through *another* war zone, and am on my way to a third. My father's had his leg nearly blown off, and I've found out that my brother's also been badly wounded and that my mother has a brain tumor. Oh, and almost single-handedly, my sister's solved the Caelian problem."

He turned to look at her, forcing a small smile. "There's also the minor point that my entire family's been branded as traitors," he added. "You tell me. How *should* I be doing?"

"You should be looking at the half-full side of the glass," Jin told him soberly. "Two war zones, yes, and you survived both of them. So did the rest of your family."

"I suppose," Lorne said, a knot forming in his stomach. "You really think the Qasamans can regrow all that muscle and skin on Dad's leg?"

Jin shrugged. "Carsh Zoshak is pretty sure they can. They've also told me they can remove my tumor just fine."

Lorne grimaced. "Not exactly high-confidence ways of phrasing it."

"Life is uncertain," Jin said. "As for the treason part, let's just see what happens. As Dr. Croi pointed out, Governor Treakness's last-minute blessing on Nissa Gendreves was hardly intended to cover the situation we all found ourselves in."

"But we *did* still give top-secret Worlds technology to the Qasamans."

"With the tacit agreement of Harli Uy and the rest of the Caelian hierarchy," his mother reminded him. "Under the circumstances, I rather think they'll be on our side in any future political confrontations with the Dome."

"Certainly after Jody's had a few weeks to work her charm on them." Lorne shook his head. "I still can't figure out how I'm supposed to feel about leaving her there alone."

"What alone?" Jin scoffed. "She's got Geoff, Freylan, and a whole planetful of Caelians who have this crazy notion that they owe a debt of gratitude to the Broom family. She's also got Rashida Vil."

Lorne felt his mouth drop open. "*Rashida* got left there, too?"

"You didn't know that?" Jin frowned. "No, of course you didn't— you were helping get your father aboard when that was decided. No, Harli needed someone to translate between him and the prisoners until Warrior can send back to his demesne-lord to arrange to have them taken off. Since we don't need a pilot anymore, Siraj Akim ordered Rashida to stay on Caelian for the duration."

Lorne grimaced. "You sure he didn't just decide to leave a hostage as a guarantee of Qasama's good behavior?"

"There may have been some of that," she conceded. "It's a very Qasaman way of thinking. You might as well start getting used to it. As for Jody, would you really rather we had brought her with us into yet another war zone?"

"I know, that sounds ridiculous," Lorne said. "That's why I'm having trouble knowing how to feel about it."

"Well, if I were you, I'd put that one out of my mind right now," Jin said firmly. "You saw her face—she wasn't about to leave Freylan and Geoff to experiment on those Djinn combat suits without her. It would have taken all of us *plus* Harli's Cobras to drag her out of there."

She reached over and patted his knee. "And I'd put all the rest of it out of my mind, too," she added. "You're hungry, you're tired, and you're suffering the emotional roller coaster that comes of being in the middle of combat. Trust me—I've been there. Food, and then sleep, are the order of the day."

"Okay." Lorne hesitated. "Mom . . . do we really have a chance?"

"To win this war?" Jin shook her head. "I don't know, Lorne. What I *do* know is that when you stood there in that meeting and said the Qasamans were the most well-equipped of all of us, you were speaking truer words than even you knew. They have soldiers, they have weapons, they have whole underground cities."

"Cities, huh?" Lorne said, his mind flashing back to all the backbreaking hours of travel through Aventine's drainage conduits.

"Whole cities," Jin confirmed. "*And* they've got Djinn."

Lorne swallowed. "And now they've got Cobras. *If* they can get them deployed fast enough."

"I think they can," Jin said. "The Qasamans probably already know which of their people have the personalities to be Cobras, which will cut out most of our usual two-week screening process. Isis will cut the two weeks of implantation to five days, and their accelerated-learning drugs will probably cut the usual nine-week training regimen by at least two thirds. Maybe more."

"*If* that stuff really works."

"Oh, it works just fine," Jin assured him. "Ghofl Khatir and Rashida Vil learned to fly that Troft transport in a single evening. There'll probably be side effects, but it'll work."

She squeezed his knee. "And those Cobras are going to make a huge difference."

"Three hundred of them?" Lorne asked skeptically. "To defend a whole planet?"

"Yes indeed." Jin smiled tightly. "Because the invaders will be coming back prepared to deal with the people and weapons and Djinn. But they won't be ready for Cobras."

"Maybe," Lorne said. "I just hope it'll be enough."

"So do I," Jin said. "I guess we'll both find out."